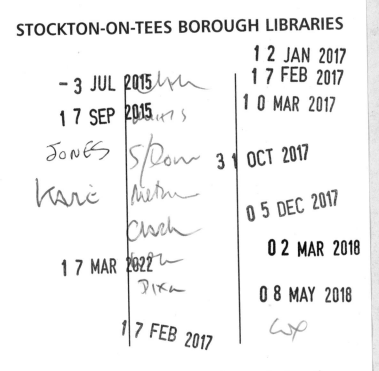

Mills & Boon, an imprint of Harlequin (UK) Limited,
Eton House, 18-24 Paradise Road, Richmond, Surrey TW9 1SR

INNOCENT IN THE REGENCY BALLROOM
© Harlequin Enterprises II B.V./S.à.r.l 2013

Miss Winthorpe's Elopement © Christine Merrill 2008
Dangerous Lord, Innocent Governess © Christine Merrill 2009

ISBN: 978 0 263 90614 1

052-0513

Harlequin (UK) policy is to use papers that are natural, renewable and recyclable products and made from wood grown in sustainable forests. The logging and manufacturing processes conform to the legal environmental regulations of the country of origin.

Printed and bound
by CPI Group (UK) Ltd, Croydon, CR0 4YY

Christine Merrill lives on a farm in Wisconsin, USA, with her husband, two sons and too many pets—all of whom would like her to get off the computer so they can check their e-mail. She has worked by turns in theatre costuming, where she was paid to play with period ballgowns, and as a librarian, where she spent the day surrounded by books. Writing historical romance combines her love of good stories and fancy dress with her ability to stare out of the window and make stuff up.

In The Regency Ballroom Collection

Miss Winthorpe's Elopement

Author Note:

I can't point to any one place or idea that inspired me to write the story of Penny and Adam. But I started on a day when I really just wanted to sit by myself and read. That is probably why I have a book-loving heroine. There is nothing quite like the feeling of sitting down with a good book, although I can't seem to read as many as I buy. Penny's overstocked library is definitely inspired by my own.

I don't normally use pictures as inspiration, but the little china figurine in Penny's sitting room really exists. I don't own anything like it, but I wanted something that would remind me of long afternoons I spent in an aunt's living room, surrounded by 'breakables'. I found just the thing, searching the internet: a figurine so fussy that it seemed the polar opposite of serious scholarship.

I hope you enjoy *Miss Winthorpe's Elopement* as much as I did. Come back soon, to discover what happens to Adam's friend Tim.

To Sean:
For doing his homework on the
Greek classics. Without you, honey,
I'd have to do all my own research.

Chapter One

In the quiet of the library, Penelope Winthorpe heard the front doorbell ring, and set her book carefully aside, pushing her glasses up the bridge of her nose. She smoothed her sensible, bombazine skirt. Then she stood and strolled toward the front hall.

There was no reason to rush since hurrying would not change the results of the trip. Her brother had accused her of being too prone to impulsive actions. Seeing her hare down the hall every time the front door opened would reinforce his view that too much education and too much solitude were affecting her nerves.

But her package was two days late, and it was difficult to contain her anticipation. She rose eagerly with every knock at the door, hoping each one to be the delivery she'd been expecting.

In her mind, she was already holding the package, hearing the rustle of crisp, brown paper, running her fingers along the string that held it in place. She would cut the twine with the scissors on the hall table, and the book would be in her hands at last. She imagined she could smell the fresh ink and the paper, caress the leather of the binding, and feel the gold-embossed title under her fingertips.

And then, the best part: she would take it back to the library and cut the pages open, spread them carefully, turning each one and catching glimpses of words without really reading, not wanting to spoil the surprise, even though she knew the story, almost by heart.

At last, she would ring for tea, settle into her favourite chair by the fire, and begin to read.

It would be heaven.

When she got to the hall, her brother was sorting through a stack of letters. The post had come, but there was no sign of a package from the book seller.

'Hector, did a delivery arrive for me? I had expected it by now, but I thought perhaps it might come with the post.'

'Another book?' He sighed.

'Yes. The latest printing of *The Odyssey*.'

Her brother waved a dismissive hand. 'It came yesterday. I sent it back to the shop.'

'You did what?' She stared at him, incredulous.

'Sent it back. You already have it. I did not deem it necessary.'

'I have translations,' she corrected. 'This was in the original Greek.'

'All the more reason to send it back. I dare say the translations will be much easier for you to read.'

She took a deep breath and tried counting to ten

before speaking, to control her rash tongue. She made it almost to five before blurting, 'I do not expect to have trouble with the Greek. I read it fluently. As a matter of fact, I am planning a translation of my own. And, since I cannot translate words that are already in English, the new book will most certainly be necessary.'

Hector was looking at her as though she had sprouted a second head. 'There are many adequate translations of Homer already available.'

'But none by a woman,' she responded. 'I suspect that there are insights and subtleties I might bring to the material that will be substantially different than those already available.'

'Inferior, perhaps,' countered her brother. 'The world is not clamouring for your opinion, Penny, in case you haven't noticed.'

For a moment, the truth of that statement weighed heavy on her, but she shook it off. 'Perhaps it is because they have not yet seen what I can accomplish. I will not know until I have tried. And for that, I will need the book I ordered. Which only cost a few pounds.'

'But think of the time you would spend wasted in reading.' Hector always considered such time wasted. She remembered his discomfort in the schoolroom, and his desire to escape from it as soon as possible, when their father was ready to leave the business in his hands. That a printer had such a low opinion of books never ceased to amaze her.

'For some of us, Hector, reading is not a waste of time, but one of life's great pleasures.'

'Life is not meant to be spent in pleasure, Penelope.

I am sure, if you put your mind to it, that you can find a better way to use your time.' He looked her up and down. 'While you needn't be so frivolous as some young girls who are hellbent on matrimony, you could devote your time to higher pursuits. Helping with the poor, or the sick, perhaps.'

Penelope gnashed her teeth and set to counting. It was not that she had a distaste for charity work. It was certainly necessary. But it only showed how awkward she was around people, both rich and poor. And it served as a continual reminder to all that she was properly on the shelf, with no hope of a husband or children of her own to tend to. It felt like giving up.

Although, perhaps it was time.

And yet, she reminded herself, if she meant to give up, she could do it just as successfully at home, in front of the fire, alone except for her Homer.

This time, she made it to eight before speaking. 'It is not as though I do not wish to contribute to society,' she argued. 'But I think that what I can do for the scholarly community is just as valuable as what I might accomplish tending the ill. And I do make regular donations to the church. The help that does not come by my hand can come from my purse instead. There have been no complaints.'

Her brother glared in disapproval. 'I believe there are complaints, Penelope, although you may think that it is possible to ignore them, since they come from me. But Father has left me in charge of you and your inheritance, and so you must listen to them.'

'Until such time as I marry,' she added.

He sighed. 'We both know the unlikelihood of that, Penny. I think it is time that we accept it.'

We meant *her*, she supposed.

'It is one thing to be a bluestocking for a time. But I had hoped that you would have put such nonsense behind you by now. I do not expect you to spend your whole day at the dressmakers, or in idle gossip. But to spend no time at all on your appearance and to fill your head with opinions? And now, Greek?' He shook his own head sadly. 'Someone must put a stop to this nonsense, if you will not. No more books, Penny. At least not until you can prove to me that you are ready to grow up and accept some responsibility.'

'No books?' She felt the air leaving the room. She supposed it was as some girls might feel if their strict older brothers had said, 'No gowns. No parties. No friends.' To be denied her books was to be left companionless and unprotected in a hostile world. 'You cannot speak to me thus.'

'I believe I can.'

'Father would never have allowed it.'

'Father expected you to have started a family by now. That is why he tied your inheritance to the condition of your marriage. You have not yet found a husband. And so control of you and your money belongs to me. I will not see you fritter away the fortune that Father left to you on paper and ink.'

'A few books are hardly likely to fritter away a fortune, Hector.'

'Only a few?' He pointed to the stack on the table next to the door. 'Here are "a few books", Penny. But there are more in the dining room, and the morning room and the parlour. And your room as well, I dare say. The library is full to overflowing.'

'As it was when Father was alive, Hector. He was a man of letters. What I have added to the collection hardly amounts—'

'What you have added to the collection is hardly necessary. There are books enough to last a lifetime already in your possession.'

Perhaps if she read as slowly as her brother did... But she held her tongue and began to count again.

'And now you are buying books that you already own. It must stop, Penny. It really must. If we are to share this house in peace, I will have no more of it.'

She lost count and her temper failed her. 'Then I do not wish to live with you a moment longer.'

'I fail to see what choice you have.'

'I will marry. Someone more agreeable than you. He will be sensible and understanding, and will not begrudge me a few pounds a month for my studies.'

Hector was looking at her with pity again, but his tone was sarcastic. 'And where will you find such a paragon, dear sister? Have you forgotten the disaster of your come-out Season? Even knowing of the substantial fortune attached to it, once you opened your mouth, no one would have you. None of them was good enough for you. You are too opinionated by half. Men want a woman who will follow where they lead, not one who questions her husband's wisdom and ignores the house and the servants because she is too busy reading.'

It had been four years, and the sting of embarrassment still rose to the surface at the mention of the utter failure that had been her Season. 'But surely there is a man who wishes an intelligent wife. Someone with whom he can converse.'

Hector sniffed in disapproval. 'At such time as you find him, you are welcome to marry. But I do not see you in pursuit of such a man, nor is he in pursuit of you. Since you show no inclination to leave your desk, unless he comes stumbling into the house by mistake, it is unlikely he will find you. And thus, I am left to make your decisions for you.

'I will not push you into society, for we both know that would be hopeless. But neither will I encourage you to further education, since what you have gathered so far has caused you nothing but trouble. Good day, sister. I suggest you find something to occupy your hands, and you will see no need to busy your mind.' And he went back to reading his mail.

She was dismissed. *One, two, three…* She retreated to the stairs before she could say something that would further solidify her brother's opinions.

He was right in one thing, at least. He was entitled to make monetary decisions for her, until she could find another man to take the responsibility from him.

Not that she needed any man to do so. She was quite smart enough on her own. Smarter, she suspected, than her brother was. His hand with the family business showed none of the mastery that her father had had.

Her father loved the books he printed and bound, loved everything about the papers, the inks, and the bindings. He turned the printing of even the simplest invitation or calling card into a statement of art. And to her father, a finished volume was a masterwork.

Four, five, six… To her brother, it would never be more than profit and loss. And so, there was more loss than profit. Given a lifetime, Penny expected to see her own part in the inheritance disappear, pound by pound, to cover the shortages that would occur from his mismanagement.

Of course, it was her mention of the fact at dinner the evening before that had caused her brother's sudden interest in bringing her to heel.

Seven, eight, nine… It was unbearable. She could not live out the rest of her life under Hector's thumb, sneaking books into the house on the sly and hoping that he did not notice. To live by his rules would be impossible.

Ten.

Which left her one choice in the matter: she must marry. Even the thought of her brother's edict and the lack of books made her throat tighten in panic.

She must marry quickly.

She walked to the corner of the room and tugged the bell pull three sharp times, then turned to her wardrobe for a valise, tossing in travelling clothes from the collection of half-mourning that she had never quite managed to leave behind, although her father had been gone for two years.

In a few moments, there was a discreet knock upon the door.

'Come in, Jem.'

The senior footman looked uncomfortable, as he always did when summoned to her rooms. He had often expressed a wish that she would find a ladies' maid, or some other confidant. She had reminded him that she would do so at such time as she needed her hair dressed or a ribbon ironed. But if she needed wise counsel, she would always call upon him.

'Miss?' He stood uneasily at the door, sensing a change in the air.

'I need you to hire a carriage and prepare for travel.'

'You are going out, miss?'

She gave him a fish eye. 'I would not need a carriage, else.'

'Are we going to the book seller's, miss?' He had overheard the conversation in the hall, she suspected. And balked at doing something in direct opposition to her brother's wishes.

'No, Jem. I am not permitted to do so.'

He sagged with relief.

'So I mean to limit myself to something my brother cannot possibly object to, since he has given me permission. He wishes me to be behave as other young ladies do.'

'Very good, Miss Penny.'

'And so we are going to go and find me a husband.'

'Lost with all hands…' Adam Felkirk, Seventh Duke of Bellston, stared at the paper in front of him and watched it shake with the trembling of his hands. He tried to remind himself that the loss of almost one hundred lives far outweighed the loss of the cargo. Had the wives and families of the ship's crew been in some way prepared for the possibility of this tragedy? Perhaps. But he had certainly been foolishly unready for the fact that his investment was a risky one.

A shipment of tobacco from the Americas had seemed like a sensible plan when he had put down the money for it. The spring lambing had not gone well, and his tenants' crops were not likely to thrive in the dry weather they had been having. But tobacco was almost guaranteed to bring in more money. It was a valuable commodity, if one could pay to have it brought to England. He could sell it for a healthy profit, and the money would tide him through this year and the next.

And now, the ship was sunk, and he was ruined.

He could not help but feel that it was his own fault. God was punishing him for the mistakes of the last year, and punishing those around him as well. The burns on his brother's arm were continual memories of his faithless actions and the fire he had caused by them.

Then summer had come and the crops had failed, and he was left with the decision to waive the annual rents or throw his tenants out into the street for non-payment. When they were already hungry, what good did it do to anyone to leave them homeless as well?

And now, one hundred innocent lives were lost because he had chosen what he thought was a sensible investment.

He must face facts and tell his brother that there was nothing left. Nothing at all of what their father had left them. The house was mortgaged to the rooftop and in need of repair. There would be no income this year, and he'd gambled what was left in the bank and lost all in a risky investment.

He was out of ideas, out of money, and afraid to take another step forwards, lest it bring disaster to some unsuspecting soul that might take his side.

He ordered another whiskey. If his calculations were correct, he had enough left in his purse to get stinking drunk. And not another penny, or a way to get one for at least a year. The innkeeper might allow him credit for the room, assuming by the cut of his coat that he was good for the debt. But soon the bill would come due, and he would have to stack it with the rest, unable to pay it.

Other than his father's watch, and the signet on the fob, he had only one thing of value. The insurance on his miserable life.

His hand stopped shaking as the inevitable solution occurred to him. He was an utter failure as a duke, and a man. He had brought shame and ruin to his family. He had betrayed a friend, and been well punished for it. The gentlemanly thing to do would be to write a letter of apology and blow his brains out. Let his brother, William, have the coronet. Perhaps he could do better with it.

Of course, it would leave Will with all the debts and the additional expense of burying Adam. And the cleaning of the study from the final mess he'd made with his suicide.

But what if the present duke should die by accident, while travelling on business? Then his brother would be left with the title and a tidy sum that might cover the debts until he could find a better source of income.

Adam thought again how unjust it was that the better brain of the family had found its way into the younger son. Will had inherited wisdom, forethought and an even temper. But all the stubborn impulsiveness and pigheaded unwillingness to take advice was lodged in his own thick skull.

And Will, God love him, had not an envious or covetous bone in his body. He worshipped his older brother, although heaven knew why. He was content to see Adam make as big a mess as possible of the whole thing, never offering a word of criticism.

But no more. His brother would make a fine duke. Let Will step up and do his part to keep the estate solvent, for Adam was more than sick of trying.

But it was up to Adam to step out of the way and allow his William to come forward and take his place.

Adam set down the newspaper. He was resolved. A simple accident would solve many problems, if he had the nerve to follow through. But how best to go about it?

He ordered another whisky. As he drank, he felt the glow in his head fogging rational thought, and numbing the pain of the failure. And realised he was well on the way to the first step in his plan. Raise enough Dutch courage to do the deed, and create the level of befuddlement in his body to convince anyone that cared to ask that this was an unfortunate accident, and not a deliberate act. He finished his drink and ordered another, staying the hand of the barman. 'Leave the bottle.'

The duke could hear the faint rumble of the coaches entering and leaving the busy courtyard. He imagined the slippery cobbles under his expensive boots, and how easy it might be to fall. And the great horses with their heavy hooves, and even heavier carriage wheels...

It would not be a pleasant death. But he doubted that any death was pleasant, when it came down to the fact.

This would at least be timely, and easy enough to arrange. He poured himself another stiff whisky. He might be thought drunken and careless. But many knew him to be that already. At least they would not think him a suicidal coward.

Very well, then.

He took one final drink. Stood and felt the world tipping under his feet. Very good, indeed. He doubted he could make too many steps. He dropped the last of his coin on the table, turned to the tavern keeper and offered an unsteady bow. 'Good evening to you, sir.'

And goodbye.

He worked his way toward the door, bumping several patrons along the way and apologising profusely, before he made it through the open door of the inn.

He could hear a carriage approaching, and deliberately looked in the opposite direction, into the sun. Now he was blind, as well as drunk. All the better, for his nerve could not fail if he could not see what was coming.

The sound was getting louder and louder and he waited until he could feel the faint trembling in the ground that told him the coach was near.

Then he started forward, ignoring the calls of the coachmen.

'Here, sir. Watch where you are going.'

'I say, look out!'

'Oh, dear God!'

And his foot slipped from under him, sending him face down in front of the approaching horses.

Chapter Two

Penelope felt the steady rocking of the carriage, but the rhythm did nothing to lull the sense of dread growing in her. They had been travelling north at a steady pace toward Scotland, stopping at inns and taverns to dine or pass the night. And yet she was no nearer to her goal than when she had been sitting in front of the fire at home.

Jem's misgivings had eased only slightly, once he realised that he was not expected to be the groom. 'You cannot hire a husband as you would hire a coach, Miss Penny.'

'How hard can it be?' Penny announced, with an optimism that she hoped would carry her through the trip. 'I think disappointments in the past were the fault of expectations on the part of myself and the gentlemen involved. I wished a soulmate and they wished a biddable female. I shall never be biddable, and the fact was emphasised by the surrounding crowd of prettier, more agreeable young ladies. After the lack of success in London, I am willing to accept that there will not be a soulmate in the offing.'

The footman stared at her, as if to say it was no concern of his, one way or the other.

She continued. 'However, if I mean to hire a man to do a job of work? Times are hard, Jem. As we go further north, there will be many men seeking employment. I will find one and make my offer.'

Jem could hold his tongue no longer. 'I hardly think that marriage should be considered a chore, miss.'

'My brother assures me often enough that marriage to *me* is likely to be such. And that is just how I mean to phrase it to any worthy gentleman I might find. It will be the simplest of jobs, really. He has but to sign some papers, and spend a few weeks in my presence to pacify my brother. I will pay him amply for his time. And I will require nothing in the way of marital obligations. Not sobriety, or fidelity, or drastic change in lifestyle. He can do just as he pleases, as long as he is willing to marry.'

'A man is not likely to be so easily managed as that, miss.' His tone was warning, but the meaning was lost on her.

'I fail to see why not. It is doubtful that he will have any designs upon my person. Look at me, Jem, and tell me honestly that you expect me to be fighting off the forced affections of some man, if he has freedom and enough money for any woman he wishes.'

The footman looked doubtful.

'But I have brought you along to protect my honour, should my surmise be incorrect,' she assured him.

The elderly footman was not mollified. 'But when you marry, the money will no longer be in your control. It will belong to your husband.' Jem gestured to fill the empty air with scenarios, all of which foretold doom.

'I have no control of the money now,' Penny reminded him. 'If there is a chance that I can find a husband who is less resolute than my brother has become, then it is well worth the risk. I will need to act fast, and think faster. But I dare say I will find a way to take the reins of the relationship before my intended knows what I am about.'

He was not convinced. 'And if the choice proves disastrous?'

'We shall cross that bridge when we come to it.' She glanced out the window at the change in scenery. 'Will we be stopping soon? I fear we are getting near to Scotland, and I had hoped to find someone by now.'

Jem signalled the driver to stop at the next inn, and Penny crossed her fingers. 'It will help if I can find a man who is slow of wit and amiable in nature. If he is given to drink? All the better. Then I shall allow him his fill of it, and he will be too content to bother with me.'

Jem looked disapproving. 'You mean to keep the poor man drunk so that you may do as you will.'

She sniffed. 'I mean to offer him the opportunity to drink. It is hardly my fault if he is unable to resist.'

Jem rolled his eyes.

The carriage was slowing, and when she looked out the window, she could see that they were approaching an inn. She leaned back against her seat and offered a silent prayer that this stop would be the one where she met with success. The other places she had tried were either empty of custom or filled with the sort of rugged brawlers who looked no more willing to allow her freedom than her brother was. Her plan was a wild one, of course. But there were many miles to travel, and she only needed to find one likely candidate for it to prove successful.

And surely there was one man, between London and Gretna, who was in as desperate a state as she. She had but to find him.

Suddenly, the carriage jerked to a stop, and rattled and shook as the horses reared in front of it. She reached out and caught the leather strap at her side, clinging to it to keep her seat. The driver was swearing as he fought to control the beasts and shouting to someone in front of them as things began to settle to something akin to normal. She shot a worried look at Jem in the seat across from her.

He held up a warning hand, indicating that she keep her place, and opened the door, stepping out of the carriage and out of sight to check on the disturbance.

When he did not return, she could not resist, and left the carriage to see for herself.

They had stopped before the place she had expected, several yards short of the inn. But it was easy to understand the reason. There was a body, sprawled face down in the muck at the feet of the horses, which were still shying nervously. The driver held them steady, as Jem bent to examine the unconscious man in the road.

He appeared to be a gentleman, from what little she could see. The back of his coat was well cut, and stretched to cover broad shoulders. Although the buff of the breeches was stained with dirt from the road, she was sure that they had been new and clean earlier in the day.

Jem reached a hand to the man's shoulder and shook him gently, then with more force. When there was no response, he rolled the inert figure on to his back.

The dark hair was mussed, but stylish, the face clean shaven, and the long slender fingers of his hands showed none of the marks of hard work. Not a labourer or common ruffian. A gentleman, most certainly. She supposed it was too much to hope that he was a scholar. More likely a rake, so given over to dissolution that, left to his own devices, he was likely to drink himself to death before they reached the border.

She smiled. 'He is almost too perfect. Put him into the coach at once, Jem.'

Her servant looked at her as though she'd gone mad.

She shrugged. 'I was trusting to fortune to make my decision for me. I hoped that she would throw a man in my path, and she has done just that. You must admit, it is very hard to doubt the symbolic nature of this meeting.'

Jem stared down at the man, and nudged his shoulder. 'Here, sir. Wake up.'

His eyes opened, and she could not help but notice the heavy fringe of lashes that hid the startlingly blue irises. The colour was returning to the high-boned, pale cheeks. He looked up into the blinding sun, and released a sigh. 'There was no pain. I had thought…' Then the man looked past Jem, and smiled up at her. 'Are you an angel?'

She snorted. 'Are you foxed?'

'It depends,' he muttered. 'If I am alive, then I am foxed. But if I am dead? Then I am euphoric. And you—' he pointed a long white finger '—are an angel.'

'Either way, I doubt you should lie here in the road, sir. Would you care to join me in my carriage? I am on a journey.'

'To heaven.' He smiled.

She thought of Gretna Green, which might be quite lovely, but fell far short of Elysium. 'We are all journeying towards heaven, are we not? But some of us are closer than others.'

He nodded, and struggled to his feet. 'Then I must stay close to you if the Lord has sent you to be my guide.'

Jem tossed the man a handkerchief, and he stared at it in confusion. Finally, the servant took it back, wiped the man's face and hands and brushed off his coat and breeches. He turned the man's head to get his attention and said slowly, 'You are drunk, sir. And you have fallen in a coach yard. Are you alone? Or are there friends to aid you in your predicament?'

The man laughed. 'I doubt any of my friends could help me find my way to heaven, for they have chosen a much darker path.' He gestured around him. 'None of them is here, in any case. I am very much alone.'

Jem looked disgusted. 'We cannot just leave you here. You might wander into the road again, if there is no one to stop you. And you seem harmless enough. Do you promise, if we take you along with us, not to bother the young mistress?'

'Take liberties with such a divine creature?' He

cocked his head to the side. 'I would not think of it, sir, on my immortal soul, and my honour as a gentleman.'

Jem threw his hands in the air and stared at Penelope. 'If you mean to have him, miss, I will not stop you. He appears to be a drunken idiot, but not particularly dangerous.'

The man nodded in enthusiastic agreement.

'Your brother will have my head if I'm wrong, of course.'

'My brother will not hear of it. He will not take you back, Jem, once he realises that you have helped me. You had best stay with me and hope for a favourable outcome. If we succeed, I will reward you well for your part in this.'

Jem helped her and the man back into the body of the coach, climbed in and shut the doors behind him. They set off again, and the man across from her looked surprised by the movement, before settling back into the squabs.

She smiled at him. 'I don't believe I asked your name, sir.'

'I don't believe you did.' He grinned at her. 'Adam Felkirk. And what am I to call you?

'Penelope Winthorpe.'

'I am not dead, then?' He seemed vaguely disappointed.

'No. Are you in some sort of trouble?'

He frowned. 'I most certainly am. Or will be, if I wake sober in the morning.' He smiled again. 'But for now, I am numb and free from care.'

'Suppose I could promise you enough brandy that you need never to be sober again?'

He grinned. 'At the moment, it is a most attractive proposition.'

'Brandy, Jem. I know you have some. Give it to Mr Felkirk.'

Jem looked horrified that his mistress would force him to acknowledge the flask in his pocket, and even worse, that she would require him to part with it. But he gave it over to the man in the seat next to him.

Felkirk nodded his thanks. 'If she is an angel, then you, sir, are a saint.' He raised the flask in salute and drank.

She examined him. He had an insubstantial quality. Harmless and friendly. She had feared that Jem spoke the truth when he had said that a real man might be more difficult to manage than the one she had imagined for her purpose. But Adam Felkirk seemed easy enough.

'Thank you for your kind words, Mr Felkirk. And if you wish more brandy, then do not hesitate to inform me.'

He smiled and drank again, then offered the flask to her.

She took it and considered it for a moment, before deciding that drink would not help her gain the courage to speak. 'But that is not all.' She tried a smile that was welcoming and friendly, since seduction seemed inappropriate for her purpose. 'You could have fine clothes as well. And a pretty mistress. Money always in your pocket, and a chance to do just as you please, in all things, at all times.'

He grinned at her, and she was taken aback by the whiteness of his smile. 'You truly are an angel, darling. And leading me to a heaven most suited for a man of my tastes. I had imagined something more pious.' He pulled a face. 'Downy clouds, flowing robes. Harps and whatnot. But heaven, as you describe it, sounds more like a fine evening in London.'

'If that is what you wish, you may have it. Whenever you want. I can relieve you of all cares. But first, you must do one thing for me.' She handed the flask back to him again.

He took it and drank deeply. 'As I suspected—it was far too pleasant to be heaven. And you are not an angel, but a demon, come for my soul.' He laughed. 'But I fear the devil might have that already, so what can I do?'

'Nothing so dire.' She smiled again, and told him her plan.

It was not at all clear that the truth was reaching him. He was smiling back at her, and nodding at the appropriate times. But with each sip of brandy, his eyes lost a little of their glitter. And, as often as not, he looked out the window rather than at her.

When she reached the word marriage, his eyes focused for a moment, and he opened his mouth. But it was as though he'd forgotten what it was he meant to say. He looked absently at her, then shrugged and took another drink, and his smile returned.

The carriage pulled to a stop, and Jem hopped down to open the door, announcing that they had arrived at Gretna Green. She stared at the man across from her, 'Do you agree to my terms, Mr Felkirk?'

'Call me Adam, my dear.' He was staring at her with increased intensity, and for a moment she feared that he meant a closer relationship than she intended. And then he said, 'I am sorry, but I seem to have forgotten your name. Oh, well. No matter. Why are we stopping?'

'We are in Gretna Green.'

'There was something you wanted me to do, wasn't there?'

'Sign a licence?' she prompted.

'Of course! Let us do that, then. And then we shall have some more brandy.' He seemed to think it was all jolly fun, and reached for the door handle, nearly losing his balance as Jem opened it in front of him. The servant caught his elbow and helped him down out of the coach, before reaching a hand up to help Penny.

When they were on the ground together, Adam offered his arm to her. She took it, and found herself leading him, steadying him, more than he ever could her. But he went along, docile as a lamb.

She led him to the blacksmith, and listened as Jem explained to the man what was required.

'Well, git on wi' it, then. I have horses ta shoe.' He looked critically at Penny. 'Da ya mean ta ha' him?'

'I do,' she said formally, as though it mattered.

'Yer sure? He's a drunkard. They cause no end a trouble.'

'I wish to marry him, all the same.'

'And you, sir. Will ya ha' the lady?'

'Marriage?' Adam grinned. 'Oh, I say. That is a lark, isn't it?' He looked down at her. 'I cannot remember quite why, but I must have intended it, or I wouldn't be in Scotland. Very well. Let us be married.'

'Done. Yer married. Na off with you. I ha' work ta do.' He turned back to his horses.

'That is all?' Penny asked in surprise. 'Is there a paper to be signed? Something that will prove what we have done?'

'If ya wanted a licence, ya coulda staid on yer own side o' the border, lass.'

'But I must have something to show to my brother, and the solicitors of course. Can you not provide for us, sir?'

'I canna write, so there is verra little I ca' do for ya, less ya need the carriage mended, or the horse shoed.'

'I will write it myself, then. Jem, run back to the carriage and find me some paper, and a pen and ink.'

The smith was looking at her as if she were daft, and Adam laughed, patted the man on the back and whispered something in his ear, offering him a drink from the brandy flask, which the Scot refused.

Penny stared down at the paper before her. What did she need to record? A marriage had taken place. The participants. The location. The date.

There was faint hammering in the background and the hiss of hot metal as it hit the water.

Their names, of course. She spelled Felkirk as she expected it to be, hoping that she was not showing her ignorance of her new husband by the misspelling of her new surname.

She glanced down at the paper. It looked official, in a sad sort of way. Better than returning with nothing to show her brother. She signed with a bold hand and indicated a spot where Jem could sign as witness.

Her new husband returned to her side from the forge, where he had been watching the smithy. He held a hand out to her. 'Now here, angel, is the trick if you want to be legal. Not married without a ring, are you?' He was holding something small and dark between the fingers of his hand. 'Give over.' He reached for her.

'I think your signature is all that is needed. And that of the smith, of course.' She smiled hopefully at the smith. 'You will be compensated, sir, for the trouble.'

At the mention of compensation, he took the pen and made his mark at the bottom of the paper.

'Here, here, sir.' Her husband took another drink, in the man's honour. 'And to my wife.' He drank again. 'Your Grace.'

She shook her head. 'Now, you are mistaking me for someone else, Adam. Perhaps it would be best to leave off the brandy for a time.'

'You said I could have all I wanted. And so I shall.' But there was no anger as he said it. 'Your hand, madam.' He took her left hand and slipped something on to the ring finger, then reached for the pen.

She glanced down. The smith had twisted a horse-shoe nail into a crude semblance of a ring, and her hand was heavily weighted with it. Further proof that she had truly been to Scotland, since the X of the smith held no real meaning.

Adam signed with a flourish, beside her own name. 'We need to seal it as well. Makes it look more official.' He snatched the candle from the table and dripped a clot of the grease at the bottom of the paper, and pulled out his watch fob, which held a heavy gold seal. 'There. As good as anything in Parliament.' He grinned down at the paper and tipped the flask up for another drink.

She stared at the elegant signature above the wax. 'Adam Felkirk, Duke of Bellston.'

'At your service, madam.' He bowed deeply, and the weight of his own head overbalanced him. Then he pitched forward, striking his head on the corner of the table, to fall unconscious at her feet.

Chapter Three

Adam regained consciousness, slowly. It was a mercy, judging by the way he felt when he moved his head. He remembered whisky. A lot of whisky. Followed by brandy, which was even more foolish. And his brain and body remembered it as well, and were punishing him for the consumption. His head throbbed, his mouth was dry as cotton, and his eyes felt full of sand.

He moved slightly. He could feel bruises on his body. He reached up and probed the knot forming on his temple. From a fall.

And there had been another fall. In the coach yard.

Damn it. He was alive.

He closed his eyes again. If he'd have thought it through, he'd have recognised his mistake. Carriages were slowing down when they reached the inn yard. The one he'd stepped in front of had been able to stop in time to avoid hitting him.

'Waking up, I see.'

Adam raised his head and squinted into the unfamiliar room at the man sitting beside the bed. 'Who the devil are you?'

The man was at least twenty years his senior, but unbent by age, and powerfully built. He was dressed as a servant, but showed no subservience, for he did not answer the question. 'How much do you remember of yesterday, your Grace?'

'I remember falling down in front of an inn.'

'I see.' The man said nothing more.

'Would you care to enlighten me? Or am I to play yes and no, until I can suss out the details?'

'The carriage you stepped in front of belonged to my mistress.'

'I apologise,' he said, not feeling the least bit sorry. 'I hope she was not unduly upset.'

'On the contrary. She considered it a most fortunate circumstance. And I assure you, you were conscious enough to agree to what she suggested, even if you do not remember it. We did not learn your identity until you'd signed the licence.'

'Licence?'

'You travelled north with us, your Grace. To Scotland.'

'Why the devil would I do that?' Adam lowered his voice, for the volume of his own words made the pounding in his skull more violent.

'You went to Gretna, to a blacksmith.'

He shook his head, and realised immediately that it had been a mistake to try such drastic movement. He remained perfectly still and attempted another answer.

'It sounds almost as if you are describing an elopement. Did I stand in witness for someone?'

The servant held the paper before him, and he could
see his shaky signature at the bottom, sealed with his
fob and a dab of what appeared to be candle wax. Adam
lunged for it, and the servant stepped out of the way.

His guts heaved at the sudden movement, leaving
him panting and sweating as he waited for the rocking
world to subside.

'Who?' he croaked.

'Is your wife?' completed the servant.

'Yes.'

'Penelope Winthorpe. She is a printer's daughter,
from London.'

'Annulment.'

'Before you suggest it to her, let me apprise you of
the facts. She is worth thirty thousand a year and has
much more in her bank. If I surmise correctly, you were
attempting to throw yourself under the horses when we
met you. If the problem that led you to such a rash act
was monetary, it was solved this morning.'

He fell back into the pillows and struggled to
remember any of the last day. There was nothing there.
Apparently, he had fallen face down in the street and
found himself an heiress to marry.

Married to the daughter of a tradesman. How could
he have been so foolish? His father would be horrified
to see the family brought to such.

Of course, his father had been dead for many years.
His opinions in the matter were hardly to be considered. And considering that the result of his own

careful planning was a sunk ship, near bankruptcy, and attempted suicide, a hasty marriage to some rich chit was not so great a disaster.

And if the girl were lovely and personable?

He relaxed. She must be, if he had been so quick to marry her. He must have been quite taken with her, although he did not remember the fact. There had to be a reason that he had offered for her, other than just the money, hadn't there?

It was best to speak with her, before deciding on a course of action. He gestured to the servant. 'I need a shave. And have someone draw water for a bath. Then I will see this mistress of yours, and we will discuss what is to become of her.'

An hour later, Penelope hesitated at the door to the duke's bedroom, afraid to enter and trying in vain to convince herself that she had any right to be as close to him as she was.

The illogic of her former actions rang in her ears. What had she been thinking? She must have been transported with rage to have come up with such a foolhardy plan. Now that she was calm enough to think with a clear head, she must gather her courage and try to undo the mess she'd made. Until the interview was over, the man was her husband. Why should she not visit him in his rooms?

But the rest of her brain screamed that this man was not her husband. This was the Duke of Bellston, peer of the realm and leading figure in Parliament, whose eloquent speeches she had been reading in *The Times* scant weeks ago. She had heartily applauded his opinions and looked each day for news about him, since he seemed, above all others, to offer wise and reasoned governance. As she'd scanned the papers for any mention of him, her brother had remarked it was most like a woman to romanticise a public figure.

But she had argued that she admired Bellston for his ideas. The man was a political genius, one of the great minds of the age, which her brother might have noticed, had he not been too mutton-headed to concern himself with current affairs. There was nothing at all romantic about it, for it was not the man itself she admired, but the positions he represented.

And it was not as if the papers had included a caricature of the duke that she was swooning over. She had no idea how he might look in person. So she had made his appearance up in her head out of whole cloth. By his words, she had assumed him to be an elder statesmen, with grey hair, piercing eyes and a fearsome intellect. Tall and lean, since he did not appear from his speeches to be given to excesses, in diet or spirit.

If she were to meet him, which of course she never would, she would wish only to engage him in discourse, and question him on his views, perhaps offering a few of her own. But it would never happen, for what would such a great man want with her and her opinions?

She would never in a million years have imagined him as a handsome young noble, or expected to find him stone drunk and face down in the street where he had very nearly met his end under her horse. And never in a hundred million years would she expect to find herself standing in front of his bedchamber.

She raised her hand to knock, but before she could make contact with the wood, she heard his voice from within. 'Enter, if you are going to, or return to your rooms. But please stop lurking in the hallway.'

She swallowed annoyance along with her fear, opened the door, and stepped into the room.

Adam Felkirk was sitting beside the bed, and made no effort to rise as she came closer. His seat might as well have been a throne as a common wooden chair, for he held his position with the confidence of a man who could buy and sell the inn and the people in it, and not think twice about the bills. He stared at her, unsmiling, and even though he looked up into her eyes it felt as though he were looking down upon her.

The man in front of her was obviously a peer. How could she have missed the fact yesterday?

Quite easily, she reminded herself. A day earlier he could manage none of the hauteur he was displaying now. Unlike some men, the excess of liquor made him amiable. Drunkenness had relaxed his resolute posture and softened his features.

Not that the softness had made them any more appealing. Somehow she had not noticed what a handsome man she had chosen, sober and clean, shaved and in fresh linen. She felt the irresistible pull the moment she looked at him. He was superb. High cheekbones and pale skin no longer flushed with whisky. Straight nose, thick dark hair. And eyes of the deepest blue, so clear that to look into them refreshed the soul. And knowing the mind that lay behind them, she grew quite weak. There was a hint of sensuality in the mouth, and she was carnally aware of the quirk of the lips when he looked at her, and the smile behind them.

And now he was waiting for her to speak. 'Your Grace...' she faltered.

'It is a day too late to be so formal, madam.' His voice, now that it was not slurred, held a tone of command that she could not resist.

She dropped a curtsy.

He sneered. 'Leave off with that, immediately. If it is meant to curry favour, it is not succeeding. Your servant explained some of what happened, while he was shaving me. It seems this marriage was all your idea, and none of mine?'

'I am sorry. I had no idea who you were.'

He examined her closely, as though she were a bug on a pin. 'You expect me to believe that you were unaware of my title when you waylaid me to Scotland?'

'Completely. I swear. You were injured in the street before my carriage. I was concerned for your safety.'

'And so you married me. Such a drastic rescue was not necessary.'

'I meant to marry someone. It was the intent of the trip.'

'And when you found a peer, lying helpless in the street—'

'As I told you before, I had no idea of your title. And I could hardly have left you alone. Suppose you had done harm to yourself?'

There was a sharp intake of breath from the man across the table from her and she hoped that she had not insulted him by the implication.

'I am sorry. But you seemed insensible. You were in a vulnerable state.'

'And you took advantage of it.'

She hung her head. 'I have no defence against that accusation.' She held out the mock licence to him. 'But I am prepared to offer you your freedom. No one knows what has occurred between us. Here is the only record of it. The smith that witnessed could not read the words upon it, and never inquired your name. I will not speak of it, nor will my servant. You have but to throw it on the fire and you are a free man.'

'As easy as that.' The sarcasm in his voice was plain. 'You will never trouble me again. You do not intend to reappear, when I choose to marry again, and wave a copy of this in my face. You will never announce to my bride that she has no legal right to wed me?'

'Why should I?' she pleaded. 'I hold no malice towards you. It is you that hold me in contempt, and I richly deserve it. Do I wish to extort money from you? Again, the answer would be no. I have ample enough fortune to supply my needs. I do not seek yours.'

He was looking at her as though he could not believe what he was hearing. 'You truly do not understand the gravity of what you have done. I cannot simply throw this on the fire and pretend nothing has happened. Perhaps you can. But I signed it, with my true name and title, and sealed it as well. Drunk or sober, for whatever reason, the result is the same. I am legally bound to you. If my name is to mean anything to me, I cannot ignore the paper in front of me.'

He stared at the licence, and his eyes looked bleak.

'You are right that no one need know if I destroy it. But I would know of it. If we had been in England, it would be a Fleet marriage and would mean nothing. But by the laws of Scotland, we are man and wife. To ignore this and marry again without a formal annulment would be bigamy. It matters not to me that I am the only one who knows the truth. I cannot behave thus and call myself a man of honour.'

She willed herself not to cry, for tears would do no good. They would make her look even more foolish than she already did. 'Then you shall have your annulment, your Grace. In any way that will suit you. I am sorry that scandal cannot be avoided, but I will take all the blame in the matter.'

'Your reputation will be in ruins.'

She shook her head. 'A spotless reputation has in no way balanced my shortcomings thus far. What harm can scandal do me?'

'Spotless?' He was eyeing her again. 'Most young girls with spotless reputations have no need to flee to Scotland for a hasty marriage to a complete stranger.'

'You thought I was…' Oh, dear lord. He thought she was with child, which made her behaviour seem even more sordid and conniving then it already was. 'No. That is not the problem. Not at all. My circumstances are…' she sought a word '…unusual.'

'Unusual circumstances?' He arched his eyebrows, leaned back and folded his arms. 'Tell me of them. If we have eliminated fortune hunting, blackmail and the need to find a father for your bastard, then I am out of explanations for your behaviour.'

He was staring at her, waiting. And she looked down into those very blue eyes, and, almost against her will, began to speak. She told him of her father. And her brother. The conditions of her inheritance. The foolishness over the book. 'And so, I decided that I must marry. It did not really matter to whom. If I could find someone on the way to Scotland… And then you fell in front of the carriage.'

He was looking at her most curiously. 'Surely you hoped for better than a total stranger.'

'Once, perhaps. But now I hope only for peace and quiet, and to be surrounded by my books.'

'But a girl with the fortune you claim…'

It was her turn to sneer at him. 'A plain face and disagreeable nature have managed to offset any financial advantages a marriage to me might offer. Only the most desperate would be willing to put up with me, for I can be most uncooperative when crossed.

'Since I know from experience that I will refuse to be led by my husband in all things, I sought someone I could control.' She looked at him and shook her head. 'And I failed, most dreadfully. In my defence, you were most biddable while intoxicated.'

He laughed, and it surprised her. 'Once you had found this biddable husband, what did you mean to do with him?'

'Gain control of my inheritance. Retire to my library and allow my husband to do as he chose in all things not pertaining to me.'

'In all things not pertaining to you.' He was staring at her again, and it occurred to her the things he might expect from a woman who was his wife. Suddenly, the room felt unaccountably warm.

She dropped her eyes from his. 'I did not wish for intimacy. But neither did I expect fidelity. Or sobriety. Or regular hours, or even attendance in the same house. I had hoped for civility, of course. But affection was not required. I did not wish to give over all of my funds, but I certainly do not need all of them for myself. If they remain with my brother, in time I will have nothing at all. I have thirty thousand a year. I should suspect that half would be more than enough for most gentlemen to entertain themselves.'

Again, there was an intake of breath from the man across from her. 'Suppose the gentleman needed more.'

'More?' She blinked back at him.

'One hundred and fifty thousand, as soon as possible.'

One hundred and fifty thousand. The number was mind-boggling, but she considered it, doing the maths in her head. 'I should not think it would be a problem. I have savings. And I do not need much to live on. While it will reduce my annual income considerably, it will leave more than enough for my needs.'

He studied her even more intently, got up and walked slowly around her, considering her from several angles. Then he returned to his chair. 'If I go to your brother and present myself as your husband, which indeed I am, then you would give me one hundred and fifty thousand pounds and the freedom to do as I wish with it?'

'It is only money. But it is my money, and I can do as I will.' She looked back into his eyes, searching for anything that might give her a clue as to his true nature, and hoping that it aligned in some small way with the man who had written such wonderful speeches. 'I should as soon see you have it as my brother, for I am most angry with him. You may have as much money as you need. If you agree to my other conditions, of course.'

He met her gaze without flinching. 'Why would I have to do that? Now that I am your husband, I can do as I please with all the money. You are a woman, and lost all say in the matter when you were foolish enough to wed a stranger.'

'There was the flaw in my plan,' she admitted. 'I expected to find a man slower in wit than the one I seem to have married. A drunken fool would be easy enough to gull. I could distract him with pleasures of the flesh. By the time he sobered enough to realise the extent of his good fortune, I meant to have the majority of my assets converted to cash and secured against him.'

She looked as closely at him as he had at her. 'But you are likely to know better. And I have given you the licence that proves your right to control my money, should you choose to exercise it. In truth, I am as much at your mercy now as you were at mine yesterday.'

There was a flicker of something in his eyes that she could not understand.

She said, 'You say you are a man of honour. And so I must appeal to your better nature. If you wish it, you may destroy the paper in front of you or we can go to London and seek a formal annulment.

'Or we can go directly to my bankers, and you can

take control of the fortune, which is your right as my husband. If so, I beg you to allow me some measure of freedom, and the time and money necessary to pursue my studies. The choice is yours.'

She thought to dip her head in submission, and decided against it. She waited in silence, watching for some sign of what he might say next. And the look in his eyes changed gradually from one of suspicion, to speculation, to calculation and eventually to something she thought might be avarice. He was thinking of the money. And what he might do with it, God help her.

It was a day too late to inquire what that might be. She had found the man, drunk as a lord in a public place. Who knew what vices he might be capable of? If she had not cared to discover this yesterday, it did no good to care now. And if his lechery and drunkenness were strong enough to run through the whole of her money, then it would prove to her brother just how foolish she was.

At last, he spoke. 'When you found me, I was near the end of my rope. An investment that should have returned enough to tide me and my estate through the coming year had failed, utterly. I have responsibilities. People are depending on me for their welfare. And I am destitute.

'Or was, until you appeared and offered me this opportunity. What I need to do may take a larger portion of your money than you had hoped to part with. But I hope it will be a temporary loss. My land is fertile most years, and returns more than enough to live in luxury. Had I not gambled with the profits, hoping for an increase, I would not be in need of your help.'

Gambling? Although it did not please her, it made perfect sense. Many men of considerable wealth lost all over a green baize table. She could but hope that she might hide some of the money from him, or perhaps, through sound advice, she might prevent him from making a similar mistake in the future.

He was waiting for some response on her part, and she gave him a faint nod of understanding.

He continued. 'In exchange, you shall be a duchess, which will make it possible to do largely as you please in all things. No one will dare to question your actions or your spending, least of all me. If you do not have cash in hand, no one will deny you credit. The bills will come to me, to be paid at such time as we have the funds for them.'

Doing business on credit went against her nature. But the prospect of freedom beckoned, and hope flared in her. 'And my studies?'

'If you do not wish to question my diversions, then what right would I have to question yours?'

As her husband? He would have every right in the world. But he was being most reasonable about things, so she held her tongue on the literalities. 'I doubt we would have much in common—in the matter of diversions, I mean.'

He nodded. 'Quite possibly not. We might live comfortably as strangers, although in the same house.' There was no sense of remorse as he said it. 'But I see no reason that we cannot succeed at it. As long as we have no intention of impeding each other's pleasure, we might manage well together. Certainly better than some couples I know who seem bent on ensuring their spouse's misery.'

It seemed so cold, when stated thus. But her new husband seemed content with it. He did not care that she wished to be alone with her books. And looking at his full lips and the seductive light in his blue eyes, she suspected the less she knew about his activities when he was not in Parliament, the happier she would be.

She ventured, 'It sounds most pleasant when you describe it thus.' Which was not precisely true. 'And very much what I was hoping for.' Which was. It was exactly what she had hoped for, and she must not forget the fact.

He smiled in return, although there was a frozen quality to his face that made her unsure. 'Very well, then.' He reached out a hand to her, and she stared at it for a moment before offering him her own. He took it and shook. 'We are in agreement. Let us hope that this union will prove mutually beneficial.'

'Will you be ready to start for London today?'

He started at the impertinence of her request. He was not accustomed to having another set his schedule.

She hesitated. 'I admit to being most eager to bring the news of my marriage to my brother. And my bankers, of course.'

He remembered the money, and his resistance to her suggestion evaporated. 'Today would suit me nicely. Have your footman prepare the carriage.' He nodded in such a way that she knew the interview was at an end and she was dismissed.

Adam watched his new wife exit the room and sank back into his chair, exhausted. What in God's name had he just agreed to? He'd sunk so low as to marry a cit's daughter, just to get her money.

And a cool voice at the back of his head reminded him that it was better than his first plan, if it meant that he could be alive to correct his mistake and rebuild his fortune. He had been given a second chance and would make the most of it. There would be money in the bank before his creditors noticed that there had been an absence. And by next year, the drought would be over, the coffers refilling and the present state of penury no more than a bad dream.

And he would be a married man. What was he to do with—he struggled to remember her name—Penelope Winthorpe?

He shook his head. She was Penelope Felkirk now. And there was nothing to be done, according to her. She wished to be left alone.

He was more than willing to grant her wish. He could not very well parade her in front of his friends as the new duchess. He'd be a laughing stock.

He immediately felt guilty for his pride. He'd be a laughing stock in any case, knowing his circle, who often found the humour in the misfortunes of others. Let them laugh. It would not matter, if he managed to save the estate.

But it pained him that they might laugh at her, as well, with her unfashionable clothes, her spectacles and outlandish ideas. To what purpose did the world need another translation of Homer? The majority had had more than enough of that story, by the time they'd left the schoolroom. And yet she was still worrying over it.

But he could find no indication that she meant him harm, by picking him up out of the street. In truth, she had saved his life. And her money would save his land as well.

What would people think of it? She was most obviously not his sort, in temperament or in birth. She was nothing like the ladies of the *ton* that he usually chose as companions. The world expected him to marry someone more like Clarissa Colton: beautiful, worldly, and with wit that cut like a razor. He shuddered.

Perhaps it told him something of his true mental state that he had married Clare's opposite. Penelope Winthorpe's clothes were without style, and her manner was bookish and hesitant. And her looks?

He shook his head. She'd called herself plain, but it was not truly accurate a definition. Plainness implied a commonality with the norm. A face unmemorable. And that did not describe his new wife.

Her looks…were disturbing. Her hair was too pale, almost white. Her skin as well, from too much time spent indoors with her books. And her spectacles hid eyes that were bright and far too observant. He wanted to know what she saw when she looked at him, for she had been studying him most intently. It was like being pierced to the soul, when her eye had held his. A gimlet, not a razor.

The intelligence in that gaze was daunting. And in her words as well. He'd have expected it from another man, but to hear such reasonable behaviour from a woman? There had been no nonsense. No tears behind the lashes. No attempt to appeal to him with her frailty. Their interview had been a frank meeting of intellectual equals.

Her presence had been both calming and stimulating. The combination made him uneasy. It was far too much to take before one had had one's morning tea.

But it shouldn't matter, he reminded himself. He needed nothing more from her than her money, and she needed nothing from him but his name. There would be scant little time staring into those disquieting eyes over breakfast. If she did not care for his title, then she need not concern herself with society, after the briefest introduction. And he would be spared the expenses of time or money that were involved in the keeping of a wife in the height of fashion.

And it dawned on him that there were other responsibilities in the taking of a wife that had nothing to do with the purchase of jewels and the redecoration of the manor.

There should be children.

He thought of her eyes again, and imagined a brood of little eyes following him with that same direct stare: dangerously clever children with insatiable curiosity. The prospect intrigued him, but it was not something he was likely to experience, if their current plan went forwards.

It came as somewhat of a relief to know that the title could follow another branch of the family tree. He had his brother as heir. That had been a fine plan yesterday. And if not William, then perhaps William would marry and have sons of his own. Good-tempered and intelligent children, just like their father. Any of those might do for the next duke.

Very well, then. He would take her back to London, or let her take him. And if what she said was true, he would sort out the money, right enough. And once she and her books were safely stowed at Bellston, then he could return to his comfortable old life. They would live, happily ever after, as was told in folk tales.

Just not with each other.

Chapter Four

The carriage ride to London was nothing like the one to Gretna. The trip outbound had been more excitement than misgiving, since she was convinced of the soundness of her plan and the immediate improvement it would bring to her life.

But now that she had succeeded, she found it most disquieting. Jem had been relegated to a seat beside the driver, leaving her alone with her new husband with a morose shake of the head that showed no confidence in a brighter future.

The man seated across from her was not the drunkard she had rescued on the way to Scotland. That man had been relaxed and friendly. His posture was familiar, as was his speech.

But when sober, the duke continued to behave as a duke. She hoped he was still feeling the effects of the liquor, for his expression was most forbidding, and she hoped it was not she that had put the look of disgust on his face. Or, worse yet, that his foul mood was habitual. Perhaps it was only the strain of travel, for they had been almost two full days on the road.

For whatever reason, her new husband sat rigidly in his seat across from her, showing no desire to close the distance between them.

And in response, she felt repelled from him.

It was foolish to care on that account. Jem's original fears were quite the contrary to the truth. He had imagined her wrestling a brute for her virtue in the back of a moving carriage. But this man no more desired the physical contact of his spouse than she did herself.

The chatty voyage to Gretna had been replaced with an uninterested silence that she suspected could stretch the length of the trip and far into the future.

And it was all right with her, she reminded herself. Once they were settled, she would return to her books and would appreciate a husband who was not likely to interrupt her work with demands for her attention.

Still, there were things that must be decided before they arrived in London. And that would be impossible without some communication.

She cleared her throat, hesitating to speak.

He looked up at her expectantly.

'I was wondering if you had considered what we might do once we reach London.'

'Do?'

'Well, yes. I wish to go to my bank, of course. And make my father's solicitors aware of my change in status.'

He nodded.

'But once that is done? Well, we cannot very well

live with my brother. There is room, of course, but I doubt that it would be in any way comfortable...'

He was staring at her and she fell into embarrassed silence. He spoke. 'When we arrive in the city, we will be going directly to my townhouse, and can make the financial arrangements after that.'

'Your townhouse.'

'Of course.'

She readied an objection, but paused before speaking. He was her husband, after all. And a man used to being obeyed. Insisting on her own way in this was liable to meet with objections. She said, 'Wherever we reside, I will need room for my collection of books, which is quite substantial. And a quiet place to study. A London townhouse might not be the best choice...'

He sighed, quite out of patience with her. 'Perhaps not the ones you have seen. But I assure you, the Bellston property in London is more than sufficient. We will not be staying there for long, since no one of any fashion is in London at this time. We will adjourn to the manor, once you have settled your business.'

'Manor?'

He was still looking at her as though she were an idiot. 'My home. I have a hunting lodge near Scotland, as well. I was visiting there when you found me. But there is no reason for you to see it at this time or ever, if you have no interest.'

'A manor,' she repeated.

His expression had grown somewhat bemused. 'And where did you think I lived, madam? Under a bridge?'

'I did not think on it. At all.' And now she looked

foolish. It annoyed her even more that she probably was. She had acted in a fit of temper, without considering the consequences.

'So you truly gave no thought to my title.' There was still a touch of amazement in the statement, as though he found the fact hard to comprehend, even after two days' trying. 'The peerage has both responsibilities as well as advantages. A title such as mine comes with a reward of land. In many years, it is a gift, but in some, it is a burden. In either case, I cannot simply walk away from it to indulge a whim.'

'A burden?'

'A recent fire has left portions of the manor house unlivable. Repairs are in effect, even as we speak. Expensive repairs,' he added significantly.

She nodded, understanding his most specific request for funds.

'Most of the house is livable, but I have business to complete in town. And so we will remain for a time in London, and reside in the townhouse. You will find space ample for your needs, I assure you.'

'That is good to know.' She was not at all sure that it was, but there was little she could do to change it.

'We will go to your bank as soon as you wish. You will introduce me as your new husband, and I shall need to make it clear to my solicitors that I have taken a wife. I doubt we can escape without the marriage becoming an *on dit,* for it is rather irregular.'

And there was another thing to worry about. She had not taken into account that his social life would be disrupted by the sudden marriage. No wonder he seemed cross. For her part, the idea was more than a little disturbing.

He continued. 'As soon as is possible, we shall retire to the country. We will take your books, of course. Have no fear of that. I doubt anyone shall wonder very much about us, once we are out of the public eye. I will need to return for Parliament, next session. But whether you choose to accompany me is your own affair.'

She searched his plan for flaws and found none. After the initial shock of it wore off, of course. She had expected to choose her own dwelling, and that her circumstances might diminish after leaving her brother's home. Why did she need a large house when a smaller one would suit her needs? But a manor...

'Did you have a better solution?' There was a touch of acid in the tone, but it was said mildly enough, considering.

He had taken pains to assure her that she would not lose her books. The least she could do was attempt to be co-operative. 'No. No. That is most satisfactory.'

'Satisfactory.' His mouth quirked. 'My holdings are not so rich as some, but I assure you that you will find them much more than satisfactory, once the improvements have been made.'

'Of course.'

Silence fell again. She looked down at her hands and out at the passing countryside, trying to appear comfortable. So, she was to be lady of a manor in the country. What part of the country? She had forgotten to ask. It would make her appear even more ignorant, if she waited until they were packed and driving toward it, to inquire.

Of course, once she was back in London, it would be easy enough to find the information, without having to ask her husband.

Unless her failure to ask made her appear uninterested in her new spouse…

It was all becoming very confusing.

He cleared his throat. 'This brother of yours. Is he a printer as well?' There was a pause. 'Because the servant mentioned that your father had been. And I thought, perhaps, family business…' He trailed off, displaying none of the eloquence that she had expected from him. Apparently, he was as uncomfortable in his ignorance as she was with hers.

She smiled and looked back at him. 'Yes. It is a family business. My father loved it dearly, and the books as well. And reading them, of course. He and Mother named us from the classics. My brother's name is Hector. Father always said that education was a great equaliser.'

'It is fortunate that a lack of education does not work in the same way. I was sent down from Oxford. It has had little effect on my status.'

They fell silent, again. She longed to ask why he had been forced to leave Oxford, but did not wish to seem impertinent. Was he like her brother had been, unimpressed by her desire for scholarship?

If so, he was biding his time before making the fact known. He'd had ample opportunity in the last few days to point out her foolishness over the translation. But he had said nothing yet.

'Marriage is also a great equaliser,' he said, to no one in particular.

Did he mean to refer to her sudden rise in society? If so, it was most unfair of him. She looked at him sharply. 'Apparently so. For once we reach the bank, your fortune shall be the equal of mine.'

She noted the flash of surprise in his eyes, as though she had struck him. And she waited with some trepidation for the response.

Then his face cleared, and he laughed. And suddenly she was sharing the carriage with the man she thought she had married. '*Touché*. I expect I will hear similar sentiments once my friends get wind of our happy union, but I had not expected to hear them from my own wife. I recommend, madam, that you save some of that sharp tongue to respond to those that wish to offer you false compliments on your most fortunate marriage.'

People would talk.

Well, of course they would. Why had she not realised the fact? And they would talk in a way that they never would have had she married the drunken nobody she was seeking. She was a duchess.

She would be noticed. And people would laugh.

A hand touched her, and she jumped, and realised that she had forgotten she was not alone in the carriage. She looked up into the face of her new husband, and read the concern on his face.

'Are you all right?' He said it very deliberately, as though he expected her to misunderstand. 'For a moment, you looked quite ill.'

'It is nothing. We have been travelling for some time, and the trip…' She let her words drift away, allowing him to make what he would of them.

'Shall I tell the driver to stop?'

'No, really. I will be fine.'

'Perhaps if we switch seats—a change of direction might help.' He took her hands and pulled her up off her bench, rising and pivoting gracefully in the tight space of the rocking carriage, to take her place and give her his. Then he pulled the shade on the window so that the moving scenery did not addle her gaze.

'Thank you.' She did still feel somewhat faint at the realisation of what she had done by marrying, and the impact it might have on the rest of her life. The distant and strange idea occurred to her that her husband was being most helpful and understanding about the whole thing. And that it might be nice to sit beside him, and rest her head against his shoulder for a time, until the world stopped spinning around her.

Which was a ludicrous idea. He was solicitous, but he had done nothing to make her think she was welcome to climb into his coat pocket. She looked at him again, even more beautiful in his concern for her, and closed her eyes against the realisation that they were a ridiculous study in contrast. A casual observer could not help but comment on it.

If he noticed the clamminess of her hand, which he still held, he did not comment, but reached out with his other hand as well, to rub some warmth back into the fingers. 'We will be in the city soon. You will feel much better, I am sure, once we have had some refreshment and a change of clothes.'

She certainly hoped so, for she doubted that she could feel any worse.

Chapter Five

When she opened her eyes a while later, the carriage was pulling up in front of a row of fine houses, and he tapped on the door, waiting for the servants to open it and put down the step. Then he descended and offered his hand to her. 'My dear?'

She reached out nervously to take it, while her mind raced to argue that she was in no way dear to him. The endearment was both inaccurate and unnecessary.

He saw the look in her eyes, and said, before she could speak, 'It might go easier with the servants if we maintain a pretence of familiarity. They will obey you, in any case. They would be foolish not to. But all the same…'

She nodded. 'Thank you, Adam.' There. She had said his name.

A footman opened the door before them, and she entered on the arm of the duke, who greeted the butler with a curt, 'Assemble the staff. Immediately.'

The man disappeared. He reappeared a short time later, accompanied by what Penny assumed must be the cook and the housekeeper, and, as she watched, an assortment of maids and footmen appeared from various entrances, lining up in an orderly row behind them.

She counted them. It must be a great house, as he had said, to need a staff so large. The home she had managed for her brother had made do with a staff of four. She reminded herself with some firmness that they were only servants and it did not do to show her fear of them.

The duke looked out over the small crowd assembled. 'I have called you all out from below stairs for an announcement. On my recent trip north, things did not go quite as expected.' He paused. 'Actually, they went much better than I expected. I married.'

There was an audible gasp from the room, before the servants managed to regain control of their emotions.

'May I present her Grace, the Duchess of Bellston—'

Before she could stop herself, she felt her knees begin to curtsy to the non-existent duchess, and her husband's hand came out to lift her back to her feet.

'—formerly, Miss Penelope Winthorpe. In celebration of this fact, you may all take the rest of the day off, to do as you will.'

There was an unexpected moment of tension.

'With pay, of course,' he added, and she could feel the staff relax again. 'We will be dining out. You need do nothing on our behalf until breakfast.'

The gasp had turned to a murmur of excitement, as the staff realised their good fortune.

'Three cheers for his Grace and the new lady of the

house.' The butler made an offer of 'huzzah' sound subdued and polite, but she accepted it with pleasure, as did her husband. 'Thank you. And now, you are dismissed. Enjoy the rest of your day.'

As quickly as they had gathered, the staff evaporated.

She looked at him, waiting for some indication of what was to be done next.

He glanced around him, seeking inspiration. 'Perhaps, a tour of the rooms would be in order. And then we will refresh ourselves, before a trip to your bankers.'

She nodded. 'An excellent plan. Please, your Grace, lead the way.'

He flinched. 'Remember, I am to be Adam to you. And you shall be?' He cocked his head to the side. 'Do you prefer Penelope, or are you a Penny?'

'Penny.'

'Then Penny it shall be, and whatever small endearments I can muster. Come, Penny.' There was a hesitation, as though he was struggling with a foreign language. 'Let me show you your home in London.' He led her down a short corridor, to doors that led to a parlour, which was grand; and a dining room, grander still, with room to seat twenty people. At the back of the house were a study, and a morning room.

'And this shall be yours.' He gestured into the sitting room, hesitating in the doorway as though he were afraid to enter.

She could understand why. Whoever had decorated the room had been the most ladylike of ladies. The furniture was gilt and satin, with legs so delicately turned that she was almost afraid to sit on it. If she chose a second sandwich at tea, the settee might collapse from the additional weight. And the desk, which would need to hold her books and writing materials, looked as though it might faint dead away, if expected to hold anything more serious than social correspondence. The other tables in the room were too small for anything larger than a rosebud, which would have to be candy pink to match the horrible silk upon the walls. The total was so sweet it made her teeth ache to look at it.

She looked in disgust at the ormolu clock on the mantel, which was supported by tiny gold goats and overflown with cherubs.

In response to her glare, the clock chimed the quarter hour, if such a stubbornly unobtrusive bell could be considered a chime.

She looked to her husband and struggled to speak. The correct response should have been 'thank you'. But it was quite beyond her. Eventually she said, 'It is very—pretty.'

He nodded in apology. 'We can find you furniture more suitable for work, and install additional shelves.' He pointed to a rather foolish collection of porcelain shepherds that graced a corner of the room. 'The bric-a-brac and nonsense can be dispensed with, if you wish.'

She looked dubiously around her.

'The room itself is large enough, is it not?'

She tried to ignore the design, and focus on the dimensions. It was larger than the one she had been using. She nodded.

'Very good, then. Redo it to suit yourself. I expected nothing less than that, from whatever woman I married. The rest of the house as well. If you see something that does not suit your tastes, it is well in your power to change it.' He paused. 'Except for my rooms, if you please. I would prefer that my bedroom and study remain as they are now.'

'I think that is not an issue. For I have seen nothing so far that needs alteration, and have no desire to change everything for change's sake.' She neglected to point out that, since any cosmetic changes to the house were to be made with her money, it hardly seemed like a sensible use of the funds. 'But this—' she gestured into her new work room '—must go.'

'Thank you.' He seemed relieved as well. There had a been tension in his back that eased as she said the words, and she suspected the first marital hurdle had been jumped with ease. He made no effort to open the door to his study, and she suspected that he wished some areas of his life to remain unviewed as well as untouched.

Fair enough.

'Let us go upstairs, then, and see the bedrooms.' He led her up the wide marble staircase and turned to the left, opening a door for her. 'These will be your rooms. There is a bedroom, a dressing room and a small room for your maid.'

None of which had been aired, she noted. The fireplace was cold and empty, and there was an uncomfortable chill in the unused room.

He noticed it as well, and wrinkled his nose. 'Well. Hmm. It seems I spoke too soon, when sending the staff away for a day of celebration. I have left no one to light you a fire.' He stepped across the room and opened a connecting door to his suite. There was a nervous pause. 'And I see the servants have brought your things to my room. They assumed…' He looked back at her, helplessly. 'This is not as it appears.'

What upset him more? she wondered—that she might think he wished to bed her, or that the servants had assumed that he would? 'It is all right. We will work things out between us, somehow.'

He nodded. 'Do you wish to change? You are welcome to use my room. There is a basin of fresh water. And clean towels. I could send for a maid to help you… Oh, damn. If you need help, I suppose, I…'

She imagined the feel of his hands at her back, undoing buttons. 'No. Thank you. I have become most adept at managing for myself, if there is no one to help me. If you will give me but a few minutes?'

He nodded and stepped aside, allowing her access to his room.

As the door shut behind her, she went hurriedly to the portmanteau on the floor and chose a fresh gown, struggling briefly with the closures at her back and slipping out of the travelling dress. Then she splashed some water from the basin on to her face, slipped into the new gown and used her brush to arrange her hair as best as was possible.

She could not help it, but glanced in the mirror behind her, examining the room. The man they had rescued from the street was obviously wealthy, but had seemed to have little care for health, his own cleanliness or welfare.

But the room behind her was orderly and immaculate. A sign of good housekeeping, perhaps. But there was more to it than that. The items in the room were expensive but well used and well cared for. The style and arrangement were elegant but simple. The whole suggested a well-ordered mind in repose. It gave her some level of comfort, knowing that her new husband's private rooms looked as they did. This was what she had expected from the Duke of Bellston.

She opened the door to the wardrobe and examined the line of coats and neatly hung breeches and trousers, and the row of brightly polished boots. Expensive, but not gaudy. The man was well tailored, but not a dandy. If he had sunk his fortune because he was prone to excess, there was no indication of it here.

From behind her, he cleared his throat.

She whirled, shutting the wardrobe door behind her.

'I am sorry. I knocked, but obviously you did not hear. Is there something you needed?'

That would cause her to snoop in his closet? He did not finish the sentence, allowing her a scrap of pride to hide her embarrassment. 'No. I am quite finished, thank you.'

'Then I would like to use my room as well, if you do not mind...' There was a hint of challenge there, but his face showed bland inquiry.

'I'll just wait downstairs. In the sitting room?'

'Thank you.'

She turned and exited the room before he could see the blush on her cheek, retracing her steps to her room on the first floor.

Adam waited for the click of the door latch before struggling out of his coat. It would be easier to call for his valet and admit that he had spoken in haste when releasing the staff. But he could manage to do for himself, if his wife had done so. And a day of leisure for the servants would unite them in support of the new mistress, and quell fears of upheaval and negative gossip. The minor inconvenience would be worth the gains in goodwill. He untied his cravat and tossed it aside, washing his face in the basin. Then he chose fresh linen, managing a sloppy knot that he hoped looked more Byronic than inept. He glanced behind him at the open door of the wardrobe.

She'd been searching his room. The thought should have annoyed him, but instead it made him smile. His new bride had a more-than-healthy curiosity. He walked over and pulled a coat off its hanger to replace his travelling clothes. Then she'd likely have been disappointed. There was nothing to see here. No skeletons. And not, fortunately, the bodies of any previous wives. Perhaps he should reassure her, lest she think him some sort of Bluebeard.

He glanced at her portmanteau on the floor beside the bed. Two could play at that game. Although what he expected to find, he was not sure.

He laid his hand on a spare gown, a clean chemise, a night rail, trimmed with embroidery and lace. It was all to be expected. Neatly folded and cared for, even though his wife travelled without a maidservant. The case was large and very heavy for only a few days' travel. But that was very like a woman, was it not? To pack more than was absolutely necessary. His hand stopped short of the bottom of the bag.

Books. Homer. Ovid. A book of poetry, with a ribbon tucked between the pages so that the reader would not lose her place. Not the readings of a mind given to foolish fancy.

He replaced things carefully, the way he had found them, and turned to go to meet her in the sitting room. She was as studious as she claimed, if she could not manage a few days without some sort of reading material. And it was well that she had brought her own to his house. There were many books he fully intended to read, when he had leisure. But for the life of him, he could not think what they would be, and he certainly did not have anything to read in the London house that held any enjoyment. It probably made him look a bit odd, to be without a library but well stocked in Meissen shepherds. But there was little he could do to change that now.

He approached her room in trepidation. The door was closed. Should he knock or enter freely? It was one of many decisions they would have to make together. If they did not mean to live as most married couples, then boundaries of privacy would have to be strictly observed.

At last, he settled on doing both: he knocked and then opened the door, announcing himself and thinking it damn odd that he should need to do it in his own house.

His wife looked up from a book.

'You have found something to read?' he said, and wished he did not sound so surprised at the fact.

'There were a stack of books on the shelf, here. Minerva novels. And Anne Radcliff, of course.' She glanced around her. 'Overblown and romanticised. They are most suited to the décor.'

'They are not mine,' he said, alarmed that such things even existed on the premises.

'That is a great comfort. For I would wish to rethink our bargain were they yours.' There was a twinkle in her eye as she said it. 'But if you favour melodrama, I suspect that this afternoon's meetings will be quite entertaining.'

And she was correct in what she said, for the trip to his wife's bank was most diverting. He was not familiar with the location, which was far from Bond Street, nor did the men working there know him. But it was obvious that they knew his wife and held her in respect. She was ushered into a private office before she even needed to speak her request.

When her bankers entered the room, she wasted no time on introductions, but straight away announced that she had married, and that all business matters must be turned over, post haste, to her new husband.

He could not help but enjoy the look of shock on the faces of the bankers. There was a moment of stunned silence, before the men sought to resist, arguing that the union had been most impulsive and possibly unwise. They eyed him suspiciously, and hinted at the danger of fortune hunters where such a large sum was involved. Was she sure that she was making the correct decision? Had she consulted her brother in the matter?

Adam watched as his new wife grew very still, listening in what appeared to be respectful silence. Although there were no outward signs, he suspected the look of patience she radiated was a sham. And at last, when they enquired if she had obtained her brother's permission to wed, her cool exterior evaporated.

'Gentlemen, I am of age, and would not have needed my brother's permission if the decision to take a husband had taken a year instead of a day. In any case, it is too late now, for I cannot very well send the man away, explaining that our marriage was just a passing fancy on my part. Nor do I wish to.

'May I introduce my husband, and manager of all my finances from here on, Adam Felkirk, Duke of Bellston.'

He did his best to maintain an unaffected visage, although the desire was strong to laugh aloud at the sight of the two men, near to apoplexy, bowing and calling him 'your Grace', and offering tea, whisky or anything he might desire, hoping to erase the words 'fortune hunter' from the previous conversation.

'No, thank you. I merely wish to see the account book that holds the recent transactions on my wife's inheritance.'

The men looked terrified now, but the account book appeared, along with a cup of tea.

Adam glanced down the row of figures, shock mingling with relief. His financial problems were solved, for there was more than enough to effect repairs on the house, and tide the property over until a more favourable season. He was equally glad that he had known nothing of the numbers involved when he had wed the girl. Considering his financial condition, he feared he'd have lost all shame, fallen at her feet, and begged her to wed him, based on what he saw before him.

He looked at the line of monthly withdrawals, increasing in amount as time passed. 'Do you have any regular expenses that need to be met, my dear?'

'Not really. My brother allows me a small allowance, and I take care not to exceed it. I doubt I'll need more than twenty or thirty pounds a month.'

Which was far less than the expenditures on the account. He tapped the paper with his fingertip and glanced up at the bankers. Where was the money going? To the only man with access to the account.

Until now, that is.

Hector had not touched the principal, as of yet. But Penny had been correct in her fears. If measures were not taken, there would be no fortune left to hunt.

He smiled, as condescending and patronising as he could manage. 'You gentlemen were wise to be concerned with the prudence of my wife's decision. But you need concern yourself no longer. Please prepare a draft, in this amount…' he scribbled a number in the book '…and send it to my bankers. I will give you the direction. The rest can remain here, as long as the investments continue to be as profitable as they have been. But under no circumstances is anyone to have access to the account other than myself.' He glanced at Penelope. 'Or my wife, of course. She has my permission to do as she pleases in the matter. Should she send any bills to you, please honour them immediately.'

He shot a sidelong glance at Penelope, and watched her eyes go bright and her mouth make a tiny 'O' of surprise.

He smiled. 'Is that to your satisfaction, dear?'

'Very much so.' The smile on her face was softer than it had been, with none of the hesitance that he had seen in her from the first day. Her body relaxed enough so that her arm brushed the sleeve of his jacket.

She trusted him. At least, for now.

And it cleared the doubts in his own heart, that he had married her for her money. Her fortune could stay separate from his, and he would leave her the control of it. With the look she was giving him, he felt almost heroic.

He was quite enjoying it.

After the success at the bankers, Penny had hoped to feel more confidence when confronting her brother. But as she entered the house, she could feel all the old fears reforming in her. Living here had felt a prison, as much as a haven. And her brother's continual reminders that this was all she would ever know, since no one would want her, had reinforced the iron bars around her.

And now, after only a few days away, the house felt strange. It was as though she were visiting a friend and not returning to her home. She had not realised how thoroughly she had put it behind her, once she made her decision. But it was comforting to think that there would be no foolish longing for the past, now that she was settling into her new life. Once she had her clothing and her things, there was no reason to return again.

She rang for servants, signifying that a maid should be sent to her room to pack her belongings, and sent Jem and another footman to the library with instructions for the crating and removal of her books and papers.

In the midst of her orders, her brother hurried into

the room and seized her by the arm. 'Penny! You have returned, at last. When I realised that you were gone I was near frantic. Do you not realise the risk to your reputation by travelling alone? Especially when you gave me no indication of where you were going. I absolutely forbid such actions in the future. I cannot believe…' Hector appeared ready to continue in his speech without ceasing, and showed no indication that he had recognised the presence of another in the room.

It annoyed her to think that he cared more about her disobedience than he did her safety. She pulled away from him, and turned to gesture to the man in the corner. 'Hector, may I present my husband, the Duke of Bellston. Adam, this is my brother, Hector.' She hoped she had not hesitated too much on the word Adam. She did not wish to appear unfamiliar with the name.

Hector ran out of air, mid-sentence, taking in a great gasp before managing, 'Husband?'

'Yes,' she replied as mildly as possible. 'When last we spoke, I indicated to you that I intended to marry, to settle the question of who should control my inheritance. And so I have married.'

'But you cannot.'

'Of course I can. I am of age, after all.'

'You cannot expect me to take a stranger into our home, on the basis of such a brief introduction.'

Her husband stood the rebuke mildly.

'Of course I do not. I have come for my possessions and will be moving them to my new home as soon as is possible.'

'Your new home.' Apparently, her brother was having some problem following the speed of events.

'Yes, Hector. I will be living with my husband, now that I am married.'

'You will do nothing of the kind. I have had more than enough of your nonsense. This is what comes of too much learning. Ideas. And telling jokes that are in no way funny. You will go to your room, and I will apologise to this gentleman, whoever he may be. And tomorrow, we will all go to the solicitors and straighten out the mess you have created.'

This time, she did not even bother to count. 'I will go to my room, Hector. To gather my clothing. From there, I mean to go to the library and the study, and empty them as well. And then I will be gone from this house and your presence. You have no power over me to stop it. And that, Hector, is what comes of not enough reading.'

His face was growing red, and he was readying a response.

And from behind her, she heard her husband, quietly clearing his throat. His voice was mildness and reason itself. 'Perhaps, Penny, it would be best if you saw to your packing, while I speak to your brother.'

She had the most curious feeling that he had issued a command, although it showed in neither his face nor his voice.

She opened her mouth to object, and then remembered how effectively he had dealt with the bankers. If he wished her to leave the room, then perhaps there was a reason for it. It would serve no purpose, challenging him in front of her brother. That would only prove Hector's point: that she had been foolish to marry in the first place. She blinked at Adam for a moment, then shrugged her shoulders and said, 'Very well.' And then she left the room, shutting the doors almost completely behind her.

Then she turned back and put her ear to the crack.

Her husband waited for a moment, giving her enough time to get to her room, she suspected. And then he waited even longer.

When the silence became oppressive, Hector blurted, 'Now see here, sir—'

Adam responded, 'The correct form of address when speaking to me is "your Grace". Perhaps you did not know it, since you obviously have little acquaintance with the peerage. But since we are family now...' disdain dripped from the last words '...you may call me Adam.'

Hector snorted. 'You cannot expect me to believe that Penny has been gone from the house less than a week, and has returned not only a married woman, but a duchess.'

Adam said, 'Your belief is not a requirement, Mr Winthorpe. The marriage exists. The bankers have been informed of it, and I have taken control of my wife's inheritance.'

This last seemed to give her brother pause, for he took a moment before letting out a weak laugh. 'But you cannot wish to be married to my sister. She is a nothing. A nobody.' There was another pause, and his tone changed. 'Albeit, a very wealthy nobody. And that could not possibly have influenced your decision when seeking such a humble bride—'

'Stop right there.' Adam did not shout, but the command in the tone was no longer an implication. 'I recommend that you pause to think before speaking further.' His voice dropped to just above a whisper. 'Here are the facts, and you would do well to remember them. Penelope is neither a nothing, nor a nobody. She is her Grace, the Duchess of Bellston. It will do you no good to hint that I am after her fortune, since she has gained as much, if not more, than I have by the union.'

There was another long pause, to allow the facts to sink into the thick skull of her brother. And then Adam said, 'But you have lost by her marriage, have you not? I've seen the books at the bank, and the withdrawals you have been making to keep your business afloat.'

Hector sputtered, 'I've done nothing of the kind. Those monies were for Penelope's expenses.'

'Then it shall not matter to you in the least that I am willing to take the management of the monies out of your hands. I can take care of my wife's bills without your help. You need trouble yourself no further with the management of her funds, but devote the whole of your time to business.' Her husband's tone clearly said, 'Dismissed.'

Penny covered her mouth to stifle a laugh.

But her brother refused to yield all. His voice rose to near a shout. 'All right, then. Very well. She has married and you have taken her money, and her as well. I wish you luck, your Grace, for you will find her fractious nature, her impulsive temper and her unending stubbornness to be more curse than blessing. She may pack her clothes and leave immediately, if she is so eager to do it. But she shall leave the books where they are. I have no intention of allowing her to put the contents of the family library into trunks and carry them from the house.'

Her husband seemed to consider on it, and then replied, with a neutral, 'If she wishes it, then it shall be so.'

Her brother shouted back, 'But it will leave the shelves empty!'

Adam responded quietly, 'That should not present much of a problem. You are a book printer, are you not? Bring home something from work to fill the shelves. I doubt it matters much what the titles may be, if one has no intention of reading them.'

If her brother recognised the insult to his intelligence, he let it pass without comment. 'This has nothing to do with whether I wish to read the books in question.'

'I thought not.'

'It is the value of the things. Do you know how many pounds has been spent to furnish that room?'

'Quite a few, I should think. She purchased many of those books herself, did she not?'

'When I could not manage to stop her.'

Adam's voice was cool reason. 'Then I see no reason that she need purchase them twice to stock the library in her new home. It is not as if she will be returning here to study.'

And still her brother would not give up. 'See here, you. You cannot think to take her from her family.'

'That is generally what happens when one marries,' Adam said, in a bored drawl. 'There is something in the

Bible about it, although I cannot say I remember the words. She is cleaving unto me, now. You have nothing to say in the matter of her future.'

Penny could almost imagine the wave of his hand, as he dismissed her brother's argument.

'Only because you have stolen her from me,' Hector snapped.

'Stolen her?' The duke laughed out loud. 'How long have you known your sister, sir? Is there some chance that you are adopted, or that she is some changeling, recently added to your family? I have limited acquaintance with her, I'll admit. But in that time I have learned enough to know that it would be exceptionally difficult to steal her from a place she wished to be, or to dissuade her from a path she had chosen for herself.'

'But that does not mean that I will allow her to behave foolishly.'

She was angry before she could even remember to count, and grabbed the door handle, ready to push her way back into the room and tell her brother that, after all that had been said and done, he had no right on earth to control her.

But Adam cut in before she could move. 'You have no authority over my wife. Penelope shall arrange for the transport of the library and the rest of her things to my townhouse. She shall do so at her own pace and in her own way. If I hear of any interference from you in the matter, if you place even the slightest obstruction in her way, I will take whatever action is necessary to thwart you, and it shall be my goal, henceforth, to see that you regret the impertinence. Are we in agreement?'

His voice held a cold fury that she had never heard before, and he was every bit the man she had imagined from *The Times*, so powerful that he could move the country with a few words.

Hector appeared to have been struck dumb, and so Adam answered for him. 'Very good. Our interview is at an end. I will be waiting in the carriage, should Penelope need me for anything. Which, for your sake, Mr Winthorpe, I sincerely hope she does not.'

Which meant he would be coming out into the hall in a moment, and he would realise that she was so lost to all manners as to listen at keyholes on private conversations. And, even worse, he might see the effect his speech had upon her, for her heart was fluttering so that she could hardly breathe.

She turned and sprinted towards the library, ducking into the open door, only to collide with Jem, knocking a case of books from his arms. The sound of the crash mingled with his bark of objection at people charging around the house and not watching where they were going.

Which in no way covered the faint chuckle she heard from the hall as her husband passed by on his way to the exit.

Chapter Six

Her heart was lighter, now that she had faced her brother at last. But empty as well. Hector was furious, and she'd cut herself off from the only home she'd ever known. It would have happened eventually, she supposed. Just as it should have happened four years before. But she had been prepared then. Now, the sudden marriage and all that came with it made her feel more alone than she had been, even though she had a life's companion to share it with.

And what a strange companion she had chosen. It had been much fun to watch him in action against her adversaries. And she hoped that her current feelings for him were not too apparent, for the afternoon's appointments and the masterful way he had handled things had left her breathless and not quite herself. She had half a mind to throw herself upon him, in a display of affection that would be most inappropriate towards a man who was nearly a stranger to her. And she feared that, if she spoke, she was liable to ramble on and sound as foolish as a schoolroom miss.

Her husband was seated opposite her in the hired carriage with a faint smile on his face, showing no effects of the day's changes. When she said nothing, he spoke. 'We have done a good day's work, I think. Your money is taken care of. Your things will be brought to the house tomorrow. I recommend that we send your manservant on his way, and attend to our supper, for we have missed tea, and I am feeling quite hungry. I can recommend several restaurants...'

Eating in public. She had always found it difficult to relax when in a crowd, and sitting down to a meal surrounded by strangers seemed to amplify those feelings. Suppose she were to order the wrong thing, use the wrong utensil when eating or break some other rule that would make her appear gauche to the duke or the people around them? If she took a simple meal in her rooms at the townhouse, she need have no worries of mistake. She would beg off, and save her husband the embarrassment of being seen with her. She said, 'I am accustomed to eat at home of an evening.'

'And I am not,' he said, with finality. 'I belong to several clubs— Boodle's, White's, Brooks's—and frequent them most evenings when I am in town. Of course, I cannot very well take you there. No ladies.' He stopped to consider his options.

So many clubs. It gave her a good idea where his wealth might have run to. And why he had needed so much of hers. 'It is more economical to dine at home,' she offered.

He raised an eyebrow and said, 'I imagine it is on such nights as the servants are engaged. My kitchen is most fine. You will know that soon enough. But remember, I have released the staff for the evening. You may go back, if you wish, and explain to them that economy requires they return to work.'

She gave a small shake of her head.

'I thought not. In the future, you may dine at home, as you wish. But do not be terribly surprised if I do not join you there, for I prefer society to peace and quiet. And tonight, we will dine out to celebrate the nuptials. That is only natural, is it not?'

She nodded hesitantly.

'I thought you would agree.' He smiled again, knowing that he was once more without opposition and gave directions to the driver.

On entering the restaurant, they were led by the head waiter to a prominent spot with the faintest murmur of 'your Grace'. Penny was conscious of the eyes of the strangers around them, tracking them to their table.

Her husband's head dipped in her direction. 'They are wondering who you are.'

'Oh, no.' She could feel the blood draining from her face and a lightness in her head as the weight of all the eyes settled upon her.

'My dear, you look quite faint.' He seemed genuinely concerned. 'Wine will restore you. And food and rest.' He signalled the waiter. 'Champagne, please. And a dinner fit for celebration. But nothing too heavy.' When his glass was filled, he raised it in toast to her. 'To my bride.'

The waiter took in the faintest breath of surprise, as did a woman at a nearby table, who had overheard the remark.

'Shh,' Penny cautioned. 'People are taking notice.'

'Let them,' Adam said, taking a sip. 'While you packed, I arranged for an announcement in tomorrow's *Times*. It is not as if it is to be a secret.'

'I never thought…'

'That you would tell anyone besides the bank that you had wed?'

'That anyone would care,' she said.

'I have no idea what people might think of your marriage,' he responded. 'But if I marry, all of London will care.'

She took a gulp of her own wine. 'That is most conceited of you, sir.'

'But no less true.'

'But there must be a better way to make the world aware than sitting in the middle of a public place and allowing the world to gawk at us,' she whispered.

He smiled. 'I am sorry. Have I done something to shame you, Penelope?'

'Of course not. We barely know—'

He cut her off before she could finish the sentence. 'Are you embarrassed to be seen with me?'

'Don't be ridiculous. You are the Duke of Bellston. Why would I be embarrassed?'

'Then I fail to understand why we should not be seen dining together, in a public place. It is not as if I do not wish my wife at my side.'

She was readying the argument that, of course, he

would not wish to dine with her. He was a duke, and she was a nobody. And he was every bit as beautiful as she was plain. And if he meant to embarrass her by showing the world the fact...

And then she looked at the way he was smiling at her. It was a kind smile, not full of passion, but containing no malice. And she imagined what it would be like, if he had dropped her at the townhouse, and gone on his merry way. Perhaps he would mention casually to some man at a club that he had wed. And there would be a small announcement in the papers.

People would wonder. And then, someone would see her, and nod, and whisper to others that it was obvious why the duke chose to leave his wife alone. When the most attractive feature was a woman's purse, you hardly need bring her along to enjoy the benefit.

Or, they could be seen in public for a time, and people might remark on the difference between them. But they would not think that the eventual separation of the two was a sign that he had packed her off to the country out of shame.

He watched as the knowledge came home to her. 'People will talk, Penny. No matter what we do. But there are ways to see that they speak aloud, and then lose interest. It is far less annoying, I assure you, than the continual whispering of those who are afraid to give voice to their suspicions.'

The plates arrived, and he offered her a bite of lobster on the end of his fork. 'Relax. Enjoy your dinner. And then we will go home.'

She took it obediently and chewed, numb with

shock. *Home. Together. With him.* The thoughts that flitted across her mind were madness. After the rough start in Scotland, her new husband was proving to be almost too perfect. In the space of a few hours, he had gained for her everything she could have wished. And now, if he would only let her go home and seclude herself in that horrible pink room before she said something foolish... If he insisted on staring at her as he had been with those marvellous blue eyes, and feeding her from his own plate as though she were a baby bird, who could blame her if she forgot that the need for familiarity was a sham, and began to think that deeper emotions were engaged.

There was a very subdued commotion at the entrance to the room, and Adam looked up. 'Aha. I knew news would travel quickly. But I had wondered how long it would take.'

A man strode rapidly toward them, weaving between the tables to where they sat. He noticed the space, set for two, and turned to the nearest empty table, seizing a chair and pulling it forward to them, seating himself between Penny and the duke. Then he looked at Adam and said, without preamble, 'When did you mean to inform me? Do you have any idea how embarrassing it is to be at one's club, enjoying a whisky and minding one's own business, only to have the man holding the book demanding that I pay my wagers on the date of your marriage? Of course I insisted that it was nonsense, for there was no way that such a thing would have occurred without my knowledge.'

Adam laughed. 'Ah, yes. I had forgotten the wagers.'

He looked sheepishly at Penny. 'I stand to lose a fair sum of money on that as well. I had bet against myself marrying within the year.'

Gambling, again. And losing. Another confirmation of her suspicions. 'You bet against yourself?'

He shrugged. 'I needed the money, and thought it must be a sure thing. But when I found you, darling, I quite forgot—'

'Darling?' the man next to her snapped. 'So it's true, then? You ran off to Scotland to get a wife, and told me nothing?'

'It did not occur to me until after,' Adam answered. 'Penny, may I present your brother-in-law, Lord William Felkirk. William, Penelope, my wife, the new duchess of Bellston.'

William stared at her, reached for his brother's wine glass and drained it.

William was a younger version of her husband. Not so handsome, perhaps, but he had a pleasant face, which would have been even more pleasant had it not been frozen in shock by the sight of her. Penny attempted a smile and murmured, 'How do you do?'

Will continued to stare at her in silence.

Adam smiled in her direction with enough warmth for both of them, and then looked back to his brother. 'Manners, Will. Say hello to the girl.'

'How do you do?' Will said without emotion.

'Penny is the heiress to a printer, here in London. We met when I was travelling.'

She could see the alarm in his eyes at the word printer, followed by a wariness. He examined her closely, and glanced from her to his brother. 'You were not long in the north, Adam. The trip lasted less than a week. Your marriage was most unexpected.'

'To us as well.'

He stared back at Penny, daring her to confirm the story. 'My brother never spoke of you.'

Her gaze dropped to her plate. 'We did not know each other for long before we married.'

'How fortunate for you to find a duke when you chose to wed. You must be enjoying your new title.' He had cut to the quick with no fuss.

'Frankly, I do not give it much thought.'

'Really.' He did not believe her.

Adam took a sip of wine. 'William, Penny's feelings on the matter of her sudden elevation to duchess are none of your concern. Now, join us in our celebration, for I wish you to be as happy as I am.' His voice held a veiled command.

Adam signalled for the waiter to bring another glass and plate, and they finished the meal in near silence, and William made no more attempts to question them.

Adam rubbed his temples and did his best to ignore the dull pain behind his eyes. It had been the longest meal of his life. First, he had needed to calm Penelope, who was clearly unaccustomed to the attention of the other diners. But he had done a fair job charming her back to good spirits. It had been going well, until Will had come and set things back on edge.

He'd had a good mind to tell his brother that the middle of a public dining room was no place to air the family laundry. If he could not manage to be a civil dinner companion, then he should take himself back to whatever foul cave he'd crawled from, and let them enjoy their food in peace.

When it was time to leave, William offered his carriage, and when they arrived at the townhouse, he followed them in, without invitation.

Adam should have refused him entrance, after his reprehensible behaviour in the restaurant. But if Will had anything to say on the subject of his brother's marriage, it might as well be said now and be over with, when the servants were away.

They were barely over the threshold before Will said, 'We must speak.' He glanced toward the study, then to Adam, totally ignoring the other person in the room.

Penny was aware of the slight. How could she not be, for Will made no effort to be subtle? She said, with false cheer, 'I will leave you two alone, then. Thank you for a most pleasant evening.'

Liar. But at least she was making an effort, which was more than he could say for his own family.

Penelope was barely clear of the room before William muttered, 'I will send for the solicitors immediately and we will put an end to this farce before anyone else learns of it.'

'The study, William,' he snapped, all patience gone.

They walked down the corridor, and he gestured Will into the room, slamming the door behind them.

Will paced the floor, not bothering to look in his direction. 'It has been only a few days, has it not? And most of that time, spent on the road. No one of importance has seen, I am sure. I will consult the lawyers, and begin the annulment proceedings. You will spend the night at your club, safely away from this woman.'

'I will do no such thing. I have no intention of leaving this house, and there will be no more talk of annulments.' Adam stalked past him, and threw himself into the chair behind the desk.

'You've lain with her already, have you?'

'That is none of your business, little brother.'

William nodded. 'I thought not. It is not a true marriage, but you have too much pride to admit the mistake.'

'This has nothing to do with pride.'

'Neither does it have to do with a sudden affection.'

Adam laughed. 'Affection? You expect me to marry for love, then?'

Will ceased his pacing and leaned over the desk, his fists planted on the wood. 'I think it is reasonable that there be at least a fondness between the two people involved. And it is plain that none exists between the two of you. You sat there at dinner with a false smile, pretending nothing was wrong, and she could barely look up from her plate.'

'We have an understanding.'

'That is rich.' Will snapped. 'She married you for your title, and you married her for her money. We can all claim the same understanding, for the fact is perfectly obvious to everyone who cares to look.'

'It is more complicated than that.'

'Do you mean to enlighten me as to how?'

Adam thought of the condition he'd been in when he'd made the decision to marry. And the condition just before, when he'd meant to end his life. 'No, I do not. That is something between my wife and myself.'

'Your wife.' Will snorted.

Adams hands tightened on the arms of his chair until he was sure that his fingers must leave marks in the wood. 'My wife, William. And I will thank you not to take that tone when referring to her. Despite what it may appear, I did not marry her for her money, any more than she sought to be a duchess. That we are both so blessed is a most fortunate occurrence, and I have no intention to annul. Lord knows, the estate needs the money she brings with her, and she has no objections to my using it.'

'So you will tie yourself to a woman that you do not love, just to keep the estate going.'

Adam stared at him, hardly understanding. 'Of course I would. If it meant that I could rebuild the house and protect the tenants until the next harvest time. Her money will mean the difference between success and failure this year.'

'What are the tenants to you, Adam? It is not as though they are family. And the manor is only a house.'

'It is my birthright,' Adam said. 'And I will do what is necessary to protect it. If it were you, would you not?'

William stared back at him, equally confused. 'I thank God every day that your title did not come to me. I have no desire to possess your lands, Adam.'

'But if it were to fall to you?' he pressed.

'Do not say that. For that would mean that you were dead. You are not ill, are you? Your line of questioning disturbs me.'

Adam waved his hand. 'No, no, I am not ill. It is only a rhetorical question. Do not read so much into it.'

'Then I will answer truthfully. No, I would not marry just for the sake of the title. Do not think you can marry for money to a woman you cannot bring yourself to bed, and then force me to be Bellston when you die without an heir. I would as soon see it all revert to the crown than become a slave to the land, as you are.'

Slavery? It was an honour. How could Will not understand? 'Search your heart and answer again. For it is quite possible that the whole thing will come to you, at any rate.'

Will waved the suggestion away. 'Not for long. If you mean to escape your responsibility with a hypothetical and untimely death, then two of us can play the game. I would rather die than inherit.'

Adam paused to thank God for the timely intervention of Penelope and her wild scheme. His death would have served no purpose if it had forced Will to take such action as he threatened. And he would not have wanted the heir he saw before him now. Will had always seemed so strong. Why had he never noticed that he was selfish as well?

Will continued. 'I suggest again that you seek an annulment if you do not wish for a legitimate heir from this poor woman. It is not fair to her, nor to me, for you to play with our fates in such a way, so that you can buy slate for your roof.'

Adam tried one last time. 'But if it falls to you…'

'I will take whatever measures are necessary to see that it does not.'

Damn it to hell. Here was another thing that he would have to contend with. Until now, he had assumed that there would be no problem with the succession. He had thought no further than the immediate crisis, just as he had thought no further when attempting suicide.

He must learn to play a longer game if he wished to succeed.

He looked to his brother again. 'I do not mean to abandon this life just yet, so you need not fear an inheritance. I had no idea that you felt so strongly about it.'

'I do.'

'Very well, then. No matter what may occur, you will not be the next duke. But neither do I intend to abandon my current plan just yet. The heir situation will sort itself out eventually, I suspect.'

'Do you, now?' His brother laughed. 'If you think it can sort itself out without some intervention on your part, then you are as cloth-headed as I've come to suspect. You wife is waiting in your bed, Adam. Let the sorting begin.'

Chapter Seven

Penny tried to put the mess downstairs behind her as she climbed the stairs to her room. William Felkirk had made little effort to disguise his distaste for her and was no doubt pouring poison in his brother's ears on the subject of marriage to upstart title hunters.

There was little she could do about it if Adam chose to listen. An acquaintance of several days and a trumped-up marriage were not equal to a bond of blood. She could only wait to see if he came to her room to explain that it had been a mistake, that he was terribly sorry, and that they would be undoing today's work in the morning.

She looked at her bedchamber and sighed, nearly overcome with exhaustion. No matter the outcome, she needed a warm bed and a good night's sleep. But the room in front of her was as cold and dark as it had been earlier in the day. If there was fuel available, she could manage to lay her own fire, but she could see by the light of her candle that the hearth and grate were empty. Not an ash remained.

She looked in trepidation at the connecting door to her husband's room. If she could borrow some coal and a Lucifer from his fire, and perhaps a little water from the basin, she could manage until the servants came back in the morning.

She knocked once; when there was no answer she pushed the door open and entered.

The bed had been turned down and a fire laid, despite the servants' day off. It was warm and cheerful, ready for occupation, and nothing like the room she had just left. There was a crystal bowl on the night table filled with red roses, and stray petals sprinkled the counterpane. Their fragrance scented the room.

Her portmanteau was nowhere to be seen, but her nightrail lay on the bed, spread out in welcome.

The door to the hall opened, and she looked back at her husband, leaning against the frame.

'My room is not prepared,' she said, to explain her presence.

He ran a hand through his hair in boyish embarrassment. 'The servants assume…'

She nodded.

He shrugged. 'You can hardly expect otherwise.'

'And what are we to do to correct the assumption?'

He stared at her. 'Why would we need to do that? That a man and a wife, newly married, might wish to share a bed is hardly cause for comment. But that a man and a woman, just wed, do not? That is most unusual. More gossip will arise from that than the other.'

She looked doubtful. 'I wondered if that might not matter to you so much now you have spoken to your brother.'

'Whatever do you mean?'

'That perhaps, now that you are back in your own home, you might wish to call a halt to our marriage. It is not too late, I think, to have second thoughts in the matter. And I would not fault you for it.'

'Because my brother does not approve?' He made no attempt to hide the truth from her. Although it hurt to hear it, his honesty was admirable.

He stepped into the room and closed the door behind him. 'What business is this of Will's? When he takes a wife, he will not wish me to trail along, giving offense and offering advice where none was requested. I recommend that you ignore Will as I intend to.' He moved across the room to a chair, sat down and set to work removing his boots.

Very well, then. There had been no change in her status. But what was to happen now? Did he mean to change in front of her? She was torn between embarrassment and a growing curiosity. How far did he mean to take their marriage? They had discussed nothing like this on the road from Scotland.

Then he stood up and walked across the room in his stockinged feet, locked the door and dragged the heavy comforter from the bed across the room to his chair. 'It shall not be the finest bed in London, but I have had worse.' He gestured to the rose-strewn mattress on the other side of the room. 'Be my guest.'

She sat on the edge of the bed and watched him as

he divested himself of coat and waistcoat, untied his cravat and undid his cuffs. He sat down again, slouching into the chair, long legs stretched out before him, wrapped the comforter around his body, and offered her a sketch of a salute, before closing his eyes.

She blew out her candle, placed her spectacles on the night table beside the bed, removed her slippers and stretched out on top of the sheets, arms folded over her chest.

From across the room, her husband's voice came as a low rumble. 'Is that how you mean to sleep? It cannot be comfortable.'

'For you either,' she said.

'But at least I am not fully dressed. Shall I call someone to help you out of your gown?'

'I can manage the gown myself, for I am most limber and can reach the hooks. But that would leave the corset, and I fear the lacing is too much for me. If we do not wish the servants to gossip, then I think not.'

He sighed and got out of his chair. 'I shall help you, then.'

'That would be most improper.'

He laughed. 'For better or worse, madam, I am your husband. It is the most proper thing in the world.'

She hesitated.

'It will look much stranger to have the maid undo the laces tomorrow than to let me do it tonight. Here, slide to the edge of the bed, and turn your back to me.'

She sat up and crawled to where he could reach her, turning her back to him. She could feel his touch, businesslike, undoing the hooks of the bodice and pushing it open wide until it drooped down her shoulders. She tensed.

'You needn't worry, you know. I will not hurt you or damage the gown.' He laughed softly. 'I have some small experience with these things. In fact, I can do it with my eyes closed if that makes you feel more comfortable.'

It would be ludicrous to describe the sensations she was experiencing as comfort. It would have been comforting to have the efficient, easily ignored hands of a maid to do the work. She would have climbed into bed and not thought twice about it.

But a man was undressing her. And since he had closed his eyes, it seemed he needed to work more slowly to do the job. He had placed his hand on her shoulders and squeezed the muscles there in his large palms before sliding slowly over the bare skin of her upper back and down the length of the corset to the knot at the bottom. He reached out to span her waist, and she drew a sharp breath as he undid the tie of her petticoat and pushed it out of the way. Then he leaned her forward slightly, and his fingers returned to the corset to work the knot free.

She could feel it loosen, and tried to assure him that she could manage the rest herself, but no breath would come to form the words.

He was moving slowly upwards, fingers beneath the corset, pulling the string free of the eyelets, one set at a time. She could feel the warmth of his hands through the fabric of her chemise, working their way up her body until the corset was completely open.

There was a pause that seemed like for ever as his hands rested on her body, only the thin cotton between his touch and her skin. And then he moved and the corset slipped free. She folded her arms tight to her chest, trying to maintain some modesty before it fell away to leave her nearly bare.

'Can you manage the rest?' His voice was annoyingly clear and untroubled.

She swallowed. 'I think so. Yes.'

'Very well, then. Goodnight, Penelope.'

And she heard him returning to his chair.

She squinted at him from across the room, until she was reasonably sure that his eyes were closed and he would see nothing. She hurried to remove her clothing, throwing it all to the floor and diving into her nightgown and under the sheets, safely out of sight.

She settled back on to the bed, pulling the linens up over her and waiting for sleep that did not come. The fire was dying, and the chill was seeping into the corners, though her skin still tingled with the heat from his touch.

It probably meant nothing to him. He was familiar with women's garments and the removing of them. He had done what he had done many times before, albeit with different results.

Her unwilling mind flashed to what it would have been like, if she was anyone other than who she was. His hands would be as slow and gentle as they had been while undoing her dress. Only, when the laces of the stays were undone, he would not stop touching her. Instead, he would lean forwards, and his lips would come down upon her skin.

She stared at the canopy of the bed, eyes wide, unable to stop the pictures playing in her mind and the phantom feeling of his hands and his mouth. Her body gave an uncontrollable shudder in response.

Across the room from her, her husband stirred in his chair, and rose, moving through the darkness towards her.

Without warning, the comforter dropped upon her body, and his hands smoothed it over her, tucking it close about her. Warmth flooded her, the warmth of his own body, left in the quilt. She sighed happily.

He returned to his chair, stretched out and slept.

Chapter Eight

When she awoke, light was seeping through the cracks in the bed curtains, which had been drawn at some point during the night. She could hear movement, and hushed voices from the other side. She sat up and placed her ear to the crack, so that she could listen.

Her husband. Talking to a servant, who must be his valet. Arranging for someone in the staff who would serve as a lady's maid, temporarily, at least. Perhaps permanently, since he was unsure if her Grace had servants of her own whom she wished to bring to the household. He had not discussed the matter with her.

The valet hurried away, and the door closed. She could hear her husband approaching the bed, and she pulled back from the curtain.

'Penny?' He said it softly, so as not to startle a sleeper.

'Yes?'

'May I open the curtains?'

'Yes.' Her voice was breathless with excitement, and she cleared her throat to cover the fact. As the light streamed in and hit her, she rubbed her eyes and yawned, trying to appear as though she had just awakened.

Adam was wrapped in a dressing gown, and she could see flashes of bare leg when she looked down. She must remember not to look down, then, for the thought that he was bare beneath his robe made her feel quite giddy.

'Did you sleep well?' He was solicitous.

'Very. Thank you. Your bed is very comfortable.' She glanced in the direction of the chair. 'I am sorry that you did not have the same luxury.'

Which might make it sound like she had wanted him there. She fell silent.

He ignored the implication. 'I slept better than I have in a long time, knowing that the financial future of my property is secure. Thank you.' The last words were heartfelt, and the intimacy of them shocked her.

'You're welcome.' She was in the bed of an incredibly handsome man, and he was thanking her. 'And thank you. For yesterday. For everything.'

He smiled, which was almost as blinding as the sunlight. Why must he be so beautiful, even in the morning? A night sleeping upright in a chair had not diminished the grace of his movements or dented his good humour. And his hair looked as fine tousled by sleep as it did when carefully combed.

She dreaded to think how she must appear: pale and groggy, hair every which way, and squinting at him without her glasses. She reached for them, knocking them off the night table, and he snatched them out of the air before they hit the floor and handed them to her, then offered the other hand to help her from bed.

She dodged it, and climbed unaided to the floor, pulling on her glasses.

'It will be all right, I think,' he said, ignoring her slight. 'We have survived our first day in London as man and wife. It will be easier from now on.'

Perhaps he was right. She went through the door to her own room to find it bustling with activity. Her clothing had arrived, and an overly cheerful girl named Molly was arranging a day dress for her, and had a breakfast tray warming by the fire. When she went downstairs, the first crates of books had arrived and were waiting for her in the sitting room. She had marked the ones that she expected to be the most important, opened those, and left the others lined up against a wall to obscure the decorating. The rest she could arrange on the shelves that had held the china figurines. She handed them, one piece at a time, to a horrified Jem to carry to storage, until his arms were quite full of tiny blushing courtiers, buxom maid servants and shepherds who seemed more interested in china milkmaids than in china sheep.

Jem appeared torn, unable to decide if he was more horrified by the overt femininity of the things or the possibility that he might loose his grip and smash several hundred pounds' worth of antique porcelain.

She waved him away, insisting that it mattered not, as long as they were gone from the room and she could have the shelves empty.

She gestured with the grouping in her hand, only to glance at the thing and set it down again on the table, rather than handing it to the overloaded servant. The statue was of a young couple in court clothes from the previous century. The man was leaning against a carefully wrought birdcage, and had caught his lover around the waist, drawing her near. She was leaning into him, bosom pressed to his shoulder, her hand cupping his face, clearly on the verge of planting a kiss on to his upturned lips.

And Penny's mind flashed back to the previous evening, and the feel of her husband's hands as they had touched her back. What would have happened if she had turned and pressed her body to his?

Jem shifted from foot to foot in the doorway, and she heard the gentle clink of porcelain.

'Never mind,' she said. 'You have more than enough to carry. I will keep this last one for now. Perhaps it can serve as a bookend.' She placed it back on the shelf, pushing it to the side to support a stack of books. *The Maid of Hamlet. The Orphan of the Rhine.* She'd kept the Minerva novels. Her lust-crazed Germans were supporting a shelf full of fainting virgins.

She sank back on to a chair, defeated by rampant romance.

There was a commotion in the hall, breaking through the silence of the room, and coming closer as she listened, as though a door had opened and a dinner party had overflowed its bounds. She could hear laughter, both male and female, and her husband by turns laughing and attempting to quiet the others.

At last there was a knock on the closed door of her room before Adam opened it and said with amused exasperation, 'Penelope, my friends wish to meet you.'

She did not know how she imagined the nobility might behave, but it had never been like this. The crowd pushed past the duke and into the room without waiting for permission to enter. The women giggled and pulled faces at the great piles of books, and one man leaned against a pile of open crates, nearly upending them on to the floor. Only the last to enter offered her anything in way of apology: he gave an embarrassed shrug that seemed to encompass the bad manners of his friends while saying that there was little he could do about it one way or the other.

'So this is where you've been keeping her, trapped in the sitting room with all these dusty books.' A pretty blonde woman in an ornate, flowered bonnet ran a critical finger over her library.

'Really, Barbara—' the laugh in Adam's response sounded false '—you make it sound as though I have her locked in her room. I am not *keeping* her anywhere.'

'She is keeping you, more like.' An attractive redhead made the comment, and Penny stiffened.

The woman clarified. 'I imagine the bonds of new love are too strong to break away, Adam. I wonder if you will manage to leave your house.'

Penny returned her cold smile. That had not been what she'd meant at all. It had been a slight on her wealth, followed by sarcasm. She was sure of it.

But Adam ignored it, smiling as if nothing had been said, and Penny vowed to follow his example.

Her husband gestured to his friends. 'Penelope, may I present Lord John and Lady Barbara Minton, Sir James and Lady Catherine Preston and my oldest, and dearest, friend, Lord Timothy Colton, and his wife, the Lady Clarissa.' He gestured to the cruel redhead and the man who had acknowledged Penny earlier. Adam smiled proudly at the man, and then looked to Penny. 'You will get along well with Tim, I think, for he is also a scholar. Botany. Horticulture. Plants and such. No idea what he's doing half the time. Quite beyond me. But I am sure it is very important.' Adam waved his hand dismissively, and Tim laughed.

Penny didn't understand the reason for her husband's pretended ignorance or the meaning of the joke. But clearly it was an old one, for the others found it most amusing. The room dissolved in mirth. It was like finding herself in a foreign land, where everyone spoke a language that she could not comprehend.

When their laughter had subsided, Clarissa spoke again. 'And what shall we call you?' The woman reached out to her, and took both her hands in what seemed to be a welcoming grip. Her fingers were ice cold.

'I know,' said Lady Barbara. 'We could call you Pen. For Adam says you like to write. And you were a book printer's daughter.'

Lady Catherine rolled her eyes. 'You write on paper, Bunny. Not in books.'

Clarissa looked down at Penny with a venomous smile. 'Surely not "Penny", for you are not so bright as all that.' There was a dangerous pause. 'Your hair, silly. It is I who should be called Penny.' She released Penny's hands and touched a coppery curl, smiling past her to look at Adam.

Penny watched, with a kind of distant fascination. Clarissa's gesture had been blatant flirtation, and she seemed not to care who noticed it. Yet her husband, Timothy, paid it no attention. He seemed more interested in the books on the table before him than his wife's behaviour to another man.

Adam ignored it as well, avoiding Clarissa's gaze while answering, 'But it is not your name, is it, Clare? Penny was named for the loyal wife of Odysseus. And she is worth far more than copper.'

There was an awkward pause.

Clarissa responded, 'So we assumed. We can hope that you are worth your weight in gold, Pen, for you will need to be to equal your husband's spending.'

And then they all laughed.

One, two, three… Penny felt shame colouring her skin compounded by anger at Clarissa and her own husband, and the pack of jackals that he had allowed into her study to torment her. She wanted nothing more than to run from the room, but it would only have made the situation worse. So she forced a laugh as well.

Her response would not have mattered, for now that she had wounded, Clarissa ignored her again and returned her attention to the duke. 'Darling Adam, it is so good to see you back amongst us. It is never the same when you are not here. London is frightfully boring without you, is it not, Timothy?'

Her own husband was looking at her with a sardonic twist to his smile. 'Would that you found such pleasure in my company as you do in Adam's, my darling.' He turned to Adam. 'But I missed you as well, old friend. Without you, times have been sober, as have I. We must put an end to that sorry condition as soon as possible. White's? Boodle's? Name your poison, as they say.'

'White's, I think. This evening?'

'Of course.'

Clarissa stamped her foot. 'You will do nothing of the kind. I expect you to dine in this evening. With us.' She made little effort to include her husband in her invitation. And none to include Penny, literally turning away to shut her out from the group.

Adam eluded her gaze again, speaking to the room rather than the woman before him. 'We would, but I believe my wife has other plans.' There was the subtlest emphasis on 'we', to remind Clarissa of the change in status. And then he glanced at Penny, waiting for her to confirm what he had said.

She tried to imagine herself responding as Clarissa had. She would say something clever, about how divine it would be to spend an evening at table with a woman who her husband held so dear. And there would be the same ironic tone that the others were using, to indicate an undercurrent of flirtation, and proof that she knew what was what. It would anger Adam, but he would admire her fearlessness. And it would enrage Clarissa. Which would be strangely pleasing, for Penny found herself taking an instant dislike to the woman.

Instead, she replied haltingly, 'Yes, I fear I am most busy. With my studies. And will be unable to get away.'

'You cannot leave your books.' Clarissa turned and

glanced down at her, then looked back at the others as if Penny's social ineptitude had been more than confirmed. 'But you do not mind if Adam comes without you, of course.' The woman dared her to respond in the negative.

And here was where she must admit defeat, ceding the field with the battle barely begun. Although why she would feel the need to fight for this, she had no idea.

Before she could answer, Adam spoke for her. 'My darling wife would have my best interests at heart, no matter what she might say, for she wishes to see me happy. And since I have already expressed a desire to go to White's with Tim, she would not think to drag me into mixed society, no matter how pleasant it might be for her.' He glanced back to his friend. 'Eight o'clock, then?'

If Tim was relieved, he did not show it, only smiling in acknowledgement of the plan. And then he smiled at Penny with unexpected warmth. 'Do not worry, my dear. No gels allowed at White's. I will keep your new husband on the straight and narrow. As long as you have no objection to cards and whisky.'

Penny searched again for a clever reply that would not come. 'Of course, not. Whatever Adam wishes…'

Clarissa was clearly piqued. 'It does not do, Penelope, to give a man latitude in these things. It leads them to take one too much for granted.'

Adam snapped back at her, 'On the contrary, Clarissa, a man is more likely to give his affection to one who can manage, on occasion, to put the needs of others before her own selfish desires.' Adam was looking straight into the woman's eyes for once, and

Penny realised, with sickening clarity, why he had been avoiding the contact.

They were lovers. They had been, or soon would be—it mattered not which. While Adam might smile at the wives of the other men in the room and laugh at their foolishness, he dared not acknowledge Clarissa, for when he looked at her, the guilt was plain in his eyes for all who cared to see.

After the brief lapse, he looked away from her again, and proceeded to act as though she were not in the room with them.

Penny looked to the others, watching the silent messages flash between them. Those who were positioned to see Adam's expression passed the truth to those who could not, with furtive glances and hungry smiles. Only Timothy appeared oblivious to what had happened, his attention absorbed by a volume of Aristotle.

And then the moment passed, and Adam stepped around Clarissa to stand behind his own wife. 'I am lucky to have married such a gracious woman, and hope never to take the fact for granted.'

Penny felt the mortification rising in her, forming a barrier between her and the outside. Was she expected to put her needs so far to the side that she must condone his adultery?

And then her husband put his hand upon her shoulder, as a gesture of affection and solidarity, and she jumped, as though she had been burned.

There were more sidelong glances and more wicked smiles. Suddenly Lord Timothy cut through the silence, shutting his book with a snap. 'Yes, Adam. We must offer you congratulations on your amazing luck. And it is good that you recognise it, for a man is truly blessed when he has the love and respect of such an intelligent woman.' He turned to the others in his party. 'And now, ladies and gentleman, we should be going, for we are quite destroying the peace of the household and keeping her Grace from her studies.'

'Let me show you out.' Adam took the lead, and the others fell obediently in behind him. Clarissa made as if to stay behind, but her husband held the door for her, making it impossible for her to linger.

When she was gone, Lord Timothy turned back into the room, and favoured Penny with another brief, encouraging smile. 'Good day to you, Penelope. And good fortune as well.' And then he was gone, shutting the door behind him.

She sank back on to the settee, weak with confusion. Adam had seemed so kind. He was good to her. Affectionate, in a distant sort of way. And in a short time it had become easy to imagine the affection blossoming into something warmer. Never passion. She could not hope for something so ridiculous. But love, in the classical sense. A respect for each other that might lead to a mutually satisfying relationship.

But how could she ever trust a man that would betray his best friend? And what did he mean for her, in any case? They had talked in Scotland about living as amiable strangers. And then he had paraded his lover under her nose, allowed her to be the butt of his friends' jokes, then glossed it over with fine and empty words about mutual respect.

If this was how fashionable society behaved, then she had been right in her decision to turn her back on it. But what was she to do if society hunted her out and continued to harass her?

She could hear her husband's step in the hall, and prayed that, for once, he would abide by his earlier promises, go to his study, and leave her in peace.

But instead he opened her door without preamble and shut it tightly behind him, then glared at her. He was angry. She could see it flashing in his eyes, and noted the stiffness of his back, as though his movements were containing some sudden physical outburst. His tone was curt. 'I wish to speak of what just happened here.'

'Nothing happened, as far as I noticed.'

'Exactly.' He frowned. 'And those around us took note of the nothing. It will be quite the talk of the town.'

'They took note of so many things, I am at a loss as to which one you refer to. Could it have been when you informed them of my monetary worth to you?'

'I misspoke. I had intended to praise your virtues, and the words went wrong.'

'Perhaps because I have so few virtues to extol. Since you cannot discuss my birth or my beauty, I should thank you on the compliment to my purse.'

'Believe me, Penny, I do not wish to call further attention to your wealth. It is not a point of pride that my friends suspect I married beneath me to get to your money.'

'Beneath you?' she snapped. 'When I discovered you, you were face down in a stable yard and under the horses. To marry beneath yourself, you would have to look quite a bit further than the daughter of a cit. There was not much lower you could have sunk.'

He flinched. 'I will avoid fulsome praise of you in the future, for I have no talent for flattery. In any case, it is wasted on one who makes no attempt to hide her distaste of me.'

'*I* have a distaste of you? Whatever do you mean?'

He glared at her. 'I might have been face down in the muck when you found me, but in marrying me, you got control of your inheritance and bagged a title. You understand, do you not, that many men would not be nearly so tractable as I have been towards you? We get on quite well, considering. And I did not mean to insult you in any way, nor do I plan to in the future. But I expect the same in return.

'It is one thing, madam, to refuse my affection, when we are alone. You avoided my hand this morning, but I thought, "Perhaps she is shy. I must give her time to trust me." But it is quite another thing to shrink from my merest touch when we are in public.'

'I did nothing of the kind.'

He reached to touch her hand, and she pulled away from him.

He smiled, coldly. 'Of course not, my dear. You are just as welcoming now as you were before. I touched your shoulder, and you looked to all the world as if I had struck you.'

'I thought it was agreed—'

'When I agreed to a marriage in name only, I did not realise that you found me so utterly repugnant that you would deny me all physical contact. Nor did I expect that you would make the fact known to my friends.'

'You do not repel me.' No matter how much she might wish he did.

'Oh, really? Then you had best prove it to me. Take my hand and assure me.'

She stared at the hand he held out to her, the long fingers curled to beckon, but she made no move to take it.

He nodded. 'I see. Most comforting.'

'I do not see why it is so important to you.' *You have her attention. Why must you have mine as well?*

He stared back at her until she met his eyes. 'I am a proud man. I do not deny it. It does not reflect well on either of us to have the full details of our relationship as public gossip. We are married, and I hope to remain so. The time will pass more easily for both of us if you can bring yourself to be at ease in my company, at least when we are in public. I will not bother you at home any more than is necessary.'

There was frustration and anger in his eyes, but they were still the same compelling blue, and just as hard to resist as they had been when she had trusted his motives. 'How can I do this?' she asked herself, as much as she did him.

His shoulders relaxed a little. 'You could, on occasion, smile while in public. I would not expect unceasing mirth. Merely as pleasant a face as you wear when we are alone. And if my hand should happen to brush yours, you need not flinch from it.' He raised his hand in oath. 'I promise to treat you with the care and respect due my wife and my duchess.' And then he offered it to her again.

She closed her eyes, knowing in her heart what his respect for his wife was worth, if he could not respect the marriage of another. Then she reached tentatively out to put her hand in his.

She heard him sigh, and his fingers closed over hers, stroking briefly before pushing her hand back until they were palm to palm and he could link fingers with her. He squeezed. 'There. Feel? There is nothing to be afraid of. I mean you no harm.' His other hand came to her face, and the fingertips brushed lightly against her cheek. 'I only wish for you to leave others with the impression that there is some warm feeling between us. Nothing more. That perhaps we might share something other than an interest in your money. Help me undo my foolish words.' His hand touched her hair and stroked to the back of her neck, and he moved close enough so she could feel his breath on her skin, and the change in the air against her lips as he spoke.

'This is much better, is it not?' His voice was low and husky, as she had never heard it before, barely more than a whisper.

She opened her eyes. He was right. When he was this close and looking at her, it ceased to matter how he looked at other women. She could feel the magnetic pull to be even closer. She had but to lean in a few inches, and his lips would be upon hers.

Which was madness. She had to resist yet another urge to jump away from him in alarm, and watched as his pupils shrank, and the soft smile on his face returned to its normal, more businesslike form. He withdrew slowly, with easy, unruffled grace. 'Very good. That is much more what I had hoped for. I do not expect you to fall passionately into my arms as a false display for visitors. But if we could at least give the appearance that we are on friendly terms, I would be most grateful.' His fingers untwined and his hand slipped away from hers.

'Most certainly. For I do wish to be on friendly terms with you in more than appearance.' She sighed, and hoped it sounded like a longing for her books, and not for renewed contact. 'And now, if you will excuse me? I must return to work.'

'Of course.'

Adam left the room, closing the door behind him, and moved quickly down the hall. Hell and damnation, it had been an unbearable morning. First, the invasion of his friends, before he'd had a chance to explain to Penny how things were likely to be. Although she probably suspected, what with the way Clarissa had been making a fool of herself, with no care for the fact that Tim was in the room with them.

Penny must think him a complete fraud. She had looked around the room, at his friends and at Clarissa, and had seen it all. She'd read his character in a glance and must regret her decision.

And he, who had always been so sure of his words, even when nothing else would go right for him, had stumbled so egregiously as to let it appear that he had married her for money. If possible, it was even worse than the truth to say such a thing. He had allowed her no dignity at all. And he had seen the mocking light in the eyes of his friends when she had flinched from his touch.

He had been foolishly angry, at himself and at Clarissa, and had taken it out on Penny for not offering affection that he had not earned. But what had he been about, just now? Had he been trying to teach her some kind of lesson? Hopefully, it had been lost on her, if he had. He should have come back to her and taken her hand in a most friendly fashion, and tried to mend the breach he had caused. He should have assured her that although he had been guilty of grave transgressions, it was all in the past, and that he meant to be a better man.

Instead, he had touched her hair and forgotten all. What sense was it to talk when there were soft lips so close, waiting to be kissed? And she had closed her eyes so sweetly, allowing him to observe the fine lashes and the smooth cheek and the sweetness of her breath as it mingled with his. It was a matter of inches, a bare nod of the head to bring them into contact with his own, and to slip his tongue into her mouth and kiss her until she reacted to his touch with the eagerness he expected in a wife.

He shook his head again. Had he forgotten whom he was speaking of? If he needed to persuade his own wife to let him hold her hand, then passion-drugged nights were not likely to be in the offing.

Not while he remained at home, at any rate. Perhaps it had been too long since last he visited his mistress. A man had urges, after all. And he was neglecting his if his own wife began to tempt him more than someone else's. An afternoon relaxing in the arms of his paramour would clear his mind, which was clouded with misdirected lust, and make it easier to decide what to do about the impossible relationship with Clarissa and the unwelcome attraction to Penelope.

He called for a carriage and set out to regain control of his emotions.

As he passed out the door, he saw Penny's manservant, who stood at the entrance to the house, wearing the Bellston livery as though it were as great an honour as a night in the stocks. He looked at Adam and bowed with as much respect as the other servants, while conveying the impression that the lady of the house was worth two dukes.

Adam glared back at him. 'Jem, isn't it?'

'Yes, your Grace.' And another bow.

Damn the man. Adam fished in his pocket and came up with a handful of banknotes and forced them into the servant's hand. 'I have an errand for you. Go to the bookseller's. And buy my wife that damned copy of Homer.'

Chapter Nine

In the two years they had been together, Adam's mistress, Felicity, had been a most accommodating and entertaining companion. But now, as he looked at her, he could not seem to remember why. She was beautiful, of course. There was little reason to have her otherwise. While she might not be the most enchanting conversationalist, he employed her to listen, not to talk. And so it mattered little.

She greeted him as she always had, with a passionate kiss. Her perfect hands reached out to stroke him and to smooth his brow.

And to search his pockets, as well. 'What did you being me, Adam?' Her smile was as satisfied as a cat's.

He smiled back. 'And why must I have brought you anything?' Although, of course, he had.

'Because you always do, my darling. I have come to expect it. And there is the little matter of your recent marriage.' She experimented with a pout, but her heart was not in it. 'You could at least have told me your plans. Even though it does not change what we share, it is not pleasant to be surprised when reading *The Times.*'

He nodded. 'I am sorry. I never intended for my situation to change so suddenly, or I would have fore-warned you.'

She nodded. 'It was love at first sight, then.' Clearly, she did not believe it any more than he did, but it was sweet of her to give him the benefit of the doubt.

'Rather. Yes.'

'Then, let us celebrate.' She kissed him again with an ardour guaranteed to arouse.

But the irony of the situation washed over him, and it was as though he were watching the kiss from a distance, rather than being an active participant in it. To be celebrating one's wedding in the arms of a Cyprian was probably sin enough for God to strike him dead on the spot. When their lips parted, he laid his against her ear and murmured, 'Then you no longer wish to see your gift?'

'I wish to see it, if you wish to show it to me,' she said, the most co-operative woman in his life.

He guided her fingers to the breast pocket of his jacket, to the package he had purchased on the way to her flat.

She was immediately distracted and withdrew the bracelet from the jewel box in his pocket. 'Adam, it is magnificent. The size of the diamonds. And the clarity.' She examined it with the eye of a professional. 'Th-thank you. It is quite the nicest thing you have ever brought me.'

He must have chosen well, if he had made a whore stammer. 'I am glad you appreciate it.'

For it cost me more than all your other gifts put together. Now that I can borrow from my wife's purse, money does not matter. And she will not care that I am here, for I have bought her a book. The truth sickened him, even as he thought it. And again, it was as though he was viewing the scene from a distance.

His mind might be shamed by what he had done, but his body cared not, and awaited the reward forthcoming after a gift.

And his mouth agreed with neither of them. As though he had no control over it, it announced, 'Yes. Of course. I thought, under the circumstances, an extra expenditure was called for. For you see…'

And his mouth proceeded, unbidden, to explain that now that he was married, their relationship had indeed changed. Since it was unlikely that he would be able to spend much time in her presence, it was hardly fair to keep her. The lavish gift was meant as a parting token. The apartment would be available for her use until such time…

His body howled in disappointment, and called him all kinds of fool, but still the words would not stop. And with each one, his conscience felt lighter.

His mistress was taking the whole thing annoyingly well.

She shrugged. 'I suspected as much. When a man gets it into his head to marry, his priorities change. And we have been together for quite some time, have we not?'

He started. She sounded bored with his attentions. The fact that she bored him as well was small consolation.

'And you have always been most considerate of me, and very generous of spirit. Should you need similar companionship in the future, I would not hesitate to recommend you as a protector.'

It sounded almost as if she was giving him references. 'And I, you.' He stuttered. 'Recommend, I mean. Should you need…'

He returned to his townhouse, numb with shock. The day was not turning out as planned. His old friends annoyed him. He'd just denied himself an afternoon of pleasure for no logical reason. And he still had no idea how to deal with his new wife. He returned home, because he could think of nowhere else to go. There was no joy in lunching alone, but his clubs would be too full of people, asking questions he did not desire to answer. At least in his own house he could have the consolation of solitude.

He was over the threshold before he remembered that he no longer lived alone. He had handed his hat and stick to the servant, and was halfway down the hall when he heard the rattle of tea things from the sitting room. Her door was open.

Too late, then, to take back his hat and back out of the door. Perhaps she would not notice if he quietly went to his rooms.

And then his wife peered into the hall. 'I was just sitting down to tea. Would you care to join me?'

'Thank you.' Once again, his mouth had said something that came as a surprise to him.

'I will have the butler bring another cup. You look in

need of refreshment. Come. Sit down.' And she graciously welcomed him to sit in his own home.

Her home as well, he reminded himself. She had every right to be taking tea in the room he had promised was solely for her use. And she was performing her duty as wife to see that he was provided with his. What right did he have to complain?

He sat down on the sofa next to her and waited in silence, while she pulled a tiny table closer to him and prepared his cup as she'd seen him take it. 'Biscuit?'

He stared at the unfamiliar thing in front of him.

She responded without his asking, 'I am accustomed to take sweets in the afternoon. These are a favourite of mine. I find the lemon zest in them most refreshing, so I have given the recipe to Cook. But if you would prefer something more substantial...'

'No. This is fine. Thank you.'

She was staring at him now. And he raised his eyes from his cup, to stare back at her.

'I am sorry for suggesting it,' she remarked, 'but is something the matter? You seem rather out of sorts.'

'What business is it of yours?' he snapped. And immediately regretted his outburst.

She was unfazed. 'Only that, earlier in the day, you said you wished to be friends.'

'I said I wished to appear to be friends. That is an entirely different matter.'

Again, she was unfazed, but answered thoughtfully, 'As you wish. Although it is sometimes easier to keep up the appearance, if an actual friendship exists.' There was no tartness in her voice. Merely a statement of fact.

He rubbed his brow with his hand. 'I apologise. Of course, you are right. I had no call to snap at you.'

'As you wish. I was not offended by it. It is I who should apologise to you for intruding on your peace. I merely wished to thank you for sending Jem to get my book. It was nice that you remembered.' She fell silent and allowed him to enjoy his tea.

But the silence was almost more discomforting than the noise, for it allowed him to feel the guilt again, although he could not imagine what it was that pained him.

'You are not disturbing my peace, Penny. But I fear I disturbed yours. I think—it may be possible that I am not comfortable when at peace. I must always be doing something to keep back the quiet. Thus, I released my ill-behaved friends on you this morning.'

She chuckled. 'We are an unsuitable pair, are we not?'

'Opposites attract.' But he could not manage to sound as sure as he wished.

'But at least our political views agree. It would be most difficult to respect you if—'

'Our politics?' It was his turn to laugh. 'To what purpose does a woman have political views?'

'To no purpose, other than that I live in this country, and am concerned with how it progresses. While I am not allowed to vote, there is nothing to prevent me from reading the speeches and governmental proceedings in *The Times*. That I cannot do anything to forward my views is no fault of mine.' She cast her eyes downwards, and then favoured him with a sidelong glance through her lashes. 'As a weak woman, I must pray that the country is in good hands.'

He felt the small thrill along his spine that he always got when a woman was trying to capture his attention. Could it be? He looked at her again. There was a faint smile on her face, and an even fainter flush on her pale skin.

His wife was flirting with him. Over the proceedings of the House of Lords.

It was an unusual approach, and unlikely to be successful. It would be easy enough to prove that she knew nothing of the subject with a few simple questions. And then, if she truly wished to flatter him, she could return to safer subjects favoured by other women of his female acquaintance: the colour of his eyes, or the cut of his coat and how well it favoured his shoulders. 'So you agree with my politics, do you?'

'Most definitely. Your grasp of economy is most erudite.'

'And you feel that the country is competently governed? For having seen the political process up close, I sometimes have my doubts.'

'Well, as far as I can tell, Lord Beaverton is a fool,' she said. 'He has little understanding of domestic trade, and even less of international issues. And he seems to disagree most vehemently with you on the subject of cotton imports.'

'Because he has interests in India,' Adam supplied. 'He is feathering his own nest.'

'Well, your interchange with him sounded most spirited. Although, if you could clarify a certain point…'

He had wondered when she would allow him to

speak, for she seemed to have no understanding of the conversational gambit that encouraged a woman to listen more than she spoke. Her first question was followed by another, and then another. And some were of a level of complexity that he was required to refer to a gazetteer in his study, and other references as well.

And soon it seemed easier just to move the tea things and conversation to his desk. He ceded her the chair, for he sometimes found it easier to think while on his feet, and she peppered him with questions while he paced the room.

There was a discreet knock at the door, and the butler entered. 'Your Grace? You have guests.'

A head appeared around the back of the servant. Tim was there, and he could see other friends crowding behind him in the hall. 'Have you forgotten, Adam? Dinner at the club?'

He glanced at the clock on the mantel. How had it got to be so late? 'It will be the work of a moment, and I will be ready to go.' He glanced down at Penny. 'Of course, if you wish, I will cancel.'

She shook her head. 'That is all right. I prefer to remain at home.' He thought he detected a trace of wistfulness in her answer.

'If you are sure?'

She nodded again, gathering her tea things from his desk. 'I should be going back to my room, after all. I meant to accomplish more today.'

'I am sorry if I distracted you. Until tomorrow, then.' And before he knew what he was doing, he'd bent and kissed her on the cheek.

She turned as pink as the walls of her sitting room, but she did not flinch from him. In fact, the smile he received in reward was quite charming, before she remembered that there were others present, and hurried across the hall and into her study, closing the door.

In retrospect, he'd have been better to have remained at home, for that seemed to be where his mind resided. The strange day only served to accent the commonness of the evening. The boring conversation and stale jokes of his friends were punctuated with exclamations of 'Adam, why must you be so glum?'

The constant reminder that he was not himself only served to make his mood darker.

When they were at cards, and Minton had presented some outlandish political position, Adam had snapped, 'Really, John, if I wished to talk politics, I'd have stayed home with my wife. She, at least, has some idea of what she is talking about.'

There was an amused murmur in the crowd around him, as though he had confirmed to the men around him that his sudden marriage had addled his mind. Only Tim looked at him and nodded with approval.

Soon after, a servant arrived, bearing a note on a salver for Tim. His friend unfolded the paper, grew pale, and asked a servant for his hat and gloves. 'I must make my apologies. I am called home. There is an emergency.'

'Nothing serious, I hope,' Adam said.

'I suspect it is little Sophie. She has been sick again. And I am a little worried.' Judging by Tim's agitation, minor worry did not describe his true state of mind.

Adam stood up. 'I will go with you. We will take my carriage to save time, and I will return home once your mind is at rest.'

But on arrival at the Colton home, they discovered the true nature of the emergency. All the lights were blazing, and from the salon came the sound of voices, laughter, and a soprano warbling along with the piano-forte.

Tim swore softly and with vehemence threw his hat into a corner and stalked into the room with Adam following in his wake.

His wife seized him by the arm, forcing a drink into his hand and announced to the gathering, 'Here they are! As I told you, they were detained.'

Adam was close enough to hear Tim murmur to his wife, 'You knew my intentions, and yet you brought me home to play host to a gathering that is none of my making.'

She responded through clenched teeth. 'And you knew my intentions. I wished for you and your friend to dine at home this evening. Do not cross me again, or you shall live to regret it.'

'More so than I do our marriage?' Tim laughed loud enough for the guests to hear, although they could not make out his words. 'That would be an impressive feat, madam.'

'You know how creative I can be.' She turned away from Tim, and reached for Adam, linking her arm in his and pulling him forwards. 'Come along, Adam. Do not think you can escape so easily. Have a drink with us before you go.' She was pressing against him in a way that must be obvious to her husband, and smiling up at him too brightly.

He eased free of her grasp, stomach churning, unable to look his friend in the eye. 'A glass of wine, then. Only one. And then I must be going home.'

Clarissa said, loud enough for all to hear, 'Ah yes. Hurrying home to your bride, Adam. Just when will she be making an appearance in society? People are beginning to think that the woman is a product of your overheated imagination.'

'You know full well, Clare, that she wished to remain at home, for you spoke to her this morning.'

'But, Adam, everyone is dying to meet her. I have told them so much about her. They are aflame with curiosity. Penelope is the daughter of a cit,' she informed the group gathered around them. 'And from what I've been told, she is very rich. But she will not mix with us, I'm afraid. She is far too busy to be bothered. Adam's wife is a bluestocking.' The last was said with enough pity to make the other revelations pale in comparison.

He was expected to say something at this point, but was at a loss as to what. Most of what Clarissa had said was perfectly true, although it sounded far worse coming from her mouth. And she had probably used his absence to embroider what facts she had with as many scurrilous fictions as she could invent. So he seized upon the one thing he could safely refute. 'Really, Clarissa. You make her sound so exclusionist that she should be a patroness at Almack's. She is at home tonight, reading *The Odyssey* in the original Greek. I bought her the book this afternoon as a wedding gift. But she'll mix with society soon enough.'

And then, he could not help himself—he added a fabrication of his own. 'We are planning a ball, and I suspect most of you will be invited to it. Then you can meet her and see for yourself.'

The crowd nodded, mollified, and there was an undercurrent of curiosity in the gossip that stole the thunder from Clarissa's tales. Bellston rarely entertained. The new duchess might be an eccentric, but no one would dare comment on the fact if it meant losing the duke's favour and missing a chance to attend an event that would be eagerly anticipated by everyone of importance in London.

Everyone except the Duchess of Bellston.

Penny sat at the vanity in her bedroom, which she had transformed, with the help of a strong lamp, into a makeshift writing desk. The work had seemed to fly this evening, with words flowing out of her mind and on to paper as easily as if the text were already in English and she was only copying down what she saw. Perhaps it had been the gift of the book that had inspired her. Adam could be so effortlessly kind that she scolded herself for thinking ill of him earlier in the day.

Or perhaps the intellectual stimulation of strong tea and good conversation had freed her thoughts.

That was all it had been, of course. Any stimulation she might have felt, beyond her intellect, was girlish fancy. She had always admired the Duke of Bellston. To see the actual man in front of her, moved by his subject matter until he'd all but forgotten her existence, was more invigorating than she'd imagined. He'd invited her into his study, allowing her past a barrier of intimacy that she had not expected to cross, and for a time she'd felt she was very much in his confidence.

And then he had kissed her. Thank the Lord that their conversation had been at an end, for she doubted that she would have been able to string two thoughts together after that buss on the cheek.

She had gone back to her sitting room and curled up on the sofa and opened the book, ready to enjoy his gift, only to have her eyes drawn, again and again, to the kissing couple on the bookshelf. She must have looked as dazed and eager as that when he'd left her.

And it had not stopped him from going out, she reminded herself, returning to cool logic. Not that there was anything wrong with being apart in the evenings. How would she get any work done if he forced her to accompany him everywhere, like a dog on a leash? She enjoyed her work.

And she had been quite satisfied with her progress once she left the sitting room, which seemed to attract foolish fantasy like a normal library attracted cobwebs. She could work without fear of interruption in her bedroom.

Certainly without fear of interruption by her husband. If he preferred to be elsewhere, in the company of others than herself? That had been their plan, had it not? She could hardly blame him for it. An evening of cards at an all-male club was hardly cause for jealousy on her part.

And if she was not mistaken, he was arriving home; through the open window she heard the sound of a carriage stopping in front of the house, and the faint sound of her husband's voice as the footman greeted him at the front door. She glanced at the clock. Barely eleven.

She had not expected him so soon. It had been later than this when they'd returned to the house on the previous evening, and he'd proclaimed it early. Was tonight's behaviour unusual?

Not that she should care. She hardly knew the man, and his schedule was his own affair.

But he had come home. Not to her, precisely. But he was home, all the same. Perhaps it would not be too forward to go downstairs in search of a cup of tea, and pass by the door to his study to see if he remained up. She got out of her chair, reached to tighten the belt of her dressing gown, and, without thinking, straightened her hair. Then she laughed at herself for the vanity of it.

With her hand on the doorknob, she stopped and listened. But, no. There was no need to seek him. He was climbing the stairs, for she could hear him on the landing, and then he was coming down the hall carpet toward his room. She waited for the sound of his bedroom door, opening and closing.

It did not come. He had walked past his room, for she had been unconsciously counting the steps and imagining him as he walked.

And then he stopped, just on the other side of her door. She waited for the knock, but none came. Perhaps he would call out to her, to see if she was asleep, though he must know she was not, for the light of her lamp would be visible under the door.

If she were a brave woman, she would simply open the door and go after the cup of tea she had been imagining. Then she could pretend to be surprised to see him, and inquire what it was that he wanted. She might even step into the hall, and collide with his body, allowing him to reach out a hand to steady her. Perhaps he would laugh, and she would neglect to step away, and she would know if he merely wished to continue their discussion, or if there was some other purpose for his visit.

But she was not a brave woman, and she was foolish to think such things, since they made no sense at all. There was a perfectly logical explanation for his being there, which he would no doubt tell her in the morning at breakfast. If she waited, she could save herself the embarrassment of making too big a thing out of something so small.

But all the same, she kissed the palm of her hand, and then silently pressed it to the panel of the door, holding it very near where the cheek of a tall man might be.

Then she heard his body shift, and his steps retreating down the hall, and the opening and closing of the bedroom door beside her own.

Chapter Ten

When she woke the next morning, she found herself listening for sounds from the next room and hoping for a knock on the connecting door. Surely Adam would come to her as soon as he was awake, and explain his behaviour the previous evening?

But she heard only silence. Perhaps he was a late sleeper, or simply did not wish to be disturbed.

When she could stand to wait no longer, she called for her maid. She would go downstairs and wait for him at breakfast. But when she arrived in the breakfast room, she was told that his Grace had been up for hours, had had a light meal and gone riding in the park.

Very well, then. If he had wished to speak to her, it had been nothing of importance. Or perhaps she had only imagined it, for things often sounded different through a closed door. Whatever the case, she would go on with her day as if nothing had happened.

She gathered her papers from her bedroom and

returned them to the sitting room, where the morning light made working easier. And in daylight, with her husband nowhere about, there seemed to be fewer romantic fantasies clouding her mind. But to avoid temptation, she turned the figurine of the lovers to face the wall.

She had barely opened her books before there was a quiet knock on the door, and a servant announced a visitor, offering a card on a tray.

Lady Clarissa Colton.

The card lay there on the tray before her, like a dead snake. What was she to do about it? 'Tell the lady that Adam is not at home.'

The servant looked pained. 'She wished specifically for you, your Grace.'

'Then tell her I am not—'

'Hello.' Clarissa was calling to her from the hall. She laughed. 'You must forgive me, darling. I have viewed this as a second home for so long that I quite forget my manners.'

'I see.' Penny had hoped to load those words with censure. But instead they sounded like understanding and permission to enter, for Clarissa pushed past the servant and came into the sitting room.

She sat down next to Penny, as though they were confidants. 'Adam and I are old friends. Particularly close. But I'm sure he must have told you.' Clarissa was smiling sweetly again, but her eyes were hard and cold. She reached out to take Penny's hands, giving them a painful squeeze. 'And when I heard the good news, I simply could not stay away.'

'News?'

'Yes. He told us last night, at the party. Everyone was most excited.'

'Party?' Obviously, there was much Adam had not told her. And now, she was left to parrot monosyllables back to Clarissa, until the horrible woman made the truth clear.

'Ooo, that is right. You did not know of it.' Clarissa made a face that was supposed to represent sympathy, but looked more like concealed glee. 'Adam came to our house last night after dinner. Not for the whole evening, as I had hoped. But he could not bear to disappoint me. The man is beyond kind.'

Far beyond it, as far as Penny was concerned.

'We knew you would not mind, of course, for you did not wish to come. In any case, he told us about the ball.'

'Ball?' She had done it again. Why in heaven could she not find her tongue?

'That you will be hosting, to celebrate your marriage. I am sure it will be the most divine affair. Your ballroom is magnificent, is it not? And Adam uses it far too seldom...'

Obviously, for she was not even sure of its location since her husband had neglected to show it to her. She nodded mutely, along with the flow of Clarissa's words.

'It is more than large enough to hold the cream of London society. We will begin the guest list this morning, and the menu, of course. And in the afternoon, we can see about your gown.' She glanced down at Penny's sombre grey day dress. 'I do not know what fashion was like where you came from—'

'I came from London,' Penny interjected.

'But these clothes will hardly do. We must fit you with a new wardrobe, gloves, perhaps a turban for evening. With an ostrich feather. You will adore it, I am sure.'

Penny was quite sure that she would look ridiculous with her hair dressed in plumes. And that was probably the point of the suggestion.

'We will go to my modiste, together. And I will instruct her on just how you must look, to display your true self to the world.'

There could not be a more horrifying prospect than that. Must she be polite to this woman, for the sake of her husband? Or could she say what she thought, and risk making a powerful enemy?

'Penelope. So sorry to intrude, I had no idea you were entertaining.' Adam stood in the doorway, still in his riding clothes, expression unreadable.

'That is all right, dear. You are not interrupting anything of importance. Only discussion of our ball.'

Discussion had been a charitable way to describe it. 'Clarissa says that you announced it at her home last evening. It was most unwise of you to give the secret away before we set a date.' *Or before telling your wife*.

He seemed to pale ever so slightly at being caught out. Then he regained his smile and said, 'So sorry, darling. I could not help myself.'

'Really?' They would see about that. 'No matter. Clarissa has come to offer her help in the matter, if I need it.'

Adam smiled again. 'How kind of her. But I am sure you have the matter well in hand, so she needn't have bothered.'

Clarissa laughed. 'Don't be ridiculous, Adam. She will have no experience in handling a gathering of this sort. She knows nothing of our set, or what will be expected of her. And you have thrown her into it, assuming that she will not embarrass herself. It will be a disaster.'

Penny hardly dared breathe, for fear that Clarissa would notice how close to the truth she had come.

But Adam waved his hand and shrugged. 'I doubt it is so hard as all of that, and Penny is a most enterprising and intelligent woman. No need for you to bother about it. But thank you for your concern. Let me show you out, and we will leave my wife to her work.'

'I could not think to leave the poor creature in the state she's in.' Clarissa spoke as if Penny was not in the room. 'At least convince her to leave her books long enough to go shopping, like a normal female.'

'You were going shopping, eh? Well, I know how much you enjoy that, and we mustn't keep you from it. Perhaps, some day, when Penny is finished with her book, you may come back for her. But for now…' Adam reached out a hand to her.

Clarissa weighed, just for a moment, continuing the argument against the chance to be nearer to Adam, if only for the short walk to the door. Then she smiled up at him and said, 'Very well, then. There is nothing for it—if you wish me to go, I must go.' She rose, and linked her arm with his. 'And perhaps you can be persuaded to tell me what I must purchase, so that I look my finest when I return for the ball. I do wish to look my best when in your presence.'

She watched them leave the room, Clarissa smiling brightly and leaning on Adam as if she could not manage to walk the few steps to the door without his support.

Penny did not realise that she was still clutching a pencil in her hand until the thing snapped under the pressure of her fingers. The gall of the woman. The infernal nerve. To come into her house, to point out her flaws and to rub her face in her husband's perfidy. The rage simmered in her, as she waited for Adam to return.

Before he was near enough to speak, she met him in the hall, and demanded, 'What is going on?'

'Penny. The servants.' He said it as though the lack of privacy should be sufficient to contain her temper.

But she was having none of it. 'The servants might also want to know the amount of extra work you have brought to this house, for you have certainly set us all a task. We are to have a ball, are we? Do we even have a ballroom? Clarissa seems to think so, but I do not know, myself.'

His ears turned slightly red, which might indicate embarrassment, but nothing showed in his voice. 'It is on the third floor. We have not had time for a whole tour—'

'Because we have been married less than a week. I have lived in this house for only two days, and at no time do I remember any discussion of our hosting an entertainment.'

He backed her into the sitting room, and shut the door behind them. 'The subject came up yesterday evening.'

'When you were at Clarissa's party. Another thing you made no mention of.'

'And *I* do not remember, in any of our discussions, the need to inform you of my whereabouts at all times. In fact, I specifically remember our agreeing that our social lives would remain separate.'

'An agreement which you chose to violate when you invited all of London to our house and neglected to inform me. While I can hardly complain over your choice of *entertainments* last evening, it embarrasses me when your *hostess* chooses to come to my house and make me aware of them.'

She glared at him, and watched the guilty anger rise in his face. 'I do not like what you are implying.'

'I did not think you would. But that is hardly a denial, is it?' She waited, praying that he would tell her she was wrong, and dishonoured them both by thinking such horrible things.

Instead he said coldly, 'It does not suit you to be jealous over something that was over before we even met.'

The admission, and the easy dismissal of her feelings, made her almost too sick to speak. 'I am not jealous, Adam. What cause would I have? You know that our relationship is not likely to be close enough to merit jealousy. But I am disappointed, and more than a little disgusted. I had thought you a better person than that. And to carry on in such an obvious fashion, under the very nose of a man you claim as friend…'

'Perhaps, if I had married a woman who wished to be at my side, then there would be no cause to wonder at my relationship with another man's wife.'

She laughed in amazement. 'It is all my fault, then?

That you choose to make a fool of yourself over a married woman?'

'I am not attempting to make a fool of myself. I am endeavouring, as best I can, to make our marriage seem as normal as possible to the rest of the world. But apparently I am failing—already there has been talk about you.'

'Only because Clarissa spreads it, I am sure. Better that they should talk about me than the two of you.'

He made no effort to correct her. 'If we do not appear together in public, and supremely happy, everyone will say that I am keeping you out of sight because you are an embarrassment to me.'

'What do I care what people think of me?'

'Apparently nothing, or you would not look as you do.'

One, two, three… She closed her eyes, to stop any chance of tears, and continued her counting. She had known he would say something about her looks eventually. How could he not? But she had hoped, when the time came, it would be as a casual statement of the obvious. Then she would be better prepared, and could agree and laugh the pain away. But he had been so good about not commenting. To have it thrown back in the heat of anger had taken the breath from her and her argument with it.

She made it all the way to nine and then blurted, 'If you had a problem with my looks, then you should have thrown the licence on to the fire when we were in Scotland. There is nothing I can do to my appearance to make it a match for yours. No amount of money will turn a sow's ear into a silk purse.'

He waited until she was through with her outburst, and then said, 'Do not turn soft on me, now that I need you to be strong.' There was no kindness in his voice, but neither did he seem angry. 'Our initial plan will not work. At least, not while we are in London. And so I am making another, and I expect you to obey me in it. If you do not wish to follow my advice, I will allow Clarissa to return and badger you into your new role as duchess. She is better qualified to teach you how to navigate in society than any other woman I know. But she can be amazingly stubborn and surpassingly cruel. Do you understand?'

She bit her lip and nodded.

'First, you will not, nor will I allow you in future to, refer to yourself as a sow's ear, a lost cause, wasted effort, nothing, nobody, or any of the other terms of scorn. Self-pity is your least attractive feature, and not one I wish to see displayed in my home for the duration of our marriage.'

When she was sure her eyes were dry, she opened them and glared at him.

'Very good. You look quite like a duchess when you are angry with me.'

She could not tell if he meant to be amusing, but she had no desire to laugh.

He stared down her body. 'Is all your clothing like this?'

She nodded. 'Practical. Easy to care for.'

'Dull. Ugly. Drab.'

'I put foolish things aside when my father died.'

'And how long ago was that?'

'Two years.'

'Two years,' he repeated. 'And you are still dressed in mourning. You are a bride, Penny. And to see you dressed so is an insult to me. It is as though I pulled you from weeping on a grave, and forced you to marry.'

'Very well,' she said. 'I will wear my old things. I have more than enough gowns in storage, hardly used since my come-out.'

'But they must be…' he added quickly on his fingers '…at least five years old.'

'They are not worn, so I have not needed to replace them.'

'But hardly the first stare of fashion.'

She laughed bitterly. 'As if that would matter.'

He let out a growl of exasperation. 'You listened to nothing of what I just said. Very well, then. My patience is at an end.' He seized her by the wrist and threw open the door.

She pulled her hand away. 'What do you think you are doing?'

'What someone should have done a long time ago. You are coming with me this instant, Penelope, and you will remedy the sad state of your wardrobe.'

'There is nothing wrong with the clothing I have. It is clean and serviceable.'

'And totally unfitting for the Duchess of Bellston.'

'I never asked to be the Duchess of Bellston, and I fail to see why I should be forced to conform to her needs.'

It was Adam's turn to laugh. 'You are the duchess, whether you planned it or no. When you decided to pull a stranger from the street and marry him, it never occurred to you that there might be complications?'

She sneered. 'Of course. I suspected if I was not careful that I would have a husband eager to waste my money on foolishness. I was willing to allow it to such a degree as it did not interfere with my comfort or my studies. And I was right to be concerned, for you have breached both boundaries with this request.'

As she watched, her husband became the duke to her again, drawing in his power in a way that was both intriguing and intimidating. His voice dropped to a barely audible murmur. 'Well, then. I am glad I have fulfilled your worst fears. We must set something straight, if we are to live in harmony.'

He meant to dictate to her? Reason fled her mind, and was replaced with white-hot rage. He had no right to do this, no right to tell her who she must be, if she was to be his wife at all. *One, two, three…*

'The wardrobe I am suggesting is in no way wasteful. Think of it as a uniform, nothing more. You wish to be left in peace? Then you will find it easier to deflect notice if you can play the part of a duchess with reasonable facility. The clothing I am suggesting will make this easier and not more difficult.'

Four, five, six…

'It will be expensive, but I have seen the statements from your bank, and you can most certainly afford it. If it helps, think of it as no different than you would allow me to purchase for my mistress. You had allotted an expense of this amount, hoping to keep me occupied so that you could work. Think for a moment the level of stubbornness and bullheadedness that you must project if you allow me to spend the money, but will only berate me for it if I wish to spend it on you.'

Seven, eight, nine…

'I take your silence for assent.' He rang for a servant and ordered the carriage brought round. 'I will deposit you at a modiste, and you can work out, between you, what is best done. I care not for the details, as long as the project is completed.'

Ten. And still she could not find a hole in his argument.

'And if you balk or resort to tantrums, I will throw you over my shoulder and carry you there, for you are behaving as a spoiled child over something that any other woman in the world would enjoy.'

The nerve of the man. Very well, then. She would go to the dressmaker, get a few simple gowns in the same vein as those she owned, and escape the ridiculous display that he intended for her.

She rode in silence with him, still irritated by his insistence on controlling a thing that he could know nothing about. Before her come-out, she had had more than her share of pushy dressmakers, shoe sellers and haberdashers, all eager to force her to look a way that did not make her the least bit comfortable. She had lacked the nerve to stand up to them, and had felt no different than a trained pony at the end of it, paraded about to attract a buyer.

And it had all come to naught.

The carriage pulled to a stop in front of an unassuming shop in a side street, far away from the hustle of Bond Street. Adam stepped down and held out his hand for her, but she would not take it. Unlike some women she could name, she could manage to walk without the assistance of Adam Felkirk.

The horses chose that moment to shy, and she almost fell into the street.

But her husband caught her easily, and pulled her into his arms, and safely to the ground. Then he had the gall to smile at her. 'This is what happens when you try to resist me. There is no point in it. I suggest you surrender, now.'

She glared at the shop in front of her. 'And do you come here often to purchase clothes for women? Or is this the store that Clarissa was threatening me with?'

'I have never been here before, and I have no idea where Clarissa would have had you go. This shop was frequented by my mother.' His smile turned to an evil grin. 'She decorated the sitting room that you enjoy so well. Since it does not matter to you what you wear, the fact should not bother you at all.'

She had a momentary vision of herself, clothed in bright pink organza, and could not control her grimace.

Adam nodded. 'I will leave you to it, madam, for you know best what to do. But do not think you can return home without purchases, for I am taking the carriage and the driver will not return for you for several hours.' He looked at her servant, hanging on the back of the carriage. 'I will leave Jem with you.' He tossed the man a sovereign. 'When the carriage comes back, if you can carry the purchases in one trip, she has not bought enough. Tell the driver to leave and return in another hour.'

And her own servant, who she should have been able to trust, pocketed the coin and bowed to his new master.

Adam looked to her again. 'When you are home, we will discuss the ball. Do not worry yourself about it. My mother had menus and guest lists as well. I am sure they will serve, and we can pull the whole thing together with a minimum of bother.'

Chapter Eleven

$\mathcal{P}$enny watched the carriage roll away from her. Damn the man. He knew nothing about anything if he meant to pull a ball together with the help of a woman who, she suspected, had been dead far longer than her own father. Clarissa was right: it was a disaster in the making.

And what was she to do for the rest of the afternoon, trapped here? If she had known his intent was to abandon her, she'd have brought something to read. She stepped off the street and into the shop.

A girl dropped the copy of *Le Beau Monde* that she had been paging through and sprang to her feet behind a small gold desk. She said, with a thick French accent, 'May I be of assistance, your ladyship?'

The girl sounded so hopeful, that Penny found it almost pleasurable to introduce herself with her new title. It made the girl's eyes go round for a moment, and then her face fell.

'Your Grace? I believe there has been a misunderstanding. You husband the duke must have been seeking my predecessor in this shop.'

'There is no Madame Giselle, as it says on the door?'

The woman laughed. 'Unfortunately, no. Until her death, she was my employer. She had been in this location for many years.'

'And before she died, you were…'

'A seamstress, your Grace. Madame died suddenly. There was no family to take the shop, and many orders still to fill. It made sense to step out from the back room and become Madame Giselle, in her absence.' The French accent had disappeared to reveal the Londoner underneath. Apparently, she'd taken more than the shop when she'd come out from the back room.

The girl took her silence as hesitation. 'We are not as fashionable as we once were, I'm afraid. I will understand, of course, that you prefer to go elsewhere. I can recommend several excellent modistes who are frequented by the ladies of your class.'

If she was not careful, she'd get her chance to shop with Clarissa. Penny's eyebrows arched in surprise. 'No wonder you are not as busy as you should be. For when one is in trade, one should never turn down commerce, especially an order as large as the one I am likely to make.' When she had come into the shop, she had had no intention of spending money. But suddenly, it seemed the most natural thing in the world.

'A large order?' the dressmaker repeated, dumbly.

'Yes. Day dresses, travelling clothes, outerwear and ball gowns. I need everything.'

'Do you wish to look at swatches?'

She gritted her teeth. 'It does not matter. Choose whatever you wish. And styles as well. I do not have any idea how to proceed.' And then she prepared for the worst.

The girl ran her through her paces, draping her in fabrics, and experimenting with laces and trims. And Penny had to admit that it was not as bad as it could have been, for the girl made no attempt to force her into gowns that did not flatter, but chose clothes that would suit her, rather than poking and pinching to get her to fit the fashion.

The choice of shops had been most fortunate, although Adam could not have known it. Now if she could find a way around the inconvenience of dinner and dancing for a hundred or so of her husband's friends... The man was cracked if he thought he could use his mother's guest lists. The names on it were likely to be as dead as her modiste.

Penny glanced down at the girl, who was crouched at her feet, setting a hem in the peach muslin gown Penny was modelling. 'Giselle?'

'My real name is Sarah, your Grace,' she said, around a mouthful of pins. 'Not as grand as it should be. But there is no point in hiding the truth.'

'Sarah, then. Do you have family in service?'

'My mother is housekeeper at Lord Broxton's house.'

One of her husband's adversaries in Parliament, but closely matched in society. It would do to go on with. 'It seems, Sarah, that I am to throw a ball. But I am no more born to be a duchess than you were born a French-woman. If I had guest lists and menus from a similar party, it would help me immensely. No one need know, of course. And I would be willing to pay, handsomely.'

Jem was summoned from the street and given a note from Sarah, and directions to the Broxtons' kitchen door.

He was back in a little more than an hour, with a tightly folded packet of papers containing names and addresses of the cream of London society, and the menus for a variety of events.

Penny sat comfortably on a stool in the back room and smiled at Sarah, who was throwing a hem into another sample gown. 'This is turning out to be a surprisingly productive trip, and not the total waste of time I had suspected. If I am careful, and can avoid any more of my husband's outlandish plans for me, I might still manage an hour or two of work.'

Adam would no doubt be irate when he saw the clothing that that woman was making for her. It did not in any way remind her of the dresses worn by the ladies of his circle. The colours for evening were pale, and the sprigged muslins she had chosen for day dresses hardly seemed the thing for a duchess.

Although just what duchesses wore during the day, Penny was unsure. Whatever they liked, most likely.

She gritted her teeth again. Or whatever their husband insisted they wear. But Sarah had seemed to know her business, despite the lack of customers. She had loaded Penny up with such things as were ready, more than enough petticoats, bonnets, and a few day dresses that had been made for samples, but fit so well they might have been tailored for her.

She inquired of the total, not daring to imagine how much she might have spent.

She saw the wistful look in the girl's eye as she said, 'The bills will be sent to your husband, of course. You needn't worry about anything, your Grace.'

Of course not. For nobility did not have to concern themselves with a thing so mundane as money. But she had taken much of the poor girl's sample stock, and there would be silks to buy, and lace, and ribbon to complete the order.

And since she was the Duchess of Bellston, it could all be had on credit while the false Madame Giselle found a way to pay her creditors with aristocratic air. Her husband, who had been so eager for this wardrobe, would send the girl some money in his own good time. She must manage as she could until then.

Penny reached into her reticule, and removed a pack of folded bank notes, counting out a thick stack. 'Here, my dear. This should go a fair way in covering the materials you will need. You may send the balance directly to my bank for immediate payment. Do not hesitate to contact me, should you need more. If I must do this at all, I would that it be done right and wish you to spare no expense.'

She saw the visible sag of relief, and the broadening of the smile on the face of the modiste.

When the carriage returned, and Jem saw the pile of boxes, he looked at her with suspicion, and gestured to an underfootman to throw them on to the carriage and tie them down. 'I'm to spend all my time, now that you're a "her Grace" two steps back and carrying your ribbons?'

'If it makes you feel better, Jem, think of it as charity work, just as my brother always wanted me to do. Or perhaps as economic investment in a small business.'

Jem stared sceptically at the boxes. 'I'm thinking, at least ladies' dresses are lighter than books.'

'Well, then. You have nothing to complain about.'

She had chosen to wear one of her new dresses home, a simple thing in pale pink muslin, with a rose-coloured spencer. The matching bonnet was a work of extreme foolishness, with a shirred back and a cascade of ribbons, but it seemed to suit the dress and she did not mind it overmuch. When she walked up the steps to the townhouse, it was a moment before the man at the door recognised her, and smiled before bowing deep.

Very well. The transformation must be startling. Adam would be pleased. She was certain of it. And he would admire the way she had managed the ball with a minimum of effort.

And then she remembered it did not matter at all to her what Adam thought. The whole of this production was an attempt to fool society into believing in their sham marriage, and put up a united front for his spurned lover, Clarissa.

If she was truly spurned. It was quite possible that Penny had wandered on to the scene in the middle of a contretemps and things would be returning to their despicable normal state at any time. If she allowed herself to care too much about her husband's good opinion, she would feel the pain of his indifference when he was through with her.

She hardened her heart, and walked down the hall to her husband's study, pushing open the door without knocking.

He was not alone. Lord Timothy was there as well. They had been deep in discussion over something, but it came to a halt, as she entered. 'I have returned. As Madame Giselle would say, *"C'est fini".*' The men stared at her as she pulled the bonnet from her head and dropped it on to her husband's desk. She reached into her reticule and removed the papers. 'Here is the list of guests for your ball. Add any names I have missed to the bottom of the list. Dinner will be buffet, but there will be no oysters, because it is too late in the season. You have but to choose a date. You know your social schedule better than I. For my part, I mean to be studying every night, for the foreseeable future. Which means any night you choose for this ball is equally inconvenient.

'Once you have decided, send the cursed guest list to the printer yourself. If you do not know where I wish you to take it, I will tell you, in no uncertain terms.' She looked down her nose at her husband, in what she hoped was a creditable imitation of a *ton* lady. 'Is that satisfactory, your Grace?'

Her husband stared at her in shocked silence. Lord Timothy grinned at her in frank admiration and supplied, 'Oh, yes. I should think so.'

'Very well, then. I shall retire, in my mildly pink dress, to my incredibly pink sitting room, put my feet on a cushion and read Gothic novels. I do not wish to be disturbed.' She turned to cross the hall, only to have Tim bound ahead of her to open the door.

Before it shut behind her, she heard a noise from the study that sounded suspiciously like a growl.

Chapter Twelve

$Adam$ stared through the open door of his study at the closed door across the hall. The silence emanating from the room was like a wall, laid across the threshold to bar his entrance. She spoke to him no more than was necessary, ate in her rooms and politely refused all visitors. She had succeeded in achieving the marital state that they had agreed on, allowing herself total solitude, and deeding complete freedom to him. He could do as he wanted in all things. His life was largely unchanged from the one he had before the marriage, with the exception of a near-unlimited supply of funds.

Why did he find it so vexing?

Perhaps because he had grown tired of that life, and had been quite ready to end it by any means available. Sick to death of playing, by turns, the wit, the lover or the buffoon for a series of false friends. Bone weary of dodging the insistent affections of Clarissa, who refused to believe that he looked back on their affair with regret and self-disgust.

And Tim, still at his side as a true friend and adviser. He chose to play the absentminded academic, more interested in his books and his conservatory than in the people around him. He pretended no knowledge of what had occurred between Adam and his wife, until such moments as he let slip an idle comment or odd turn of phrase to prove he knew exactly what had occurred, and was disappointed, but not particularly surprised.

Adam had hoped that the introduction of Penelope to his life might lead to a lasting change. She had qualities most unlike the other women of his set: sweetness, sincerity and a mind inquisitive for things deeper than the latest fashion. And she had seemed, for a time, to hold him in respect. He must present a much different picture in *The Times* than he did in reality. For though she claimed to respect Bellston, the politician, it had taken her a week to become as disgusted with Bellston, the man, as he was himself.

A servant entered, offering him a calling card on a silver tray.

Hector Winthorpe.

It was some consolation to see that the card was impeccably done, for Adam had sent the invitations for the ball to the Winthorpe shop. And he had grudgingly added Hector's name to the bottom of the guest list, as a good faith gesture. The man would not fit, but what could be done? Hector was family and they must both get used to it. But what the devil was he doing, coming to the house now?

Adam gave his permission to the servant and in a moment, Hector entered the room without making a bow, then stood too close to the desk, making every effort to tower over him.

Adam responded with his most frosty expression and said, 'If you are searching for your sister, she is across the hall. But it is pointless to try, for she refuses visitors when she is at work.'

'You have had no better luck with her than I did, I see, if she is shut up alone in a library. But I did not come for her. I wish to speak to you.'

'State your business, then.'

'It is about this, your Grace.' There was no respect or subservience in the title, as the man slapped the invitation to the ball on the desk in front of him.

'A written response of regrets would have been sufficient.'

'Regrets? It is you, sir, who should have regrets.'

Adam stared back, angry, but curious. 'And what precisely should I regret, Hector? Marrying your sister? For I find I have surprisingly few regrets where she is concerned.'

Hector sniffed in disapproval. 'Because she has given you your way in all things, I suppose. And because you care naught for her happiness, you have no guilt of the fact. If you felt anything at all for her, you would know better than this.'

Adam stared down at the invitation, truly baffled now. 'I fail to see what is so unusual about a small gathering to celebrate our nuptials.'

'Small?' Hector shook his head. 'For you, perhaps.

But for my sister, any gathering over two is a substantial crowd.'

'That is ridiculous. I have noticed no problems.' Which was a lie, but he could not give the man the upper hand so easily.

Hector let out a disgusted snort. 'If you noticed no problems with my sister, it is because she is a proud woman, and does not wish to admit to them. Did you not think it strange that she wanted nothing more from you than a chance to lock herself in her study and read?'

'Not overly,' he lied again, thinking of his first suspicions of her.

'Or that an argument over something so simple as a book would drive her to such extreme action as marrying a total stranger?'

There was nothing he could say that would cover the situation, and he certainly could not tell the whole truth, which reflected badly on the man's sister as well as himself. 'It has not proved a problem thus far.' He turned the argument back upon its sender. 'Do you think she chose unwisely?' And then he waited for the apology that must surely come.

'Yes, I do, if you mean to trot her out before your friends as some sort of vulgar joke.'

'How dare you, sir!'

Hector continued to be unabashed by the situation. 'It was too late, by the time she brought you to our home, to insist that you answer this question. But what are your intentions toward my sister, if not to make her the butt of your jokes?'

Adam smiled bitterly. 'I do not mean to fritter away

her fortune, as you were doing. You were keeping her unmarried and under your control so that you could pour her money into your business.'

The shot hit home, and he saw rage in Hector's eyes. 'I am not proud of the fact that the business is in trouble, sir. And I did, indeed, borrow the money from her trust without inquiring of her first. It was wrong of me, for certain. But I did not need to keep her unmarried to plunder her fortune. She did quite a fine job of scaring away any potential mates when she had her come-out. Her subsequent isolation was all her own doing. As of late, it had become quite out of hand. When I attempted to correct her on this, she lost her temper and went to Scotland. Apparently, she was looking for any fool that would have her. And she found you.' Hector said the word as though his sister had crossed the border and picked up not a husband, but some exotic disease.

Adam refused to rise to the bait. 'She can be rash, of course. But I fail to see what is so serious in her behaviour that would cause you to censure her or deny her simple purchases. It was wrong of you, just as was the theft of her money.'

'What do you know of her social life before you married her?'

Adam tried to think of anything he could say that would make him sound like he was an active participant in his own marriage, who had taken the time to get to know his wife, either before of after the ceremony. At last he said, 'Nothing. Other than her reasons for wishing to marry, and that she was interested in translating the classics, she has told me nothing at all.'

'Did you not think it odd that she has had no visits from friends, congratulating her on her marriage?'

He had not questioned it. But of course, there should have been guests to the house. If it had been any other woman, her friends would have beaten a path to the door, eager to meet the peer and bask in the reflected glow of Penny's rise in stature. 'I thought perhaps she had cast them off as unworthy. Now that she is a duchess…'

He could not manage to finish the sentence. He had thought no such thing. It was impossible to imagine Penny, who had little interest in her title or anyone else's, being capable of such cruelty to her friends.

Hector was silent, letting the truth sink in. And then he confirmed Adam's new suspicions. 'She has received no visitors because there is no one who has missed her. No one has expressed concern at her absence, or will wish her well on her good fortune. She has no friends, sir. None.'

'That is strange.' He could not help but say it, for it was. 'There is nothing about her that would indicate the fact. She does not complain of loneliness. Nor is there any reason that people might shun her society.'

'That is because she has been most effective at shunning the society of others. Her behaviour in public is, at best, outlandish, and at worst disturbing. When Father tried to give her a come-out, she made such a fool of herself that before the Season was complete, she had taken to her bed and was unwilling even to come down for tea. We hoped, with time, she would calm herself. But by the next year she was even more set in her ways than she had been. Small gatherings made her nervous, and large groups left her almost paralysed with fear.'

Hector looked at Adam with suspicion. 'And so it went, until she went off to Scotland in a huff, and came back with you. You will find, once you get to know her, that no fortune will make up for deficiencies of the mind.' His smile twisted with cruelty. 'Or do you claim some sudden deep affection for the girl that caused you to sweep her from her feet?'

Once again, Adam was trapped between the truth and the appearance of the thing. 'I can say in all honesty that I did not know of her fortune when I married her. And as far as my deep and abiding affection for her…' the words stuck in his throat '…you will never hear me claim otherwise, in public or private.'

Hector smiled and nodded. 'Spoken like a politician. It is not a lie, but it tells me nothing of what really happened.'

Adam stared at him without answering.

'Very well.' Hector tapped the invitation on the desk. 'You will not explain. But as a politician, you must be conscious of how her behaviour will reflect on you. It might be best to cut your losses, before she exposes herself, as she is most sure to do, and brings scandal down upon you.'

Adam drew in a breath. 'Cut my losses. And how, exactly, do you propose I do that?'

Hector smiled. 'You may think it is too late to seek an annulment. But you can hardly be expected to remain married, if there is any question as to the mental soundness of one of the parties involved. Think of the children, after all.'

'And if I cast her off?'

'I would take her back, and make sure she had the care she needed.'

When hell freezes. 'And you will take her money as well, I suppose.' Adam made a gesture, as if washing his hands. 'You are right, Winthorpe. I am growing worried about what a child of this union may be like. Suppose my heir should take after you? If that is not reason to remain childless, I cannot think of a better one. And as for any balls or entertainments we might choose to have? Such things are between myself and my wife and none of your affair.' But he felt less confident than he had before.

Hector threw his hands in the air. 'Very well, then. On your head be it if the poor girl drops on the dance floor in a fit of nervous prostration. Do not say you were not warned. The wilfulness of marrying was her doing. But you, sir, must take credit for the damage from now on.' And with that, he collected his hat and left the house.

Adam stared across the hall and felt a wave of protectiveness for the woman behind the closed door. Her brother was even more repellent than Adam had imagined, and he understood why she might have been willing to risk a stranger over another moment with Hector.

His accusation was a ploy to regain control of her fortune, of course. But suppose his wife was as frightened of society as her brother claimed? It explained much of Penny's behaviour, since they had been married. She was obviously happier alone with her books. It would be terribly unfair of him to expect her to stand before his friends as hostess.

Unfair, but necessary. People would talk, of course. There was no stopping it when Clarissa was egging them on. The longer his wife hid behind her studies, the louder the voices would become, and the crueller the speculations. A single evening's entertainment would do much to settle wagging tongues.

But the sight of her, frozen in terror in front of a hundred guests, would do nothing to help and much to hurt. Hector was right in that, at least. He must avoid that, at all costs.

He rose, crossed the hall and knocked upon her door, opening it before she could deny him.

She was seated in a chair at the tiny writing desk in the corner, attired in a pale blue gown that must have been one of the purchases he had forced upon her. He doubted it would win favour to tell her that the colour and style suited her well, although, in truth, they did. She looked quite lovely in the morning sunlight, surrounded by books.

She set down the volume she had been reading, pushed her glasses up her nose and looked up at him with cool uninterest. 'Is there something that I can help you with?'

How best to broach the question? 'I was wondering—are preparations for the ball progressing well?'

She nodded, and he felt the tension in the air as she stiffened. 'As well as can be expected. The invitations have been sent, and replies are returning. The hall is cleaned, the food is ordered.'

'I thought…perhaps we could cancel the plans, if it is being too much trouble.'

She was looking at him as though he had lost his

mind. 'After all the trouble of choosing the food, deco-rating the hall, and sending the invitations, you now wish me to spend even more time in sending retractions?'

'No. Really, I—'

'Because if you think, at this date, it is possible to stop what you wished to set in progress, you are quite mad.'

He closed his eyes and took a deep breath, vowing to remain calm in the face of her temper, no matter what might occur. 'I do not wish to make more work for you, or to take you from your studies. I swear, that was never my goal. My decision to hold the ball was made in haste, and without any thought to your feelings or needs. It pains me greatly that you heard of it from someone other than myself, for it further displayed my carelessness in not coming to you immediately to explain.'

'Apology accepted.' She turned back to her books, as though to dismiss him.

'Your brother was here. In my study, just now.'

That had her attention. She looked up at him in surprise. 'Whatever did he want?'

'He came to throw my invitation back in my face and tell me that you were unfit to attend such an event, much less be the hostess. And that I was a brute for forcing you into it.'

She laughed with little confidence and no mirth. 'It is a pity I was not there to thank him, his faith in my emotional stability has always meant so much to me.'

'What happened when you had your Season to give him such ideas?'

'It was nothing, really.'

'I do not believe you.'

She shook her head. 'I was a foolish girl…'

He stepped farther into the room, moving toward her without thinking. 'You might have been impetuous. But I cannot imagine you a fool. Tell me the story, and we will never speak of it again.'

'Very well.' She sighed. 'The truth about my come-out—and then you will see what a ninny you have married. I have always been awkward in crowds, more comfortable with books than with people. But my father admired my studiousness and did nothing to encourage me to mix with others my age. It was not until I was seventeen, and he sought to give me a Season, that the problems of this strategy became apparent.'

Adam pulled a chair close to hers, sat down beside her, and nodded encouragingly.

'Mother was long past, and there was little my father or brother could do to help me prepare for my entrance into society. Father engaged a companion for the sake of propriety, but the woman was a fifty-year-old spinster. She knew little of fashion and nothing of the ways of young ladies, other than that they needed to be prevented from them. I was more than a little frightened of her. I suspect she increased the problems, rather than diminishing them.'

She paused and he wondered if she meant to leave the story at that. He said, 'So you had your come-out, and no one offered. Or were you unable to find someone to suit yourself?'

She shook her head. 'Neither is the case, I'm afraid.

Any young girl with a dowry the size of mine could not help but draw interest. Father dispensed with the fortune hunters, and encouraged the rest. And at the end of the summer, there was a young man who seemed to suit. He was a lord of no particular fortune, but he seemed genuine in his affection for me.' She looked up at him, puzzled. 'It was so easy, when I was with him, to behave as the other girls did. The crowds were not so daunting. I grew to look to the parties and balls with anticipation, not dread. And I did quite enjoy the dancing…' Her voice trailed away again.

She had been in love. Adam felt a bolt of longing at the idea that his wife had known happiness, before she had known him.

She came back into the present and smiled at him, bright and false. 'And then I overheard my beloved explaining to a girl I thought a friend that, while he loved this other girl above all things, he would marry me for my money, and that was that.

'A sensible girl might have ignored the fact and continued with what would have been a perfectly acceptable union. Or broken it off quietly and returned to try again the next Season. But not I. I returned to the room and told the couple, and all within earshot, that I thought them as two-faced as Janus for denying their hearts with their actions, and that I would rather die than yoke myself to a man that only pretended to love me for the sake of my money. Then I turned on my heel, left the assembly rooms and refused all further invitations. My mortification at what I had done was beyond bearing. I had not wanted to draw attention to myself. I only hoped to find someone who would want me for who I was. Was it so much to ask? But my brother assured me that I had shamed the family. No one would have me, now I'd made such a cake of myself.' She smiled, wistfully. 'The last thing I should have done, to achieve my ends, was behave in a way that, I'm sorry to say, is very much in my character.'

Adam felt the rage boiling in his heart and wished that he could find the man who had been so callous to her, and give him what he deserved. Then he would pay a visit to her brother, and give Hector a dose of the same.

She swallowed and lifted her chin. 'Of course, you can see that I have learned my lesson. I expected no such foolishness when I married you. If we must hold a ball and make nice in front of your friends, so be it. As long as there is no pretence between us that the event means something more than it truly does.' She lowered her eyes and he thought for a moment he could see tears shining in them, although it might have been the reflection of the afternoon light on her spectacles.

And he reached out spontaneously and seized her hand, squeezing the fingers in his until she looked up at him. 'I would take it all back if I could. Throw the invitations on the fire before they could be sent. You must know that I have no desire to force you into behaviours that will only bring back unpleasant memories. It was never my intention to make you uncomfortable or unhappy. And if there is anything I can do to help...'

Perhaps he sounded too earnest, and she doubted his sincerity. For when she looked at him, her face was blank and guarded. 'Really, Adam. You have done more than enough. Let it be.'

But damn it all, he did not want to let it be. He wanted to fix it. 'The ball will go on. There is no stopping it, I suppose. But in exchange, I will do something for you.'

She was staring at him as though the only thing she wished was that he leave her alone. What could he possibly do? It was not as if he could promise her a trip to the shops. She had made it clear enough what she thought of them, when he had forced her to go the first time. And if her mind had changed and she wished such things, she could afford to purchase them for herself.

And then, the idea struck him. 'At the ball, we will announce that it is our farewell from society, for a time. We will be repairing to our country home. There, you will have all the solitude you could wish for. It is Wales, for heaven's sake. Beautiful country, and the place where my heart resides, but very much out of the way of London society. Your books can be sent on ahead, to greet you in the library when we arrive. Between the house and the grounds, there is so much space that you can go for days without seeing a soul. Dead silence and no company but your books, for as long as you like.'

Her eyes sparkled at the sound of the word 'library'. And she seemed to relax a bit. 'This will be our only party, then?'

'For quite some time. I will make no more rash pronouncements in public without consulting you first.'

'And we may go the very next day?' She seemed far more excited by the prospect of rustication, than she did by the impending ball.

'If you wish it.' He smiled. 'And we will see if you prefer it to London. But I warn you, it is frightfully dull at Felkirk. Nothing to do but sit at home of an evening, reading before the fire.'

She was smiling in earnest now. And at him. 'Nothing to do but read. Really, your Grace. You are doing it far too brown.'

'You would not be so eager if I told you about the holes in the roof. The repairs are not complete, as of yet. But the library is safe and dry,' he assured her. 'And the bedrooms.'

And suddenly, her cheeks turned a shade of pink that, while very fetching, clashed with the silk on the walls. To hide her confusion, she muttered, 'That is good to know. The damage was confined, then, to some unimportant part of the house?'

And it was his turn to feel awkward. 'Actually, it was to the ballroom. When I left, it was quite unusable.'

And her blush dissolved into a fit of suppressed giggles. 'It devastates me to hear it, your Grace.'

'I thought it might. I will leave you to your work, then. But if you need help in the matter of the upcoming event, you will call upon me?'

She smiled again. 'Of course.'

'Because I am just across the hall.' He pointed.

'I know.' She had forgiven him. At least for now. He turned to leave her, and glanced with puzzlement at a lone remaining Meissen figurine, turned face to the wall and occupying valuable space on his wife's bookshelf. He shook his head at the carelessness of the servants, and turned it around, so that it faced properly into the room. 'I will send someone to have this removed, if it annoys you.'

She shook her head. 'Do not bother. I have grown quite used to it.'

Chapter Thirteen

The night of the ball had finally arrived, and Adam hoped that his wife was not too overwrought by the prospect. He had nerves enough for both of them.

Clarissa would be there, of course. He combed his hair with more force than was necessary. Another meeting with her was unavoidable. He could not hold a party and invite his friend, only to exclude his wife. There was very little to do about Clarissa without cutting Tim out of his social circle entirely. And he could hardly do that. They had been friends since childhood. Tim's unfortunate marriage to the shrew, and Adam's regrettable behaviour over her, had done nothing to change it, although Adam almost wished it had. It would have been so much easier had Tim called him out and shamed him in public, or at least cut him dead. But the veneer of civility, when they were together at a social gathering, was a torture much harder to endure.

He hoped that the presence of Penny, and success of the evening, would cool the look in Clarissa's eye.

There was a change in the light that fell upon the table, and a discreet clearing of a throat.

He looked up into the mirror to see his wife standing in the connecting doorway behind him.

He didn't realise he had been holding his breath until he felt it expel from his lungs in a long, slow sigh. It was his wife, most certainly. But transformed. The gown was a pale green, and with her light hair and fair skin, she seemed almost transparent. As she came towards him, he imagined he was seeing a spirit, a ghost that belonged to the house, that had been there long before he had come.

And then the light from his lamp touched the gown and the sarsenet fabric shifted in colour from silver to green again, and the silver sequins sparkled on the drape of netting that fell from her shoulder to the floor.

Even her glasses, which had seemed so inappropriate and unfeminine when he first met her, completed the image as the lenses caught the light and threw it back at him, making her eyes shimmer.

His friends would not call her a beauty, certainly. She was most unlike all the other women who were lauded as such. But suddenly it did not matter what his friends might say. It only mattered what he knew in his heart to be true—she looked as she was meant to look. And now that he had removed her from whatever magic realm she had inhabited, he was overcome with the desire to protect her from the coarse harshness of the world around them.

She had reached his side, and tipped her head quizzically to the side. 'Is it all right?'

He nodded and smiled. 'Very much so. You are lovely.'

'And you are a liar.' But he could see the faint blush on her cheek as she said it.

'You're welcome. It is a most unusual gown. Vaguely Greek, I think, and reminiscent of the Penelope of legend. And therefore, most suitable for you. Are you ready to greet our guests?'

'Yes.' But he saw the look in her eyes.

'And now you are the one who is lying.'

'I am as ready as I am ever likely to be.'

'Not quite. There is something missing. I meant to deal with it earlier, but I quite forgot.'

He removed the jewel box from where he had left it in the drawer of his dresser. 'It seems, in the hurry to marry, that we forgot something. You have no ring.'

'It is hardly necessary.'

'I beg to differ. A marriage is not a marriage without a ring. Although the solicitors and banks did not comment, my friends must have noticed.'

She sighed. 'You do not remember, do you? You gave me a ring, when we were in Gretna. I carry it with me sometimes. For luck.' She pulled a bent horse nail from her fine silk skirts and slipped it on to her finger. 'Although perhaps I need the whole shoe for it to be truly lucky. I do not know.'

He stared down at it in horror. 'Take that from your finger, immediately.'

'I had not planned to wear it, if that is your concern. It is uncomfortably heavy, and hardly practical.'

He held out his hand. 'Give it here, this instant. I will dispose of it.'

She closed her hand possessively over it. 'You will do nothing of the kind.'

'It is dross.' He shook his head. 'No, worse than that. Dross would be better. That is a thing. An object. An abomination.'

'It is a gift,' she responded. 'And, more so, it is mine. You cannot give it me, and then take it back.'

'I had no idea what I was doing. I was too drunk to think clearly. If I had been sober, I would never have allowed you to take it.'

'That is not the point,' she argued. 'It was a symbol. Of our…' She was hunting for the right word to describe what had happened in Scotland. 'Our compact. Our agreement.'

'But I have no desire for my friends to think I would seal a sacrament with a bent nail. Now that we are in London, I can give you the ring that you by rights deserve.'

She sighed. 'It is not necessary.'

'I believe that it is.'

'Very well, then. Let us get on with it.'

Another proof that his wife was unlike any other woman in London. In his experience, a normal woman would have been eager for him to open the jewel case on his desk, and beside herself with rapture as he removed the ring. The band was wide, wrought gold, heavy with sapphires, set round with diamonds. 'Give me your hand.'

She held it out to him, and he slipped it on to her finger.

It looked ridiculous, sitting on her thin white fingers,

as though it had wandered from the hand of another and settled in the only place it felt at home. She flexed her hand.

She shook her head. 'I retract what I said before. In comparison, the horse nail is light. This does not suit.'

'We can go to the jewellers tomorrow, and get it sized to you.'

'You do not understand. It fits well enough, but it does not suit me.'

'It was my mother's,' he said. 'And my grand-mother's before her.'

'Well, perhaps it would suit, if I were your mother,' she snapped. 'But I am your wife. And it does not suit me.'

'You are my wife, but you are also Duchess of Bellston. And the Duchess wears the ring, in the family colours of sapphire and gold.'

'*My* mother was happy with a simple gold band,' she challenged.

'*Your* mother was not a duchess.'

'When your mother worked, did she remove the ring, or leave it on? For I would hate to damage it.'

'Work?'

'Work,' she repeated firmly.

'My mother did not work.'

'But, if you remember our agreement, I do.' She slipped the ring off her finger and handed it back to him. 'My efforts here are hardly strenuous, but a large ring will snag in the papers and could get soiled, should I spill ink. It is not a very practical choice.'

'Practicality has never been an issue,' he admitted.

'It is to me. For I am a very practical person.'

'I am aware of that.'

She looked at the box on the table, which was large enough to hold much more than a single ring. 'Is there not another choice available that might serve as compromise?'

He re-opened the box, and turned it to her. 'This is a selection of such jewellry as is at the London address. I dare say there is more, in the lock rooms at Bellston.'

She rejected the simple gold band she saw as being a trifle too plain for even the most practical of duchesses, and chose a moonstone, set in silver. It was easily the least worthy piece in the box, and he wondered why his mother had owned it, for it was unlike any of her other jewellry. His wife ran the tip of her finger lightly along the stone: a cabochon, undecorated, but also unlikely to get in the way of her work. 'I choose this.'

'Silver.' He said it as though it were inferior, but then, at one time, he might have said the same of her, had he not been forced to recognise her. And he would have been proved wrong.

'At least I will not feel strongly, should I damage it. And for formal engagements, I will wear your mother's ring. But not tonight.' She slipped the moonstone on to her hand, and it glittered eerily.

'It suits you,' he conceded.

'I suspected it would. And it is better, is it not, than if I wore the horse nail?' She admired the ring on her hand and smiled.

He smiled as well. 'I feared, for a moment, that you might do it, out of spite.'

'I am not usually given to act out of spite,' she said. He laughed.

'Well, perhaps, occasionally.' Then she laughed as well, and surrendered. 'All right. Frequently. But I shall be most co-operative tonight, if you shall take me to Wales tomorrow.'

'A bargain, madam.' He reached out and took her hand. 'Let us climb the stairs and await our guests.'

Whoever had selected the top floor of the house for a ballroom had not made the most practical of choices, but Adam had to admit that the tall windows, front and back, provided a splendid view of London below, and the night sky above. He felt Penny tense as the first guests arrived, and thought to offer her a last chance to return to her room and avoid the evening. But he saw the determined look in her eyes and thought better of it. She meant to hang on, no matter what, although the bows and curtsies of the guests and polite murmurs of 'your Grace' were obviously making her uncomfortable.

He reached out and laid a hand on her back, hoping to convey some of his strength to her. She was able to suppress the brief flinch of surprise he could feel, when his fingers touched the bare skin above her gown. And then he felt her slowly relaxing back against his hand, and step ever so slightly closer to him, letting him support and protect her.

He smiled, because it felt good to know that, whatever else she might feel, she trusted him. And it felt good as well, to feel her skin beneath his hand. He shifted and his hand slid along her back, and it was smooth and cool and wonderful to touch. The flesh warmed beneath his hand as the blood flowed to it.

And he found himself wondering, would the rest of her feel the same? If he allowed his fingers to slip under the neckline of her gown, would she pull away in shock, or move closer to him, allowing him to take even greater liberties?

'Adam? Adam?'

He came back to himself to find his wife staring up at him in confusion. Her eyes shifted slightly, to indicate the presence of guests.

'Tim and Clarissa, so good to see you.' He smiled a welcome to his friend and nodded to the woman beside him. 'Forgive me. My mind was elsewhere.' He could feel Penny's nervousness under his hand and drew her closer to him.

And as the introductions droned on, his mind returned to where it had been. It might have been easier to concentrate, if he did not have the brief memory of her, changing clothes in his bed. She had been very like a surprised nymph in some classic painting. Beautiful in her nakedness, and unaware of the gaze of another. And he had allowed himself to watch her, for even though she was his wife, he had not expected to see that particular sight again.

And now, of all times, he could not get the picture from his head. While the object of the evening was to prove to his social circle that he admired and respected his new wife, it would not do to be panting after her like a lovesick dog. A few dances, a glass of champagne, and he would retire to the card room, to steady his mind with whisky and the dull conversation of his male friends.

* * *

It was going well, she reminded herself, over and over again. She had survived the receiving line, and, except for a moment where Adam behaved quite strangely, it had been without incident. Clarissa had been quite incensed that Adam had not paid her a compliment. But he had barely seemed to notice the woman. It gave her hope that perhaps the worst was over, and that she need see no more of Clarissa after tonight.

She looked around her, at the throng of people enjoying the refreshments, and at the simple buffet, which was anything but. There was enough food for an army, if an army wished to subsist on lobster, ice-cream sculptures and liberal amounts of champagne. The orchestra was tuning, and soon dancing would begin.

Adam was surveying the room from her side. 'You have done well.'

'Thank you.'

He hesitated. 'I understand that this was difficult for you.'

'It was not so bad,' she lied.

He smiled sympathetically and whispered, 'It will be over soon, in any case. The sooner we begin the dancing, the sooner they will leave.'

'We must dance?' What fresh hell was this?

'Of course. It is our ball. If we do not dance, they will not.'

'Oh.' She had been so convinced that she would embarrass herself with the preparations for the party, or disgrace herself in the receiving line, that she had forgotten there would be other opportunities for error.

He took her hand in his and put his other hand to her waist. 'I know it goes against your nature,' he said. 'But let me lead.'

She remembered not to jump as he touched her, for it would be even more embarrassing to demonstrate again that she was not familiar with the feel of his hands on her body. He seemed unperturbed as he led her out on to the floor. 'You have nothing to fear, you know. Even if you stumble, no one will dare comment. I certainly shall not.'

She nodded, to reassure herself.

'Have you waltzed before?'

She could only manage a frantic glance up into his face.

'It does not matter. The music is lovely, and the step is easy to learn. Relax and enjoy it. One two three, one two three. See. It is not a difficult.'

He was right. It was simple enough, when one had so commanding a partner. In this, at least, she could trust him to lead her right, and so she yielded. And he turned her around the dance floor, smiling as though he enjoyed it.

She tried to match his expression. Perhaps that was the trick of it. She had but to act like she was having a pleasant evening, and people would trouble her no further.

'You are a very good dancer,' he remarked. 'Although not much of a conversationalist. I cannot keep you quiet when we are alone together. Why will you not speak now?'

'All these people…' she whispered helplessly.

'Our guests,' he answered.

'Your guests, perhaps, but they are strangers to me.'

'You met them all in the receiving line just now. And yet they frighten you?'

She managed the barest nod.

He laughed, but squeezed her hand. 'You are quite fearless in your dealings with me. Perhaps it will help you to remember that I am the most important person here.'

'And the most modest.' She could not help herself.

He laughed again, ignoring the gibe. 'At any rate, they all must yield to me. And since I intend to yield to you, you have nothing to be afraid of.'

'You yield to me?'

'If you wish, we will cancel the evening's entertainment, and I will send the guests home immediately.'

'For the last time: no. It would be even more embarrassing to do that than to stand in front of them as I do now, looking like a goose.'

He nodded. 'At least you are speaking to me again. Even if you are lying. Your obedient silence just now was most disconcerting. And you do not look like a goose. Do not concern yourself.'

'We are the centre of attention.'

He glanced around. 'So we are. But it cannot be very interesting for them, to stare at us and do nothing. Soon they will find other diversions. See? The floor is beginning to fill with couples. And others are returning to the buffet. Crisis averted. They no longer care about us. As long as the music is good and the wine holds out, they will entertain themselves and we are free to enjoy ourselves for the rest of the evening in peace.'

It was true. The worst was over. She could pretend that she was a guest at her own party, if she wished, and allow the servants to handle the details.

And as he spun her around the room, she relaxed at the sight of smiling faces and happy people.

And there was Clarissa, staring at her with death in her eyes.

He turned her away, so that she could no longer see, and they were on the other side of the room by the time the music stopped. When they parted, he brought her hand to his lips, and she could feel the look of pleasure on her face when he'd kissed the knuckles. And then he turned to part from her.

'You are leaving me alone?' She could not hide the panic in her voice.

He nodded. 'Our job as host and hostess is to entertain the guests, not each other. There is nothing to be afraid of, I assure you. Continue to smile, nod and say "thank you for coming". Much of your work is done.' He smiled again. 'And I swear, once you have done this thing for me, I am yours to command.'

She squared her shoulders and lifted her chin, prepared to meet the horde that had infested her home.

He nodded. 'Very good. If you need me, I will be in the card room, hiding with the other married men. Madam, the room is yours.'

She fought the feeling of disorientation as she watched him go, as if she was being spun by the elements, with no safe place to stand. But she admired the way her husband moved easily through the crowd, stopping to chat as he made his way to the door. Smiling and nodding. Listening more than he spoke. He was an excellent example to her.

What had she to fear from her guests? It was not as it had been, during her come-out, when all the women were in competition, and the men were prizes. The race was over. And, without trying, she had won first place.

She thought how miserable she had been at those balls, and how awkward, and how good it had felt to find a friendly face or hear a hostess's word of welcome or encouragement.

And then she scanned the crowd. There was the daughter of an earl, barely sixteen, excited by her first invitation, but terrified that it was not going well.

Penny made her way to the girl's side. 'Are you enjoying your evening?'

The conversation was unlike anything she'd ever experienced. The girl was in awe of her. The conversation was peppered with so many 'your Grace's' and curtsies, that Penny had to resist the urge to assure the girl that it was not necessary. She was a nobody who had stumbled into a title.

She smiled to herself. The less said on that subject, the better. She had the ear of the most important man in the room. She could do as she pleased. And it pleased her that people like the girl in front of her should be happy. They talked a bit, before she gently encouraged the girl to a group of young people near to her age, and made a few simple introductions. When she left, the girl was on her way to the dance floor with a young man who seemed quite smitten.

After her initial success, Penny threw herself into the

role of hostess as though she were playing a chess game, with her guests as the pieces. Penelope Winthorpe had been an excellent player, and loved the sense of control she got when moving her army around the board. This was no different. Tonight she could move actual knights, and the ladies accompanying them, urging weaker pieces to the positions that most benefited them. While her husband was able to engage people more closely, she enjoyed the gambits she could arrange in a detached fashion. It made for a harmonious whole.

Perhaps that had been her problem all along. She had never been a successful guest. But that did not mean she could not be a hostess.

'Your Grace, may I have a dance?'

She turned, surprised to see her brother-in-law. 'Of course, Will.' She stammered on the familiarity, and felt her confidence begin to fade.

He smiled, and she searched his face for some shred of duplicity or contempt. 'Penelope?' He gestured to the floor. Since she was rooted to the spot, he took her hand, leading her to the head of the set.

She watched him as they danced, comparing him to his older brother. He was not unattractive, certainly, and moved with grace and confidence. But he lacked his brother's easy sense of command. When they reached the bottom of the set and had to stand out, he leaned closer and spoke into her ear. 'I owe you an apology.'

She looked at him without speaking.

'When I found that my brother had married in haste, I told him to get an annulment. I was convinced that you would both regret the decision.'

'I had no idea,' she replied blandly.

He smiled. 'I suspected you had, for I saw the look in your eyes when you left us that night. I am sorry I caused you pain. Or that I meddled in something that was none of my affair to begin with. It is just that…' he shook his head '…Adam has always had an excellent head for politics, and I cannot fault him for his dedication to responsibilities as Bellston. But in his personal life, he has always been somewhat reckless. He thinks last of what would be best for himself in the distant future, and seems to see only what is directly in front of him.'

She shrugged. 'I cannot fault him for that. I, too, have been known to act in haste.'

'Well, perhaps your tendencies have cancelled each other. You appear to be a most successful match.'

She looked sharply at her new brother. 'We do?'

'You are just what my brother needs: a stable source of good advice. He speaks well of you, and he appears happier than I have seen him in a long time.'

'He does?' She tried to hide her surprise.

'Indeed. He is at peace. Not something I am accustomed to seeing, in one so full of motion as Adam is. But his activity in society brings him near to people that are not as good as they could be. Compared to the foolish women that normally flock to his side, you are a great relief to a worried brother. And I can assure you, and your family, if they are concerned, that in my brother you have found a loyal protector and a true friend. I am glad of your union, and wish you well in it.'

'Thank you. That is good to know.' Impulsively, she

reached out and clasped Will's hand, and he returned the grip with a smile.

Her eyes sought her husband on the other side of the room, and she smiled at him as well.

He returned a look that indicated none of the affection that Will had described. Perhaps her new brother was mistaken.

The music ended. 'I will leave you to your other guests, then. I suspect we will have ample time in the future to speak.' And Will took his leave of her.

Another guest asked her to dance. And then another. At last she excused herself from the floor to check on the refreshments. And found Clarissa, standing in her way.

'Penelope, darling. What a charming party.'

There was no way to cut the woman, no matter how much she deserved it. Penny pasted a false smile on her face and responded, 'Thank you,' then went to step around her.

Clarissa reached out to her, in what no doubt appeared to the room as a sisterly gesture of warmth, catching both hands in hers. Then she pulled her close, to whisper what would look to observers like a girlish confidence. 'But if you think it makes any difference to your standing in society, you are wrong.'

Penny summoned her newfound bravery. 'My position in society is secure. I am Duchess of Bellston.'

'In name, perhaps. But in reality, you are a trumped-up shop girl. People know the truth, and they can talk of little else this evening.'

She had heard nothing, and she had been to every corner of the room. It must be a lie, intended to wound her.

But there was no way to be sure.

Then she thought of what Will had said, and tossed her head in her best imitation of someone who did not give a jot for what people 'said'. 'Let them talk, then. They are most unaccountably rude to be doing so in my home while drinking my wine and eating my food.'

'They are saying nothing more than what your husband has said.'

It was her worst fear, was it not? That he felt she was beneath him. And she feared it because it was based in truth. Clarissa must have guessed as much or she would not speak so.

But there was nothing she could do about it now. So she favoured Clarissa with her coldest look, and said nothing.

'He is taking you to Wales, is he? Very good. I heartily approve. You must go home and complete your work which is, no doubt, noble and of much scholarly import.' The last words were sarcastic, as though Penny's life goal was so much nonsense.

'But no matter what you mean to do, I doubt that Adam means to stay with you in isolation, if there are other more entertaining opportunities open to him. He will come back to London, or find a reason to go to Bath, or somewhere else.

'And the minute he does, you will know that he is coming to me. He was happy enough before you arrived on the scene. And he is even happier, now that he has your money. He has told us as much. He simply needs to get you out of the way, so that he may spend it in peace.'

Penny controlled the flinch, for the last words struck as hard as any blow.

Clarissa continued, 'Adam is happy. And I am happy with Adam. You have promised to be happy with your books. You have nothing further to add to the discussion, other than regular infusions of gold.'

Penny struggled to speak. 'And is Timothy happy?'

'Timothy?' Clarissa laughed again.

'Yes. Timothy. Your husband.'

'He is glad to see Adam back, for they are great friends.'

'And it must be very handy for you to share such affection for Adam. They are good comrades, are they not? And if you seek to be unfaithful, how handy that it be with your husband's best friend.'

Clarissa was unaffected. 'Why, yes. It is most convenient.'

'Until you get caught at it. And then there will be the devil to pay, Clarissa. The scandal will be enormous.'

'Caught? Caught by whom exactly? Dear me, Penelope. You make it sound as though we are likely to be run down with a pack of hounds. How diverting.'

'Your husband,' Penelope hissed. 'You must be mad to think that you can carry on in front of him and remain undiscovered. And if you believe, for one minute, that I will allow you to drag my name, and the name of my husband, through the muck with this public display, you are even more mad. This is my first and final warning to you, Clarissa. Stay away from Adam. Or I will tell Timothy what is going on, and he will put an end to it.'

Clarissa laughed, and it was no delicate silvery peal

of ladylike mirth, but a belly-deep whoop of joy. 'You mean to tell my husband? About me and Adam? Oh, my dear. My sweet, young innocent. You do not understand at all, do you? My husband already knows.'

Penny felt her stomach drop and thought with horror that she was likely to be sick on the floor of her own ballroom. What a ludicrous scene that would be. Clarissa, or any of the other ladies of her husband's acquaintance, would have managed a genteel faint.

'Clarissa, we must dance. You have monopolised our hostess long enough.' Lord Timothy was standing behind her, and she prayed that he had not heard what his wife had been murmuring, for the situation was quite mortifying enough.

'But I was having such a lovely chat with Penny.' Clarissa's voice was honey sweet.

'I can see that.' Tim's was ice and steel. 'She bears the look of one who has experienced one of your chats, darling. Drained of blood, and faint of heart. Remove your claws from her and accompany me.' He laid a hand on Clarissa's wrist and squeezed. 'Or I will pry them loose for you.'

Clarissa laughed and released her, then turned to the dance floor. 'Very well, Timothy. Let us dance. So long as it is not a waltz. I am saving the waltzes for someone special.' Then she walked away as though nothing had happened.

Penny stood frozen in place, watching her, and felt Tim's hand upon her shoulder. 'Are you all right?' His face was so close to her that his cheek brushed her hair.

'I will see to it that my wife goes home early. And then we will speak. Until then, do not trouble yourself.'

She nodded without speaking.

He eased away from her, passing by to follow his wife. In a tone loud enough to be heard by people passing, he said, 'Lovely party, your Grace. I never fail to find entertainment on a visit to Bellston.'

Chapter Fourteen

Penny closed her eyes, and focused on the sound of the room, rather than the faces of the people in it. She had thought things were going so well. But now, it was impossible to tell friends from enemies. When she was seventeen, the falsehoods and sly derision had come as a surprise. But she knew better now. When she looked closely at those around her, she could see from the strained expressions on the faces of her husband's friends that she did not fit in.

And the looks of suspicion, jealousy and disdain seemed to follow, wherever Clarissa had been. The woman could spread discord like a bee spreads pollen.

Damn them all. She would send the guests away, just as Adam had told her she could. And never, ever, would she submit to such torture again. In time, Adam would forget about her, since it was obvious that he wished to be elsewhere. If it mattered so much to him that there be entertainment in his house, he would have been at her side when she was all but attacked by his mistress.

She steadied her breathing. To call a sudden halt to the proceedings would be even more embarrassing than to continue with them. If there were any left in the room that were not talking about her, they soon would be, once she drove them from her house and slammed the doors.

She would retire herself, then. It was embarrassing for a hostess to abandon her guests. But she found herself—suddenly indisposed. Too ill to continue, no doubt due to the stress of the event. People would understand. Some would know the cause of the indisposition, but not all. She might still save some small portion of pride.

She had but to find her husband, and tell him that it behoved him, as host, to rise from the card table, and attend to his guests, for she could not hold up another instant.

She exited the hall and was almost in the card room before she knew what she was about. The sound of male laughter echoed into the hallway.

It would be embarrassing to invade the privacy of the men, but it could not be helped. It was her house, after all. Even if she might need to continually remind herself of the fact.

She paused in front of the partially open door, standing behind it, and taking in a deep breath, scented with the tobacco smoke escaping from the room. And without intending to, she heard the conversation, escaping from the room as well.

'Of course, now that Adam is an old married man, he will not be interested in cards or horses. I dare say your new bride does not approve of your track losses, Bellston.'

There was general laughter.

'She has not yet had the chance to approve or disapprove of them, Mark. We have been married a short time, and even I cannot lose money so fast as that, despite my dashed bad luck. When one is throwing one's money away, it takes time to pick a horse that can do the job properly.'

'You took little enough care in the finding of a wife, Adam.'

So she was no different than choosing a jade. Anger mingled with shame at the hearing of it.

'Indeed. You were alone when you left London. Wherever did you find her?' It was her husband's friend, John.

'She found me, more like. I was not even looking.' Her husband's voice.

She drew back from the door. Her father had often told her that people who listened at keyholes deserved what they heard. She should retreat immediately if she did not want Clarissa's stories confirmed.

'She must have a fat purse, then, for you to marry so quickly.'

She could feel her cheeks reddening. *One, two, three…*

'Her father was a cit?' Another voice, edged with curiosity.

Four, five, six.

'In printing, I believe,' her husband answered. 'Books and such. My wife is a great reader. Probably through his influence.'

Someone laughed. 'What does a woman need with reading?'

Idiot. Her fists balled.

'I wouldn't know, myself. But she seems to value it.' There was the faintest trace of sarcasm in her husband's voice. And she relaxed her fists. 'I imagine it proves useful, if one does not wish to appear as foolish as you.'

'But it must take her time away from other, more important things,' John responded. 'Her appearance, for example. She is a bit of a quiz.'

Her husband, and his damned friends, sniping and backbiting, as she had seen them on the first day. She would not cry, she reminded herself. She was a grown woman, in her own house, and she would suffer these fools no longer, but go into the room and remind her husband who had paid for the party.

And then she noticed the silence emanating from the room. John's comment had been followed by a mutter of assent, and some nervous laughter, that had faded quickly to nothing.

Her husband spoke. 'I find her appearance to be singular. Her eyes, especially, are most compelling. Not to everyone's taste, perhaps, but very much to mine. You might wish to remember that, in future, if you wish to visit my home.' The warning in his voice was clear, and she imagined him the way he had been when he stood up to her brother. Quiet, but quite frightening.

Her jaw dropped.

There was more muttering in the room, and a hurried apology from John.

Her husband spoke again. 'If any are curious on the matter of how I came to be married so quickly after my recent financial misfortunes, and to one so wealthy as my wife, let me clarify the situation, that you may explain it to them. It was a chance meeting of kindred souls. The decision on both our parts was very sudden, and on my part, it had very little to do with the size of her inheritance. I consider myself most fortunate to have found so intelligent and understanding a woman, and must regret that circumstances imply an ulterior motive. Would anyone else care to comment on it?'

There were hurried denials from his friends.

'I thought not. Furthermore, I do not expect to hear more on the subject of my wife's family. Her brother is in trade, and our backgrounds are most different. But I wished the woman I married to be worthy of the title, and with sufficient character to bring pride to my name. I am more than happy with my choice. Would that you are all as lucky as I have been.'

Nervous silence followed, and someone cleared his throat.

Then, when tension had reached a near-unbearable point, she heard the sound of shuffling cards, and her husband drawled, 'Another hand, gentleman?'

She could feel the tension release, as the men rushed to offer assent.

She leaned her back to the wall, and let the plaster support her as the room began to spin. The Duke of Bellston found her 'singular'. Whatever did that mean? If another had said it, she'd have thought it was faint praise, and that the speaker had been too kind to say 'odd'.

But from Adam's lips? It had sounded like 'rare'. As though she was something to be sought for and kept safe.

She could not help the ridiculous glow she felt at the knowledge. The most important man in the room thought she did credit to his name. And there had been no false note when he had said he was happy.

She walked slowly down the short hall, toward the ballroom. At the doorway, the butler came to her with a question about the wine, and she answered absently, but with confidence. She could not help smiling, as she went back to her guests, and even managed to stand up for another dance when her husband's brother offered.

The evening was drawing to a close, the crowd already thinning, and it did not really matter if the guests liked her or not. They were leaving soon, and she would be alone with a man who, she smiled to herself, thought she was 'singular'. She looked up to see her husband returning to the main room to seek her out. He took her hand to lead her to the floor for a final dance, but paused, with his head tipped to the side, staring at her.

'Your Grace?' she responded, and smiled back at him.

He shook his head. 'Something is different. What has occurred?'

'I do not know what you mean.'

'You have changed.'

She glanced down at her gown, spreading the skirt with her hand, and shrugged back at him. 'I assure you, I am no different than when we left our rooms earlier today.'

He smiled. 'Perhaps I should have chosen my words more carefully. You are transfigured. I was gone from the room for a short time, and I return to find I've missed a metamorphosis.'

She laughed then, and looked away, remembering his words from earlier. And she could feel the heat in her cheeks as she answered, 'Is this transfiguration a good thing? For not all of them are, you know.'

'I hope so. For you are looking most…well… hmm… I assume you had a pleasant evening.'

'Well enough. But better, now that it is over.' She saw Lord Timothy, staring significantly at her, from across the room. 'If you will excuse me. I think your friend wishes to speak to me.'

'Very well.'

Adam watched her back as she walked away from him and toward the stairs. There was definitely something different about her. A sway in her hips, perhaps? Or a toss of her head as she turned. And her colouring was better. Where she had been deathly pale at the beginning of the evening, to the extent that he feared she might faint in his arms, now there were roses in her cheeks, and a sparkle in her eye. She was smiling as she walked away from him, and he heard her laugh in response to something that Tim had said to her.

The whole impression was most fetching, if a bit disconcerting. As he looked at her, he found himself comparing her with the few ladies remaining in the room. He found the others wanting. She would never be known as a great beauty, but she was certainly handsome. Tonight, she was displaying a strength of character and a confidence that had been lacking in the early days of their marriage. She glanced back at him from her spot beside Tim, and her smile was spontaneous and infectious.

And he had got the distinct impression, when she'd greeted him just now, that she had been flirting with him.

He scanned what was left of the crowd to see if any had noticed, or if there might be some explanation for the change in behaviour. His eye caught his brother, and he signalled him with a nod of his head.

Will crossed the room to his side, smiling and relaxed. It appeared he had also enjoyed the party. 'The evening went well.'

'That is good to know.' Adam indicated his retreating wife with an inclination of his head. 'Penelope did well, I think.'

Will smiled after her. 'So it seems. She is looking most fine this evening.'

Adam nodded agreement. 'What put such colour in her cheeks, I wonder? I spent much of the evening in the card room, and too little time with her.' That his absence might have contributed to her good mood was more than a little irritating.

'Perhaps it was the dancing. I had opportunity to stand up with her on several occasions. She is most adept for one who spends so much time amongst her books. And an intelligent conversationalist, once she overcomes her shyness. It was why I was so opposed to your match. You are a gad, not much for sitting home of an evening, while she would like nothing better. It is not the recipe for a happy union, when two partners are so dissimilar.'

'As you know, with your vast experience as a married man.'

His brother ignored the gibe. 'But I rescind my former feelings on the subject. She seems to be warming to her job as hostess. And once she began to open up to me, I found her views on scholarship to be most refreshing.'

'She opened up to you.'

'Yes. As the evening wore on, she was most chatty. We had several opportunities to speak, as we danced.'

'Oh.' He remembered seeing her, clasping his brother's hand, and the look she had given him, as though she wished him to see. Did she mean to make him jealous? She had succeeded.

Will continued. 'It is good that you plan to allow her to continue with her work. She is correct: her views have value. I most look forward to reading her translation when she completes it.'

Adam searched his heart for a desire to read Homer, in any form, and found it wanting. He could still remember the sting of the ruler on the back of his hand, for all the times he had neglected his studies to go riding, or attempted them, only to miss a conjugation. And now, Will would be there to appreciate the work, once Penny had completed it.

Damn him. But that was ridiculous. He had nothing to fear from his brother. Will would rather die than come between him and his new wife. He should be happy that Penny would have someone to talk to.

Then why did he feel so irritated that she was talking to him tonight? Adam had left her alone to fend for herself. And she had done it, admirably. By the end of the evening, he'd heard murmurs about what a fine hostess she had been, and the people wishing him well had sounded sincere and not sarcastic. The evening had been a success.

And now, his brother could not stop prattling on about his wife's finer qualities, as though they were any business of his. '…and a lot in common with Tim as well. Perhaps when you go home, she will have opportunity to see his research, for I think she would find it fascinating. He was a dab hand at languages when you were in school, was he not?'

'Tim.' *Oh, dear God. Not him as well.*

'Yes. They went off together, just now, while we were speaking? Probably looking for a quiet corner where they can conjugate verbs together.' Will laughed.

'Not if I can help it.' And Adam left his brother to search out his wife.

Chapter Fifteen

'Fair Penelope.' Lord Timothy was being most effusive in his praise, and she wondered if he were the worse for drink. 'I have sent my wife home, and she will bother you no further.'

'You wished to speak to me?'

He caught her hand, and slipped it through the crook of his arm, then led her away from the ballroom. 'In your sitting room, if that is all right. Somewhere we can be alone.'

'What do you wish to say that requires privacy?'

'Things I do not wish others to hear.' He led her past her husband, who was deep in conversation with his brother, and hardly aware of his surroundings. 'Perhaps I wish to be the first man of the *ton* to attempt a flirtation with you. I expect there shall be many, and do not wish to lose my chance, for lack of courage.'

She tried a laugh, and failed. 'If that was meant as a joke, I fear it was not very funny. I do not wish you to flirt with me, now or ever, if that is truly your intent.'

'A pity.' He sighed. 'We would likely do well together, just as our spouses suit each other. For we are studious and bookish, and not at ease in society. Just as they are mercurial and charismatic.'

'It was true what she said, then. You know about them.' Then Penny stopped to look around, afraid that a guest might have heard her speak.

Tim hurried down the last flight of steps and pulled her down the hall and into her own room, shutting the door behind them. 'I am many things, Penelope, but I am neither blind, nor foolish. I was well aware of what happened. Clarissa made certain of it.'

'It does not bother you that your wife is so flagrant in her attentions to other men?'

He sighed. 'Many of the couples in my set have such agreements. We married for reasons other than love. She was rich, as well as beautiful. I have been able to finance my studies.' He grimaced. 'Although she makes me pay dearly for them.'

'And you all look politely the other way when there is something you do not wish to see?'

'Precisely.'

'But if I make the slightest social *faux pas*?'

'Then you will be the talk of the town. You are already notorious for aspiring to a better class than you were born to. People like Clarissa wish to see you fail, to prove that you do not belong. Then they may continue to feel superior.'

'Timothy, this is grossly unfair.'

He nodded. 'But do not believe what she told you. You did well tonight.'

She ignored the compliment. 'It is not particularly moral of you all to allow such chaos and infidelity in your midst.'

'You must have a very limited understanding of society to think so, my dear.'

'I never claimed to have one. Not your idea of society, at least. In the circles I moved in, people did not work so at playing false. My mother loved my father, and my father loved her. They were a most happy couple, until she died. And I would swear they were faithful; even after she was gone, my father did not seek the company of women, or wish to remarry. He threw himself wholeheartedly into his work.'

Timothy laughed. 'Perhaps that is the problem, for we have no work to throw ourselves into. Idle hands, as they say, my dear. Clarissa is proof of that, for she has never done a moment's real labour, but is the devil's handmaiden if there is mischief to be made.'

Penny did not wish to speak ill of the man's wife, and attempted, 'I am sure that she has many qualities that I will consider admirable, once I know her better.'

'And I came here to warn you not to bother. You will never get from her other than you got tonight. Backbiting, sly innuendoes, threats and tricks. If you show weakness, she will use it against you. Once she finds a chink in your armour, she will strike there, to bring you all the pain she can. That is the only reason that she wants Adam back, now that he has finally come to his senses. It amuses her to drive a wedge between me and my oldest friend.'

Penny seized on the only hopeful note in the speech. 'So they are no longer together?'

'Not for some time. But she is persistent, and I feared he would weaken. When he returned from Scotland with you, I was much relieved.'

Penny shook her head. 'It is no love match. Do not expect him to choose me, should there be a choice to be made.'

'And yet, he says he did not marry for money, and I believe him.'

She weighed the truth, and the burden of keeping the secret from one who could help her understand. At last she said, 'We are married because I tricked him. I needed a husband to gain control of my fortune. When I found him, he was face down in a coach yard. It appeared he had tried to throw himself beneath the carriage and make an end of it. He said something about gambling and bad debts when he was sober enough to talk. But he was far too drunk to know what was happening at the time of the actual marriage.'

'It was not binding, if he was too drunk to agree.'

'That was what I thought. I offered to let him go. But he felt an obligation. I needed a husband, and he needed money. And since we were already married, we struck a bargain and came back to London.' She looked sadly at Timothy. 'I am sorry to disappoint you, if you were expecting a grand romantic tale. But that's the truth of it.'

'Nonsense. He is yours if you want him, and Clarissa has no hope. I know him better than I know myself. And I have seen the way he looks at you.'

She laughed. 'What way is that?'

'Like a man in love. You are good for him, Penelope. No matter how things appear, you must not lose heart, for Clarissa is no threat to you.' Tim caught her hand and held it in his.

She laughed. 'You are mad.'

'Adam may be too big a fool to tell you, just yet. But not so big a fool as to pass you by for that harridan I am shackled to. What happened pains him greatly, and I am sick to death of seeing the guilt in his eyes when he looks at me. Make him forget, and you will help us both.'

'But why do you bother, Tim? I am sure he would not blame you if you could not forgive him.'

Tim smiled. 'I know how much of the blame lies with my wife. Clare angled after him for years before she finally trapped him. It was a wonder he held out as long as he did.'

'But she was not the only one at fault,' Penny said.

'True enough. And try as I might, I cannot help but forgive him. I'm sure you have noticed by now that he is a most likeable fellow, especially when you wish to be angry with him. Very persuasive. Has he told you what happened, to get him sent down when we were at school together?'

'No.' She tried to hide her curiosity.

'It was all my doing.' Tim shook his head. 'I was a heavy drinker in those days. And one night, while deep in my cups, we got to brawling with each other in a public house, like common ruffians. That was over a woman as well, for it is the only reason we ever argue. Missed curfew. And gave him the worst of it. Blacked his eye and nearly broke that handsome face of his. It was all around the school that I assaulted Bellston's heir. Added to my lack of academic attention, I deserved a one-way ticket home. But somehow, Adam managed to convince the deans that it was all his fault. Took the whole blame. Issued the apologies, paid the bills, put some ice on his black eyes and allowed himself to be sent home in disgrace to face his father. Told me, if I loved science so much, I had best get about proving it, for with no title and no money, I would need an education to secure my future. But since he was to be duke, he could be as big a fool as he liked and no harm would come of it.'

Tim smiled and shook his head. 'Couldn't well be angry with him after that. You will see what he is like, if you haven't already. When he tries, let him charm you. You will not regret it, I promise you.'

There was a rather loud sound of someone clearing his throat in the hallway, and then the door opened and her husband walked into the room.

Adam glanced at them, as though not noticing anything unusual, and said, 'I was looking for a book, for the trip tomorrow.' He looked at her. 'Perhaps you could recommend something?' And to his friend, 'Or you, Tim. For I assume that is why you are secluded with my wife. So that you may talk books, without boring the rest of us.' There was a touch of menace in her husband's voice that she had never heard before.

'Of course,' Tim answered innocently. 'For what other reason would one choose to be alone with such a lovely woman? Not making you jealous, am I?'

'Do I have reason to be?'

'I think I might have reason to be jealous of you. But that is between you and your wife. Good luck, old friend, as if you need any more. And goodnight.' Tim let go of her hand, and rose to leave.

Adam watched him with suspicion. 'Close the door behind you, please.'

He waited until his friend had gone down the hall and was out of earshot. And then he said without warning, 'I will not let you cuckold me in my own home.'

'Would you prefer that I do it elsewhere?' She had almost laughed at the ridiculousness of it before she realised he was serious.

He did not raise his voice, but she could tell that his temper was barely contained. 'You know what I meant. I would prefer not to have to kill a man over you. Especially not that one.'

'Kill Tim? Adam, listen to yourself. Have you gone mad?'

She could hardly recognise the man before her, for his eyes were dark and his face more grim than she had ever seen it. 'Do not be flip with me. If you do not set that young puppy straight, I will be forced to deal with him on the field of honour, the next time I wander in on the two of you.'

'For holding my hand? That is rich, after what he has suffered from you.'

'Which is another reason I do not wish to hurt him. He has not, as yet, done anything I cannot overlook. But I suspect it is only a matter of time before I will have reason to act. I beg you to stop it, to prevent me from having to do so.'

She rolled her eyes. 'As if it would matter to you. From what I gather, in talking to your friends, the nobles of your acquaintance have the morals of cats in an alley. Not one wife amongst them is faithful, and all the husbands have mistresses.'

'That is different,' he answered.

'I fail to see how. It is not as if we married for love, unless that is a mandatory precursor to the level of infidelity I have seen. Ours was a purely financial arrangement, and I thought we were of an understanding on the subject of sexual attachments. I told you it did not matter to me.'

'And do you remember my saying, in response to you, that what you did would not matter to me? Because I did not. I was under the impression that while you intended for me to find a mistress to deal with my personal needs, you meant to stay home alone with a good book.'

'So the situation is agreeable, so long as it benefits you and not me?' she said.

'I fail to see how it does, since I have not yet taken advantage of the liberties you seem so eager to allow me.'

She grew even more confused. 'You have no mistress?'

'Not at this time.'

'Nor any other…'

'No.'

'Since we married, you have not—'

'I said, no,' he snapped.

'I do not understand.'

'Nor do I,' he responded. 'But that doesn't mean I

wish for you to take a lover after less than a month of marriage. You cannot expect me to sit idly by and do nothing about it.'

Her argument ran out of fuel, and her anger cooled. But his argument became no clearer. And so she said, 'Your friends do not seem overly bothered by their wives' conduct.'

'My friends all have several children. Any inheritances or titles have been assured. Their wives have performed the duties, which you have expressed no interest in. They have earned latitude.'

'And is that the only problem? You think that I encourage Timothy too soon?'

'People will say that turnabout is fair play, and I am getting a taste of what I deserve. And they will question the legitimacy of my heir, should there be one, even if I do not.'

She smiled at the nonsense of it. 'But I have no intention of getting myself with child.'

He shook his head. 'You are wise in many things, but there is much you do not know. Let me try to explain. First, you understand that you do not get yourself with child, it is a collaborative effort.'

'I do not plan to collaborate.'

He sighed. 'If you have feelings for Timothy, or any one else, for that matter, these feelings could lead you to a place where collaboration is inevitable.'

'I am not so easily led, Adam,' she said.

He shook his head. 'At one time, I thought I was as wise as you think you are now. A private conversation, a shared joke, the touch of a hand in friendship, or a waltz or two in public would lead to nothing. It was all innocent flirtation that I could stop before it got out of control. But considering our histories, you should sympathise with how easy it can be to respond poorly in the heat of the moment. And there is much heat in a forbidden kiss.'

He sank down on the couch, his head in his hands. 'The next morning, I realised what I had done, and could not bring myself to look in the mirror. I was too ashamed. And that wasn't the last time. I could not seem to stop it until I had driven myself near to ruin and hurt family and friends with the indiscretion.

'And I am not as noble as my good friend Timothy, to be all understanding and forgiveness. Should he try to do to me what I did to him, I am more like to put a ball through him in the heat of anger than look quietly aside. I do not wish it to end thus.' He looked up at her, in desperation. 'If you truly prefer him to me, tell me now, and I will request the annulment that you once offered. Then you will be free to do as you like.'

'I would make you pay back the money you have used,' she countered.

'You would have no right to do so. An annulment will make it as if you have never been married. Control of your estate would revert to your brother. I think he would consider the debts I incurred to be money well spent. The man would be more likely to kiss me than you would.' He put his hand on hers. 'I do not like Hector, and have no desire to aid him in controlling you, but neither will I allow you to shame me in public or ～stroy an already fragile friendship.'

～he shook her head in amazement. She could not

decide which was stranger: her husband's jealous raving, or the twisted logic of the upper class. 'So if any man speaks to me, you will be convinced that I am unfaithful, like all the other wives. And then you will corner me to rant, as you have tonight, although you have no reason.'

He gave her a sad smile, and nodded.

She continued. 'And although in time you are likely to stray from me, I will be allowed no indiscretions at all, for you do not wish people to think that your heirs are illegitimate. You understand that there is no point in suspecting the legitimacy of your children until you have some?'

And now, he was looking at her with speculation. The silence drew out long between them.

'But if you did, that would mean…' Her pulse quickened in response. 'Oh, no.'

'We could remain unfortunately childless, I suppose. And celibate. And hope that my brother marries and produces. But that is a lot to assume. If there is any hint of infidelity on your part, annulment will continue to be an option.'

'You mean to hold that over my head for the rest of our lives?'

'If necessary.' The intensity of his gaze grew. 'Or we could try another way.'

Her pulse was racing now, as it began to occur to her that he was serious in what he was suggesting. 'That was most definitely not part of the original bargain.'

'When you planned to marry, you must have considered the possibility.'

Strangely, she had not. She had assumed it would be hard enough to get a man to the altar, and that any so doing would not be the least interested in sexual congress with her, if other opportunities presented themselves. But the need for succession had not been part of her plans. And now, Adam was looking at her in quite a different way than he did after political discussions in the study. He was looking at her as a woman, and she remembered what Tim had said to her.

She sat down beside him, afraid to meet his gaze lest he see how she felt about him. 'I'd never have married a duke had I known it would become so complicated.'

'I am sorry to have inconvenienced you,' he said, not the least bit contrite. 'But I will need an heir. Once one has married, it makes sense to look at the obvious solution to the problem.'

'And you would…with me…and we…'

He nodded. 'Two male children are preferable, but one might be sufficient. If it was a boy, and healthy. If the first is a daughter, then…'

'But that would mean…we would…more than once…'

'Most certainly. Repeatedly. For several years at least.'

Repeatedly. She sat there, eyes round, mouth open, mind boggled. Unable to speak at all.

He continued. 'When you think of it, a sacrifice of a year or two, against the rest of your life, is not so long a time. You are rich enough to have nannies and governesses to care for any offspring. It would in no way interfere with your studies, for it must not be too hard

to keep up on reading while in your months of confinement. What else would you have to do?'

'And once you have an heir…'

'Or two,' he prompted.

'Then I am free to do as I like?'

'We both will be. The marital obligations are fulfilled. Gossip is silenced. We can go our separate ways,
as planned, even while remaining under the same roof.'

'Like everyone else.'

'If we wish.'

He was right, which made it all the more maddening. After the initial display of temper, he had presented
his case most rationally. He was not asking more than
an average husband would expect. She had been the one
to make the unreasonable request. But he was quite
upfront about his willingness to return to her plan, once
the niceties were performed. Other than the absolute
terror she felt, when she thought of what they would do
together, she could find no flaw in his logic.

She stared at him. 'And you are willing to…with me.'

'Of course.' He said it as though the fact somehow
answered her question.

'But when we married…there was no plan to… I
never expected that you would want…'

He smiled. 'If I had found the idea repellent, I would
never have agreed to continue with the marriage. And
I will admit, as we have grown familiar with each other,
I have been giving the matter some thought. I have no
wish to force you, of course. But neither can I stand idly
by while you take a lover.'

If he was to be believed, he had been faithful to her,

despite opportunity and temptation, for the brief duration of their marriage. And it must be true, for he would gain nothing by lying, since she did not care.

But if she did not care, then why was the idea so flattering? As was the idea that he was seriously considering… She looked at him, sitting beside her, with the candlelight in his eyes, and the beginnings of a beard shadow on his pale cheek. He was the most beautiful man she had ever seen. She could not help an uncontrollable attraction. It was why she had learned to look at him as little as possible, much as one learned not to stare directly into the sun.

'Are you planning to answer today?' he asked. 'Because you have been quiet for a very long time, and I find it unnerving. If you wish more time to consider, I will understand.'

'No. No, really I am fine.' Tim had said she should let him charm her. And he was only asking her to do what she had secretly wanted for quite some time.

'And?' He made a gesture, as if to coax more words out of her.

'Oh. Yes. And… Well… Although I did not expect it, I do not see anything unreasonable about your request. You are right. I will inform Tim, if he should flirt with me again, that his attentions are inappropriate. And I will…'

He raised his eyebrows, and gestured again.

'Accede to your request for…' she searched for a word that was not too embarrassing '…collaboration.'

He smiled. 'Thank you. Shall we begin?'

'Now?' She slid down the couch to be as far away from him as possible.

'I fail to see why not.' He slid after her to be near to her again, and covered her hands with his. 'I do not mean to take you here, if that is what frightens you. Now that I have your consent, it is not as if we need to rush.'

'Oh.' Her heart was hammering as his hands stoked up her arms, to touch her shoulders.

'But I do find you quite fetching this evening. Which gave rise to the jealousy of a few moments ago. I feared that other men had noticed what I was seeing in you. For how could they not? Can you forgive me?'

She blinked.

'It was foolish of me. You should not have to bear the brunt of my mercurial temper.'

She blinked again, and took a shaky breath.

'I am afraid I have an overly passionate nature. But as such, it would be most out of character for me if I did not try to steal a kiss or two, to celebrate our last night in London and your successful entrance into society.'

'A kiss.' The words came out of her mouth on a sigh. And she nodded.

'Or two.' He reached behind her, to undo the hooks of her gown.

'Then why…?' She started forward, which only brought her closer to his body, and his hands worked to loosen her stays, proving again his knowledge of lady's underthings.

'I have been told that, although they are lovely, ball-gowns tend to be rather constricting. It will be easier for you to relax if we undo your lacing.'

'Oh.' Perhaps he was right, for it was becoming difficult to catch her breath, especially when he held her the way he was doing now.

He felt her trembling, and rubbed his cheek against hers and whispered, 'You have not been kissed before?'

'You did, once. When we first came to London.'

He reached out, and took the glasses off the bridge of her nose, folding them up and setting them aside. 'This will be very different, then.' As his lips moved from her temple down to her mouth, she quite forgot to breathe. And her sudden gasp for air pulled his tongue into her open mouth, which, judging by the way he was using it, seemed to be his object, all along.

He pushed her back into the cushions of the couch, and the kiss became harder, and he sucked, to bring her tongue to him, urging her to stroke and lick in return. This was no ordinary kiss, for there was no sweetness in it, just raw desire. And she opened herself to it, loving the feel of him, wanting her and claiming her for his own.

And suddenly she realised the true reason he had opened her gown, for in her movements under him, her breasts had slipped out of the low bodice, and he was massaging them with his hands, and teasing the tips with his fingers, until she squirmed under him. Then his kiss travelled from her chin, to her neck, to her bare shoulder, before his hands cupped her breasts to bring the nipples, one by one, into his mouth. He settled his head against her, and began to suckle at them, the stubble on his chin rough against them, and the hair of his head, so very soft in contrast. His mouth pulled hard upon them, until she was arching her back, and moaning in pleasure. And then she felt the feeling rush through her body until it left her trembling in his arms.

As he looked up and smiled at her, the clock on the mantel struck three. 'That is enough for tonight, I think.'

She tried to ask him what he meant, in stopping, but the words that came out of her were unintelligible.

'Technically, I think I have fulfilled my promise.' He was still smiling. 'For that was one kiss. Two at most. I don't recall stopping at any point in the last hour. Do you?'

An hour? Had it been so long? She shook her head.

'I could go longer, but it is late, and we are travelling tomorrow, as I promised. But your initial response was most favourable. I think it bodes well for our future together.'

Their future? If tonight had been an indication of things to come, then she hoped the future was not distant. 'When?'

His smile broadened. 'I am not sure. There is an art to these things. I would not want to hurry, but neither am I willing to wait too long. Some time after we have gone home, and can lie in our own bed for as long as we like, taking pleasure in each other.' His hand dipped to her skirt, and he raised the hem. 'You may let me know when you are ready.' His fingers trailed up her leg, until they were above her knee and had searched out the top of her stocking. He ran his fingertips lightly along the bare skin above the silk, before untying her garter. The stocking slipped, and he pressed the pad of his thumb against the naked flesh of her inner thigh.

She felt her legs trembling at the touch, and moaned in response.

'Not that way, although it is music to hear, darling.' He pulled the ribbon down her leg and waved it in front of her. 'You will be ready when you are brave enough to take this back from me.' And he tucked it into his coat pocket, and offered her his hand. 'Now sit up, so that I may put your clothing back together, and we will go upstairs to let the maid take it apart again.'

Chapter Sixteen

The next day he sat across from her in the carriage, watching as she watched the road. She was not the uneasy traveller that had returned with him from Gretna. As the city passed away to be replaced by villages and open road, he watched her taking in the changing landscape, returning to her book time and again, only to gaze back out the window. She was as happy in leaving London as a normal woman would be to go there.

He shook his head and smiled to himself. Last night's conversation had been more than strange. If it had been any other woman in the world, the solution would have been easy. The merest suggestion on his part, and an assignation would have been guaranteed. That he should have to explain the obvious, quietly and politely to his own wife, and then wait for her assent, was an idea beyond comprehension.

But he had not realised, until last night, that their plan

to remain apart was a disaster in the making. It had never occurred to him that his wife might have favourites, just as his friends' wives did. That he had no right to expect her fidelity nor method to encourage it had struck him like a thunderclap.

And to see his best friend at her side, so far from the ballroom, had churned up all the feelings of guilt that he had been trying to hide. If only Tim had told him not to be an idiot when he'd questioned him. But he had laughed it off, and given him a knowing look that said, 'It would serve you right.'

Adam must nip it in the bud immediately. He was not without charm. He had been told he was surpassingly handsome. And he was a duke, damn it all, which should be more than sufficient for even the most selective of wives. He would bring the sum total of his experience to bear on the problem and the inexperienced printer's daughter would melt in his hands like butter.

Was already melting, come to that. He'd felt her kisses the previous night, and seen the stricken look she had given him when he'd stopped.

This morning, she sat there, her lips swollen and chapped from his kiss, and watched him when she did not think he would notice. This was much more of what he expected. She had not noticed him before, and he had not realised how it had annoyed him.

Now she was aware. Sexually aware of him. Watching his hands and thinking that they had touched her. Watching his mouth and knowing that it would kiss her again. And wondering about the garter that lay coiled in his pocket, and what she might be willing to do to get it.

He had wondered about that himself. He had imagined her response would be stiff and awkward, and perhaps a little cold. But the image of warm butter was more apt. Hot and delicious.

He licked his lips, and she followed the movement of his tongue with fascination, before looking away and feigning interest in her book.

It would not be too very long before she was as eager to give herself to him as he was to take her. He would do as he willed with her for as long as he liked— for a lifetime, if necessary—and there would be no more of this nonsense about taking lovers and leading separate lives.

And it all would be settled before the first snows fell, and his wife realised that her main sources of entertainment for the long winter months would be visits from his brother Will, and their good neighbour, Tim. He would have no peace in his own home if he could not trust the woman he had married when she was out of his sight. And while he wished, in many things, he could emulate the fine character of his friend, he had no wish to marry for wealth, only to have the woman put horns on him and make him the laughing stock of London.

They pulled into an inn yard for the evening, and he helped his wife from the carriage and told Jem to arrange food for them, a private sitting room, and a single bedroom.

The servant could not hide his brief look of surprise, and followed it with an insolent glare before doing as he was bid. Later, after Penny was safely inside, he caught up with his wife's servant, slouching the baggage toward the rooms. 'Here, fellow. I wish a word with you.'

Jem turned and set the bags on the floor and then straightened. For the first time, Adam noticed the bulk of the man, who stood several inches taller than he did, and was broad and strong of back, despite his advancing age. The servant glared down at him, too close for a bow in the enclosed space of the hallway, and touched his forelock. 'Your Grace?'

'Just now, in the courtyard. I did not like the look you gave me when I gave you instruction.'

'So sorry, your Grace. I will endeavour to improve myself in the future.' But the man was still looking at him as though concluding that one good slap would be all it might take to send the title to Will.

Adam straightened as well, putting on the air of command that served him so well in the House of Lords. 'It is no business of yours where your mistress sleeps. Or if we might choose to put aside the ridiculous arrangement created by Penny in favour of something closer to sanity. From this point forward, we will be acting as other couples do, and not as two strangers pretending to be married.'

Jem's eyes narrowed, and he said, 'Very good, your Grace. Because all intelligent people aspire to a union that is the current mode of the day: full of luxury, casual carnality and pretence, but devoid of any sincere feeling between the parties involved. Unless one is to count the contempt you seem to have for one another. My mistress has never wanted more than her parents had: a true meeting of the minds and a deep and abiding affection, strong enough to transcend the bonds of life itself. When her father died, your Grace, it held no fear for him, for he was convinced that his wife waited for him on the other side. That is what my mistress expected. When she found she could not have it, then she wanted to be left alone, and in peace.'

The servant looked down upon him again, as if he were still face down in the muck of the inn yard. 'And in the end, she will have to settle for you.' He picked up the bags that he had dropped, balanced them easily on his shoulders, and started down the hall. 'This way to your room, your Grace.'

She was waiting for him, there, in the tiny sitting room that connected to the room where they would sleep. A supper had been laid for them on the low table: cold meat pies, cakes, ale for him and tea for the lady.

And as he came to her, she hastily set down the mug of ale, and wiped some foam from her lips. She looked down, embarrassed. 'I'm sorry. You must think me frightfully common.'

He smiled. 'For doing something that you enjoy?'

When she looked back at him, there was fear in her eyes. A desperation to please him that hadn't been there before the party. She hadn't given a damn for what he thought of her then. But things had changed. 'I suspect the wives of your friends do not steal ale from their husband's mug when he is not looking.'

He sat down next to her. 'They do things far worse.' He tasted the ale. 'And this is quite good. We can share it, if you like.' He set the mug between them, and reached for his plate. His sleeve brushed against her arm; instead of shying from him, as she once might have done, she leaned to be closer.

And when she did it, his heart gave a funny little leap in his chest. He covered the feeling by taking another sip of ale. Not knowing how to proceed, he said, 'I spoke to my brother last night as the guests were leaving. Apparently, you told him how your work was progressing.'

She gave a little shake of her head. 'I am afraid I am not very good at small talk. I'm too little in public to have the knack of it.'

'No,' he corrected quickly. 'It was all right. More than all right. He was most impressed by you, and told me so. Still a little surprised, of course, that I found a woman with a brain who would have me.'

She laughed. 'What an idea, that the Duke of Bellston could not attract a woman of intelligence. I used to read the papers, and imagine what it would be like to meet you. I was sure that your wife would need her wits about her at all times if she were to speak to you at all.'

'Then you must have been sorely disappointed to find so little challenge...' He stopped. 'You used to imagine *me*?'

She put her hand to her temple, to hide her embarrassment. 'There. The truth is out. I sat at home reading Greek, and shunning society, spinning girlish fancies over a man who I would never meet. I assumed, by the wisdom of his speeches, he must be long married, and perhaps already a grandfather. I would never dare speak to him. But perhaps, if I could ever find the nerve, I would write to him with a question concerning his position on something or other, perhaps pretending to be my brother, or some other male, and he might deign to answer me.'

'And then you found me drunk in the street, and I hauled you to London and ignored you, and then forced you to dress in ribbons and dance with my friends, while I sat in another room, playing cards.' He laughed until tears came to his eyes, and when he noticed she was still pink with mortification, he pulled her close, and hugged her to him until he felt her laugh as well.

Then he buried his face against her neck, and murmured, 'I hope we are close enough now that, if you have any questions, you will not feel the need to submit them in writing.'

She said, 'I…think whatever I meant to ask you has gone quite out of my head.'

'Speak of something you know, then. For I do love the sound of your voice.' He breathed deeply, taking in the scent of her hair.

'Do you want me to ask for my garter, now?' It was the barest whisper, fearful, but full of hope as well.

And it tugged at his heart, to know how hard she had been trying to be what he wished, and how little he had done to make it easy for her. 'No games tonight.' He put his arms around her. 'Come. Sit in my lap. Tell me about your work. What is it about this Odysseus fellow that makes him worth the attentions of my Penelope?'

She hesitated at first, and then did as he said, wrapping her arms around his neck and whispering the story to him. He relaxed into the cushions of the divan, and thought what a great fool Odysseus must have been to get himself so cursed that he couldn't find his way back, and to waste time with Calypso or Circe when everything he needed was waiting at home.

When she finished, it was late. The fire was low and the candles were guttering. She lay still against him for a moment, and then said, 'I have talked too long.'

He stroked her head, and pulled a pin from her hair. 'Never. But it is time for bed. Let me help you.' He pulled more pins from her hair, uncoiling braids and combing them out with his fingers. He had never seen it down before, and the softness surprised him. He ran his fingers through the length of it, and closed his own eyes. 'Silk. I have never felt anything so soft.'

'It is too fine,' she argued. 'If I do not keep it tied, it tangles.'

He brought the strands to his face, breathing the scent of it and letting it cascade through his fingers. 'I will braid it for you again. Later.'

She reached out to him, and caught the end of his cravat, and undid the knot, letting it slide through her fingers to the floor. The gesture was carelessly erotic, although she seemed to have no idea of the fact. Then she slid from his lap and stood up, starting toward the bedroom and looking back over her shoulder at him.

He rose as well, stripping off his coat and waistcoat, and undoing his shirt. Then he went to stand behind her, and she held her long hair out of the way as he undid her clothing. She was very still as he worked, loosening hooks and lacings, pushing her gown off her shoulders and to the floor, kissing the back of her neck. Then he went to sit on the end of the bed, pulling off his boots and stockings, and undoing the buttons on his trousers.

He looked up at her, still standing where he had left her, the firelight outlining her body through the lawn of her chemise. She was watching him. Her eyes travelled slowly over his body. He could feel her gaze, like the touch of fingers, on his shoulders, his chest, his stomach and lower. Then she removed her glasses, holding them tightly in her hand, and closed her eyes.

He stood up and took them from her. 'Would you like me to put out the lights?'

'Please.'

He set them on the table beside the bed and blew out the candles, one by one, until the room was lit only by the fire. 'There. Now we are both a bit blind, and there is nothing to be afraid of. Remove your shift, and climb into bed.' He removed his trousers, hung them over a nearby chair, then threw back the covers and climbed in himself.

She waited until he was settled, and then quickly stripped off the last of her clothing, draping it over the end of the bed and going around to her side. Her movements were slow and sure, for she had believed him when he said he was near blind. But he could see her well enough: the hair, pale as moonlight, trying and failing to hide her full breasts, slim waist and soft, round hips.

She climbed into the bed, and he threw the covers back over her and pulled her close to bring her forehead to his lips. She trembled a little and so he said, 'Do not worry. I will do nothing tonight that will alarm you. We can wait until we are home to be more intimate. But I wish very much to touch you.'

'And kiss me again?'

'Once or twice.'

'I would like that. Very much.' And she turned her open mouth to his.

He kept his movements slow and gentle. His tongue stroked hers and traced the edge of her teeth, and his hands massaged her neck and her shoulders, making her muscles relax and her body melt into his. He let his hands slide lower down her back, and cupped her to him as he thrust his tongue into her mouth.

Instinctively, she parted her thighs and tried to get closer still, until he had to stop for a moment, to remind himself that he meant to go slowly, and not take what she was offering.

He pushed away from her, rolling her on to her back, and she moaned, reaching to bring him close to her again. He pulled himself up to kneel between her parted legs, and let the covers fall away so that he could watch her as he played with her breasts. If she had been shy of him before, she had forgotten it, and looked up at him with love-drugged eyes as he stroked her, catching her lip between her teeth as he teased her nipples, and stroking her own hands up the sides of her body to squeeze his hands on her, encouraging him to be less gentle.

He took her permission and kneaded and pinched, until she was writhing on the bed, her hips bucking as her body begged to be loved. The sight was making him dizzy with lust and painfully hard.

He fell upon her then, pushing her body back on to the bed, and burying his face against her breasts, letting his teeth do what his fingers had, and sliding his hands between her legs to stroke her, gripping her thighs and spreading them wider, sliding his thumbs up to part the hair and find her most sensitive places. He could feel her heart, beating under his cheek, and waited until he was sure that it must be near bursting it was so loud. And he lifted his face from her breast and swore to her that it would be ever like this between them, if she would trust him and let him love her as she deserved. Then he thrust, filling her with his fingers.

She was hot and tight, and he imagined the feeling of sliding into her body, night after night, and waking to her sweet smile, day after day, knowing that she would always belong to him. And he heard her cry out and collapse against his hand, sated.

He released her and slipped up her body to kiss her upon the mouth again, and she gasped and laughed. 'That was magnificent.'

He rolled off her, and said, 'That was just the beginning. Here, turn over and let me do up your hair.'

'My hair?'

'To give me something else to do with you.' He reached out and pulled the length into a messy braid. Then he wrapped it around her to tease her breasts with the end. 'For if I do the things I am thinking of, we will get no sleep at all, and you will have a most uncomfortable ride tomorrow.'

She yawned. 'That sounds very wicked.' And then she settled back into him, grinding her hips against him, and driving him one step closer to insanity. 'But I am very tired. Perhaps you may show me tomorrow.' She yawned again. 'I think I shall very much want to reclaim my garter.'

'I sincerely hope so.' And he lay back against the pillows and cradled his wife's body to him for a night of delicious agony.

Chapter Seventeen

The next day, Penny watched her husband dozing on the other side of the carriage. He said he had not slept well, but he did not seem overly bothered by the fact.

She, on the other hand, had had an excellent night's sleep. Her body could remember every kiss and every touch from the previous evening, and it woke hungry for more. The feeling was aggravated by the gentle rocking of the carriage. She was excited enough by the prospect of the new home that her husband had described to her. But the nearness of him, and the promise that they would be alone together from now on, left her nearly overcome.

Adam started awake, and looked out of the window, smiling and pointing to a marker that he said indicated the edge of his property.

He leaned his head out of the window of the carriage, closed his eyes, and inhaled deeply. Then he looked sheepishly back at her. 'You will find it embarrassingly sentimental of me, I'm sure. But I find that the air smells sweeter in Wales than anywhere in England. And is not the quality of the sunshine brighter than that in the city?'

She thought to comment on the coal burning in London, and the noise of the traffic, which were impediments to the climate and perfectly rational explanations for the changes he described. If the Welsh air smelled of anything, she suspected it was sheep, for there were flocks in many of the pastures they were passing. She smiled at him. 'Black sheep?'

He grinned at her and nodded. 'Perhaps it is symbolic.' He looked critically at the flocks. 'But there are not as many as there should be. It was a hard winter, with a late spring and a dry summer.' He shook his head.

She looked out the window at the land they were passing. The year had obviously been difficult. The fields and gardens were not as green as she expected them to be, nor the crops as large. But the tenants appeared happy; as the carriage passed, people in the fields looked up and smiled. They dropped curtsies, removed caps and offered occasional shy waves.

And Adam smiled back and surveyed the land with a critical eye and a touch of possessiveness. He had missed it. And no matter how at ease he had seemed in London, he belonged here.

The carriage slowed as it came up the long curved drive and pulled abreast of the house, and he leaned forward in his seat as though his body strained to be even closer to home. When the footman opened the carriage door, he stepped out, forgetting her. He was immediately surrounded by a pack of dogs, barking, wagging and nudging him with wet noses for his attention. He patted and stroked, calling them by name and reaching absently into a coat pocket for treats that he was not carrying.

She watched him from the door of the carriage as he was drawn like a lodestone to the open front door. And even the butler, whose kind were not known for their exuberant displays of emotion, was smiling to see the return of the master of the house.

Adam took a step forwards, and then froze and turned back to her, embarrassment colouring his face. He strode back to the carriage and reached up to offer her his hand to help her down, making a vague gesture that seemed to encompass his brief abandonment of her. Then he laughed at himself and kicked the step out of the way, held both hands out to her and said, 'Jump.'

She stared at him in amazement. 'Why ever for?'

'Trust me. I will catch you.'

She shook her head. 'This is nonsense.'

'Perhaps. But the sooner you do it, the sooner it will be done. Now, do as I say.'

He showed no sign of relenting, and at last she closed her eyes, and stepped from the carriage into open air.

He caught her easily under the arms, and let her slide down his body until her slippered feet were standing on his boots. The closeness of their bodies was shocking, and she meant to pull away, but he was smiling down at her with such ease that a part of her did not wish to move ever again.

He said softly, 'There are customs about brides and

thresholds, are there not? You must not stumble, or it would be bad luck to us both.'

She pointed to the house. 'I see no reason to hold to superstition. There is nothing wrong with my legs, and the way is not strewn with disaster. I think I can manage.' But it felt good to be held so close to him.

'You have been very lucky for me, up 'til now. It is better to be safe than sorry. Perhaps it were best if I were to see you safely into the house.' And before she could object, he scooped an arm beneath her knees and had lifted her into his arms.

She surprised herself by squealing in delight. She should have demanded that he let her down immediately, and that it was all highly undignified. But instead, she wrapped her arms around his neck, tipped back her head and laughed into the Welsh sunshine. The crowd of dogs still milling about them had to jump to nudge and sniff her as well. And even as he took care to guide her through the pack, she could feel the strain of his body, wanting to go faster and take the last few steps at a run to be inside his house again.

As they passed the butler, the man bowed to her as well as her husband, and murmured, 'Your Grace, welcome home. And welcome to you as well, your Grace. May I offer my congratulations?'

Adam nodded, as though his heart were too full to speak, and held her even closer, before taking the last step that brought them both into the house. Then he set her down and took her by the hand to lead her into the entry, where the servants were assembled.

The introduction was easier than it had been on the

first day in the townhouse, and she hoped that this was a sign that she was adjusting to her new role as well. Although it might have had something to do with the change in the man beside her, who was neither as distant nor as superior. When he smiled with pride as he spoke to the staff, she had a hard time distinguishing whether it was happiness with them, or his eagerness for them to meet her. And she could not help but smile as well.

At last, he held out his hand in a broad gesture and said, 'Your new home,' as though the manor were a person and the introduction would result in a response.

She looked up at the high ceilings, and the wide marble steps that led to the second floor of rooms and a portrait gallery above them.

She could feel his hesitation next to her. He wanted her to like it. And how could she not? It was the grandest house she'd ever seen. Although the idea that it was to be her home was faintly ridiculous.

'The roof needs new slate,' he said in apology. 'But that is the way it is with all old homes. Something is always in need of repair. And nothing has been done in decoration for many years. But the part that is undamaged by the fire is warm and clean, and I find it most comfortable.'

Comfortable? She looked at him. If one found museums to be a comforting place, perhaps. But museums were not so different really than… 'May I see the library?' she asked hopefully.

'Certainly. I believe your books have already arrived.' He led her down the hall and opened a door before them.

She poked her head into the room. Books. Floor to ceiling. Some shelves were so high that a set of brass steps was necessary to reach them. But there was plenty of space for the contents of the crates that stood stacked by the door. A fire had been laid in the grate, and the warmth of it extended to the oak table at the middle of the room. There was space for her papers, ample lamps to light the words. Comfortable chairs by the fireside where she could read for pleasure when she was not working. And the heavy rug beneath her feet was so soft and welcoming that she was tempted to abandon the furniture and curl up upon it.

'Will there be sufficient room for your collection, or shall we need to add extra shelves?'

Without thinking, she had been counting the empty places, and reordering the works. 'There is ample room, I am sure.'

'And here.' He walked to a shelf by the window, and pulled down a battered volume. 'You will not need it, for I think you are well stocked in this. It is left over from my own school days.' He looked at it sadly. 'Which means it has seen very little use.' He handed her a schoolboy's edition of Homer, in the Greek.

She stared down at the book in her hand, and then up to the man who had given it to her. When he was at home, he was a very different person. No less handsome, certainly. The light from the windows made his hair shine, and his eyes were as blue as they had been. But the cynical light in them had disappeared. He seemed younger. Or perhaps it was that he did not seem as arrogant and unapproachable after the previous night.

'It is all right, then? Do you think you can be happy here?'

Happy? It was a paradise. She hardly dared speak.

'Of course, there is more. I haven't shown you your rooms yet.' He led the way out of the library and down the corridor.

She peered in the next room as they passed.

'My study,' he answered. And this time, he opened the door wide so that she could see the desk within. 'It connects to the library. As does the morning room on the other side. I had thought, perhaps you might wish to use it as well, should the library not prove to have sufficient space.' He backtracked down the hall and opened another door. 'It is rather…' He waved a hand at the decoration, which was rococo with gilt and flowers, and a ceiling painted with cherubs and clouds. 'My mother, again.' He looked at her. 'And there are more of the damn china shepherds.'

She reached out to touch a grouping that was very similar to the one she had left in London, a court couple, locked for ever in passionate embrace. She ran a finger along it and felt the heat of the kiss in her body. 'That is all right. I think I am growing used to them.'

He gestured her out of the room and led her down more halls to a music room, separate rooms for dining and breakfast, another parlour, and a formal receiving room. Then he took her up the stairs past the portraits of his family to a long row of bedrooms and opened a door near the end. 'This is to be your room. If you wish.'

It was beautifully appointed, and larger than the one

in the townhouse, but of a similar layout. She looked for the connecting door that should link her room to his. 'And where do you sleep?'

He looked away. 'I am not particularly sure. I had used this room, for a while. But I could choose another. Here, let me show you.' He took her into the hall and opened the door to what must have been the master suite. A strong smell of smoke crept out into the hallway.

He sniffed. 'Better than it was, I'm afraid. The real damage is farther down the hall. But your room is not affected. Let me show you the worst of it.' He seemed to steel himself, gathering courage, then led her down the corridor to the left, and as they walked the odour of smoke got stronger. The line of tension in her husband's back increased. He quickened his pace as they reached the end of the corridor, and threw open the heavy double doors at the end.

He caught her, before she could attempt entrance, for there was little floor to step on. The hall seemed to end in open air before him. She was looking down into what must have been the ballroom before the fire. The light in the room had a strange, greasy quality as it filtered through what was left of the floor-to-ceiling windows on the back of the house. Some of the panes were missing, leaving spots of brightness on the floor and walls. Some were boarded shut, and some merely smoke-stained and dirty. At the second-floor level, there were bits of floor and gallery still clinging to the outer walls. From a place near the roof, an interloping bird sang.

'Oh, my.'

'It was beautiful once,' Adam remarked, bitterness in his voice. 'The retiring rooms were off this hall, card rooms and galleries for musicians. A staircase led up from there.' He pointed to a blank space opposite them.

'How did it happen?'

'There was an accident. After a ball. One of the candleholders was overbalanced, and the flames touched the draperies.' He stopped and swallowed, then started again. 'The truth. You should hear it all, before we go further. It was I who caused it. The party was over, and most of the guests had gone. And I followed Clarissa to the second floor, so that we could be alone. My room is just down the hall and I thought…' He could not look at her, as he spoke. 'But she chose the musicians' gallery. I had too much wine that night, and was thinking too slowly to realise that the acoustics would be excellent. Tim was searching for her, to take her home. He must have heard it all. She made no effort to be quiet that night. And when I cautioned her, she laughed and asked what did I think she'd meant to happen.

'I pushed her away from me, and she overturned the candles. I pulled her clear of the fire, but the flames spread quickly. Fortunately, the walls on this side of the house are old and stone. The damage was limited to this room, and the rooms above and below. And smoke damage to my bedroom, of course. Divine justice.'

'Was anyone hurt?'

Adam seemed to flinch at the thought. 'Will has a burn on the back of his arm, gained from fighting the fire. A beam fell upon him.'

She looked up at the roof, and the badly patched holes, and piles of new lumber on the floor below. 'And this is why you needed the money?'

'Not a thing has gone right since the night of the fire. It was as if I was cursed. I invested. Badly, as it turns out. In tobacco. The ship sank, and my hopes with it. The profits should have been enough to repair the house and account for the failure of this year's crop.' He reached out and took her hand. 'And then I met you. Before that, I had no idea how to go on.'

She looked at him, and at the wreckage before them. 'And you swear, this is over.'

He smiled sadly. 'Nothing brings you to the knowledge that you are behaving like a fool quite so fast as burning your house half to the ground, and seeing your brother nursing injuries that were a result of your stupidity in chasing after another man's wife. And I saw the look on Tim's face that night. Yet he insists on forgiving me, which is the worst punishment of all.'

She tugged at his sleeve. 'Close the doors on this mess, then. Let us go downstairs and find supper.'

Chapter Eighteen

$\operatorname{\mathscr{O}\!}$

He took her to the formal dining room, which was set for two. And she watched as the servants went through their paces, attempting to impress their new mistress with speed of service and excellence of presentation.

She wondered what Jem thought of it all, and if they had managed to force some work out of him, or had he found a warm corner somewhere to sleep. Perhaps she could find a post for him, something that involved short hours and long naps.

And while her husband might think of them as being totally alone in Wales, she found the room crowded with servants. There were footmen behind each chair and a regular influx of courses arriving and departing. She watched Adam, who was staring at the contents of his plate, but doing very little with it. He must think himself alone, for he seemed to have forgotten her entirely. Instead, he cast furtive glances in the direction of the damaged wing, as though he could sense it through the walls.

By the look in his eyes, he had been wrong. He might think that things were over, and managed to keep them at bay when he was in London and could keep busy enough to ignore them. But his good spirits had begun to evaporate the moment he had opened the door to the ballroom. She wondered how many rooms of the house held bad memories for him. She imagined Clarissa, as Tim had described her, attempting to trap Adam in an indiscretion. The music gallery had been an excellent choice, if she wished discovery.

But had it been the first attempt? Or had she taken every opportunity she could to embarrass her husband and create talk? Penny might be forced to see her own husband starting at ghosts of memory in every room of their home.

Why must the woman have been so beautiful and so audacious? So without shame as to be unforgettable? How was she expected to compete? When they were together, in the inn, Penny had felt like the only woman in the world to him. And in scant hours, he had forgotten her.

The idea angered her, and she prepared to count, when it occurred to her that, in fighting this battle, a measured and thoughtful response would not win the day. If she thought at all, she would never have the nerve to act.

She looked back at Adam, who was staring into his dessert in confusion, as though wondering where the earlier courses had got to. She slid her chair closer to his, so that they might not be overheard. 'Adam. Darling. I was wondering if you had given thought as to where we would sleep?'

He started, and looked up at her. 'I am sorry. I had forgotten. You must be tired after such a long journey. You will take the mistress's suite, of course. I will find somewhere.' He shrugged. 'One of the guest rooms. I doubt I will sleep well this first night.' He gave her a tight, pained smile. 'I had hoped to be in better spirits. There are uneasy memories. But do not let me disturb you.'

She pulled her chair closer still, until their knees were touching under the table. 'You are disturbing me very much, husband. For I was rather under the impression that you would be disturbing me tonight. And I find the prospect of a lack of disturbance…most disturbing.'

He started again, as if waking from a bad dream. 'You still wish…' He raised his eyebrows.

'To reclaim my garter. If you still have it, of course. The way you are acting, I am beginning to suspect that you have forgotten where it is.'

He looked at her, with the long slow smile he used to charm her into so many things, and said, 'I have it on my person, at this moment.'

She took a large sip of wine, to steady her nerves. 'Really? I do not believe you. Show it to me.'

The roguish light was back in his eyes again. 'You must find it for yourself, if you are so curious to see it.'

She toyed with her glass and gauged the locations of the servants, and how much they were likely to see. It was some small consolation that, should any word reach the outside about the indiscretions of the Duke of Bellston, from now on they would involve the duchess as well.

Then she took another drink, casually dropped her hand below the table as though to adjust her napkin, and ran her fingers up her husband's leg.

He choked on his water and gripped the edge of the table. When he had regained his breath, he whispered, 'What the devil are you doing?'

'What you suggested I do,' she whispered back. 'Where else would you wear a garter? You know where it was when you removed it.' Her hand travelled farther up his thigh and his face went white as the blood left it.

'But I do not feel anything.' She gathered all her nerve and thought about last night at the inn. And then she sent her hand higher up his thigh, under his napkin, and undid two of the buttons on his trousers, slipping her hand into the gap. After a few seconds she said, 'And while this is very interesting, I do not think it is a garter, either.'

'Out!'

She sought to remove her hand, but he pressed down on it through the napkin, trapping it where it was.

He turned his head to the footmen at the door, 'Go. All of you. We do not need you. Thank the cook. Wonderful meal. But no more. Do not bother to clear away, just go. And lock the door behind you.'

When he heard the click of the latch, he sighed and leaned back in his chair. Then he closed his eyes and said in a hoarse voice, 'You may continue looking.'

She undid some more buttons, moved the napkin, and peeked beneath the table. When he caught her looking, she said, 'Last night, it was very dark. And I was not wearing my glasses.'

'Oh.'

His response to what she had said sounded quite like a moan, and she smiled in triumph. She looked again, as she felt him shuddering under her hand as she stroked him. 'Shall we play hot and cold?'

'Very hot,' he murmured, and tore at the knot on his cravat.

'I am still looking for the garter, silly. I do not think you have it hidden here at all.'

With one hand, he yanked at the buttons on his waist-coat, and the other cupped the back of her head, dragging her mouth to his for a desperate kiss. When his chest was bare, he pulled her empty hand to his heart, and she stroked the hair on his chest, and the nipples hidden in it. He broke the kiss and guided her mouth down to them, letting her bite and suck as he had done for her, while he fumbled at the closures on her gown, swearing as he fought to dispense with her clothes.

Had she unbalanced him to that degree? A feeling of power rushed through her, along with desire, and she could feel her body readying itself for what was to come. Her breasts ached to be touched, and as she stroked him she could feel the heat building inside her, where he would soon be.

She stopped what she was doing and enjoyed the moment, and then looked at her husband. She'd thought him a master of seduction. But tonight the tables were turned, and he could not undo the simple knot that held her stays in place. 'Really, Adam. If you cannot manage, perhaps I shall go to my room and send for the maid.'

'You will do no such thing.' He grabbed her hands and placed them firmly on his knees, bending her over the arm of his chair. 'Do not move.' And then he seized a knife from the table in front of them, and slit the lacings of her corset from bottom to top.

She sat up and took a deep breath, which he stole with another kiss and then pulled the thing free of her, and threw it on to the floor. She stood up and let the gown follow it, and then he grabbed her by the waist and lifted her to sit on the table, kissing her face, her throat and her breasts. Between the kisses he undid the last button on his trousers. Pushing them out of the way, he panted, 'Sorry, darling. Most undignified. And not as gentle as I should be. I cannot help myself.'

He could not help himself. And he was talking to her. She took a breath to calm her nerves, and then pulled up her chemise and spread her legs, leaning back to tip her hips up. 'Stop talking and take me.'

'Say that you love me,' he whispered. 'I want to hear you say the words.'

And it was surprisingly easy to tell him the truth. 'I love you,' she whispered back.

This time, he was the one to groan, 'Soon.' And he kissed her again, rough and insistent. So she reached out and put her hand to him again, and mimicked the strength of his kiss. She could feel herself losing the boundary between what she was feeling, and what he must be feeling as he found her with his fingers and thrust.

She rocked her hips against his hand, and let him fill her, as the feelings grew inside of her, and his sex grew slippery in her palm.

'Very soon,' he whispered. His hips thrust toward hers until the head of his sex rested against her, and she writhed against it, stroking so that it rubbed her body where it felt most right. She was trembling with excitement, balancing on the edge of something wonderful. He removed his fingers from her, clutching her hip with his hand to steady her, and bring her closer to him.

The emptiness frustrated her, and she stroked harder, feeling him tremble, and rubbed herself with him until his sex slipped against the opening to her body, making her gasp.

And he said, 'Now,' and drove into her.

There was a shock of pain, and he kissed her until it hardly mattered, and the tension grew in her again. He pushed her back to brace her hands on the table so that her hips stayed steady, put his hands on her breasts and thrust, over and over again, staring into her eyes.

She leaned back and wrapped her legs around him so that the friction of their bodies changed, driving her wild with touches that were never long enough. But they brought her close again, so very close. And when he shuddered against her and stopped, she moaned in protest until he stroked her with his thumb and took her over the edge.

When she came back to herself, they had moved very little. She held him inside her, her legs wrapped around his waist, and he was leaning over her on the table, staring down into her face.

He dropped a kiss on her lips, and glanced around the shambles they had made of dinner. What clothing they had managed to remove was scattered around them, chairs were tipped, and goblets were knocked over on the table. He reached beside her, and fed her a candied apricot from the dessert tray, watching her mouth with interest as she ate. 'In case you are wondering,' he said, 'I had intended something a bit more sedate for our first evening together.'

'Oh, really?' she touched her tongue to her lips, and waited as he offered her a bit of cake.

He furrowed his brow. 'I believe my original plan was to seduce you at my leisure, and render you docile and agreeable through lust.'

'And my garter?'

'Is tied around my shirt sleeve, for I thought, perhaps, you would summon the nerve to help me off with my jacket.'

'And what do you think of your plan now?' She shifted her legs to grip him tighter.

He sighed and smiled. 'It is an utter failure. You control me body and soul. Command me.' And he looked supremely happy to have lost.

She released him, and offered her hand to him, so that he could help her down from the table. 'Take me to our bedroom.'

His smile broadened and he scooped up her dress and tossed it over her head. Laughing and whispering, they collected the rest of the discarded clothing and a plate of cakes. Then he opened the door, checked the hall to make sure it was empty and they ran from the room together, not stopping until they were safely behind the closed bedroom door.

Chapter Nineteen

Adam came down to the breakfast room and took his usual seat. His coffee was already poured, the mail was stacked beside the plate, and his wife was seated at his side. Life was as close to perfect as any man had a right to expect.

Penny was as happy in Wales as he had known she would be, even more so now that they had each other. For a month, they had awoken every morning, tangled in the sheets and each other, breakfasted together, and then he went to his study, and she to the library. He could read his paper, ride out to inspect the property, or argue with the workmen who had begun renovations on the ballroom, knowing that when he came back, his steadfast Penelope would be waiting for him.

They had not yet made love in the library, perhaps because he had spent so little time there, before Penny had come to the house. She had learned the measure of him, on that first night. And now, if she felt he was growing morose, or attempting to dwell in the past, she had but to lock the door and show him a flash of garter, and he was lost to the world.

But any suggestions made in the library would be of his own doing. He looked up into her face, startled by the thought, and smiled as he caught her looking at him.

'Excuse me?'

'What?'

'Was there something…?'

They spoke in unison, to cover their mutual confusion, and fell silent at the same time.

'The eggs,' he lied. 'I bit down on a piece of shell.'

'I will speak to Cook.'

'Do not worry, it is nothing.'

She nodded and looked down into her plate.

'They are very good eggs today,' he supplied. 'The best I have ever tasted, I think.'

'You say that every morning.' She went back to her breakfast. But she was blushing.

At some point, he would have to return to London, or share her with the world. But not just yet. For now, they were the only two people on earth, and it was enough. He opened the first letter on the stack, and a folded sheet dropped on to his plate.

…torment me no longer. For I cannot live without
the perfection of your body, the taste of your kiss,
the sound of your voice as you call my name…

He recognised his own hand, and remembered the letter well. It had been drunken folly to have written it.

He should have thrown it on the fire rather than sent it. And it was hardly the most damning thing he put to paper in the months before the fire.

It was accompanied by another sheet, with a single line.

Come to me at Colton, or I shall go to her.
Clare

She had followed them to Wales.

'Something interesting in the mail?' Penny did not look up from her tea.

'Nothing important.' Perhaps he had grown better at concealing his feelings from her, for she did not seem to notice that the room had gone cold, or that his mouth had filled with smoke and ashes.

'Then I will leave you to it, and return to work.' She raised her eyebrows. 'Ithaca calls.'

'With its rosy fingers of dawn?'

'There must be a better way to say that,' she said, and wandered down the hall, lost in thought.

He stared back at the letter in front of him, and then threw it into the fireplace, watching the edges curl and the words disappear. He poked at the bits of ash until there could be nothing left of them to read.

Then he went to the stables to saddle a horse.

The Colton property abutted his, and as he rode toward it, he could feel the tightening in his chest. He should have spoken the truth to Penny, and got it over with. Soon she would be seeing Clarissa again, and that it would be impossible to avoid contact, if the Coltons had returned to Wales.

But it was very unlike them to be here in the summer. Clare much preferred Bath. He had not been prepared for the letter, and he had no response at hand. Perhaps the situation was not as bad as it seemed. He could assess, and return to Penny by lunch, with an explanation.

Tim's house seemed as it always did, preternaturally quiet. There was nothing to indicate that the family was in residence, although what he expected to find, he was not sure. Tim must be out riding in the hills. Probably trying to avoid his wife.

The servant allowed him entrance and took him to the sitting room without introduction.

Clare was waiting for him, lounging on a divan in dishabille, her dressing gown artfully arranged to display a length of bare leg, the globe of a breast, and the barest hint of nipple, peeking from the ruffles of lace. 'Adam. At last.'

Her voice raised the hairs on the back of his neck, just as it always did, and he wondered how he could have mistaken the feeling for passion. 'Clarissa. Why have you come here?'

'Because it is my home.'

'It is Tim's home. And you loathe it. You have told us often enough.'

'Then I will be honest. I came because I missed you.' She pulled a pretty pout, which made her look more like a spoiled child than a seductress. 'It has been so long.'

'Barely a month.'

'Why did you leave London?'

'You should know that. I sought to be where my wife would be happiest.' *And to be where you were not.*

'Timothy would not let us travel home to be near you. He insists on staying in the city, although it is unbearably hot, and everyone of fashion is leaving.'

'Go to Bath, then. Somewhere that suits you.'

She sighed. 'I did not want Bath. I longed for the comforts of home. If he does not wish to follow, I cannot very well force him. He may stay in the city with the children for all I care.'

'You left your husband and your children as well.' Adam shook his head in disgust.

She shifted, allowing her robe to fall open, so that there could be no mistake of her plans for the next hour. 'I am totally alone, if you still fear discovery. My servants know better than to talk. And your wife spends most days poring over her books, does she not? No one will be the wiser.'

'I thought I made it clear that there would be nothing more between us.'

'On the contrary. You think that by saying nothing, and running away from me, you can end what we had together. If you truly wanted to end it, you would have told me so, outright. But I think you are afraid to speak to me. You are still not sure what you will say to me, Adam, when we are alone. And I have your letters, you know. I read them often. I know the contents of your heart.'

He felt a wave of humiliation, remembering the things he had written to her. Words he wished he'd have saved for the woman who deserved them. 'That is all in the past, Clare. If you must hear me speak the truth plainly, before you believe it, then listen now. Anything that there was between us is at an end. I will not come crawling back to you like a whipped dog. I have a wife now.'

'Why should it matter? I have always had a husband, and it did not seem to bother you.'

The mention of Tim cut at his heart. 'It bothered me a great deal, Clarissa. He is my friend.'

'And I am your lover.'

'Do not dignify what we did by calling it love. There was no higher feeling involved than lust. I disgusted myself with my behaviour.'

She laughed. 'You did not seem so disgusted at the time, as I remember it.'

'I betrayed Tim. That was why you were so eager to snare me, was it not? You enjoyed our liaisons all the more, for knowing how it would hurt your husband.'

'I viewed it as a challenge,' she admitted. 'To see if my charms were strong enough to break your fragile sense of honour. And it snapped like a twig. Now you think silence, distance and a hasty marriage is all it will take to gain your freedom.

'Do you not remember trying this trick before with me? The cold silence. You lasted for six months. And when you came back, I made you beg before I would let you share my bed.' She tipped her head to the side and smiled in remembrance. 'It was really quite amusing. I wonder what I shall make you do this time, once you grow bored with your shop clerk and you want me again.'

He heard the words and, for the first time in months, everything came clear. Suddenly, as if a bond had been cut, he felt truly free of her. And it was his turn to laugh. 'You trapped me well, with your sly affections and your subtle advances. You came to me when I was most vulnerable, when I was troubled, or lonely, or too drunk to care what I was doing. You used my weaknesses against me and took what you wanted. And afterwards, you left me broken. Cursed by my actions, ashamed of what I had become.

'But when Penny found me in that state, she gave herself to me until I was healed. She has made me, in a few short weeks, into the man I wished I was. I can never give her what she truly deserves, for nothing I have is equal to her casual generosity towards me.

'I love her, Clarissa. And I never loved you.'

She laughed back at him. Long and hard and unladylike. 'Never mind, then. For she appears to have made you into the very thing I abhor. The virtuous prig that you never were, before you met her. Your head is full of romantic nonsense. What you mistake for sincerity is emotional claptrap. I wash my hands of you.'

He felt a flood of relief. And then he saw her smile, which was sly and catlike, and knew that there was no chance in the world that he would escape so easily.

She continued. 'Since your love for her is true, I assume that you have her heart as well. So she will stand by you, head held high, while I reveal the particulars of our relationship to the world. You detailed in writing what we had done, and what you wished to do. I could send the letters to your wife, as a belated wedding gift. Or shall I leave them for Timothy some morning, mixed up with the mail? Or I could take them to our friends in London, to read aloud. Everyone will find it most diverting, I am sure.'

The idea of it turned his stomach. There was so much shame to be had in his past behaviour. Heaps of disgrace for all concerned. Timothy would no longer be able to feign ignorance, and must be moved to act. He would meet his best friend at dawn with a weapon in his hand, and attempt to defend himself for an indefensible action.

Will would shake his head in pity, as he had at the news of the marriage, and at all the other stupid things Adam had done in his life. Perhaps Adam was destined to be an eternal source of disappointment, and a terrible example to his brother.

But Penny. If Penny found out, it would be worst of all. Would she be more hurt by a full revelation from Clare, or would the *ton* throw the information back in her face some night, when she least expected it? Either way, it did not seem likely that she would wish to make love to him in the library, once she knew all the sordid details of his affair. She might return to her study and never venture forth again.

And the worst of it was that the truth could leave him relatively untouched. What did it matter what people said of him? For no matter how shocked the world might be, he was Bellston until he died.

But it would wound the people most dear to his heart.

What were the alternatives? He could return to Clarissa, to buy her silence for a time, and hope that she would grow bored enough to let him go. It would hurt the same people just as much, if not more. For how could he claim that his infidelity was meant to lessen the damage? There was no easy answer. But the choice between right and wrong was clear. Better to bear the agony, lance the wound, and allow the poison to drain, than to leave things as they were, dying from within.

He opened his eyes and stared at Clarissa. 'Do your worst, then. I should have expected no less from you, for you are wicked to the bone. Bring down the ruin upon my head. It is just as I have deserved, and I have known for a long time that there was no preventing it. What will happen will happen. But do not think that you can control me any longer with the fear of revelation. Whatever may occur, I am through with you, Clarissa.'

And he turned and left the room, feeling lighter than he had, despite the sense of impending doom.

Chapter Twenty

Penny sat in the library, watching the blur of sunlight through the leaded windows, as she cleaned her glasses with her handkerchief. Her husband had been right: the air was sweeter here, and the sunshine more bright than any place else on earth.

And then a shadow fell upon her table. Timothy Colton stood, blocking the light from the door.

She smiled and stood, reaching out for his hand. 'Timothy. Whatever are you doing in Wales?'

He was leaning against the door frame, and as her vision cleared, she took note of his appearance. He was the worse for both drink and travel. His hair was wind-blown, his coat dirty, and he smelled of whisky, though it was not yet noon. 'I live here, as does Clarissa. We are near enough to walk the distance on a clear day.' He smiled mirthlessly. 'Did your husband not tell you of the fact?'

She racked her brain, hoping that there had been a revelation, and that she had forgotten. 'No.'

'Now, why do you suppose he would forget to mention it?'

There had to be a reason. He had said that Tim was a childhood friend. And she knew that Clarissa had been there, the night of the fire. But had he told her they would be neighbours? He must have assumed she would know. 'I am sure it was a harmless omission.'

'Really. Then he did not tell you, this morning, that he has gone to my home, to be with my wife.'

'He would not,' she said.

'I was there, and saw them together myself.'

'You lie.'

'When have I ever lied to you, Penelope, that you would distrust me now?' His voice was colder than she'd ever heard it, but he did not avoid her gaze, as her husband had that morning at breakfast. 'She left me in London several days ago. When I realised where she would go, I shut up the house and came after her. It is not so easy when you have children. You cannot simply hare off to Wales, and abandon them to be with your lover. Not that my wife would care.'

'But Adam has not been with her, I would swear it.'

'His horse is in my stables now. And as I approached the house, I could see them clearly through the windows of the sitting room.'

She shook her head. 'I'm sure there is an innocent explanation for it.'

'She was lying bare before him, Penny. There was nothing innocent about the scene I witnessed.'

'Then I will ask Adam about it, when he returns.' She would do nothing of the kind. She would do her best to pretend that it did not matter to her. Perhaps Adam had eyes only for her because she was the only one near enough to see. But she had convinced herself that there would be no worries in the future. It would always be just as it had been for the last month. Now Timothy meant to spoil it all.

'And now I wish you to leave.'

He stepped around her, and shut the door. 'I am not through speaking.'

'I have nothing to say to you. If you wish to talk to anyone, it should be Adam or your wife.'

Timothy laughed. 'And now you will pretend that your husband's affairs do not hurt you. I think this matters more than you care to admit.'

'What business is it of yours?' she snapped.

'If your husband does not wish to be faithful to you? It can be very lonely, knowing that one's chosen mate has little interest. Now that you have had a taste of what marriage might mean, you will find it is very difficult to content yourself with solitude.'

'On the contrary, I much prefer to be alone.'

'If that is true, you are likely to get your wish. But Adam likes company. He is not alone this morning, any more than my wife is. Perhaps it does not matter to you, as a woman, to see your vows tossed back in your face. But I am tired of standing alone while my friend makes me a cuckold again.'

It amazed her, after all they had said to each other, after all they had done, that her husband could be so cruel. 'Challenge him, if you care so much.'

'Do you want us to duel?'

'No.'

Timothy sagged against the wall. 'Strangely, neither do I. Our friendship is over, of course. But I have pretended for so long that I did not care, that it seems foolish now to reach for a sword.' He was staring at her with a strange light in his eyes, as he had the night of the ball.

'Do you mean to reach for me, instead?' she asked.

He sighed. 'There is nothing we can do to stop them, should they wish to be together. But there is no reason for us to be alone.'

'We will be alone,' she responded. 'If we feel anything for them, we will be alone.'

'But we could be together, in shared misery.'

She shook her head. 'I am sorry. I cannot…'

He smiled, and removed a flask from his pocket, taking a deep drink. 'I thought not. And it is truly a shame, Penelope. For I feel I could grow most fond of you, should I allow myself to.' His voice was low and welcoming. 'You are a lovely woman with a quick wit and a sweet nature. You are too good for Adam, my dear. He has many admirable qualities, and has been a true friend in many things. But he is proving to have no more sense than he ever did, when it comes to women. I thought that you brought a change in him.'

'I hoped…' She choked on the words. 'I did not mean to, you know. It was all to be so easy. We both had what we wanted. And then I fell in love with him.'

'There, now.' He reached for her and drew her into an embrace that was more brotherly than passionate. 'Do not cry over him. He is not worth your tears.'

'Oh, really?' Her husband's voice from the doorway was cold.

She sprang back from Timothy's grasp, and hastily wiped at her face with her sleeve.

'It was nothing, Adam,' Penny murmured.

'Other than that you are making this poor woman miserable with your careless philanderings,' Timothy supplied.

'Hush.' Penny cringed at the description of her feelings, hauled out into the light for all to see. 'I was overwrought. It was nothing.'

'Nothing?' Adam stared at her. 'When I find you in the arms of another man, it is not "nothing", madam.'

'She was crying over you,' Tim goaded. 'I could not very well leave her, could I? Although you seemed to have no problem with it.'

'And I suppose, when it comes to comforting my wife, you are worth two of me?' Adam glared at his friend.

'Much as you are, when it comes to my wife.' Timothy glared back. 'Of course, you would have to be as good as two men, for you seem intent on keeping both women. It is hardly fair, old man.' Timothy grinned, but the smile was cold and mirthless.

'I do not want your wife.'

'That was not how it appeared this morning, Adam. After you swore that it was over and you would not be alone with her again.'

Adam made to speak, but hesitated.

Timothy nodded. 'You cannot look me in the eye and deny it, can you?'

'I was with her,' Adam admitted grudgingly. 'But it was nothing. I swear it, Tim.'

The tears rose in her throat as her husband declared his innocence to his friend. But not to her. Never to her, for she did not deserve it. She had sold the rights to his fidelity for a pile of books.

'Do you take me for a fool? I saw you plain, through the window. She was naked before you, in broad daylight.'

'It was not as it appears.'

'It never is,' Timothy responded drily. 'I believe you said that the night of the fire, as well. And I heard the whole thing clearly, although I did not see. Can you not, for once, favour me with the truth? I will at least admit that, given a little more time and the co-operation of your wife, the scene you witnessed, which was truly nothing, would have been exactly what it appeared.'

'How dare you.' Adam's fury was cold. He appeared ready to strike and Penny rushed to his side to take his arm.

'Adam, nothing happened. And no one knows of any of this. Please.'

Tim laughed, 'So what are we to do, then? Do you wish to challenge me, or should I challenge you?' And then he muttered something in Welsh that she did not understand, and spat upon the floor.

She might not have understood the words, but Adam clearly had, for he broke free of her and struck his friend, knocking him to the ground. Tim staggered to his feet with blood in his eye, ready to fight.

And at last, Penny snapped. 'You may do as you please, the both of you. And Clarissa as well. But whatever you do, you can do it without my help.'

'Penny, go to your room.' Adam barely looked at her.

'That is how it is to be, is it? You will be brother and guardian to me, and banish me to my quarters, so that you can do as you please? Take my money, then. I offered it to you freely, in exchange for peace and freedom. And I have scant little of either. But the money was not enough for you. You wanted my affection when it suited you, so that I did not embarrass you in public. And then, you needed my body to be a mother to your children. And now you expect my loyalty, while you lie with another man's wife.

'I want none of it, Adam. No more than I ever did. I want to be alone. And I would sooner see my children raised by jackals than by you or your twisted friends. I am leaving you.'

'You cannot. I will not permit it.' Her husband had turned away from his friend, no longer caring for the fight before him.

'And you cannot stop me. The bargain between us is irretrievably broken. If you thwart me today, I will try again tomorrow. Sooner or later, I will succeed in escaping you. If you wish, you may drag me back to your home by the hair, and lock me in my room. The Duke of Bellston, charming, handsome, lecherous and debauched, will need to keep his wife, and her fortune, by force. And then we will see what people say of you and your precious reputation.'

And she swept from the room.

Chapter Twenty-One

Adam thought, all things considered, that he should feel much worse. But he felt nothing. She had left the room, and taken his anger with her.

He had turned back to Tim, who must have been more than a little drunk, for he had collapsed back on to the floor, and absently offered him a hand.

Tim had ignored it and struggled to his feet, wiping blood from his mouth and on to his shirt cuff. 'There. Are you satisfied now?'

He stared back at Tim. 'Are you?'

'I think I am. For you finally look the way I feel. All these months you have spent, wallowing in ecstasy, or lust or guilt.' Tim made a bitter face. 'Never content unless you were torn by some emotion or other, and convinced that no one felt more deeply than you. Now, she will go. And you are all hollowed out.'

Adam nodded. He could feel the growing emptiness as she withdrew from him. A space that needed filling.

Tim smiled. 'Now imagine her with someone else.'

The pain of the thought was exquisite, for there was nothing to dull it. It was untouchable, like the phantom pains that soldiers claimed, in a limb that was no longer there. 'And this is how you feel?'

Tim nodded. 'Clarissa knows it, and she works all the harder to make me hurt. And yet I cannot leave her. She says, if I do, she will take the children, even though she cares little for them. They are innocents. They do not deserve such a mother.'

'She does not deserve to live. And if I cannot find a way to mend this?' Adam smiled. 'Then I will send her back to hell from whence she came.'

He offered his hand to his friend again, and Tim pushed it aside. 'It is a bit late for that, I think. I am going home, to my loving wife. You will understand, I trust, if the door is shut to you, should you attempt to visit.'

Adam nodded. 'As my door is now shut to you. But a word of warning. It all may get worse before it gets better. Your wife is none too happy with me. I refused her this morning. If you find letters to her, in my hand? They are old. Burn them without looking. For both our sakes.'

Tim nodded. 'Goodbye, then.' And he left him alone.

One, two, three... She'd had to start over on several occasions, for she was so angry that she kept losing her count. Penny stormed into her library and rang the bell for Jem. *Twenty-seven, twenty-eight*... And why did she even bother with it? For what good did it do to keep your temper, and be agreeable in all things, if someone you thought you could trust used your even nature against you?

Jem entered and looked at her suspiciously.

She waved an arm at the walls. 'Pack them up again.'

He squinted. 'Your Grace?'

'My books. Bring back the crates. Take them down and box them up.'

'Where will I be taking them, once I'm done?'

'I have no idea. Box them.'

'Are we going back to London, or the Scotland property that everyone talks of? Or is there somewhere…?'

'Away. I am going away, and not coming back. You were right all along. My idea was foolish, and now I am punished for it. So stop arguing with me and box these cursed books.'

'No.'

'I beg your pardon?'

He raised his voice. 'I said no, Miss Penny. I have put up with more than my share of nonsense from you over the years. But today it stops. I have carried these books halfway across England for you. You may not have noticed the fact, since you lift them one at a time. But as a group, they are heavy. And they are not moving another inch.'

'They are not remaining here,' she shouted, 'and neither am I.'

To this, Jem said nothing, merely fixed her with a long, hard look and stood, blocking the door.

'You refuse to pack the books? So be it. I'd probably

have a hard time sorting them from the ones that were already here. It is amazing how quickly one's things can get tangled with another's… But never mind that. Go to my room. I will send the maid for my dresses. They are unquestionably mine. Although I never wanted the cursed things in the first place.'

Jem showed no sign of obeying this order, either.

'What are you waiting for? Go!' She sounded shrill, even to her own ears.

Jem folded his arms.

'Look at me.' She pointed down at her clothes. 'How long has it been since I met him? A scant two months. And I no longer know myself. I dress differently. I act differently. I do not even live in the same city. I was totally content to spend days by myself. And now, if he leaves me for more than an hour or two, I miss him.

'Little by little, he has made me into exactly the thing that he wants, and now he is bored with me.'

'And for this reason, I must pack your things and carry them to you-do-not-know-where.' He remained unmoved.

'He does not love me.'

'I did not think you wished him to. When you dragged me to Scotland—'

'I was wrong.'

'And so you wish to compound the first bad decision by making another.' Jem shook his head in pity. 'I will admit, I had my doubts about the man at first. But given time, he will love you beyond reason, if he is does not already. It is hardly worth the strain on my back to bring your things down from your room, only to carry them back up again. If you insist on going, you may carry your own damn bags. Your Grace.' He added her title as an afterthought and left the room.

Chapter Twenty-Two

Penny glanced around the room, painfully aware of the silence. When had it become such a burden to be alone? It was what she had always thought she wanted.

She had been in the library for almost a week, leaving only when she was sure that the corridor was empty, to creep to her room to wash or to sleep.

But it had become harder and harder to avoid the inevitable confrontation. Most times, she could hear her husband prowling outside the library door like some kind of wild beast. On the first day, he had pounded on the oak panels, demanding that she open for him, and hear what he had to say. She feared he would shake the thing off its hinges with the force of the blows, but had put her fists to her ears, and shut her lips tight to avoid the temptation of answering him. For she knew if she saw him again, she would forget everything that had happened, and remember only how it felt to be in his arms. She would believe anything he told her, and trust any promise, no matter how false, if only he would lie with her again.

But after a day of thundering, his temper had passed like a summer storm, and the knocking had become quieter, more civilised. His shouts had turned to normal requests, 'Penny, open this door. We must speak. We cannot go on like this.'

And at last, it had come to her as a whisper. 'Penny, please…'

And now, for several days, there had been no sound at all. Just the ceaseless rustling of his footsteps on the carpet outside.

It was all foolishness. If he wanted to enter, there was nothing to stop him. He must have the key, for this was his house, not hers. If it was not in his possession, he had but to ask the servants, and they would open for him in an instant. He was the duke. He had proved often enough that he could do as he pleased.

But he did not. He respected their bargain. She had wanted privacy. And he had given this space to her. He would not cross the threshold without her permission. It was maddening. She had gotten exactly what she wanted: a library full of books and all the time in the world to enjoy them.

And yet she could not stop crying. The sight of her own books was torture, for she could not seem to concentrate long enough to read more than a few words. And those she managed all seemed to remind her of her own fate: unfaithful Odysseus and his myriad of excuses, weak will and false guilt. And Penelope, waiting for him, perpetually alone.

Why did it have to bother her so, that her husband had visited his lover? Nowhere in their original agreement, or in any of the bargaining that had occurred since, had there been any mention of his fidelity. She had not asked it of him, nor had he promised. She had held her own against the woman, for a time. But she had always known that the moment would come when she would lose. And she felt dead inside, knowing that when the mood had struck him, he would leave her to her books, as though she meant nothing to him.

And now, he thought that he could wait outside her door until her mood softened, and worm his way back into her good graces. He wanted the best of both worlds: a co-operative wife when it suited him, and his freedom all the rest of the time.

Out of the coldness in her heart rose an ember of burning rage. He had been the first to break the agreement. If he had but let her alone, she could have stayed in her study, and never have known or cared. If he had not insisted on coming to her bed, she would not be feeling jealousy over a thing that she had never wanted. If he had remained indifferent, or neglectful or at least absent, she would have viewed this liaison as just another example of his uninterest in her.

But he had treated her with kindness and respect, almost from the first. He had guarded her from ridicule and shepherded her through the maze of society, then he had touched her, and brought her more pleasure than she could have imagined possible.

And then he had taken it away. Given the chance, he would do so again. She must hold that thought foremost, and make sure it would not happen. The longer she stayed in this house, the more likely her heart would soften, and she would forget how it had felt to see Tim and her husband fighting for the attention of another. She would begin making excuses for it, and then all hope was lost.

She must leave while the anger was still fresh and she had the strength. With just the clothes on her back, if necessary. There was nothing holding her here but the fear of confronting him. Once it was done, she would be free. If he tried to stop her in the hall, she would push past without speaking. Let him follow her to her rooms. She would ignore him. She would slam the door in his face again, pack a valise and leave immediately.

She threw open the door, ready to cut him and walk by, but she almost stumbled. For he was not standing before her, but right there in the doorway, sitting on the rug with his legs drawn up to his chest, his back leaning against the frame.

She caught her hand against the wood to steady herself, and before she could stop, she had looked down into his beautiful blue eyes and felt the fight going out of her, as she feared it would. 'What on earth are you doing down there?'

He blinked up at her, surprised by her sudden appearance. 'Waiting for you to open this door. I assume you must go to your rooms at some point, but I have not been able to catch you, so I resolved to remain until you came out. I grew tired of pacing. It has been days, you know.' There was a faint accusation in his voice, as though it were somehow her fault that he was weary.

'I know exactly how long it has been.' She could feel each minute since last she had seen him. 'I would not still be here if I had managed to get my own servant to obey me. He is loyal to you, now, and will not help me move my things.'

'You really do mean to leave me, then?' At least he did not waste time in apologies that she would not have believed anyway.

'Yes.'

'I cannot say I blame you.' He looked away for a moment, sucked in a small breath and stood up. When he turned back to face her, he had become the distant, rather polite stranger she had known in London. He gestured to the library. 'May I at least come into the room? I'd prefer not to discuss this in the hall.'

As though there was a servant left in the house who was not aware of their difficulties. Perhaps he had forgotten how little effort he had made to hide them, when he had been shouting the details through the closed door. She almost smiled, before remembering how serious the situation was. She gestured through the open door and preceded him into the room.

He came through and shut it behind him. Then he turned to face her. His hands were folded behind his back like a penitent schoolboy. His mouth worked for a bit before he could find more words. 'Have you given thought as to where you will go? Not to your brother, I hope.'

It would be the logical choice. Hector would take her back. But he would never let her forget the mistake she had made in leaving. 'I do not think so.'

He nodded, obviously relieved. 'I am concerned for

your welfare, although I might not seem so. You understand that there may be a child involved as well?'

She had not thought of this fresh complication to her future. 'I will know soon enough.'

'And wherever you go, you will need space enough for your books.'

She looked at the shelves around her, and where she had seen friends before, now all she saw was dead weight. 'I doubt I will be taking them. Suddenly, it seems an awful lot of bother. And without knowing what the future holds for me…'

'No.' There was a wild light in his eyes, and he dropped his attempt at calm. The words rushed out of him. 'I can understand if you cannot abide my presence after what has happened, but do not tell me that you are abandoning your work because of me. There is a dower house on the grounds. You could stay there. The books could stay here. And you could visit as often as you liked.'

She considered how painful it would be to see him, and forced herself to look away. 'I would hardly have succeeded in escaping your influence if I were visiting this house as a guest for the majority of my days.'

'I could go from you, then.' His voice was bleak. 'You would have the books, and the space and quiet for your studies. I could go to London. I would not set foot upon the grounds without your permission. And I would be here no more than was necessary to run the estate.'

She stared at him. 'Does Clarissa approve of this plan? I imagine she would like to spend more time in London.'

'I do not know. Or care,' he added. 'It is a bit late to

tell you now. But I only went to her to say goodbye. If it troubles you still, the thought that we might meet in secret, I could travel abroad, or stay at the property in Scotland. It is farther away.'

'And you would leave the estate to me?'

'I would be honoured if you would accept it.'

She was confused. 'You love this house.'

He nodded.

'You are different, when you are here. It is where you belong.'

'You, as well. And if it can only be one of us in residence?' He smiled sadly. 'Then I wish it to be you. Without you, there would be no estate. And it is wrong that you should be banished from it for my misdeeds, or to suffer any discomfort because of my behaviour. It is my wish that you accept it from me, and anything else you might need. You are my wife. All that I have is yours.'

'That is ridiculous,' she responded. 'I never wanted all that you had. I have need of a quiet place to study. That is all.'

'And I thought I wanted nothing more than your money.'

'And a position in society. And an heir…'

He stared at the ground. 'Things have changed since the first day, have they not?'

'Yes.' She smiled sadly at the floor as well. 'Perhaps we could go back to the way we first planned.'

'I don't think that will work,' he replied.

She nodded. 'Too many things have changed.' She'd felt like a fool for even suggesting it, especially after banishing him from her life just a few days before. But when she was near to him, she remembered. And it was so hard to give him up.

'It would work fine, for a time,' he hedged. 'But I am afraid I cannot control my impulses sufficiently to keep our lives as separate as we had planned.'

Impulses? Even the thought made her temper start to rise.

One, two, three…

'Knowing I could not have you? The sight of you with other men, any other man, even if it was quite innocent, or you were very discreet, would drive me mad with jealousy.'

Four, five… 'What?'

He continued, ignoring the interruption. 'Before we came to Wales, I thought if I could keep you all to myself, then you would forget anyone but me. I am sorry.'

'And you did not tell me that we were neighbors to the Coltons?'

'Because I did not want you to see them. Especially not Tim, for I did not think I could trust him, given all that has happened. If the world were different, and we were all free, you would have done better to choose him, for his temperament would suit you.'

Adam's face darkened and his lips twisted in a bitter smile. 'But I find that I do not care, when you are near, what is best for you or that you deserve better. You are mine, and I want to keep you all to myself.' His smile softened as he remembered. 'It was so good, being alone with you. And you seemed content with just me for company.'

'But what about Clarissa?' She held her breath.

'The day I went to her, she sent me a letter, saying that if I would not come to her, she would come here. It would have ruined everything.' He looked up, and his face was blank. 'It wouldn't have mattered. Things are ruined, in any case. There will be less bother, now that Tim and I are quits. I will not need to pretend civility with her. She is angry, and promises to make a scandal. There are letters that I wrote to her.'

He rubbed his hand over his eyes, as though to blot out the memory. 'They are very detailed. And I would ask you, as a last favour, to destroy them without reading them should they come your way. The words are no longer true, but to read them might cause you pain.

'But if she does not send them to you, then she will circulate them freely in London next Season. You may be more comfortable if you remain here, far from the gossip of the *ton*. I am sorry, but whatever might happen, you should know and prepare yourself. Perhaps it will not matter and she will be quiet, now that she sees we are…apart.' The last word seemed to come difficult to him.

'It will not matter to your position, of course. You are Duchess of Bellston for as long as you wish to be. Nothing anyone says will change that. But people will talk. I am afraid you will find it embarrassing.' He said it as gently as possible, and his face was full of remorse.

The idea of talk, which would have appalled her a few weeks before, seemed distant and unimportant. What did it matter what people said? Nothing could hurt as bad as being without Adam. 'It does not really matter, does it, if it is all in the past? It is not as if you can change what you did, even if it was very awful.'

He looked hopeful, for a moment, and pulled one of the straight-backed library chairs to him, and sat a respectful distance from her.

'I know it is too late to say these things. But I would do anything to take back what has happened. I never wanted anything less for you than you wanted for yourself: peace and security. That you might come to harm from behaviours of mine, things that occurred long before you knew me—it pains me more than you can imagine. And if I had known, the day we met, that I would make you unhappy, I swear I'd never have married you.'

She shrugged. 'You can have no idea what you might have done, for I dare say you had little control of yourself on that particular occasion.'

'I still cannot remember the details,' he admitted. 'Only that I was convinced you were sent by God to lead me to salvation. I'd have followed you to the ends of the earth. And still would, if you would but allow it. You have brought me more happiness than I deserve.'

'I made you happy,' she repeated numbly.

He smiled and shook his head in disbelief. 'You did not realise it? Yes, you made me happy. You are unlike any woman I have ever met. Blazingly intelligent, unfailingly honest, and a rock to which I can cling in moments of turmoil. And when we are together as man and wife?' He shook his head again. 'I never knew how it felt to join in love, until you came to me.'

'Love?' she whispered.

He nodded. 'I love you, Penelope. I cannot help myself. It is not what you wanted, of course. Not peaceful or quiet at all, for neither of those virtues are in my nature. But there it is.'

He loved her. What an amazing idea. She felt the warmth of the words against her heart, growing in her, surrounding her to keep her safe, and heating her blood in a way that was not safe at all, but just as wonderful.

'And you were faithful to me,' she said, testing.

'Strangely enough, yes. I put off my mistress, I forsook my old haunts. There has been no one but you since the day we met. What Tim saw when he spied me with Clarissa was no doing of mine.'

She stepped closer and reached out a hand to him, touching his hair, and trailing her fingers slowly down his cheek. He closed his eyes for a moment, then turned his head to press kisses into her palm, seizing her hand in his so that she could not pull away.

And she felt the familiar thrill of power at the sight of him, cradling her hand as though he feared the loss of her touch. He kissed her knuckles again, and bowed his head to her. 'My fate is yours to decide, Penny. I will do as you wish in all things. I will go tonight, if you say I must. But I beg you, do not be apart from me, for I fear I shall go mad with the loss of you.'

Fierce joy was rushing through her, and desire mingled with it. And without speaking, she touched him under the chin, urging his lips up to hers and kissing slowly into his open mouth.

His breath trembled for a moment, and then his response was eager, hungry to deepen the kiss.

She pulled away, and he looked up with hope, awaiting her answer, and she looked into his eyes, and saw only herself reflected back.

When she spoke, she was pleased that her voice sounded cool, collected and very much like the ladies of the *ton* that had once beguiled her husband and not at all like she truly was: too far gone with love of him to ever leave. 'So you love me, and wish to give me all that I might desire?'

He gave the barest nod, but his eyes sparkled with shared devilment.

She reached to his throat, and undid the knot of his cravat, tugging him up out of his chair. 'Then, we have much to discuss. But first, you must give me my garter back.'

* * * * *

Dangerous Lord,
Innocent Governess

Somewhere in the writing of *Miss Winthorpe's Elopement*, it became clear to me that I was only telling half the story. The more I wrote, the more I became convinced that there was another whole book that would explain the behaviour of Tim Colton and his wife, Clare.

Perhaps Clare secretly had a heart of gold. Perhaps things weren't as they appeared between her and the Duke of Bellston. Perhaps she only needed love and, if I gave them a little time, Tim and Clare could work out their differences and live happily ever after.

Or perhaps not.

And as I wrote, I discovered that I'd been leaving myself little clues as to how unhappy they really were together and what might happen between the two of them once they were alone in Wales.

Once I stopped fighting the truth, the book all but wrote itself. My research became a weird mix: the nineteenth century, British horticulture, conservatory design and old-fashioned gothic romances. The result was the story you are about to read.

To Jo Carr.
May it always be this easy.

Chapter One

'Her Grace will see you now.'

Daphne Collingham followed the servant to the door of the sitting room, and took an involuntary breath as she was announced. Was it always this intimidating to seek employment? She certainly hoped she would never have reason to know.

Once her mission here was finished, she could return to her real life in London. And she would miss none of the Season: the parties, the balls and the tiresome chore of hunting up a husband who would meet with her father's approval. But for now she must remember that she was a humble governess, whose only intent was to make a future in caring for the children of the Colton household.

She tried not to shudder at the idea.

Perhaps it was worse for her because she knew that her petition was a sham. And while it might be rather nerve racking to meet a duchess on a social occasion, it was much more so when the duchess stood as gate-keeper to a place one wanted to enter. Even more so when one was still trying to memorise an employment history that one had bought off a stranger on a north-bound coach.

The Duchess rose as Daphne entered, which was entirely unnecessary, given their difference in class, and reached out to take her hand. 'Miss Collins.'

'Your Grace,' she responded with what she hoped was appropriate subservience.

The Duchess sank back on to the divan, and gestured her to a nearby chair. The woman in front of her looked more like a schoolteacher than the wife of a peer. But looks could be deceiving. Daphne hoped that the Duchess believed the same, for she doubted very much that she was managing to look the part of a prospective governess. Her curtsy alone should have given her away. It would have suited in a drawing room, she suspected. But she had practised curtsying like a governess in front of a mirror at the inn, and could not seem to manage it.

The Duchess narrowed her eyes as Daphne bowed to her, as though she had recognised the deficiency. It had not been unfriendly. Merely a sign that the fact had been noted, recorded and filed appropriately. The Duchess of Bellston suspected she would prove difficult.

But now, the woman was examining her references, and smiling. 'These seem to be in order. Although they refer to you as Daphne. I understood, from your original letter, that your Christian name was Mary.'

'There was already a Mary in the last house, your Grace. So they called me by my middle name, Daphne. I've grown to prefer it.'

The Duchess nodded. 'Daphne. Very pretty. And it suits you much better than Mary.'

She certainly hoped so.

The Duchess was reading more carefully. 'These are most exceptional.'

'Thank you.' She had laboured long to erase the name of their previous owner, and insert her own. The fact that they were exceptional forgeries needn't enter into the conversation.

'You have been in service long?' There was a definite upturn at the end of the sentence, as though the Duchess had her doubts. Probably the fault of that damned curtsy.

'When one enjoys one's work, the time passes quickly.'

'And you do enjoy your chosen profession, and are not doing it solely from duty, or a need to make a way for yourself?'

'I adore children.' And there was the biggest lie of all. For while she hoped that she would manage to adore her own, she had never found the children of others to be better than a necessary evil.

'Excellent,' said the Duchess, eager to believe her. 'For that is just what this family needs.' She looked at Daphne with the same searching expression she had used upon the paperwork. 'The residents of this house have undergone a loss, and the children's behaviour has

been somewhat…' she paused significantly '…diffi-
cult.'

'Difficult?' Oh, dear. It had never occurred to her
that the children would be part of the problem.

The Duchess smiled encouragement. 'But it will be
nothing to someone as experienced as you. It is just that
they will need more than rote learning and a firm hand.
They need understanding. And affection, of course.'

What they needed was justice. But Daphne nodded
enthusiastically at the Duchess's words. 'The poor dears.
One can never replace a mother, of course. But if it is
possible to provide stability, and a woman's touch?' She
gave a deprecating shrug. 'One tries.'

The Duchess let out a visible sigh of relief. 'I think
we are in agreement. While I place a high value on
education, the Coltons are bright children, and naturally
inquisitive. Advanced for their years.'

Daphne nodded, as though she understood. It was
strange that a woman who was little better than a neighbour should take such interest in another man's children.
Perhaps she thought it her duty, as lady of the land. Or
perhaps there was some other, more ominous reason that
she felt a need to insinuate herself into the household.

The Duchess continued. 'They will find their own
way. They need less help in that area than they need a
sense that they are safe and cared for.'

As long as their father was present, there was little
Daphne could do to ensure their safety. But she nodded
again.

The Duchess rose and straightened her skirts. 'If you
will just wait here, while I speak to Lord Colton, the

butler will be along shortly with some refreshment for you. When I return we will go to meet the children.' She said it with confidence, as though the hiring was a foregone conclusion, even without the consent of the master of the house. Then she turned and left the room. Daphne could hear her on the other side of the partly closed door, speaking with a servant about tea and cakes.

She let out the breath she had been holding. The first hurdle was cleared. When she had met the real Miss Collins, while travelling to Wales for a family visit, Daphne had thought it amazing good luck. Here was a woman heading straight to the place that she had really wanted to see: the home of her beloved cousin, Clarissa. And since the true governess was heartily sick of tending the children of others, it had not been hard for a persuasive young lady to talk her out of her identity.

It had cost Daphne two of her favourite gowns, a garnet brooch and the spending money she had been given for her visit. But the total was more than a year's salary for Miss Collins, and would give her an opportunity for a well-deserved rest. She could have her dreary life back, once Daphne was done with it, and no one would be the wiser.

Daphne got quietly up from her chair, and moved to the doorway. She stayed well in the shadow of the door, listening for the Duchess's steps as they turned down the corridor to the left. Her slippers clicked quietly against the marble in an efficient staccato, pausing after a few seconds. There was the sound of her voice, distant and barely intelligible, requesting entrance.

It was impossible to hear the response.

Daphne eased the door open, expecting to hear a squeak of hinge. But it moved noiselessly. It hardly mattered, for when she poked her head into the hall, there was no one to hear any sound she might make. If she was quick, she could begin her investigations, and be back in the room before a servant appeared with the tea tray. No one need be the wiser. She followed the direction of the Duchess's steps, taking care that her shoes made no noise at all as she moved, and counted off the paces she had heard the Duchess take. As she progressed, she could hear the sound of voices from an open doorway, increasing in volume as she approached.

'And just what gives you the right, Penny, to meddle in this at all?' It was a man's voice, brusque and irritable.

Daphne slowed her steps to listen.

'Do I need permission to help a friend, when I know he is in need?' The Duchess's voice had lost the edge of efficiency. It was warmer. Perhaps there was something more than friendship between the two. Daphne inched along the wall that held the door and glanced across the hall.

There was a large, gilt-framed mirror on the wall opposite her, meant to bring light to the dark corridor from the conservatory at the end of the hall. As she moved closer to the open door, she could see the reflection of the study where the two were speaking.

After a frigid pause, the man responded to the Duchess. 'Yes, your Grace, you do require permission.'

'Your Grace?' She could see the hurt on the woman's

face, as her reflection crept into view. 'Suddenly we are to be formal, Lord Colton?'

'I see no reason to pretend that engaging servants to spy upon me is an act of friendship.'

'That is not what I am doing,' the Duchess protested. And Daphne flinched. He had guessed her own purpose without meeting her, even if he was wrong about the Duchess's part in it. 'I am concerned for the welfare of the children.'

'If you were motivated by concern, you would leave them in peace. And me as well.'

She had inched forward to the point where she could see most of the room and the Duchess in profile before the desk, and the man seated in front of her. She was not sure what she expected, but it was not what she saw. Clare had described her husband as weak, anaemic, cruel. In her own mind, Daphne had seen him as a great, grey spider, pale and thin but deceptively strong, and with influence far beyond the reach of his thin grasping fingers.

But that did not fit the real Timothy Colton at all. Dark brown hair falling forward on to the healthy complexion of a man who enjoyed the sun. His shoulders did not speak of great height, but they were straight and unbent. He was quite ordinary. And if she was honest about it, rather handsome.

It seemed her adversary was nothing more than a man.

The Duchess leaned forward, on to the desk, trying to catch his gaze, which was directed sullenly downward.

'Perhaps solitude is the best way for you to deal with your grief. But must the children suffer?'

He raised his face to hers. 'Grief? Is that what you think my problem is?' He gave a bleak laugh. 'I am glad that Clarissa is gone. In time, so will the children be, if they are not already.' There was no hesitation as he spoke, no sign that he might feel guilt over speaking so about his wife of twelve years.

Daphne felt a fresh wave of hatred for the man seated behind the desk.

The Duchess whispered, almost as though she feared that there was a listener. 'We are quite aware of your feelings on the subject. It would be easier for all of us if you were not so plain about it.'

'Is that what this is about, then? An attempt to make things appear more normal than they are? Your husband is the magistrate. He would have been better off had he admitted the truth, and dealt with this when he had the chance, just after she died. I would not have faulted him for it. You can hardly blame me if you find that maintaining the lie is difficult.'

So it was just as she suspected. Her cousin's death was not the accident that everyone pretended.

The Duchess straightened, and her tone became chill. 'It does not matter to me, Tim, if you wish to wallow in your misery. I care only for the children. It will not be as easy for them as you seem to think. A female presence will be a comfort to them, if you allow it.'

'The only comfort they are likely to have will be gained far away from this mausoleum. Edmund is old enough for school, as is Lily.'

'You mean to send them away, do you?'

'I want what is best for them. And that is to be far away from the memory of their mother's last day. And far away from me.'

'Even Sophie?'

She saw the man stiffen in his chair. 'I will find a place for Sophie. She is my daughter, after all. And no concern of yours. I do not need your help, your sympathy, your friendship or your misguided attempts to make right a thing that can never be repaired.' Then he looked up out into the hall, and into the mirror. 'And I do not need a governess.'

His eyes met hers in the mirror, and for a moment, she knew what it was to face death. They were the soulless black eyes of a murderer, and they stared into her as though he had known that she was there the whole time.

She turned and fled back to the drawing room, not caring how much noise she made.

Tim Colton leaned back in his chair and folded his arms. The Duchess gave no indication that she heard the prying governess clattering off down the hall. She seemed near to explosion. 'You do need a governess, Tim Colton, if you mean to act like a spoiled child. Perhaps Miss Collins will be able to persuade you, since I cannot, that your behaviour is doing injury to the children you seek to protect. She will be an employee in this household, no matter what your opinion on the subject might be. If you resist me in this, I shall go to my husband, just as you ask. He will have you locked in your room until you can stand before the House of Lords and explain yourself. When you are gone, we will pack the children off to stay with their mother's family. Does that suit you?'

'You know it does not.' And in his own ears, his voice sounded sullen. A spoiled child's muttering, just as she had said. He had best gain control of himself, or the children would end up with the Collinghams. And the last thing he wished was for them to grow up to be just like their mother.

'Then we are agreed. I shall go back to Miss Collins and arrange for her salary. You shall put on your coat, comb your hair and come to meet your new servant.' She turned and swept from the room.

Tim sat at his desk, head cradled in his hands. Penny had made another effort to arrange his life. He supposed he was expected to be grateful for it, but felt nothing more than numb.

Perhaps she was right in it. If he was as concerned for his children as he claimed, then surely he did not wish to cause them more pain than he had already. And at this late date, an airing of the family secrets would do more harm than good.

With any luck, this latest governess would last no longer in the house than the previous one had, or the ones before that. They had all found the children 'difficult' and the master of the house 'disturbing', although he doubted that they had admitted that last fact to Penny. But on the rare occasions when they spoke to him directly, he could see that they had guessed the truth.

It was in their eyes, and in the great care they took never to be alone with him.

Once Miss Collins fled, things would return to quiet and solitude. A few months would bring them to the start of the spring term. He would pack Edmund and Lily off to the best schools he could find. And for a time, he would be alone with Sophie.

He felt his heart wrench again, wondering how much lonelier it would be when he was left to parent the silent little girl, without the buffering of the two older children. Then he pushed it to the back of his mind, and rose from his desk to greet the new governess.

As he pulled on a jacket and ran a hand through his hair, he thought of the reflection of Miss Collins in the hallway mirror. He had seen her, from the corner of his eye, moving slowly into focus, trying to glean the details of a conversation she had no part in. Was she curious as to the fate of her employment? It spoke of a desperation that was absent from the previous candidates. If the job was so important to her, then it might be difficult to dislodge her from it.

Or it could be something else. Something far more sinister. Spies listened at doors. If she came to this house to learn and not to teach, then he had another problem altogether.

As he neared the sitting room, he could hear the sound of voices through the open door. Penny was arranging the particulars. He was hardly needed. If he was lucky, he might have no further contact with the girl after this brief introduction. He stepped into the open doorway and froze in surprise, unprepared for what he saw.

The reflection in the mirror had not done her justice. It had been watery and unclear. Other than her eyes, which were curiously intense, he had not noticed anything singular about her. But in person?

He caught his breath. She was a beauty, and the failed attempt at simple clothing and stern coiffure did nothing to hide the fact. Her hair was a rich chestnut, and framed a face that was softly rounded, with full red lips and startlingly green eyes. He could imagine the curves of her body under the stiff fabric of her gown, for she had none of the sharp angles he'd come to associate with women of her class. There was nothing to hint at a privation that might have urged her to take a position. Nor did she have the pinched, disapproving look of one secretly envious of her charges' wealth.

He gripped the door frame in surprise as a wave of lust swept over him. It had been a long time since he'd been with a woman. Too long, if he had begun to harbour thoughts about the servants, especially someone brought into his house to care for his children.

But as he looked at her again, he could not resist the thought that she might be better suited for the bedroom than the classroom.

Take her there, and see.

The thought chilled him, although his blood ran hot at the sight of the girl. It did not do to give too much weight to the odd thought that might cross one's mind, in a moment of weakness.

Is it weakness or strength, to act on your desires instead of hiding from them? You were never such a coward, before.

More madman than coward, if he was hearing voices. And even more mad to listen. If what one desired was wrong, one must not succumb.

Too late for that. You are already lost. If you want the girl, wait until the house is asleep. Then go to her and take her.

No. He closed his eyes so he could no longer see the object of temptation, and willed his pulse to slow. But it only became easier to imagine the skin hidden under the plain dress, and the smooth feel of it against his, the soft lips startled open by his kiss, and the tightness of her body as he came into her.

The voice in his head gave a sigh of satisfaction. *Open your eyes and look at her, coward.*

He could feel his will weakening as he allowed himself to be persuaded. Surely she did not seek the life of a governess, unless all matrimonial options had failed. She must have resigned herself to never knowing the touch of a man. If she was lonely, and as frustrated as he was, then was seduction such a great crime?

You have done worse.

Everything inside him froze. He had done worse. And worse yet, he had escaped punishment for his crime. One could justify anything, if one could live with one's self after doing the unthinkable.

Penny turned and saw him, standing in the entrance, and gave a hurrumph of frustration at his lack of manners. 'There you are, Timothy. Come into the room and meet Miss Collins.'

'Miss Collins.' He bowed, stiffly, from the waist.

The young woman stood as he entered, and responded

with a curtsy, and a cool and professional smile. 'Lord Colton.'

'I understand you have been retained by the Duchess to see to the care of my children. It is so nice to finally meet my new employee.' He gave her a pointed look to tell her he had seen her hiding in the hall, and was annoyed by it and the Duchess's handling of the whole affair.

'And to finally meet my employer.' She responded with a look that seemed to convey her opinion of a man who cared so little for his own family that he would leave such an important decision to a neighbour.

Their eyes locked, as though in battle. For a moment, he was convinced that she had heard the voices in his head as clearly as he did himself, for she looked both disapproving and disgusted, though it was only their first meeting. Perhaps he deserved her censure. But it angered him, all the same. So he held her gaze far longer than was proper, until he was sure that she knew who was master and who was servant. At last, she broke away and cast her eyes downward. He gave a small nod of satisfaction, and said, 'Welcome to my home. And now, if you will excuse me?' And he left the room with Penny dumbfounded and his pride intact.

'That man,' muttered the Duchess in frustration and gave a small stamp of her foot.

'Indeed.' Daphne swallowed, trying to control the strange feeling she had had, as her cousin's husband had smiled at her. He had stared at her far too long, until the look in his eyes had gone from sullen to seductive. He had looked at her as a wolf might look at a lamb.

She was sure that the Duchess had not seen the worst of it, thinking the man had been rude and not threatening. For when she turned to Daphne, she had a grim smile that said she would not be crossed in this, no matter how stubborn the master of the house might be. 'Lord Colton has proved difficult on the subject of his children's care.'

'They are his children,' Daphne said softly, rather surprised at how little the Duchess seemed to care about the fact.

'Of course,' the Duchess responded. 'But recent events have left him all but unfit to care for them. As a close friend of the family, I feel a responsibility to help him through this difficult time.'

'You knew Lady Colton?' Daphne smiled eagerly. She might have an ally, if the woman had also known Clare.

'I knew her. Yes.' And now the Duchess's look was one of distaste. She offered nothing more, before changing the subject. 'But come, you must be eager to see the nursery wing and meet your charges.' She rose quickly and preceded Daphne to the door and out into the hall, as though the merest mention of the children's mother hung in the air like a bad smell.

As they walked up the main stairs, Daphne paused for a moment and glanced behind her. So this was where it had happened. She could almost imagine her cousin, who had been so full of life, lying dead below her on the floor of the entry. She shook off the image to further examine the scene of the crime. Smooth marble treads, and an equally smooth banister that might have denied an adequate grip to the woman who had struggled here.

She glanced at the floor to see faint proof that a rug had been present and was now removed. So the poor carpet had taken the blame. A loose corner, a trip and a fall. Perfectly ordinary. Most unfortunate.

But Daphne believed none of it. Clare had used the stairs for twelve years without so much as a stumble. There was nothing to be afraid of, if someone was not here to push you down. When she was finished in this house, everyone would know the truth and Clare would be avenged.

The Duchess did not notice her pause, absorbed by her own thoughts, which did not concern the unfortunate death of the mistress of the house. She gave a helpless little shrug. 'I might as well tell you, before we go any further, that there is a small problem that I have been unable to deal with.'

'Really.' There were many problems with this house, and none of them small. Daphne wondered what would incite the Duchess to comment, if the death of Clare had not.

'In my letter to you, I promised something I could not give. The bedroom just off the nursery is the one intended for the governess. Convenient to the classroom, and next to little Sophie should she need you in the night.'

Daphne nodded.

'The oldest girl, Lily, has taken the room as her own.

I have been unable to dislodge her from it. The two older children care deeply for the littlest girl. And in the absence of a regular governess they have taken the duties of Sophie's care upon themselves.' For a moment, the Duchess looked distressed, nearly to tears over the plight of the children.

Forgetting her station, Daphne reached out a hand to the woman, laying an arm over her shoulders. 'It will be all right, I'm sure.' It was comforting to see that the Duchess cared so deeply for the children, for it made her actions in the Colton house seem much less suspicious.

The Duchess sniffed, as though fighting back her emotion. 'Thank you for understanding.' She walked to the end of the hall and opened the door to the servants' stairs, looking up a flight. 'There is a small room at the top of the house. Only fit for a maid, really. But it is very close to the children. And yet, very private. There is nothing at all on this side of the house but the attics, and the one little place under the eaves. And it is only until you can persuade Lily to return to her own room.'

Daphne looked up the narrow, unlit staircase, to the lone door at the top. 'I'm sure it will be adequate.' It would be dreadful. But it was only for a few weeks. And living so simply would help her remember her position.

'Shall we go and meet the children now? I have sent word that they are to wait for us in the schoolroom.' She led the way past two bedrooms, which must be Sophie's and the one Lily had usurped, to a small but well-stocked classroom. There were desks and tables, with a larger desk at one end for her, maps and pictures upon the walls and many shelves for books.

Remembering how she had felt as a child when cooped up in a similar room, Daphne was overcome with a sudden desire to slip away from the Duchess, to lead her in hide and seek or some other diversion. Anything that might prolong the time before she must pick up a primer.

The children lined up obediently in front of her, by order of age. Daphne felt a surprising lump form in her throat. They were all the picture of her beloved Clare. Red hair, pale complexions, fine features and large green eyes. Some day, the two girls would be beauties, and the boy would be a handsome rakehell.

The rush of emotion surprised her. She felt a sudden, genuine fondness for the children that she had not expected. She did not normally enjoy the company of the young. But these were the only part of her cousin that still remained. She had to overcome the urge to talk to them of the woman they both knew, and to reveal her relation to them. Surely it would be a comfort to them all to know that Clare was not forgotten?

But then she looked again. The light behind their eyes was the same suspicious glint she had seen in the man behind the desk on the floor below. They had also inherited the stubborn set of his jaw. Without speaking a word to each other, she watched them close ranks against her. They might smile and appear co-operative. And her heart might soften for the poor little orphans that Clare had left behind. But that should not give her reason to expect their help in discovering the truth of what had happened to their mother, or in bringing their father to justice.

She smiled an encouraging, schoolteacher's smile at them, and said, 'Hello, children. My name is Miss Collins. I have come a long way to be with you.'

The boy looked at her with scepticism. 'You are from London, are you not? We make the trip from London to Wales and back, twice a year. And while it is a great nuisance to be on the road, it is not as if you have come from Australia, is it?'

'Edmund!' the Duchess admonished.

Daphne chose to ignore the insolence, and redoubled her smile. 'As far as Australia? I suppose it is not. Do you find Australia of particular interest? For we could learn about it, if you wish.'

'No.' He glanced at the Duchess, who looked angry enough to box his ears. He corrected himself. 'No, thank you, Miss Collins.'

'Very well.' She turned to the older girl. 'And you are Lily, are you not?'

'Lilium Lancifolium. Father named me. For my hair.' When she saw Daphne's blank look, she gave a sigh of resignation at the demonstrated ignorance of the new governess. 'Tiger Lily.'

'Oh. How utterly charming.' Utterly appalling, more like. What kind of man gifted his first child with such a name? And, worse yet, a girl, who would someday have to carry that name to the alter with her. Clare's frustration with the man had not been without grounds.

Daphne turned to the youngest child. 'And you must be little Sophie. I have heard so much about you, and am most eager to know you better.' She held out a hand of greeting to the girl.

The littlest girl said nothing, and her eyes grew round, not with delight, but with fear. The two older children stepped in front of her, as though forming a barrier of protection. 'Sophie does not like strangers,' said Edmund.

'Well, I hope that she will not think me a stranger for long.' Daphne crouched down so that she might appear less tall to the little girl. 'It is all right, Sophie. You do not have to speak, if you do not wish. I know when I was little I found it most tiresome that adults were always insisting I curtsy, and recite, and sit in stiff chairs listening to boring lessons. I'd have been much happier if they'd left me alone in the garden with my drawings.'

The little girl seemed taken aback by this. Then she smiled and shifted eagerly from foot to foot, tugging at her older sister's skirts.

In response, Lily shook her head and said, 'Sophie is not allowed to draw.'

'Not allowed?' Daphne stood up quickly. 'What sort of person would take pencils and paper away from a little girl?'

Edmund responded, 'Our last governess—'

'Is not here.' Daphne put her hands on her hips, surprised at her own reaction. She had not meant to care in the least about the activities of the children. But she found herself with a strong opinion about their upbringing, and on the very first day. 'You...' she waved her hand '...older children...' it took a moment before she remembered that calling them by name would be best

'...Edmund and Lily. Look through your books and see if you can find an explanation of the word *tyranny*. For that is what we call unjust punishments delivered by despots who abuse their power. And, Sophie, come with me, and we will find you drawing supplies.'

The older children stood, stunned, as though unsure if she'd meant the instruction or was merely being facetious. But the younger child led her directly to a locked cabinet, and looked hopefully at her.

'They are in here, are they?' Daphne fumbled for the keys the Duchess had given her at the conclusion of the interview, which fit the doors to the nursery and schoolrooms, the desk and its various drawers. But she could find none that would fit the little cabinet. The girl's face fell in disappointment. She patted her lightly on the head. 'Fear not, little Sophie. It is locked today. But I promise, as soon as I have talked to the housekeeper, I will remedy the situation, and you shall have your art supplies again.'

All the children looked doubtfully at her now, as though they were convinced that she would be unable to provide what she had promised.

But the Duchess was smiling at her, as though much relieved at the sudden turn of events. 'Children, let me borrow Miss Collins to finish arranging the particulars. Then she shall have all her keys and you shall have your paints and pencils.' She led Daphne back out into the hall, and squeezed her arm in encouragement. 'Well done, Miss Collins. Barely a minute in the room, and you have already found a way to help the children. You are brilliant. And a total justification of my desire to advertise in London for a woman with exemplary references, instead of dealing with the problem in the haphazard manner this family is accustomed to. I am sure you will do miracles here. You are just what is needed.'

Daphne could only pray that the woman was right.

Chapter Two

The rest of the day passed in a whirl. The Duchess helped her to find more keys, made sure that her things were sent to the little room in the attic and arranged for her salary. When it was nearing supper time, she left to return to her own home, which was only a few miles away. Daphne felt her absence. It was almost as if she had made a friend of the woman, she had been so solicitous.

But now she must strike out on her own, and find the evening meal. Which led to the question—where did the governess usually eat? She struggled to think if she had ever seen one at her own family's table, or dining with the family in the home of friends. But it was possible, even if they had been there, she would not have noticed. She doubted that they were encouraged to call attention to themselves.

She strolled down the passages of the ground-floor

rooms, and found the dining room closed and dark. Wherever the Colton family ate, it was not a formal thing. But if servants were not waiting at table, then they must be below stairs, having a meal of their own. She went to the same stairway that would lead to her room if she followed it upwards to the end. She took the stairs downwards instead, and came out into a large open room with a long oak table set for supper. The servants were already gathered around it.

She came forwards and sat down at a place somewhere about the middle, offering a cheery 'hello' to the person next to her, who appeared to be a parlourmaid.

The room fell silent for a moment, and the housekeeper looked down the table toward her. Without a word, the woman went to the sideboard for a fresh plate, for the person Daphne must have displaced. This was handed down the table, and there was much shifting and giggling as the servants around her reorganized themselves according to their rank. It appeared that servants had a hierarchy every bit as structured as that of a fine dinner party above stairs. And Daphne had wandered in and disrupted things with her ignorance.

Once things were settled again, the housekeeper, Mrs Sims, announced, 'Everyone, this is Miss Collins. She is the new governess that her Grace hired for the children.'

The staff nodded, as though they did not find the Duchess's interference to be nearly so unusual as the presence of a governess at the servants' table.

The housekeeper favoured her with another nod. 'In the future, Miss Collins, you are welcome to eat in your room or with the children. No one here will think you are putting on airs.' She said it rather as a command, not a request.

It rather put a crimp in her plans to gather intelligence below stairs. 'Thank you, Mrs Sims. I was rather at a loss today as to what was expected. But I am sure this shall be all right, tonight at least. I wished to meet you all.' She smiled around the table.

And was met by blank looks in return, and mumbled introductions, up and down the table.

'Where did the previous governess eat?' she asked by way of conversation.

'Which one might you mean? There have been three since the lady of the house died. And many more before that. They all ate in the little dining room in the nursery wing.'

'So many.' It did not bode well for her stay here. 'What happened to them? I mean, why did they leave?' For the first sounded far too suspicious.

Mrs Sims frowned. 'Of late, the children are difficult. But you will see that soon enough.'

And there was mention of the difficulties again. But in her brief meeting with them, they had not seemed like little tartars. 'I am sure they are nothing I cannot handle,' she lied, really having no idea how she might get on with a house full of children.

'Then you are more stalwart than the others, and more power to you,' said the butler, with a small laugh. 'The first could not control them. And the second found them disturbing. The third…' he gave a snort of disgust

'…had problems with little Sophie. Thought the poor little mite was the very devil incarnate.'

'Sophie?' Having met the girl, this was more than hard to believe.

'The master caught Miss Fisk punishing the girl. She had been forcing Sophie to kneel and pray for hours on end, until her little knees were almost raw with it. And the older children too frightened to say anything about it.' The housekeeper shook her head in disapproval. 'And that was the last we saw of Miss Fisk. Lord Colton turned her out of the house in the driving rain, and threw her possessions after her. He said he had no care at all for her safety or comfort, if she did not care for the comfort of his children.'

'Served her right,' announced the upper footman. 'To do that to a wee one.'

'You'll think so, if he finds reason to turn you out, I suppose?' asked another.

The boy smirked. 'I don't plan to give him reason. I have no problem with the children.'

'Or the neighbours,' said another, and several men at the table chuckled.

'The neighbours?' Daphne pricked her ears. 'Do you mean the Duke and Duchess?'

The housekeeper glared at the men. 'There are some things, if they cannot be mentioned in seriousness, are better not mentioned at all.'

The butler supplied, in his dry quiet voice, 'Relations are strained between our household and the manor.'

'But Lord Colton seemed to get on well enough with the Duchess.'

'There is nothing strange about that, if you are imply-ing so.' The housekeeper sniffed. 'The master has no designs in her direction.'

'No,' said one of the house maids with a giggle, 'his troubles were all with the Duke. Her Grace wishes to pretend that nothing is wrong, of course. But she was not here for the worst of it. If she had seen the way the Duke behaved with Lady Colton…'

Now this was interesting. Daphne leaned forwards. 'Did he…make inappropriate advances?'

A footman snickered, and then caught himself, after a glare from the butler.

But a maid laughed and said, 'It was hard to see just who was advancing on who.'

'Remember where your loyalties lie, Maggie,' murmured Mrs Sims. 'You do not work at Bellston Manor.'

Maggie snorted in response. 'I'd be welcome enough there, if I chose to go. My sister is a chambermaid at Bellston. And she has nothing but fine words to say of his Grace and his new Duchess, now that our mistress…' the girl crossed herself quickly before continuing '… is no longer there to interfere.' She looked at Daphne, pointing with her fork. 'When her ladyship was alive, I worked above stairs, helping the lady's maid with the ribbons. And let me tell you, I saw plenty. Enough to know that his lordship is hardly to blame for the way things turned out in the end.'

'Then you should know as well the reason we no longer see his Grace as a guest in the house.' The butler was stiff with disapproval.

Daphne's eyes widened in fascination as the conversation continued around the table.

'It is a wonder that Lord Colton did not take his anger out in a way that would be better served,' said a footman, 'on the field of honour.'

'Don't be a ninny. One does not call out a duke, no matter the offence.' The upper footman nodded wisely. 'There's rules about that. I'm sure.'

'In any case, weren't all the man's fault.'

The housekeeper sniffed again, as though she wished to bring an end to the conversation.

'Just sayin'. There are others to blame.'

The housekeeper tapped lightly on her glass with her knife. 'We do not speak of such things at this table, or elsewhere in the house. What's done is done and there is no point in placing blame for it.'

The table fell to uneasy silence, enjoying a meal of beef that was every bit as good as that which she had eaten at home above stairs. Daphne suspected that such meals had gone a long way in buying the loyalty of the servants, none of whom seemed to mind that the master had murdered the mistress.

One by one, the servants finished their meals and the butler excused them from the table to return to their duties. But Daphne took her time, waiting until all but the butler and housekeeper were gone. If there was information to be had, then surely they must know, for it seemed that they knew everything that went on in the house.

But before she could enquire, the housekeeper spoke

first. 'Why did you choose to eat below stairs, Miss Collins?'

'I thought, since I am a servant, it was appropriate.'

The housekeeper gave her a look to let her know that she had tripped up yet again. 'A servant now, perhaps. But a lady above all, who must be accustomed to a better place in the household than the servants' table.' Mrs Sims looked at her with disapproval. 'And a lady with a most unfortunate tendency to gossip. It is not something we encourage in this house.'

'I am sorry. I was only curious. If I am in possession of all the facts, I might be best able to help the children.'

The butler responded, 'I doubt there is anyone in possession of all the facts, so your quest is quite fruitless. But I can tell you this: the less said about their mother, the better. She was a hoyden, who got what she deserved.'

Daphne let out a little gasp. 'Surely not. The poor woman, God rest her soul.'

The housekeeper drew herself up with disapproval. 'You think that knowing the truth will help the little ones? Then here it is, or all you need to know of it. What happened to our mistress was the result of too much carrying on. The children are lucky to be rid of her, however it happened.'

So Mrs Sims suspected something was strange about the death. But the housekeeper's assessment was most unjust. 'I hardly think it is fair to believe such things, when you yourself admit that no one knows all the

facts in the situation. In the last house I was employed,
everyone thought much the same of the only daughter.
They were all most censorious, when she was guilty
of the smallest breaches of etiquette. She strayed from
the common paths in Vauxhall with one of her suitors.
And before she knew it, she was packed off to the
country in disgrace. I suspect she was no worse than
Lady Colton.'

'Do you now?' The housekeeper shook her head.
'Then you are most naïve. If the young girl you mention
was already straying on to dark paths with young men,
then *I* suspect it was for more tickle than slap. Perhaps
the late Lady Colton would have called it innocent fun
and not the death of the girl's reputation. In fact, I am
sure that my lady and the girl would have got on well
together. Clarissa Colton would have approved, for the
young lady you describe would have been taking a first
step toward becoming what she had become: a lady with
no discernible morals. It pains me to say it. But her ladyship had no sense of decency whatsoever. No respect
for herself, and certainly none for her husband.'

It stung to hear such a blunt assessment of her character. For the housekeeper seemed to agree with Daphne's
parents that her trips to Vauxhall could have put her
beyond the pale. And Mrs Sims had predicted Clare's
reaction to the thing well enough—she had said that
there was no harm in it at all. She came to her cousin's
defence. 'Perhaps, if I were married to Lord Colton, a
man so distant, so cruel and so totally lost to gentleness,
my behaviour would be much the same.'

'If you were married to him?' The housekeeper let out

a derisive laugh. 'Quite far above yourself, aren't you, Miss Collins? His lordship is not good enough.' She glanced toward the conservatory, as though she could see the master of the house through the walls separating them. Then she said softly, 'I have worked in this house for almost forty years. I have known Lord Colton since he was a boy. And there was nothing wrong with his character before that woman got her hooks into him. A bit of youthful high spirits, perhaps. A slight tendency to excess drink, and with it, a short temper. Things that would have passed, with time. But under the influence of his wife, he grew steadily worse.'

'So his misbehaviour is youthful high spirits. But the occasional straying of a girl will permanently damage her character.'

The housekeeper gave her a look that proved she thought her a complete fool. 'Yes. Because, as you can see, his problems did not render him incapable of making a match.'

'But I do not see that they have made him a good choice for a husband,' Daphne snapped in return. 'In my experience so far, he is a foul-tempered, reclusive man who cares so little for his children that he allows the neighbours to choose their governess.'

Mrs Sims frowned. 'He cares more for the children than you know. And if you care for them as well, you will see to it that the boy grows up to be the man that his father is, and the girls learn to be better than their mother, and get no strange ideas about the harmlessness of straying down dark paths in Vauxhall Gardens. Good evening, Miss Collins.'

Daphne had the strange feeling that she was being held responsible for the wayward actions of her imaginary charge, and that Mrs Sims's estimation of her skills had gone down by a wide margin.

Which made the truth seem all the stranger. What might Mrs Sims have said if Daphne'd admitted that she was the girl, and that her parents had no idea that she had elected to come to Clare's home, instead of her dear aunt in Anglesey? She was supposed to remain there until such time as her behaviour was forgotten, her reputation restored and her head emptied of Clarissa Colton's nonsensical advice.

She walked slowly up the stairs to her room. In retrospect, she had to admit that the outing to Vauxhall had been a mistake. She had been so blue, in the wake of Clare's death. And her beau, Simon, had assured her that moping at home was no way to honour her cousin's memory. But once she was alone with him in the dark, she suspected that Simon cared less for her feelings than his own. Her London social life had ended in a flurry of open-mouthed kisses, wayward hands and a slap that had brought her friends running to her aid. And then running just as fast to spread rumours of what they had interrupted.

As she looked at the three flights of stairs in front of her, she wished her parents could see what penance she had set for herself. Several weeks of hard work, with not a single ball, *musicale* or country outing to break the monotony. It had been exhausting just meeting the family and making arrangements for the position.

She suspected it was likely to be more difficult, once

she began the duties she had been hired for. Although she knew nothing of teaching, she must begin proper lessons directly, or someone would become suspicious.

Unless there was no one who cared enough to suspect her. If the governess here normally ate with the children, in the absence of a governess, did anyone eat with them at all? It seemed unlikely that their father would come upstairs and take his meal if there were perfectly good rooms for that purpose on the ground floor. And she had been introduced to no nurses or servants who had charge over them.

It appeared that they were left to their own devices. She knew little of children, other than that she had recently been one. And in her experience, too much freedom meant an opportunity for mischief, and the fostering of wilful ideas that would make the job of governess to the Coltons a difficult one.

Her candle trembled a little as she climbed the last flight of stairs, and she regretted not investigating her sleeping quarters in daylight. With its lack of windows, the narrow stairwell would be intimidating, both day and night. She certainly hoped that the room above had some natural illumination, for to be climbing from darkness into further darkness would lead to unnecessary imaginings that would make for a difficult first night.

She opened the door, and was relieved to see a bright square of moonlight from the small window opposite her. She walked across to it, and looked up into a brilliant full moon, which seemed almost close enough to touch. The ground below was distant. The shrubs and trees casting shadows that were sharp as daylight in the white light from above, giving the whole an unworldly quality, as though a day scene were rendered in black and white. She turned and looked at the room behind her, which was lit the same way.

If she were a real teacher, she might know how great an insult she was paid by these accommodations. She was all but sleeping in the attic. Half the ceiling of the room slanted, to make the space unusable for one so tall as she. Her trunk had been pushed to that side, next to the small writing desk, which held a dried-up inkwell and the stub of a candle. On the other side there was a bed, pushed in front of a door that must lead to further attic rooms. That they'd placed furniture in front of it was the only assurance given that she would not have other servants tramping through her private space when bearing things to storage. There was no proper wardrobe, only pegs for her dresses. A small mirror hung upon the wall. And that was all. If she wished for a chair for the writing desk, she would need to steal one from another room, just as she suspected the intended chair had been stolen from hers.

She sat down upon the bed and tested the mattress. It was lumpy and narrow, and certainly not what she was used to. But if one was tired enough, one could sleep anywhere. She was already at that weird combination of exhaustion and wakefulness that one got sometimes when overtired. Enervated, but not sleepy. Perhaps a book from the library would provide the necessary soporific. The light in the room was almost bright enough to read by even without a candle, and she had no curtain to block it out.

She took up her candle again, and came back down the flights of stairs to the brightly lit ground floor, and the familiar feeling of warmth and civilisation. She found a volume that she did not think too dreary from the rather intellectual holdings of the Colton library. She wished that Clare had been alive to greet her when she arrived. Then she could stay here reading before going up the stairs to a fine guest room, secure in her place as a visitor in this house, and not an intruder.

When she turned to go back to her room, it suddenly occurred to her that two choices were open to her. She had taken the servants' stairs to the ground. Surely, as governess, she was closer to family than serving maid, and entitled to use the main stairs? It would mean a flight in the open, postponing the stifling darkness that led to her room.

But it would also mean a trip down the nursery hall, past the children's rooms, before she reached the stairs to her room. She suspected it was her duty to check on them, and make sure that they were all snug in bed, resting for the next day.

Her duty. If she were really the governess, her time would not be her own. She would be responsible for the watching of the children, morning and night. The needs of the family must always come before her own.

Until such time as she revealed the truth about Clare's death. Then she need answer to no one, least of all the murderous Lord Timothy Colton. Tomorrow would be soon enough to begin the charade of watching his children. Tonight, she would have one last night of her own, no matter how mean the comforts might be.

So she went to the end of the hall and opened the door to the servants' stairs. The stairwell was narrow, and the rise steep. The first flight was just as black as the stairway to her room. She took a firm grip on her candle, tucked the book tightly under her arm so that she could grasp the handrail for safety, and began her ascent.

She could not help the chill feeling and the shiver that went through her, alone in the dark with only her candle for company. The hall doors were shut tight on all the landings, cutting the regular pathway of the servants off from the rest of the house, as though they were mice in the walls, and not a part of the household at all.

She started as she heard a door above her open, and someone else beginning a descent. The person was beyond the bend in the stairs, so she could not yet see who it was. It was ridiculous to worry, but she was suddenly taken with the notion that when she arrived at the next landing, there would be no one on the stairs above her. The ghostly footsteps would walk through her, with only a passing feeling of icy air.

What a foolish notion. More likely, it would be a footman on his way to the kitchen, or someone else sent on an errand. She would round the next corner and find nothing unusual. But she could not resist calling a hoarse 'hello?' into the darkness.

The space around her got suddenly darker, as though a candle around the corner, barely able to cut the gloom of the stairwell, had been extinguished.

Did the person above her mean to keep their identity a secret? There was no point in it, for she would come upon them with her own candle in just a few more steps.

But the footsteps had stopped as well.

She could feel her own steps falter at the realisation, before plucking up her nerves and continuing her climb. She rounded the bend in the stairs and kept climbing, eyes averted, before working up the nerve to look up at the silhouette of a man, looming on the flight above her. He was not moving, just waiting in stillness for her to pass him.

This was not normal behaviour, was it? For though it might make sense to wait while another passed, it made no sense at all to do so in silence. It turned a chance meeting into a threatening situation. Or perhaps it was only her imagination. She proceeded up the stairs, hand on the rail and eyes focused on the shadowy face of the man in front of her, watching the features sharpen in focus with each step she took.

Then she gasped. 'Lord Colton.'

'Miss Collins.' He did not move. And although she had not thought him a particularly large man, he seemed to fill the stairwell in front of her, blocking her progress. 'What a surprise to find you creeping about the house so late at night.'

His tone was insulting, and she caught herself before responding in kind, remembering that he was her employer, not her equal. 'Merely coming back from the library with a book for my room. It is sometimes difficult to sleep in a strange place.'

'And since you are educated, you sought solace in a book.' In the flickering candlelight, his smile looked like a sneer.

She nodded.

'Very well. But you had best be careful on your way. Stairs can be dangerous.'

What did he mean by that? Was it a threat? And why threaten her, for he hardly knew her? What was he doing on the servants' stairs at all? He had even less reason to be there than her.

She glared back at him, not caring what he might think. 'I assure you, my lord, I am most careful when it comes to stairs. And since lightning does not strike twice in the same place, a second fall in this house would be a most unusual circumstance indeed.' And then, without waiting for dismissal, she released the handrail that they were both holding, and went to pass him and continue her ascent.

There was not enough space to go around without brushing against him, and she steeled herself for the moment when their bodies would touch.

And suddenly he reached out to steady her, his hand on her waist. The touch was like a jolt of electricity, cutting through the fear she felt of him. For a moment, she was sure that he was debating whether to embrace her, or give the downward shove that would cause another fatal accident.

Then the moment passed, and he was helping her to find the handrail and go on her way. She continued up the stairs, hurrying her pace, all the time aware that his downward steps did not resume.

* * *

Tim waited on the stairs, frozen in place, listening to her progress. She must be in the small room in the attic, for he could hear her, passing the second-floor landing and continuing upwards. It was a lonely spot at the back of the house, far away from prying eyes and ears. No one would know if he turned and followed her.

But he did not want that, did he? For only a moment before...

He hurried down the stairs to the ground floor, shutting himself up in the study and reaching for the brandy decanter. One drink would not matter, surely. Just to steady his nerves. He poured, and drank eagerly, praying for the numbness that would come with the first sip.

For a moment, when he had heard her call out, he had been convinced it was Clare. Although he had not noticed it at the time of introduction, there was a similarity in tone, just as there was in colouring. And her voice had startled him so that the trembling of his hand had put out the candle. He'd stood, rooted to the spot, hearing those approaching footsteps, waiting for the figure that would round the corner: the vengeful spirit of his wife.

And he had not been disappointed. There were her accusing green eyes staring up at him, as though daring him to run. He had all but given up the main staircase. For that had been where he expected to see her, when she finally came for him. But the sight of her approaching on the back stairs had been totally unexpected and utterly terrifying.

When he realised that it was a mistake of the light

and his overwrought nerves, his response had been a jumble of emotions. Anger at being so foolish. And suspicion of her behaviour, which had been quite ordinary and probably an appropriate match to the strangeness of his.

And then, there had been that hint of desire, as he'd stood close enough to feel the warmth of her body and smell her scent. Longing that a touch might lead to something more than a chance meeting on the stairs.

He looked down in to the half-full glass of brandy, momentarily surprised to find it in his hand. Then he smiled and set it aside. He gave a nervous, involuntary chuckle, and ran a hand over his eyes in embarrassment. It did not say much for the state of his nerves if he could manage to work himself into such a state over nothing. There were no ghosts on the front stairs, or the back. Although she was most attractive, the governess's resemblance to Clare was superficial, at best.

The cause of all his problems was a penchant for brandy and redheads. Once he learned to leave them both alone, the remainder of his life would go easier. And he sank back into the chair, and laid his head on the desk to rest, too weak from the realisation to take either set of stairs to his room.

Chapter Three

Daphne awoke with the dawn, the rays of morning light streaming upon her bed with aggressive good cheer, making sleep impossible. It was just as well. For she suspected the real Miss Collins would have risen intentionally at this time, so that she might be washed and dressed and down the stairs to breakfast. She would be ready to start lessons before the children were half out of bed.

Daphne had never been an early riser. The best she was likely to manage was prompt, but surly. She pasted a smile upon her face and put on one of the sensible gowns that she had bought off the real Miss Collins. Then she came down the stairs to the nursery wing, walking down the hall until she found the open door to the children's dining room.

The sight of it made her smile; it was attractively decorated but informal, rather like the breakfast room in her own home back in London. The woman who had been introduced to her on the previous evening as Cook was setting eggs and ham and tea things on a side table. It was most unusual to see her doing work that would be better suited to a footman. But she gave Miss Collins a defiant look, that seemed to say, What if I am? Someone must watch out for them.

The children filed in from the hall, and Cook greeted them pleasantly, making sure that their plates were full and that everyone had enough of what they wanted. She extended her offers to Miss Collins, as though relieved to see that there would be an adult present at the meal, before excusing herself and returning to the kitchen.

Daphne smiled hopefully at the three children across the table from her, and attempted polite breakfast talk. Had they slept well? Was it not a beautiful day? Did they have enough to eat? And were they sure that they did not want a second helping of anything? Absolutely sure? Because she had no problems with delaying the lesson, and they should not feel a need to rush their morning meal.

It would have been a blessing to her if they could manage to delay lessons indefinitely. She had no more interest in sitting in a classroom as teacher than she had managed to display when she had been a student.

The children answered all questions in polite monosyllables, as though they had decided her presence was to be tolerated for the moment. But they intended to make no effort at a closer relationship than was absolutely necessary.

Eventually, her attempts at conversation were

exhausted, as was the breakfast food. She suggested that they wash their hands and make their way to the classroom, where the real business of the day could begin.

They were almost eerily agreeable to it, as though faintly relieved to be able to do something they preferred over socialising with the governess. They took what appeared to be their regular seats in the room, and folded their hands on their empty desks, waiting to be impressed.

'Very well then,' she said, and waited for something to fill the blank void in her mind as to what would happen next. Perhaps it was best to discover what the children already knew, before attempting to educate them further. 'Please, children, gather the books you have been working in and show me your progress.'

They remained unmoved, still in their seats, staring out at her.

So she reached for the nearest book, a maths primer that had given her much trouble when she was their age. She opened it, paging through the equations. 'This would probably be yours, wouldn't it, Lily?' She arched an eyebrow, for she had seen the girl's name written clearly inside the front cover. 'Show me how far you have got.' And please Lord, let it be not far, for Daphne had given up on that particular subject before she was halfway through the text.

The girl took the book sullenly and flipped through pages until she was nearly at the end.

Daphne gave a nervous laugh. 'My, my. How well

you are doing. Perhaps I will allow you to tutor your brother.'

Lily gave her a disgusted look. 'He has been this far and further for at least six months.'

Daphne narrowed her eyes. 'Then perhaps I shall allow him to tutor you. Edmund!' She smiled and turned suddenly upon the boy, to catch him making faces at his sister.

He had the grace to look embarrassed at being caught, and then his expression turned as sullen as his sister's.

'Lily says you are good at maths. Is that your best subject?'

The boy raised his chin and said, 'I prefer reading.'

'Do you? Well, we can not always do what we prefer, but I wish for our time together to be enjoyable. What is it you like to read? We will see if we can incorporate it into our studies.'

He went to the shelf and brought down a book that was almost as big as himself, and held it out to her. 'Plutarch.'

She smiled feebly. 'In Greek.'

He nodded. And she could tell by his smile that he knew he had bested her.

She turned to Lily. 'And I suppose you enjoy Plutarch as well?'

'Yes. But not so well as Edmund.'

'Then we must see what can be done to encourage you.' She pointed to the front of the room. 'Edmund. Today, you may read to us. I wish to hear you declaim. Choose your favourite passage.' She walked to the back of the room and took a seat.

The boy began in a clear, unwavering voice, reading with what she supposed was accurate and enthusiastic inflection. But the prose was, quite literally, all Greek to her. She had no idea how to correct him, or if it was even necessary. So she chose a polite and interested expression, similar to the one Lily was wearing, and folded her arms across her chest. It would be possible to spend at least an hour of the school day, if the passage was long enough. By then, she would think of some other trick with which to keep them occupied.

There was a slight pause in the reading, and Edmund said something, still in Greek.

There was another slight pause, which she suspected was just long enough for the older girl to translate something she did not expect to hear in the reading. And then she stifled a laugh.

So they had realised she knew little Greek and were going to have fun at the expense of the governess. 'Please return to the text that is printed before you.'

She must have guessed correctly, for Edmund responded with a look of surprise, and fear that she had understood whatever rude thing he had said.

She glanced over at the younger girl, Sophie. Unlike the other two, the child was doing her best to be obedient. She sat quietly, staring down at the hands folded in her lap, and shooting glances out the window, when she thought no one was looking. The poor thing clearly wanted and needed to run and play, but was afraid to call attention and risk punishment.

Yesterday, it had appeared that the girl liked to draw. Perhaps with paper and pencils, and a little peace, she would find a way to express herself. 'You do not have to sit through the lessons if they are too advanced for you, Sophie.' She spoke softly so as not to alarm the girl. 'I'm sure your turn will come with Plutarch, before too long. But for now? Perhaps you would prefer to draw instead. I promised you your art things, didn't I? And now I've got the keys, I can give them to you.'

She opened the cabinet in the corner and found a rather nice selection of pens, brushes, paints and crayons, and paper of a quality that made her almost envious of the little girl. Then she prepared a place at the table near the window, where the light would be good for drawing.

Sophie smiled in relief, and climbed up on to the chair, taking the pencil eagerly and stroking it and the paper as though they were more precious than china dolls.

Then Daphne went back to allowing the boy to teach her his Greek. Edmund continued to recite, this time with a tired voice that said that he understood well what she was trying to do, and that the whole thing bored him to tears.

There was a limit to this, she thought, before it became plain to everyone that she had no idea what she was doing in a classroom. When she had hatched the plan, she had thought that she might occupy the children for a few weeks before they caught on to her ruse. But if they had tumbled to her within hours?

The Duchess was right. They were as sharp as needles. Too clever for their own good. But since the house made little effort to hide its secrets, perhaps she would not be here long.

And what was to happen to the children, if that was so? They seemed just as stubborn about remaining in the house as their father did in sending them to school. But if their father would admit to his crime, and accept punishment for it?

Then they would have to go somewhere, wouldn't they? They could not remain in the house alone. Perhaps the Duchess would see to their education. She had no children of her own, and she seemed most fond of them.

What happened to them did not really matter, she reminded herself. For they were no concern of hers.

But perhaps they were. They were Clare's children, as well as Lord Colton's. There was a family connection to her. Perhaps she could persuade her father to take them in. Clare's parents could not do the job. They'd seemed to care little enough for what had happened to the mother, once she was off their hands. Why should they want a good home for their grandchildren?

If she meant to disrupt their lives further in the name of justice, she held some responsibility in seeing that they were cared for. She must give the matter more thought.

Edmund reached the end of his passage and returned to his seat.

'Very good,' she said. 'You read well. Let us see how you write.' She went to the shelf, and pulled down another book, and gave him a page from Homer to translate. 'And, Lily, why don't you work on your maths?

Since you seem to be managing well, you may work at your own pace.' Then she wandered to the window to check on Sophie. 'Have you finished your drawing, little one?'

The girl nodded eagerly, and held the paper out to her.

And Daphne dropped it in revulsion as she got a look at the subject.

It was Clare. Or what had been Clare. There was no mistaking the fact, for the rendering was skilful, even in the hands of a five-year-old. It was a woman's body, dead at the foot of the staircase, arms and legs at odd angles, and a head that was curiously misshapen.

Daphne crumpled the paper and threw it to the floor.

Sophie drew back in alarm, sure that she had done wrong and trembling as she awaited punishment.

The older girl gave her a look of bitter triumph. 'It serves you right for giving her the pencils. Our first governess ran screaming to Papa. The next one called her a devil. And the last one tried to beat the devil out of her, until Papa caught her at it and sent her away.'

Daphne took a deep breath and scooped up the paper from the floor, straightening out the wrinkles and laying it back on the table. 'Since I did not assign her a subject, I have little right to complain about the finished work.' She tried to ignore the subject matter and focus on the execution. Then she looked down at Sophie. 'I would not normally give lessons so advanced to one as small as you. But it is clear from looking at it that you have more than normal abilities for a child of your age.' She crouched down beside the girl and urged her back into her seat.

Sophie looked at her in confusion, tears in her eyes, still half-expecting punishment.

'It is all right,' Daphne said. 'You needn't worry. I love to draw as well. And I know how comforting it can be to sit with pen and paper, especially when one has something on one's mind. Unless I tell you otherwise, you may draw whatever you wish. Is that all right?'

The girl gave a hesitant nod.

Daphne steeled herself to look again at the wrinkled sketch. 'You have a good eye for detail and your proportions are fair. But no one has taught you about light and how to draw it.'

The girl gave her a puzzled look.

She smiled back encouragingly. 'You might think that there is nothing to see in empty air. But it is possible for the artist to show the light, by showing the shadows. Let us put figure drawing aside for now, and start with something simple, like an apple.'

She took a blank sheet of paper, and drew a rough fruit, then showed Sophie how to choose a direction for the sun, and put in shading and highlights with a bit of chalk. Then she offered the paper back to the girl. 'Now you try. Begin with round things, like apples. And then try something with angles, like the bookcase or the window frame.'

Sophie looked at her with growing amazement, as though these were the first words she had understood in hours. And then she smiled and took the pencil back in her hand, placed a fresh sheet of paper on the table and bit her lip in determination, bending eagerly over her work.

Daphne watched the older children, who were exchanging looks of surprise and confusion, as though she had interrupted the perfectly intelligible Greek with a language they could not understand. She turned to them, hands on her hips. 'I suppose this is as good a time as any to see how you children draw. Lily, show me your watercolour book.'

'I do not have one.' The girl was almost stammering in embarrassment.

Daphne fought down the feeling of triumph. 'You do not draw?'

'It is hardly necessary, for if one knows maths and languages...' Edmund said in a starchy tone.

'Your father knows those things, I am sure. And how to draw, as well. He enjoys gardening, does he not?'

'He is a botanist,' said Lily, as though deeply offended by the slight.

Daphne waved it aside, not much caring about the difference. 'Then he must know enough drawing to render the plants he works on.'

The older children's eyes grew round, as though they had never considered the fact.

'And I doubt he would like to hear that you are dismissing any element of your education as frivolous. We must work to correct our ignorance, rather than making excuses for it.' And now it was her turn to be surprised. That last had sounded rather like something her school mistresses had said to her. Perhaps all that was necessary to turn oneself into an educator was to starch one's bodice and put on a stern expression.

She smiled at the children so as not to appear too forbidding, remembering the minimal effect such lectures had had on her. 'For now, you may continue with the lessons you have. But in future, we shall see that you gain some talent for art.' She smiled at Sophie, who was dutifully drawing an apple from memory. 'After I have got the more advanced student properly settled.'

The little girl turned to her with such a look of surprise on her face that it almost made her forget her role and laugh. But then Sophie smiled, as though the words were better than rubies to her. With such talented siblings, she had never been the star pupil.

And if what the older children had said was true, she had endured far worse since Clare had died. So it helped her to draw horrible pictures to help recover from her mother's death. Was there really any harm in it? Daphne picked up the sheet of paper, considered throwing it on the fire, and then smoothed it and set it aside. If it was destroyed, the poor girl would only draw it again.

She stared down at the image of her cousin, crumpled in death. The girl had drawn it from memory, just as she had the apple. Had no one the sense to keep her away, so that she did not have to see such a horrible sight? But the picture was very informative, for it showed just what she had expected: Clare lying on her back as though she had toppled backwards, and not fallen face first as one likely would if the death were accidental.

Without realising it, Sophie might help to prove her mother's murder.

Chapter Four

Daphne took the picture and placed it between the pages of her own sketchbook. It was too disturbing to hang on the schoolroom wall, but the information in it was too important to discard. She would conceal it for now, then take it to her room where she might examine it in detail. She encouraged the children to work on what they wished, and gave only the barest supervision, assuming that they would come to little harm reading from their texts.

At lunch time, Cook delivered trays of food to the nursery dining room, and they paused in their lessons to eat. The same seemed to hold for tea, and would happen at supper just as Mrs Sims described. The household had given the children no reason to come below stairs at all, if they did not wish to. She wondered if the intent was to keep them away from their father. For if it was, it told the real truth about the loyalty of the servants to their master. They would support him, of course. They took his side in what had happened to his wife, and frowned on gossip about it.

But they feared him, feared for the children and kept them far out of his path.

When a maid had come to clear away the tea things, and they were almost ready to return to the classroom, she noticed a shadow from the doorway that fell across the room.

Lord Colton was there, observing them. She had not heard him approach, and could not shake the feeling that he had been standing there for quite some time, unnoticed. It put her on her guard. Though she doubted he had seen or heard anything of interest, it was disquieting to think him so adept at spying.

'Miss Collins.' He gave the same curt bow he had given her on the previous day, and she feared he was ready for another disquieting battle of wills.

Before he could catch it, she broke her gaze, and gave another curtsy, eyes downcast to hide her discomfort. 'Lord Colton.'

'How are the children today?'

'Very well, my lord.' She hoped that she was not expected to go into detail on their progress, for she had nothing to add.

'We shall see about that. For if I find otherwise, I will turn you out, no matter what the Duchess might say.'

She flinched at the suddenness of the threat. And when he saw her reaction, and that she was showing none of the bravado of yesterday, he gave a faint laugh and went to greet his children.

She felt her muscles tense in instinctive defence of them. They were stubborn little beasts, to be sure. But what could one expect, when they had a monster for a father? What poison had he poured in their ears about their mother? And what abuses had they undergone to leave them so suspiciously quiet?

Colton's smile changed as he approached the children. As he looked at them, the lines seemed to smooth from his forehead, and his lips were turned upwards not in a cynical parody of mirth or seduction, but with joyful anticipation. The tension in his body disappeared, making his movements easy. He seemed to become younger with each step, almost as if he were a denizen of the nursery wing and not the master of the whole house.

He came to the boy first, bending down, smiling and offering his hand, which his son took and gave a pale imitation of a manly clasp. The father asked how the studies were progressing, and the boy answered that they were satisfactory. And then Colton said something in what sounded like Latin, and the boy answered quickly and easily, as though in his native tongue.

They conversed thus, for a few minutes, and the child cast a sidelong look in her direction. They were talking about the new governess again, were they? If she lasted long enough to make a difference here, she would take an opportunity to teach the children some manners. It was quite rude to switch languages, and take advantage of the ignorance of others. Even more so when the other was your teacher and had so much ignorance to abuse.

The boy said something adamant, his jaw set in a stubborn parody of his father's.

The older man shrugged. With a half-smile, he glanced in Daphne's direction and shook his head. Then he turned to the older girl and dropped to one knee so that he could greet her face to face.

'Bonjour, Papa.' She gave him a shy kiss upon the cheek, but her smile had a wicked glint to it. She continued in French, as though she wished to prove that she could best her brother in something.

Her father answered her in the same language, and they proceeded to discuss the day. Daphne had less trouble with this, for she knew more than a little French, although the girl did speak quickly for one so young. Apparently, the day was *bon,* as was the new teacher. Although the girl was equally adamant that such guidance was not necessary, and that they would show him how well they could manage, if left to their own devices.

Her father answered with a *c'est la vie.* If *Tante Penny* wished it, then what were they to do? The children must prove that they could take care of themselves by giving no more trouble to the new teacher, for he knew what mischief they were capable of. While he did not wish her here, neither did he wish to see Miss Collins running to his study in fits, or, worse yet, to the neighbours, because his children were being naughty. But if the governess were to try any of the evil tricks that the last one had, they were to send word. He would come and deal with her, and there would be no more trouble. He looked up at Daphne, to make sure that she had understood the warning.

She looked back at him, and raised her chin a fraction of an inch to show that she did not fear him. She had to admit, if the last woman had been as bad as the servants said, the family had a reason to be less than trusting of her.

But while Lord Colton obviously disliked her, his conversation was surprisingly innocent, and he was even tempered with both children. It came as rather a surprise, for she had expected some sign of the problems there. Perhaps the children did not understand what had happened to their mother, or their father's part in it. He must be a master actor, to be so calm and pleasant with them that they felt nothing of what he had done.

And then he turned again, dropped to both knees and held his arms wide. 'And where is my little Sophie? Come here, darling, and give your papa a hug.'

She turned and looked, expecting to find the strange, haunted child warming to the sight of her father, as the other two had done. But instead, she heard a quick scurrying behind her, and felt the tug upon her skirts. When she looked down, she saw Sophie's little face turned up to hers, the tear-stained cheeks pressed tight to the fabric of her dress, fingers white and claw-like, twisted into the cloth so tightly that Daphne was afraid that there would be holes worn in it, when she managed to get the girl to release her.

And the little eyes were shut tight, screwed closed,

as the mouth murmured something silently, over and over again, like a prayer.

'Sophie, sweetheart, come here and tell me about your day.' She would have expected the tone to be more demanding, in response to such obvious disobedience. But instead it was even softer, and more gentle then it had been the first time. 'Did you draw a picture? You love to draw.' There was a wistfulness to the tone, and Lord Colton cleared his throat, and addressed Daphne directly, as though she might not have heard. 'She very much loves to draw, and is surprisingly proficient, for a girl of such small years.'

The little girl burrowed further into her skirts, clinging even tighter, as though each word from her father's mouth was a blow upon her back.

Daphne looked helplessly at the master of the house, afraid that he would demand that she pry the poor creature loose, and turn her over to him. Then she put her hand upon the head of the child in a gentle caress, and felt the girl snuggle against it, eager for protection.

Still on his knees, her employer dropped his hands to his sides in a gesture of defeat. 'No hug today then, little Sophie? Tomorrow, perhaps. I will wait.' If she wished to see the man punished for his deeds, perhaps it had already happened. He was brought to his knees before her, and his daughter's rejection was sufficient to leave him broken, his shoulders slumped, his expression downcast. As he rose to his feet, he seemed a much older man than he had when entering the room.

'It is good to see you all doing well.' He glanced at Daphne as though she were a canker in a rose. 'And so,

I will leave you in the capable hands of Miss Collins.'
It appeared she had bested him, without even realising
they were competing. Lord Colton turned to leave.

The two older children took a step forwards, as
though to stop him, but then froze in their tracks, afraid
to signal.

And young Sophie was the strangest of all. For
though she was obviously terrified of the man when he
came close to her, she watched his retreating back with
a hunger greater than the others. Daphne could feel the
girl tensing, ready to spring after the man in the doorway, to throw herself upon him like a little animal.

But if she wanted her father to stay, why would she
not just say so? It was clear that he wanted to be with
her, and the other children as well. It was only Sophie's
rejection that was keeping them away.

Daphne shook her head, confused at her response to
the scene. She was not here to make it easier to reconcile father and daughter. She was here to get the horrid
man away from them, so that they had a chance at a
normal life.

Chapter Five

Daphne rose the next day when the sun crept over the horizon, just as she had the day before. So this was to be her routine, while in the Colton house. Rise at dawn, take all meals above stairs with the children, and have what little time to herself she could, after she had readied them for bed. They had gone to their rooms easily enough after the previous night's meal. And she had taken time straightening the classroom and lingering in the dining room over a cup of tea.

Before going up to bed she had passed Sophie's room, trusting that the older children would not need her help. And through the door, she had heard faint sounds of the girl whimpering in her dreams. But when Daphne had opened the door to come to her aid, she had found a candle burning on the nightstand, and Lily, sitting on the edge of the bed, her hand on the little girl's shoulder. She'd looked up at Daphne, as though annoyed at the intrusion, and whispered, 'She will be all right in a moment. But it is best not to wake her.'

Daphne nodded. Not her choice of action, perhaps. She would have shaken the girl awake immediately. But there was nothing about the sister's actions that seemed rooted in malice. In fact, it appeared that Lily often took the role of comforter, and showed no desire to give it over to a stranger. Daphne had trusted her to do what was best and gone to her room.

Once there, she'd removed Sophie's sketch from her own book and hidden it under the folded gowns in her trunk. Should someone enter the room, it would not do to let them think she was too interested in the subject. But should she need to provide proof of what she had found, it would be invaluable.

That morning, she went to breakfast with the children, and from there to the classroom. The Duchess had been right. They were quite capable of teaching themselves. In some subjects they were clever enough to teach her. She let them proceed, helping with such few questions as they had, trying to do as little damage to their educations as possible.

But if she wasn't actually needed in the schoolroom, there was no reason she could not slip away for a short time, to begin her search of the rest of the house. She excused herself under the guise of going to the library for a book. And with one last glance at the bowed heads, she shut the schoolroom door and hurried down the hall.

She looked into the children's rooms first. There was nothing out of the ordinary in Lily's or Sophie's room, other than that the connecting door appeared to stand open at all times, in testament to the sisters' close bond. Further down the hall was Edmund's room, orderly but boyish. And beside it the cold, dark room that would be Lily's, still with some of her things scattered around, as if waiting for her to return.

She moved more slowly now. Somewhere down the hall was the master suite, and there was a risk of blundering into Lord Colton. Although at this hour he should be below in the conservatory, where she suspected he spent most of his days. She turned the knob on the door at the head of the stairs, and found his room, quiet and empty. It was ordered to the last degree, with no ornaments on the dressers, no item out of place in wardrobe or drawers. There was no wrinkle in the cover on the bed, no mashed pillow or lump in the mattress to hint that the owner of the bed might sleep restlessly, from guilt or any other reason.

If she had not known better, she would have suspected that the person whose room this was did not reside in the house. It was almost too neat to be inhabited. It was a blank. A cipher. And it was unlikely that he might be hiding anything in it. If he meant to write a journal of confession, there was not even a writing table on which to do it.

Perhaps Clare's room would be different. She glanced to the wall that had the connecting door. If the servants had not already cleared the room, there might be some evidence of the state of her cousin's mind in the days before her demise.

But when she put her hand to the knob, it did not

turn. Locked. She sighed in exasperation and exited cautiously into the hall, ready to enter from there.

Also locked.

Every room on the floor was open to her, including the master's bedroom. The only place she could not search was the room of her beloved Clare. In her mind, it became the room she most wanted to see. For there would be no reason to lock it if there was not something to hide.

She walked back down the hall to the nursery, frustrated by her defeat.

When she returned to her desk, the tea things had arrived. The children were busy, red heads bowed over the tray, pouring her a cup. They looked up as she entered with such innocent smiles that she was immediately suspicious.

So she smiled back at them, as guileless as they were, and said, 'You are preparing my tea things. That is very kind of you.' She took the cup they offered, watching the intent way they observed her, waiting for her to take the first drink.

She sat down on the small settee in the corner, and paused, with the cup halfway to her mouth, noting the rapt expression on the faces of the older two children.

'But it is hardly fair that I should be able to take tea, while you have nothing.' She set the cup down upon the tray, and, without looking at the contents, offered it to Edmund. 'You should drink before me, for you are the heir and I am but a servant.'

The boy looked at the cup with alarm.

She smiled. 'Here. Take it.' She held the cup out to him again.

He picked it up, tentatively, and sipped.

She held up a hand. 'Just swish it about your mouth for a bit.'

The boy made a terrible face, looking like he would gag rather than take another sip.

She waited for a second. 'Now spit it back into the cup, please.'

He hurried to do as he was bade.

'And smile.'

The boy opened his mouth to show a face full of bright purple teeth.

She smiled in satisfaction. 'Just as I thought. You put ink into my tea, as a trick. And you never stopped to think what might be in the ink, or that it might hurt me.'

'A little would not hurt,' Lily insisted. 'You would have spat it out. It tastes horrid.'

'Suppose I had not spat out the tea after getting a comical blue smile. Suppose I had swallowed it. Who knows what it is made of, or what harm it might have done? Do you wish to go to your father and admit that you poisoned the governess?'

Without warning, little Sophie started to cry with great gulping sobs. And both the older children looked not just guilty, but disproportionately frightened.

Daphne reached out and scooped the little one into her lap. 'There now, Sophie. No harm has been done. I am all right, as will your brother be, once he has rinsed the colour from his teeth.'

'Will you tell Father?' the older girl asked, in a hoarse whisper. 'We never meant to hurt you. We never meant to hurt anyone. Do not make him send us away.'

And Sophie cried even harder.

The situation was rapidly getting out of hand, and Daphne suspected that the real Miss Collins would have been better equipped for it. But she would manage as best she could. She put an arm around the helpless Sophie, and gestured that the older girl should sit close beside them. She glanced back at Edmund in a way that she hoped was neither angry nor judgemental, and said, 'Take some water from the pitcher and wash out your mouth. Then bring the cakes and come sit with us.'

When the children had surrounded her on the couch, she cuddled Sophie until the crying stopped, and let Edmund pass the teacakes back and forth amongst them. 'Now, there. See? I am not such a great ogre, am I? And I am not about to be a ninny and run downstairs to trouble your father with schoolroom foolishness, if you will leave off tormenting me. I have three older brothers, who most enjoyed playing pranks on their little sister. I doubt there is a trick you will try on me that I have not already experienced. But now that I am grown I had hoped that I would not be bothered with ink in my tea cup and worms in my writing desk.'

'Worms?' Edmund asked, obviously fascinated.

She nodded. 'Great long ones from the garden. My older brother Thomas shut the poor things up with the sealing wax, meaning to surprise me.' She grinned at the memory. 'I dare say it was an even bigger surprise to him when he found them in his cucumber sandwich later in the afternoon. Half of them, actually. That quite put him off worms, and cucumber sandwiches as well. To this day, he lifts the bread before he eats.'

Both the girls laughed, and Edmund followed, after a brief indignant look.

'Now, you are afraid, are you, that your father means to send you away?'

They returned solemn nods.

'You know that it is almost time for Edmund to go away to school? Possibly even past time.'

'I will not leave my sisters,' he said, looking not so much at the older girl as he did at Sophie.

'Then it is in your best interest to keep your current governess happy, rather than frightening her away. If you have someone to monitor your education here, your leavetaking can be prolonged.'

'We do not like strangers,' Edmund said stubbornly.

'You have little choice in the matter,' she answered him. 'Someone must do the job. But a stranger is not the same as an enemy, unless you wish to make me one. It might go easier for all of us if you keep me as an ally. For I mean you no harm.'

There, that was vague enough.

'And even if you must go away to school, your sisters will be in good hands.'

Of which she had no proof at all. She felt a pang of guilt. There was no telling what chaos she might make of their little lives, if she succeeded in her plans.

The children seemed to consider, and there were sly looks passed one to another. At last Lily, as the oldest, spoke for the group. 'We wish, above all else, to remain here, just as we are.'

'And while I wish you to be well educated, I am also most concerned for your happiness. I doubt that an unhappy child makes a better pupil.'

'If you could explain to Father…'

'I hardly know him well enough to make demands, or even suggestions about your education. But in time, I will try to speak to your father on the subject. I cannot guarantee that you won't be sent to board elsewhere. That is often the way of things. But I will do my best to see that your wishes are considered, rather than just the conventions of society.'

The children seemed to relax a little at this. They were looking at her differently, as though seeing her for the first time. She offered them her hands, and said, 'Do we have a bargain?'

Little Sophie announced, 'It is a bargain, Miss Collins.' They were the most words that Daphne had heard from the girl since she had arrived. They came as rather a surprise, for Daphne had begun to suspect that the girl was mute. But the phrase was spoken loud and clear enough, as though she did not wish for her meaning to be mistaken.

The other two children looked equally surprised, but shrugged their shoulders and took Daphne's hands, shaking them in agreement.

'Very good. Then I think it is time that we went back to lessons. If you can help me with the maps, we shall spend the rest of the afternoon on geography.' For she suspected that she could not make nearly such a hash

of it as she might on languages or maths. Any fool with
a pointer and an atlas ought to be able to manage the
subject without embarrassing themselves.

She'd barely begun her lesson when the master of
the house entered the room, quietly, so as not to disturb
her pupils.

But of course he did. At the sight of him the children
lost all interest in what she was saying. They turned to
look back, smiles on their faces, although Sophie's was
hesitant. It was as though she enjoyed looking upon him,
but enjoyed even more that it was from a distance, as
one might like to view a tiger in a cage.

Daphne made to stop, for there was little point in
continuing the lesson with him standing at the back of
the room, arms folded across his chest.

'No, pray continue, Miss Collins. I am very interested
in the education of my children.'

Oh, dear. The last thing she needed was for him
to take an interest in her teaching, since she had little
interest in it herself. But she soldiered on through
the lesson, pointing out locations on the big map of the
world, and sharing what little she knew of them. The
minutes seemed to drag by. But, finally, she heard a hall
clock chiming the hour. It seemed as good a time as any
to release the children to their father.

The greetings went very much as they had done on
the previous day, with the older two speaking formally
to him, and Sophie hanging back, tangled in Daphne's
skirts.

'Go, now, and prepare for dinner. And remember to wash your hands and faces,' she called after

them, thinking she sounded very much like her own governess.

'Miss Collins.'

When she turned, her employer was still in the room, staring at her with a hard expression. And she became suddenly conscious of how alone they were. 'My lord?'

'I would like a word with you. In my study.' He turned and walked from the room, not waiting to see if she followed. It surprised her to see him turn right instead of left, eschewing the main staircase, to take the servants' stairs to the ground floor. But the door to his study was very near to the bottom of them, as was his conservatory. Perhaps that explained his choice.

Once in the hall, he opened the door to his study, and allowed her to precede him, shutting it tightly behind them. Then he turned upon her, and said, 'Explain yourself.' He gave no further clue as to what he might mean. But, if possible, his expression became even more forbidding.

She struggled to think what she might have done that he'd found objectionable. There were probably a hundred things. She was unable to settle upon any one that was worse than the others. Since she did not wish to give away any more than she had to, she said, 'In what sense?'

'You are no more a governess than I am. I wish you to explain what it is that you are doing, here in my house, caring for my children.'

'I do not understand, my lord.' She carefully wiped any trace of guilt from her face, and replaced it with a look that she hoped was suitably puzzled. 'Were my references not to your liking?'

'It matters little whether I liked your papers or no, since the decision to hire you was totally that of my neighbour. And I suspect, should I look closely at your letters of reference, I would find them to be in your own hand.'

'Sir!' This was too close to the truth, so she fell back on outrage as her only defence.

He paced the room, hands waving in agitation. 'I could forgive a small mistake made when teaching maths. For who among us does not, on occasion, transpose a number, or forget to carry a one? And a mistake in French or Latin could be passed off as colloquial, were I to be in a charitable frame of mind.'

He turned suddenly, and pointed at her. 'But do not tell me you are qualified as a teacher, if you cannot find our colonies on a map.'

'Whatever do you mean, my lord?'

He snatched a ruler from his desk and brought it down with a sharp crack against the surface of the globe on the table top. 'This, Miss Collins, if you wish to know, is the former colony known as New York. And the location to which you were pointing—' he brought the pointer down again, with another loud slap '—is Canada. Which is, if I am to believe *The Times*, still a colony of Britain. And this—' he slashed with the pointer '—is the border between the two.'

She leaned forwards, and peered at the map. 'So it is,' she said weakly.

'The principal export of the area is not tobacco, which needs a much more temperate climate to thrive.'

'Well, you should know, for you have a much more complete knowledge of horticulture than I.'

He glanced at the ruler, and for a moment she feared he meant to use it upon her in anger. But he threw it aside and turned to face her.

Without thinking she took a step back, and felt her shoulders bang squarely into the wall behind her.

He smiled, realising her fear, and took another step to close the distance between them. Then he said, so softly that she doubted anyone would hear, 'Can you explain the errors you have made?'

She could hardly blame her own governesses for her inattention when the subjects had been covered in lessons. And so she muttered, 'It is just that I become nervous when I am observed.'

'Oh, really. My presence unnerves you?' And he took a step closer, until there was very little space between them at all. 'Is it just me, I wonder? Or are you flustered by other men as well?'

'Not you at all, my lord. It is just that I am unaccustomed to such attention. While teaching.'

He laughed softly, and the hairs on the back of her neck rose as he whispered, 'You are lying again and not very skilfully.'

'I swear, I am not.' But her voice became breathy as she said it, with a tone that was all wrong for the earnest denial she should mount.

'I will agree that you are not accustomed to teaching. But, looking as you do, I find it hard to believe that you are unaccustomed to masculine attention.' He was making no effort to hide an interest that she suspected had little to do with her knowledge of geography. 'A simple governess would not dress the way you do.'

She glanced down at her gown, which was one of her own, a simple day dress of pale green muslin. 'There is nothing exceptionable or immodest about what I am wearing.'

'Other than it does not belong to a servant. Is it yours, or did you steal it, I wonder?'

Now that she was ensconced in the household, she'd felt it safe to put aside the simple frocks she'd borrowed from Miss Collins, and return to wearing her own clothes. But apparently she'd been wrong, for it had made him suspicious. 'It was a gift. From a previous mistress. A cast-off.'

'But brand new.' He reached out a finger to touch the fabric at her throat. 'But what is this you have stuffed into the front of it?'

She should slap the man for such impudence. But she suspected he was only trying to frighten her, and it would not do to let him succeed. So she muttered, 'Chemisette.'

He took a pinch of the cotton, and plucked at it, and she could feel the ties give way, as he drew the neckpiece out of the gown. She found the little ruffled blouse to be oppressive and unnecessary, and there was some part of her that rejoiced at its removal. As the air touched her skin she had a flash of memory from her forbidden walks in the dark paths of Vauxhall Gardens. The sense of anticipation, and the furtive rush of desire.

Colton saw the look in her eyes, and smiled. 'You prefer it this way, don't you? It is the way you normally wear it. With your throat bare and your bodice low, so that men may admire your breasts.'

He was staring at her, and she felt her nipples tighten in response.

He nodded as though aware of her reaction. 'The gown is yours, but the modesty is false.' He looked into her eyes again. 'Tell me, now. Why did you come to my house? Nothing about you is as it seems, Miss Collins. And if you do not give me the truth, you cannot blame me for assuming the worst about you.'

She snatched the fabric from his hand, crumpling the starched cloth in frustration. 'I came to help your children, since you seem unwilling or unable to do so.' It was not a complete truth, but neither was it a total lie. Then, she risked a threat of her own. 'And if you try to remove me from my post, I shall tell the Duchess. And she shall take action.'

He stood very close to her. Too close, for she could feel the heat of his body on the bare skin of her throat. His voice was hoarse when he answered, and barely above a whisper. 'Perhaps I shall not have to remove you. It will be better if you decide to remove yourself. For you must realise that it is dangerous for you to remain under this roof with me. Time will tell if you truly care so much for my children that you are willing to risk your honour to teach them.'

And, for a moment, she knew how Timothy Colton

had been able to escape justice. For when he stared at her with those bottomless dark eyes, his threats against her felt more like promises of illicit pleasure from a man who did not care for law or sin. The sort of man who would have what he wanted, and the whole world be damned. She put her hand to his chest and pushed him away, breaking the spell of his gaze. 'I care for your children, Lord Colton, and my honour as well. But I do not now, nor will I ever, care for you. Not for your title, your money or your designs upon me.'

And then she turned and fled the room, before he could see that she was lying, yet again.

As the door closed, Tim reached out to grab his desk for support. It was as though her sudden absence had left him physically weakened. He should not have even invited her into this room, where they were alone and the door was closed. And he certainly should not have touched her. He had meant to give her a stern warning, or dismiss her without one. For though the children seemed to have no complaints, what good was a teacher who knew less than her students?

But in the absence of prying eyes, his mind had filled with strange fantasies. He had wanted to see the skin of her throat, and the bared swell of her breasts above the gown. And the foolish girl had done nothing to stop him. She had trusted her virtue to his fragile self-control.

He wished he could write to Penny and explain the problem. If she would not permit him the care of his own children, then at least she could show mercy and remove Miss Collins from his house. Send him another woman who was less attractive, older, more timid. Someone who did not stare into his soul with her cat-like green eyes, as though daring him to kiss her.

He stared at the door that she'd slammed behind her and let his lust settle into a bone-deep longing. He was not thinking rationally if he'd consider, even for a moment, admitting to the Duchess that he was unable to master his reactions to Miss Collins.

But it did not matter how he felt. After what had happened with Clare, he did not deserve female company. Better to lock himself in the conservatory, far away from temptation and the new governess. For he'd come to believe that the two things were one and the same.

Chapter Six

⤜⤛⟊⟋⤜⤛

Daphne opened the window, desperate to catch the last breath of summer air. She could see by the falling leaves that the season was almost done with its change. After the interview of the previous day, she had decided to postpone searching the ground floor for a time. It would be best to stay away from Timothy Colton, until his interest waned. She had returned to wearing Miss Collins's cast-off clothes to forestall any further harassment. But the stiffness and starchiness of them felt unnatural against her skin, just as Miss Collins's job did on her mind. Why must they stay in the boring old schoolroom, when there was so little time left to play before winter came?

After the night's rain, the room was stuffy and damp in a way that the garden would not be, for the sun had dried the grass and was burning off the last mist in the valleys that she could see in the distance. She longed to take out her own sketch pad and draw it, just as Sophie would.

And then she smiled. She had had thoughts just such as that often enough when she was a child. And there was always a nurse or governess with a stern expression to lay those thoughts to rest and send her back to her books.

But for now, she was in charge of the classroom, and there was no reason things could not be different.

'Come, children. To the garden. It is too fine a day to be trapped inside.'

They seemed to hunker down in their desks, as though they expected her to pull them out into the sunshine, against their will. 'We should stay here,' Lily said firmly. They were looking at her as though she had failed yet another test, proving herself to be less a true schoolteacher. But what sort of children were they, that they preferred the schoolroom to the trees, on the last fine day of autumn?

Daphne smiled. 'We can take our books with us and manage just as well, sitting under a tree. You do have a garden, I am sure. For I saw it as I was entering the house.'

'It is very fine, although better in summer,' said Edmund, smiling as a point of pride. 'Father has an amazing selection. Rare plants from America. And the roses of course, in all colours. And the herbs, but everyone has those.'

'Not as we do,' said Lily, warming to the idea. 'There is an entire section of it, plants brought from China. Lilies, for me. And poppies. And a lotus in a pond with fish. And there is a little pagoda that Father had built, just for us to play in.'

Edmund grinned. 'Mother said it was a waste to have the only folly in the garden be expressly for us. But Father is of the opinion that such buildings are perfect for children, but quite nonsensical for adults.'

Lily lifted her chin proudly. 'He says that it is not necessary to improve upon the beauty of nature by sticking a building in front of it.'

'What your father said is quite true. If one has a sense of the arrangement for the plants themselves, then one hardly needs more than a bench on which to sit and enjoy them.' It stuck in her throat to agree with the man. But in this, at least, he was right. And if it helped to gain the co-operation of the children, then she would ally herself to the devil. 'You sound very proud of your father's work. And very knowledgeable. You must give me a tour of the grounds.'

'It is hardly proper schooling to be wandering in the garden.' Edmund had remembered his place, and was trying to sound as stern as any schoolmaster, and convince himself that fun could have no part in learning.

She smiled at him. 'Is that your opinion, Master Ed, or some philosopher's? I suspect that the sunshine of Greece was sufficient for Plato to teach.'

'Please?' The sound of little Sophie's voice surprised them all. 'May we go to the garden?'

They all turned to look at her, and she seemed to shrink for a moment, as though she realised that speaking above a whisper had called unwelcome attention to herself. And then she squared her little shoulders and spoke again. 'May we play?'

And there was such a look of desperate hope on her little face that Daphne knew it would be impossible for Edmund to object. 'There. See? Your little sister wishes it as well. There can be no harm in one day of sunshine, can there? You can show me the plants, and then you may sit under a tree, and learn philosophy as it was first taught, with plenty of fresh air. Come.' She opened the door, and gestured them out into the hall, then closed it behind them and headed for the main stairs.

She had managed to detach them from the room, but they lagged even further behind, once they realised the path she had chosen. 'We always take the back stairs,' said Lily.

'This is shorter.'

'But we always take the back.' Her voice managed to be both firm and shrill. Daphne turned and stared at the wide-eyed little girl. Was it fear of the accident site that made her balk, months later?

She turned to them, each in turn, and saw the same nervous expressions. It would not do to upset them. But did it do them a service to foster an irrational fear? She shook her head. 'Today, I think it better that we take the main stairs. Directly down, out the front doors and on to the path to the garden. Much shorter than going all round the house. You will be outside and playing in no time.'

She smiled to show them that it was all right. 'If you are afraid, then I shall go first.' Little Sophie was cowering behind her sister, as though the thought of it was equal to the worst terror of her young life.

So Daphne reached out a hand to her. 'Come. Sophie and I will show you. Sophie, you take the banister, and I will hold your other hand. My family assures me that I am as hard to move as a marble statue, once I get an idea into my head. You will be protected on both sides.'

The girl hesitated for a moment, while desire and fear warred within her. And then she stepped forwards, and wrapped her fingers around the banister until they were as white as the stone. With the other hand, she took Daphne's fingers in a death grip, and closed her eyes.

It made things tricky, if the child meant to take the stairs without looking. But who was she to argue? So she took a step forwards that almost lifted the little girl off her feet. The child's hand loosened on the rail enough to slide, and her little feet hurried to keep up with Daphne's.

She kept up a running commentary, to put the girl at her ease. 'See? Or you would, if your eyes were not closed. Not difficult at all. Only stairs, just like the ones at the back, but safer because they are not so narrow and steep. And you do not need a candle to light the way.'

And then they were in the hall, safe and sound. Sophie opened her eyes in wonder. She turned back to her brother and sister, and her smile was so radiant that for a moment Daphne felt like a true governess, one that might know nothing of Socrates, but still managed to teach a very important lesson.

The older children hurried the last few steps with a relieved sigh, and ran ahead to open the door in front of them. She smiled to them in encouragement. 'Go on. You can find the garden better than I. Race. As fast as you can go. Without dropping your books, of course.' She tried to be stern, with little success.

The children shot past her and out the door.

She turned to follow them. But the words 'Miss Collins!' echoed behind her, bringing her to a full stop.

She turned to see Lord Colton standing perfectly still in the hallway behind her. 'My lord?' The fact that he could approach without her noticing made his continual scrutiny most disturbing. She took a step away from him, fearing that he might try to re-enact the scene of the previous day.

But the weird, seductive light in his eyes was overwhelmed by anger, and his lips were bloodless white, until he spoke. 'If you are to spend any time in this house, you will learn that I value the safety of my children over all. I will not have them upset, or put at risk in an effort on your part to prove some foolish point.'

She bristled in return, her fear of him forgotten. 'I did nothing to jeopardise the safety of the children. We merely walked down a flight of stairs.'

'The stairs are dangerous,' he sputtered, obviously uncomfortable.

It gave her a strange feeling of power to see him out of countenance. 'And I say they are not. There is nothing about them that puts a person at risk. If one is careful, the chance of an accidental fall is so small as to be moot.' She glared at him, hoping that he could see her knowledge of the truth, and her contempt for him, plain in her eyes.

'If you think it matters what *you* think in this situation, then you have an imperfect understanding of your role here. I wish for the children to use the back stairs, as they seem perfectly content in doing.' He took a step closer, until he seemed to tower over her.

He was trying to bully her again, as he had done yesterday. And she would have none of it. 'You say you are interested in your children's welfare. And yet you wish for them to use the steep, unlit stairs at the back of the house.' She smiled at him for proving her point so well. 'Then perhaps their safety does not matter so much as you think.' And she swept past him, and out of the door.

The gardens were as magnificent as the children had promised, and it took only a short time for her surroundings to calm her, and blot out the unpleasant altercation in the entry hall. Most of the flowers were finished blooming. But when she wished to know how they had looked at the height of the season, she had merely to ask. Sophie would sit with her pastels, and produce hurried sketches that were riots of colour, yet impressively harmonious in their composition.

'In summer, it must be truly splendid,' Daphne breathed, for she could not help herself.

Edmund frowned. 'Do you really think so? Mother wished for a garden more like the ones she saw in London. She was most vexed.'

'Many designers prefer a more artificial landscape, and their clients are willing to pay a great price to obey them. Your mother was interested in fashion, and the appearance of wealth. She would have followed their example.' Daphne waved a hand. 'She would have no patience for subtleties like this.' And she stopped herself, wishing she could take back an opinion about the late Clarissa Colton that, while perfectly true, was quite unflattering. And it should have been quite beyond the knowledge of Miss Collins, governess and stranger to the family. 'Or so I assume,' she added, hoping the children did not notice her slip.

'She had no patience for us,' Edmund blurted.

'I'm sure that was not true,' Daphne corrected automatically. But in her heart, she recalled the Clare Colton she had known, and feared the children were right.

'It was true,' Lily said in a voice so small and sad that for a moment she sounded more like Sophie. She reached out and took Daphne by the hand, leading her to the China garden, to see the pagoda. But instead of going to the front so that she could stoop and enter with the children, Lily led her to the back. She pointed to scratches in the red enamel work. 'When Mother learned that this was to be built for us, but that Father had included nothing for her, there was a frightful row. He said she could do what she liked inside the house, and with the town house and grounds in London. But that the glasshouses, the conservatory and the grounds here in Wales were his, to do as he liked. And that was that.' Lily ran her finger over the scratches. 'So she found a spade.'

In Daphne's mind it was easy to imagine hot-tempered Clare swinging furiously at the little playhouse, taking her anger out upon it. And she wondered if that had been the worst of it, for Edmund's eyes had gone very round, looking at the scratches, as though seeing the same thing.

Without thinking about it, she reached out to both of them, gathering one child under each arm. She said, in a resolute voice, 'Your mother was very foolish to behave in such a way. And to take her anger out upon you or your things was very wrong indeed.'

Lily sighed. 'She would not have done it had it been for Sophie alone. She said we were Father's children, but Sophie was all hers.'

Daphne cursed Clare under her breath. She wanted to remember her cousin as blithe and beautiful. Why had it been so easy to forget that, on occasion, she could be shallow and cruel? To see the truth on the faces of the children was truly sobering.

She crouched beside them, as their father had done. 'Still more nonsense. You are every bit as charming as your little sister, and just as much a part of your mother.' She pulled them into a hug, and ruffled their bright red hair. 'And far too clever for the likes of me to be teaching, although you must have realised that by now.'

'But we won't tell,' whispered Lily, and Edmund gave a solemn shake of his head. 'We like you much better than our last governess.'

'And I like you, as well.' She smiled at them. 'And I will not think anything of it, if you want to take a short break from your studies to play in the fine pagoda that your father has made for you. Winter will be here soon. Enjoy the garden while you can.'

The two older children did not need a second offer.

With a last glance of relief, they took off after their little sister in a game of hide and seek amongst the flower beds.

Daphne smiled to herself. Perhaps she had some skill as a governess after all. For she had been right to bring the children here. Removing them from the house for an afternoon had certainly done Sophie good. Her sketches were proof of that. She was using all the colours, not just the black and red that she had used to render Clare, and drawing with lines that were smooth and flowing, not jagged and tense. It was good to know that she had happy memories as well, of blooming trees and flowers.

And the pictures were exceptional, not just in execution, but in the subject matter. The variety was amazing, with samples from all over the world. Despite his obvious faults, Lord Colton did seem to have an eye for the ordering of the plants. He had managed to lay colour against colour, just as a painter might, and blend textures of bark and leaf, until she felt she could spend hours here in fascination. Nor had he neglected education. The plants were neatly tagged with genus and habitat as proof that they would live in harmony in the places from which they had come. It was a feast for an artist and scientist alike.

And without intending it, she felt a fleeting admiration for the man that had orchestrated it. It was so peaceful here. Was it even possible for the creator of such beauty to give himself over to violence?

She glanced in the direction of the conservatory, for the garden wrapped around the wing that had the glasshouse. She suspected it was a magnificent view, even from within the house. From inside the conservatory one would be able to look out on to the terraced garden and have an illusion that there were no walls at all, but that one was suspended in a glass bubble in the middle of Eden.

Or perhaps a glass cage. For there, framed in one of the large arched windows, was the master of the house. His palms were pressed flat to the glass, body straining as though in confinement. He was smiling as he watched the children at play, but it was not a happy thing to see. Then he noticed her observation of him and stared for a moment into her eyes. All expression on his face faded. And he turned and disappeared into the foliage on his side of the barrier.

Chapter Seven

When the sun began to set it grew cooler, and it was clear that they would need to come in for their evening meal. Daphne shepherded the children back to the nursery. She saw to it that they were properly washed and dressed and had the cook send them their evening meal.

It made her smile to listen to their chattering, for the fresh air had put life into them. Even Sophie was talking, infrequently, but in an almost normal tone. But as quickly as it had come the energy seemed to fade, and she knew that it meant an early bedtime.

Which left her alone. Once the children had gone, it occurred to her that she had heard no more from the master of the house on the subject of her interference with the children. It was almost a pity, for she wished he could have seen the ease with which they climbed the main stairs on their return to the house. They scampered up the steps as though they were not there, just as children should. She had had to give them the perfectly ordinary caution to walk when inside the house. They'd laughed and slowed, but given no thought to the possibility of accident or the fate that had befallen their mother. It had been as if she'd broken down a wall, and set them free from one of the cells their father had trapped them in. Now that they had tasted freedom, she doubted that it would be an easy thing for him to banish them again to the back stairs.

She viewed it as a small victory against the tyrant. She marched up the stairs to her room, full of satisfaction. Of course, she had done nothing to find the truth, as yet. But to help Clare's children was to do some justice for the woman.

Although the stories that the children had told about their mother were almost as disturbing as the problems with their father. It was a shame to think that they had not been their mother's first consideration. But to be honest with herself, she had never thought of Clare as a mother of three. In all the time they had spent in shopping, riding in the park with Clare's many admirers and attending parties and balls, she had mentioned the children so seldom that Daphne had needed to consult with Miss Collins to verify their names and ages.

While she might care for them in memory of Clare, she could not shake the feeling that her cousin would have discouraged the interest as unnecessary. But she decided to put the feeling aside as she climbed the stairs to her room, and focus on the day's success instead of what Clare might or might not have intended. It did no good to think on it, for the state of her cousin's mind at the time of her death was a thing that could not be known.

She opened her door, and sensed a change almost immediately. Her room was filled with a spicy sweet scent of flowers. And there on the night stand was a crystal vase filled with red gilly flowers, baby's breath, lilies of the valley and a sprinkling of hyacinths. She could not help the smile on her face, for the bouquet was magnificent. There were so many cut flowers in the house. She had seen orchids and roses in bowls scattered about the main rooms as though they had no worth.

But these flowers were simple and unassuming, perfectly appropriate for the tiny servant's room she occupied. She stepped forwards and buried her face in them, letting the feeling of the afternoon garden come rushing back to her. Then she felt along the table, searching for a note of explanation.

And stopped. A note was hardly necessary, for there could be only one person who had arranged for the flowers. When she had asked about a particularly fine display in the hall, Mrs Sims had said that they'd come from one of the glasshouses in the grounds. And that everything in the house was cut and displayed at the recommendation of her master.

Timothy Colton was the only one who could have sent the flowers to her.

She looked again at the arrangement. The flowers were an unusual mix of seasons. They looked well together, but were not common companions. Perhaps he had a meaning in choosing so. There was a language of flowers, was there not? It would render a note unnecessary, if he'd spoken to her using the plants. And if the garden was any indication, he was as comfortable speaking through them as Sophie was in talking with pictures.

She gave a last, lingering sniff to the heart of them, and then retreated down the stairs to the library. For if any house might have a book to explain the meaning, she was sure that this one must.

He had made it easy for her. The needed volume lay open on the main table, ready for her consultation. She looked down at the page before her. Baby's breath meant sincerity. That was encouraging, for whatever he wished to say was truly felt. Lilies of the valley were humility, which was also good. And the hyacinths? She flipped hurriedly through the pages.

Hyacinths said 'forgive me'. She covered her hand with her mouth to hide the smile. It was a bouquet of apology for his behaviour towards her in the hall. He was displaying humility before a servant, but with no loss of face and without the need to admit aloud that he had been wrong. She could not decide whether to be insulted by the subterfuge or to admire the cleverness of it. If he wished, he could always deny that there was any meaning at all. It was not as if he had given her roses. There could be nothing more innocent than gilly flowers.

Which must have a meaning as well, she supposed. She flipped to the *G* page, and did not find what she was seeking, and so tried again under the other name, carnation, and found a whole list, with each colour having a different meaning.

And her finger stopped upon red. Admiration. He felt admiration, for her?

She returned to the hall, shutting the library door behind her. Apology. Humility. And sincere admiration. Why could it not have come from any other man in the world? From Simon, perhaps, whose loutish behaviour had got her banished from London. If his few moments of stolen passion had been accompanied by a floral apology, and some sign that it had meant anything at all to him to be alone with her? That he had done what he had done because he sincerely admired her?

A tear traced down her cheek, and she wiped it away. Her friends in London felt nothing but embarrassment in knowing her, as was demonstrated by their distance before her departure. No one had come to see her off. And she doubted, even now, that they had given much thought to her absence.

But Timothy Colton had known her only a short while, and they had spoken only a handful of times, most of them marred by threats and strange behaviour. And yet, she did not doubt for a moment the truth of the flowers, or think his feelings were less than he claimed.

She hurried back toward her room, but stopped on the stairs, gripping the handrail. She was giving him too much credit in this. And there had been a fleeting moment of pure pleasure, on discovering the meaning of the flowers, and knowing their source. Was it so easy to forget the reason for this visit? The man was a murderer.

But not cold-blooded, a tiny voice reminded her. What had happened must have been a crime of passion. She could see in his treatment of the children that he was not a man given to common displays of violence.

But that did not matter. He had killed Clare.

But Clare was the one in the house prone to childish tantrums and violent behaviour, if the children were to be believed.

If Tim had acted against her, perhaps she had given him good reason. Had she done something that he had seen as a threat to his children? Whatever the reason, he had been deeply wounded by his actions, as had the whole family. The children were desperately afraid of being separated from their father, no matter what he had done. And he longed to keep them close.

She had thought she could blunder into the house, denounce the man and leave with a light heart, knowing that justice had been done. But what would that do to the children? How would the truth help anyone?

She was trembling in confusion as she climbed the last stairs to her room. Anything she had done, anything she did and anything she might do—all paths would lead to more pain for this family. And knowing that Lord Colton had tender feelings for her made it all the more complicated.

She could forgive her body's reactions to him. He was a handsome man, virile and with an element of darkness that made him all the more attractive. It was no different from falling for a rake or a rogue. The knowledge of danger made the flirtation more exciting. But her time in London should have taught her better. She must not let her mind wander into sympathy for him or allow herself to be flattered by a bouquet. A few flowers would not wipe away the stain of murder.

And perhaps she was being foolish. Admiration could mean many things. Some of them were quite simple and not the least bit romantic. He might simply be acknowledging a job well done in the garden today—his admiration of the way she had dealt with the children's fears. He might have given her the flowers without another thought about her, or the foolish romantic meaning she might construe.

She came back to her room, and saw the bouquet again, a lone spot of beauty in the otherwise grim room.

Her room.

She sat on the bed, shocked by a rush of emotions. Suddenly, she was sure that no servant's hand had touched the vase. Tim had prepared the thing himself. And then he had climbed the last lonely flight of stairs and placed it there for her to find. He would feel no compunction about it. It was his house, after all. All the rooms were his.

But she knew it was more than that. The message was clear, and there was nothing innocent about it. He had entered her room without her knowledge or permission, and left flowers so that she might know what he had done. Whatever she might think he meant by admiration, it meant more than just common praise. The man who had killed her cousin desired her. Although the meaning of the bouquet was harmless, the delivery spoke of possession, and of a man who would not be swayed by barriers of propriety if he wanted her.

She remembered the darkness in his eyes, and the way it seemed to swallow her as she looked into them. When he came for her, would she be able to resist him? And would she want to try?

Tim dug his hands into the soil on the potting table, feeling the tension leave his body and peace flow in with the scent of earth. Why couldn't everything be as simple? Sun, soil and water. And plants were happy. But people?

He was never sure. He could not shake the feeling that his lovely new employee hated him. It was not as if he hadn't given her every reason to. He had not treated her well, for he had not meant for her to stay.

But this was something more. She had disliked him from the first meeting. It was as though she'd come into the house with the feelings. And yet she seemed unfazed by his behaviour. No matter how he tried to frighten her, she remained defiant in a way that the other governesses had not. He had forbidden her to take the course of action she had taken this afternoon, and she had ignored him as though his opinions did not matter.

He smiled grimly to himself. She had been right, of course. The children were doing well under her care. In the garden, they had looked better than they had in months. And the sight of them together had moved him, for a moment, to wonder what it might be like for them to have a mother, not a nurse.

He shook his head. He'd been thinking the same such nonsense when he'd cut and arranged the flowers. But it had been worse than that, when he'd taken them to her room. If he'd intended a simple 'thank you', he could have delivered it to the classroom. Or sent a maid with it.

But he had wanted to do the thing in secret. And he'd wanted to see where she slept.

He had never been to the tiny room under the eaves. It was little better than an attic, and not at all as he imagined the governess's room to be. But with Lily in the bedroom most convenient to the nursery, the governess had made do with second best.

The small space had been full of the scent of her. He could understand why the children might thrive under her care, for there was something else in the air, as well. A lively intelligence? A lack of care? A singleness of purpose that was the same he felt when at work? He had looked about her room and felt an overwhelming sense of peace.

But quick upon it came the feeling of desire. He remembered the fire in her eyes when she looked at him as she flouted his authority and dared him to respond. She'd had opportunity enough to tell him that he was behaving improperly, or at least to show fear in the face of his advance the previous day. But she had stood her ground as though willing to see how far his emotions might take them. Perhaps she secretly wanted his kiss as much as he wanted to kiss her. How easy it would be to lie down upon the bed to await her return!

Then he would strip her bare and crush the flowers against her skin to release their scent and to mark her with the meaning of his gift. He would make love to her with all the passion and turbulence he felt in his soul. And she would give him the peace that she had shared with the children. She would set him free.

He could imagine her, under him, neck arched to receive his kisses, legs spread to receive his body, unafraid to cry out in passion, alone at the top of the house where no one might hear what they were doing.

He had left the room, frightened by the image, hurrying down the stairs until he was back in the conservatory. Once there, he shut it tight against the outside world. There were reasons to fear discovery.

What he imagined was wrong. He wished to treat a young lady of good character, a servant under his protection, as though she were a mistress, wanton and experienced, and eager for his touch. It showed how far his own character had fallen. If he had come to believe that all women were no better than Clare had been, hungry and whorish, then in the end he would treat the next woman in his life in the same manner he had treated his wife, with loathing and contempt. And the relationship would come to the same bitter end.

Chapter Eight

The next day at breakfast the children greeted her as formally as ever they had. It was as if a curtain had dropped over the success of the previous afternoon, and it was all but forgotten. Daphne cursed herself for thinking their problems would be so easily solved. While the children might be better than they had been on her arrival, their behaviour was nowhere near the boisterousness that she might call normal. And it did not help that yesterday's sunshine had disappeared, replaced by fog.

After almost a week of her pathetic attempts at teaching, Edmund and Lily seemed to have contented themselves with being self-taught. They got out their books without argument, helping each other through any difficulties. Daphne arranged Sophie's usual table for drawing, and gave her pencil and charcoals, showing her how to smudge the coal to get lights and shadows, before wiping her hands and going to the sofa. Without thinking, she took her own sketchbook in her lap and made a rough drawing of a park, shrouded in mist. She added shadows, and phantoms hiding behind crooked trees. The grimness of the subject suited her current mood.

Perhaps this afternoon she could find the time to begin her search of the downstairs. Lord Colton had nothing of interest in his room. If there was anything out of order, it would be below, in the study, perhaps. Or the conservatory, where he spent so much time. But how was she to go into his sanctum without arising suspicion?

Perhaps she should thank him for the carnations. But it might mean being alone with him in the study again. And the man she had met, when last she was called there, was not at all like the one who had attempted to speak with flowers. It was most confusing.

Sophie tugged upon her skirt, trying to gain her attention, and held papers out to Daphne, with a half-smile and eyes eager for approval.

'You have finished already?' Daphne smiled back. 'Such a clever girl you are. Let us see what you have done.' She got up from her seat and walked across the room to Sophie's table.

Sophie held the drawings out before her, and Daphne remembered, too late, that she had not given the girl a theme. Sophie had drawn her parents in a way that shocked the viewer with their dissimilarity.

The one of her father was an accurate enough rendition, although the nose was a trifle too large. He was smiling, as she had often seen him do when greeting the children. He was in shirtsleeves, probably just come from the conservatory, for Sophie had even managed to capture a smudge of dirt on the white of his cuff. His arms were outstretched and welcoming, as though he meant to scoop the viewer into them and hold them close.

For a moment, Daphne forgot all trepidations and smiled back at the picture, just as Sophie was doing.

But the one of Clare left no such feeling of peace. She supposed it was some progress that the woman in the picture did not lie dead at the foot of the stairs. Instead, she was very much alive. She was wearing a gown that Daphne recognised from their time in London. She had admired it greatly. But it had never occurred to her how inappropriate it might be, if one were mothering small children. In the picture, Clare's red hair was piled high on her head, and jewels glittered at her neck and ears. Her hands were gloved, and seemed to hover at her skirts, as though she had been caught in the act of pulling them out of reach of mud on the street. Her lips were twisted in a cold smile that conveyed utter disdain. Sophie had captured her beauty, but also her unapproachability.

But there was something else about the picture, something unaccountably wrong. At first, Clare seemed out of scale with the picture of her husband. In the drawing, she seemed overtall, her features elongated in a way that accentuated the haughty brow. It was then Daphne realised that the perspective was not so much wrong as merely different. Although she could not see his legs in the picture, Tim must have been on his knees, for he was just as he would look to a five-year-old who was meeting him on eye level as he crouched to give a hug.

But Clare had towered over her small daughter. She made no effort to hide her height or to relate to the girl on her level. The angle of view had created strange shadows, making Clare's face not just aloof, but openly hostile.

The expression, coupled with the set of the hands, and the knowledge that it all came through the eyes of a child… It made Daphne suspect that Sophie had approached too close, with hands that were less than immaculate, and been sent packing for it.

She glanced again at Lord Colton's dirty shirt, rumpled hair and easy smile.

Sophie reached out to touch the picture, wistfully. The coal smudged her fingers, and she glanced at the drawing of her mother, as though she had been caught anew, and found wanting. She hurriedly wiped her hands upon her pinafore, then looked at the smudges she'd made, and gave Daphne a look of hopeless resignation.

Daphne laughed at the girl and reached into her pocket for a handkerchief, hurrying to set her at ease. 'Drawing is messy work, isn't it? But it cannot be helped.' She took Sophie's hands in hers, wiping. Then she bent low so she could look into the girl's face. 'Your drawings are very good. You have learned much since I've been here. I am very proud of you.'

Without warning, Sophie threw her arms around

Daphne's neck and almost pulled her off balance, giving her a hug and a rather wet kiss upon the cheek.

Daphne hugged her in return and then gave her a kiss on the top of her head. She was momentarily overcome by the sweet smell of little girl and the desire to be able to sit with her, holding her tight whenever she wanted.

She realised her mistake almost immediately, releasing the girl and taking an involuntary step back. It was wrong. She had never loved children, nor had she meant to change her feelings about them. She would be gone soon, back to her normal life. Some day, perhaps she would have her own. But these were not hers to hold. She was to care for them. Not about them. And she absolutely must not develop a sense of attachment. For who knew what would happen, if she succeeded in her plans?

Sophie sensed the rejection and stepped away herself with a look that said she realised she had been bad again, and was sorry.

And impulsively, Daphne threw her fears aside and pulled the girl back to hug her again. She would sort out the details later. But for now, things would be as they were, and all would be happy. 'Do not worry, Sophie. You only startled me for a moment. Thank you very much for the lovely hug. And do not worry about dirty handprints and smudged drawings. Accidents happen all the time. No one is to blame.'

The girl gave her the most amazed look, as though the concept of an accident was a foreign one. And then she gave Daphne another hug, this one guaranteed to leave a dirty handprint on Daphne's neck. Sophie stood back and waited for the response.

Daphne laughed. 'Now that was not an accident at all. That was deliberate, you silly girl. But it came with another very nice hug and it is not terribly difficult to wash my neck. I hardly think it merits punishment. Do you?'

Sophie stood, as though considering for a moment, and then gave a solemn nod, which, as Daphne watched it, turned slowly into a smile.

'Very good. Now go wash your hands in the basin, and we shan't have to worry about it.'

By afternoon, the fog had turned to rain. It made steady streams on the window panes, and the children dozed over their books. Daphne was dozing in her chair as well. Even Sophie, who normally had no trouble entertaining herself with paper and pen, was drawing listless spirals, but showing no interest in them.

Daphne glanced at the drowsy children. If there were some way to keep them occupied, while she investigated the conservatory… And if she could distract Lord Colton as well…

A thought occurred to her. If it worked, it would be almost too perfect. She shut her book with a snap and smiled at the children. 'Enough of this. You cannot learn anything if you are barely awake. Let us have an adventure.'

The children looked at her sceptically.

'We will go downstairs, into the conservatory, and ask your father what he is working on.'

'We cannot,' Lily said, without even thinking.

'Why?'

'He is working and does not need us interfering.'

Edmund added, 'We will track the dirt everywhere and spoil our clothes.'

'Urchins,' said Sophie, in a sharp tone that made the older children start guiltily as though hearing the voice of a parent.

'Has your father told you that?' Daphne asked, feeling a sudden wave of annoyance at the man. It was little wonder that his relationship with his children was in shambles.

'The door is closed,' said Edmund firmly, as though that answered all.

'I suspect it is to keep the plants from taking a chill,' Daphne answered reasonably. 'We will go and ask him, shall we? Bring your books. And your drawing things,' she added, looking at Sophie.

The girl hopped off her stool, eager to leave the schoolroom.

The other children followed with less enthusiasm as she led them down to the east wing of the ground floor.

Although it was still raining and she could hear the low splattering of water against the multitude of glass panes, light was streaming through the glass doors at the end of the hall. She threw them open, and shepherded the children inside, then waited for Lord Colton's response. She could but hope that the presence of his family would distract him from any of the tricks he tried when she met him alone. He would be too eager for their attention to pay Daphne any mind. And he would hardly expect her to acknowledge his gift of flowers while they were there.

At the sound of their entry, he looked up from his work with a quiet curiosity, and said, 'To what do I owe the honour of this visit?'

'The children are bored with regular classes, and I felt that they might learn much more readily while in communion with nature as they did yesterday, even if it is held captive in a glasshouse.'

He grinned. 'Capital idea. I know I often gain knowledge by keeping a healthy sense of exploration.'

The children blinked at him in surprise, as though it had never occurred to them to visit their father before.

Colton ducked his head slightly, embarrassed by his enthusiasm. Then he muttered, 'If you wish, you may help me with my planting. There are aprons enough, hanging by the basin.'

Lily started forwards, and passed too close to a pot, sending it teetering on edge and dumping the plant on to the marble table. When she rushed to set it up again, a flower broke off in her hand. The expression on her face was near tears, and Sophie took a hurried step behind Daphne, clinging to her skirts.

Daphne waited for the explosion she was sure must come. There had to be something to justify the children's fear. But instead, their father gave a small sigh, righted the pot and scooped the dirt back in, bedding the plant again and pressing the soil down upon its roots. Then he smiled, picked up the flower, and tucked it behind his daughter's ear. 'You needn't look so worried,

Lily. It is a living thing. It can make a new blossom, just as easily as you can grow a fingernail. Come, let me show you its sisters.' And he took her gently by the hand and led her to a rack of similar plants in various stages of bloom.

Sophie peeked out from behind her skirt, watching the progress of the other children through the conservatory.

'Would you like to follow too?' Daphne asked helpfully.

Sophie gave a small shake of her head.

'Very well, then.' She picked the girl up in her arms, and deposited her on a bench near the windows. 'Why don't you draw some of the plants? Choose whatever subject you like. But be sure to take note of the direction of the light. Later, after you have drawn the shape, perhaps I will let you experiment with water colours.'

Sophie gave her a delighted smile and opened her sketchbook.

Daphne resisted the urge to settle herself beside the girl and enjoy the warmth of the room and the steamy smell of earth mixed with green things. It was very different here than the rest of the house, which seemed to hold itself in cold formality, aloof from the cosy work space that had been fashioned here. She wandered through the rows of plants. There were flowers, both plain and exotic. She found common greenery more appropriate in a field and vegetable plants labelled with their planting and sprouting dates. At the end of each table was a log book, kept in a neat hand, that explained the purpose of the planting, the expected results and the progress of any experiments.

It was all as orderly as the bedroom had been and quite harmless. There was nothing that might further her investigations, no concealed mystery, no sign that the owner wished them gone. She wondered what the children had been so afraid of. The only secret was that it was by far the most welcoming room in the house. It must be a blessed relief to them after the weeks they'd spent in mourning above stairs.

The older children were working close beside their father, red heads bent over the table. He spoke of the various parts of a seed, then took a pocket knife, and carefully dissected the specimen they had been admiring, handing the children a magnifying lens so that they might see. They crowded him on either side and appeared to hang on every word. But Daphne wondered if it was not more than that. They were leaning close enough to touch him. In response, he laid his hands upon their shoulders, drawing them into a semblance of a hug. He seemed more relaxed than she had seen him and it surprised her. Here, he was an eager young scientist and not the brooding lord of the manor who was so critical of her teaching.

She watched him. Being close to him here did not threaten her peace, as he did in the rest of the house. Or, at least, he disturbed her in a different way. Outside the glass doors, she had found him handsome, the frown on his face accentuating the fine structure, calling attention to the brows, the chin and the width of his shoulders. When he'd accosted her in the hall she'd felt a dark frightening pull, as though she was not sure what he meant for her should she get too close.

But here he was gentleness itself. As he worked, she could admire his smile and the light of discovery in his eyes. The strength was still there. But she could see the careful, tender way he held the plants, and her gaze was drawn to his hands, long-fingered, supple and none too fastidious. She saw dirt under his nails and the stain of plants. It surprised her that she was imagining the touch of those hands, all languid relaxation and the heat of sunshine. And how easy it would be to give in to him here.

She shook her head in disgust. Her parents would be frustrated to know that this trip had done nothing to teach her temperance and moderation. In fact, she had grown even less resolute. While she should not imagine herself yielding to anyone, Timothy Colton should be the last man on earth to occupy a place in such fantasies.

Sophie tugged on her hand and held up a pencil sketch of a nearby fern, and she smiled in response. 'Oh, my. That is very good work, Sophie. Let us show your father.'

The girl looked alarmed and gave a small shake of her head.

She smiled in comfort. 'It is all right. He will like it, I am sure. Come. See.' She walked to the planting bench and said quietly, 'Lord Colton?'

He started, as though unused to his own name, and then smiled up at her, brushing the hair out of his eyes in a gesture that was very similar to his son's. 'What is it?'

'Sophie has drawn you a picture.' It was a slight exaggeration, but she doubted it mattered. She held the paper out to him.

'*Equisetum telmateia*, from the Latin for horse.' He reached out to an odd-looking plant and plucked one of the long, fernlike leaves. 'It looks very like a horse's tail. You have captured it well, my darling Sophie.' Then he turned the leaf to her, tickling her nose with the frond until she giggled. He handed her the leaf. 'May I trade you a horse's tail for a horse's tail? For I would very much like to keep your fine drawing here, to inspire me in my work.'

The little girl's eyes widened in surprise and her smile lit up her face. And then she reached up, very cautiously, and gave her father a hug.

He was completely unmanned. His eyes opened wide as well, and then he closed them tightly. And, for a moment, Daphne was convinced that she could see tears on his lashes as he reached out to wrap his arms around his daughter. 'You must come to visit me here often. If you have enjoyed yourself,' he added hurriedly. He opened his eyes. 'All of you. Come whenever you like. I would not interrupt your studies, of course. But there is much that can be learned from nature, if you are interested.'

'You want us here?' Lily sounded more sceptical than surprised, as though there was some kind of trap involved in the simple offer.

'I always have.'

'But Mother said…' and then the girl stopped.

Colton's face darkened for a moment, and then

smoothed to glasslike serenity, and he spoke to her as though she were an adult. 'Perhaps your mother was mistaken in my wishes. You have always been welcome to enter my work area. I assumed your lack of visits was due to a lack of interest on your part. Now we know better.'

Lily gave a hesitant nod.

'And now you must go and wash your hands before your dinner. Hurry along. I understand that Cook has something exceptional planned.' He hesitated for a moment, and then said, in an offhanded way, 'You could eat with me in the dining room if you wish. It would save Cook a trip to the nursery. And Miss Collins should dine with us as well. She might enjoy dressing for dinner on occasion.'

The girls' eyes lit up, and they murmured that they would find it most interesting to dine formally, as long as Miss Collins did not object.

She assured them that she did not. 'But it will require that you wash especially well. Let us go upstairs, and I will call a maid to help you.' But as Daphne went to shepherd the children out of the conservatory, Lord Colton called her back.

'Miss Collins, if I might speak with you for a moment.'

'Of course, my lord.'

'Shut the door behind you, please.'

She nodded. He was still using the mild voice, the one he had used with the children. It would be most ineffectual, if he meant to reprimand her using such a tone.

But the door had barely latched before he'd swooped down on her, scooped her up in his arms and carried her away from it, pulling her back into the conservatory until they were shielded from the glass doors to the hallway. And then, his hands were on her face, and his lips upon hers, in a sweet, laughing, relieved kiss. 'Thank you,' he breathed.

'What?' She could barely catch her breath for the contact was there and gone so quickly that she had hardly realised what was happening. But surely, it had not been her imagination? He had kissed her, for his arms were still about her body, holding her tenderly to him.

'Thank you for bringing them to me. For bringing them back to me. Thank you.' He smoothed her hair and kissed her again, this time upon the forehead.

'Bringing them back? But they were here all along.'

'You have seen how they behave with me, when we are in the schoolroom?' He pressed his face to hers, and kissed her cheek. 'It was not always thus. Since Clarissa…' a shudder ran through him '…they fear me.'

'I know.' It did no good to lie about it.

'I would do anything, if I could take it back. If there were a way to be close to them, as I once was. But I had given up hope of it.' He smiled down at her. 'And then you came, and brought them here. They would not have come for me.'

'You are being foolish. Surely…'

He placed a finger over her lips. 'I have tried. Everything I can think of. They are as secure in the nursery room as if they are in a fortress. Just as I feel safest when I am here. It upsets them when I come to visit them there, but it upset them even more when I insisted they dine with me, or spend time with me in the evenings, in the library or sitting room. We have grown so distant that we might as well be living in different houses. And yet they seem just as resistant to the idea of leaving for boarding school.' He frowned. 'Whether they love me or hate me, they cannot live for ever in that little room.'

'It will be all right,' she said, wondering if that were true. She doubted they could forgive the murder of their mother after just a few trips to the conservatory.

Murder, she reminded herself. That was why she was here, and this was a murderer, holding her close and pressing his lips to her skin. She should be repulsed by him, not attracted. She should be shuddering in revulsion at the touch of him. But instead she was trembling with emotions that she had not experienced before.

He was so gentle, with the plants, with the children, and sometimes even with her, that it was hard to keep a hold on the truth. For Timothy Colton was not what she had expected when she had come to this house. Perhaps she had been wrong all along, and the death truly had been an accidental fall.

'It will be all right.' He murmured her words back to her, as though to reassure her. 'When you say the words, Miss Collins, I almost believe it.' And then he laughed. 'Miss Collins, though you have been here for nearly a week, I do not even know your given name.'

'Daphne,' she whispered.

'Daphne,' he whispered back. 'A nymph fair enough to tempt Apollo. You are well named, then.'

'She became a laurel tree to escape him.' Daphne whispered the only piece of the legend she could remember.

He smiled. 'Then it is only natural that I should find you in my glasshouse.' And he kissed her again. He was exquisitely gentle, as though giving her credit for more innocence than she felt. He used the barest touches to part her lips, the lightest stroke of his tongue against hers and a featherlight touch of his hands on her waist.

She felt a stirring inside her. Perhaps it was passion. Or perhaps only a desire that he hold her this way for ever, kissing her with that same reverent intensity. Then she would not have to think about the past or the future. Only the moment. And the moment was incredibly sweet.

When he pulled away, he smiled. 'Did you appreciate the flowers?'

'Flowers?' Appreciate. And his choice of words triggered a blush.

He dropped his hands to his sides. 'Oh, dear. I thought, when you came here, that you had understood my message. And that the visit was related...' And now, he looked quite thoroughly embarrassed. 'Please forgive me, for my actions were incredibly forward, if you did not mean... And even if you did, I should not have...' His words trailed away, and he put his hand to his temple and closed his eyes as though he would wish himself out of the room.

She stared in amazement. The man in the study who threatened her honour had been naught but a paper tiger. The man before her now had given a few gentle kisses, and was embarrassed at his own forwardness.

She touched her fingers to her lips. Perhaps he was not all paper. For there was resolve behind the gentleness. When he chose to, he had proved himself to be quite commanding. 'I liked your flowers very much. But I had forgotten how a visit to the conservatory might appear to you.'

And now he looked horrified that he had kissed her and was preparing another apology. Was this the man she was convinced was a killer?

She gave him her best society smile, that had captured the attention of half the men in London, and got her into so much trouble that she was sent off to rusticate. She hoped, if used judiciously on a single gentleman, that it would not do any harm. 'But I am not overly bothered by your misunderstanding me.'

'That is good.' His smile was more of a grin and really quite charming. 'A great relief, actually. I was momentarily overcome with the progress you had made with the children. And your presence as well—' He stopped. 'And you do not mind if we all dine together, this evening?'

'I should think it the most natural thing in the world.'

'Very well, then. Until this evening.' He bowed to her with none of the stiffness he had shown on her arrival. She curtsied in response, and it came off as a rather playful bob, and nothing like what was appropriate for one's employer.

But she doubted that it would matter much longer.

Tim watched, through the glass doors, as she went down the hall and up the main stairs towards the nursery suite. The turn of events had been surprising, but most welcome. Clearly, the woman was an experienced governess in many things that mattered more than giving lessons and maintaining order. He had never been so glad to be mistaken in his life. He owed her more apologies than his simple bouquet had offered. There were not enough flowers in the house to convey his shame at the way he had treated her. And, in retrospect, the scene in the study had been beyond mortifying.

And a dark voice within him whispered, *'You no longer want her?'*

Of course he did. For she was most beautiful. He had not forgotten the lure of her flesh, nor ceased to imagine their joining. But there were other methods to achieve the ultimate goal than brute force. He could court her in a normal way, slowly and gently. She got on well with the children, which was very important. He could behave as a gentleman and make her a proper offer. If she found him worthy, then she might accept. And there would be no impediment to making the kind of marriage he had always wanted.

'No impediment, now you have got rid of Clarissa.'

He pushed his knuckles against his temples, as

though the pressure could silence the words ringing in his head.

'Are you going to tell her what kind of man you are, before the wedding? Or do you mean to surprise her some night when she has angered you?'

He could feel the cold sweat upon his forehead as he struggled with the memories of his first wife. He would never hurt Daphne. She was nothing like Clare.

'The woman is different, but you have not changed. If it could happen once...'

He shook his head, because he did not want to believe. He had always been so sure of his temper. Positive that intellect conquered impulse, and moderation was more powerful than violence. And then, everything had changed.

And now, he could not be sure of anything, ever again.

Chapter Nine

Dinner was a strained affair, and not at all what she had been expecting after the time in the conservatory. Daphne took care with her appearance, not wishing to seem too eager to please her employer. There was always a chance that she had misunderstood the depth of his interest, for he had the most mercurial nature of any man she had met.

But he had kissed her.

She closed her eyes, remembering the feel of his lips. They had not been the most passionate kisses she had received. But then, most girls her age had not been kissed at all. She should have no cause for comparison. After the sudden salute upon the lips, he had got control of himself and tried very hard to give her a near-perfect first kiss. He was hardly to blame if someone else had got there before him.

She put on a gown of sea-green silk that was beautiful but demure, and prepared herself for an evening of shy looks down the table. And remembering that she was still the governess, she made sure the children were scrubbed and ready before leading them in procession down the stairs and into the dining room.

The room was beautiful. The food was perfect. And the children excited, but polite and on their best behaviour.

It was only the host who was wrong. He had taken the time to dress to perfection in a coat of black superfine, a waistcoat of deep blue brocade and a shirt so white as to be blinding in comparison. Although she was no expert, she could see that his cravat was a masterpiece. His valet must have left the floor strewn with spoiled linen before getting it right.

But the man in the suit was as different as his clothes. He was not the hot-tempered Lord Colton that she had met upon arrival, nor the warm Timothy Colton of the afternoon. This man was as cool towards her as a stranger might have been. He would not meet her eyes, seeming to be most concerned with the children and their happiness.

He treated Daphne as though she were the governess. Invisible. Just as she had wanted from the first. The fact might have been laughable had it not been so frustratingly unexpected.

The children felt the change as well, and grew more quiet and reserved as the meal went on. Her host threw aside his napkin in frustration long before the dessert course and retired, claiming illness. She and the children finished the meal in silence and returned to the nursery to prepare for bed.

It was a disaster that undid much of the progress of the last few days. Daphne frowned. Perhaps it was all too much, too soon. It had left the children overwhelmed. But she was hard pressed not to lay the failure at the feet of the one responsible: Lord Timothy Colton. It had been his sudden foul mood that had spoiled everything. The children decided to take the next day's meals back in the nursery, and returned to their usual study habits. There was very little she could do about it.

She attempted to beard the lion in his den, going down to the conservatory without the children to demand an explanation. But she found only the occasional gardener, or under-gardener, tending to the plants at the instruction of his lordship. The man in question was by turns riding, resting, walking the grounds or missing. He was avoiding both her and the children.

Had something happened to change him profoundly, between four in the afternoon and six in the evening?

She doubted it. The thing that had changed them all had happened months ago, on the night that Clare had died. Unless she managed to exorcise the malevolence, there was little chance of lasting happiness for any of them. So she returned to her original intention of solving the mystery. There were still rooms unsearched, and questions unanswered.

After lunch on the next day, she made sure the children were settled and took herself to the ground floor.

It was there that Mrs Sims found her, one hand upon a desk drawer knob in the library.

'Was there something you needed, Miss Collins?' The woman seemed surprised to find her there.

Daphne struggled a moment for a plausible answer, moving her hand out from beneath the desk. 'I'd come to see if there was another pot of ink that I might borrow, to write some letters. The one in the schoolroom is thinner than I normally use. But while I am here, there is something that you might help with. It is almost embarrassing to ask, after all this time.'

'There is no need to be embarrassed, Miss Collins. I will help, if I can.'

Daphne gave her a relieved smile. 'It is a small thing, really. I have spent so much time above stairs with the children that I am barely acquainted with the common rooms. A stranger who had stopped to see the grounds would know more about the house than I do.'

Mrs Sims smiled in return, to find the request so small. 'You would like a tour of the house.'

'If you are not too busy. The children are so good with their studies, and so obedient. They do not need me for several hours at least.'

Mrs Sims was obviously surprised at their transformed character. But then she said, 'You have done much to help them. They are good children by nature, just as their father was.' And she launched into a story of how things used to be, when the children haunted the library they were standing in, rather than hiding above.

They moved from library, to drawing room, to

morning room, and in each Mrs Sims seemed to have a story about the master or the children and how things used to be. Daphne observed carefully, but had to admit that there was little to see. The rooms were orderly. Nothing about them made her suspect that she would find secrets in the drawers, concealed panels or any other gothic nonsense.

The only thing absent from Mrs Sims's narrative was mention of the previous mistress. Apparently, the decoration of the rooms had been done by Lord Colton's mother, classically but simply. In her twelve years Clare had left it unchanged. Daphne remembered the Colton town house, which she had visited frequently. It had been in the first stare of fashion, and Clare always seemed to be changing the silk on the walls, the rugs or the furniture, to reflect any passing trend or fancy.

Of course, in all the visits Daphne had not met Lord Colton, or heard anything but unflattering commentary about him, his house and Wales in general. None of those things was as important to Clare as the fact that she be seen in the best places, with the best people, dressed in the height of fashion.

Mrs Sims was walking Daphne back towards the nursery, and they passed the bedroom that she was sure must have belonged to Clare. She could imagine what she would see there. It would be decorated as the town house had been, totally out of step with the stately pace of the rest of the house, to suit the changing taste of the occupant. But there was no good way to request a tour of it.

She glanced at the waist of the housekeeper, walking

just ahead of her. The ring of keys hanging there probably contained the solution to her problem. And as if it was a sign from heaven, the knot holding them in place appeared to be loose.

The temptation was too much to resist. 'Mrs Sims?'

The woman stopped and turned back to her with a questioning look.

Daphne pointed to a large oil on the wall. 'I have been walking past this portrait, every morning, and wondering who it might be. Did Lord Colton have a brother?'

Mrs Sims launched into another, rather animated description of the subject, Tim's father, who had been plain Mr Colton, living here until his death. It had been the death of a distant cousin that had brought the title...

Daphne stood just behind the woman, as though admiring the portrait over her shoulder. She gave the slightest tug on the ribbon that held the keyring. She could feel the keys beneath her fingers begin to slip. And with a move worthy of a London cutpurse, she collected them in her hand without so much as a jingle, and drew them slowly away, stuffing them into her own pocket.

The housekeeper was so involved in her story that she did not feel the change. Daphne kept up the pretence of interested questions before admitting that it was time for her to return to the children, but thanking Mrs Sims most sincerely for her wealth of information.

She stayed long enough with the children to be sure

that she was not needed, and then checked the hall again. The old servant had returned below stairs, and the way was clear for her to visit her cousin's room. She looked both ways, up and down the hall, before proceeding quietly to the room at the end. What explanation should she give, if she was seen entering? She could think of nothing. Perhaps something concerning the children. Although what they would want from their late mother's room, she had no idea.

She tested the door again, and found it still locked. Then she removed the purloined keys from the folds of her dress. She fitted them quickly into the lock, one at a time, until she came to the one that turned the mechanism. Opening the door, she slipped inside and closed it silently behind her.

The room was dark, for the curtains had been drawn to keep the sun from damaging the furnishings. But there were no holland covers over them, and no layer of dust. It was all neatly kept with the bed smooth and well made, as though the mistress would be returning shortly. It was an attractive room as well, with pale green silk on the wall to match the hangings on the bed.

Daphne swallowed a wave of sadness. They matched the light in Clare's green eyes as well. She could imagine her cousin choosing the colours that would show her beauty to best advantage, sitting at the dressing table as a maid fixed ribbons in her beautiful red hair.

And then she remembered the disturbing pictures that Sophie drew and shuddered involuntarily. Clare would never sit at this table again. And however horrible she might have been to the people closest to her, she had been kind to Daphne. The death of one so full of energy resonated deeply with her, as though she had lost a part of her own life.

She glanced quickly around the room as her eyes adjusted to the dim light coming from the cracks in the curtains. Then she hurried to the wardrobe, and flung open the doors to see the gowns neatly arranged, and in the bright colours that Clare had loved so well. Each drawer she opened was the same: an intimate glance into the life of her cousin, and a reminder of how suddenly and unexpectedly it had ended.

The jewel box was still sitting on the dresser. She found it odd. Tim should have taken the thing and locked it away to avoid tempting the servants. But no, when she popped the lid the necklaces, rings and ear drops lay forgotten in sparkling perfection on the velvet.

And beneath them was a small bundle of letters, tied with a ribbon.

She untied it quickly and drew the first out, stepping closer to the window to read.

My darling Clarissa,
I know I must not see you. Even writing is wrong. But how can I bear this torture? I long for a taste of your lips, the perfection of your breasts in my hands, the feel of your body when you yield to me and your cries of passion in my ears…

Oh, dear Lord.
Her hands trembled as she read the letters, and then her body, for they were more shocking than anything

she had read or seen before. On reading them, there was no doubt what had been occurring. It was all described in detail for her. As she read, the room grew hot and her clothes constricting, as though her body was licked with the flames of someone else's passion.

Each letter, in the same masculine hand.

And each one signed, Adam.

Was Adam the Duke of Bellston's given name? It had to be, for it proved so much. The reason for the estrangement between the houses. The reason for Lord Colton's jealousy. And for Clare's untimely death. It had been wrong of Clare, so horribly foolish, to openly betray her husband. But wrong of the Duke as well to betray a friend.

Perhaps, if there had been love between the two, she could understand. She read on, searching the pages for some sign that the relationship had been more than what it appeared. But he said nothing of love, just the torment of a man nearly demented with desire, and graphic descriptions of their adulterous coupling.

Seeing the words felt…wrong. She knew they were not meant for her eyes. But still, she was driven by curiosity. If there was a truth to be revealed in the letters, she would not find it by shying away from them.

Or perhaps her desire to read was merely voyeurism. It made her feel strange inside. Hot and trembling, and eager. As she read them, she could not help but imagine bare flesh and twining bodies, and to remember the feel of the stolen kisses in Vauxhall Gardens and Simon's stealthy hands playing at the bodice of her dress. What would it be like to drive a man so mad with desire that he would have reason to write her such letters? And to be so lost to decency that she would save them, and pore over them, reliving each illicit moment?

And although she knew the words were not his, her mind turned to Timothy Colton. The dark look in his eyes when he saw her. The deep, smoky sound of his laugh. His hands and lips, as they might feel upon her body if he threw restraint aside.

She took a deep breath and dragged her eyes from the letters, refolded the papers, then thrust them deep into the pocket of her skirts. The contents showed her nothing she needed, other than the name at the bottom, which was the only thing of use. She could not very well show them to the Duchess. But perhaps, if the Duke knew what she had discovered, he would be willing to treat the matter of Clare's death more seriously.

She turned to the writing desk, and pulled open the little drawer to find stationery and more letters. Things from her and from the family. And some things in Clare's hand. Notes to herself, and letters begun and then forgotten. And thrust deep into the stack, with the ink smeared, as though it had been hidden while in progress.

My darling,
My marriage has grown intolerable, and my husband near to violence. Things cannot continue as they are. I fear for my safety. I mean to come to you, with the child which I know to be yours. If you cannot give me your love, at least offer me sanctuary...

This was even more serious than what had gone before. Had she truly been with child, or was it merely a ruse to gain the Duke's attention?

And if it was true…

An angry husband. And a lover, powerful, but recently married, who would have no desire to see his reputation sullied by a woman who would not quietly disappear once he was through with her. How easy would it have been to stand by and let her husband remove the problem, and then hide the truth from gratitude?

Or worse yet, to wait until an opportunity presented itself, and then remove the problem himself. To allow suspicion to fall on the man who had been wronged. Would it be better to let him hang for his wife's death, or would guilt prevent the murderer from going so far? Just as easy to spare the life of his old friend, but allow him to remain under the cloud of suspicion. For with Timothy Colton alive, no one would ever suspect…

'What the devil…?'

Light flooded the room, catching her, and she thrust the last letter into her pocket with the others. When she turned, the interruption had come not from the hall, but from a connecting door that lead to Tim Colton's room.

He was striding towards her, face contorted with fury. 'You. I was a fool to have trusted you, to be swayed by recent events. I knew there was something wrong and chose to ignore it.' He saw her withdrawing her hand from the fold of her skirts. 'Here, thief, what did you just put in your pocket?'

She reached in quickly and grasped the ring of keys that she had taken, holding them out to him.

He caught her by the wrist. 'And what did you mean to do with those?'

'I found them,' she lied. 'On the rug in the hallway. And I meant to return them.'

'But the owner is not in this room, as you well know.' He caught her by the wrist and squeezed until the key-ring dropped upon the rug. 'You had to see, didn't you? To come to this room, of all the rooms in the house.'

'The door was locked,' she said, knowing that it did not justify her behaviour.

'Because I wished it so. But you have had no respect for my wishes in the past, so why should it matter to you now?'

'It is only a room, just as the stairs are only stairs.'

'And they both hurt, do you understand? It hurts to be constantly reminded of her, and of what happened. To come across things, perfectly ordinary things, that dredge the memories to the surface. It hurts the children. And it hurts *me*.' And for a moment, it was as if she could see inside him, and the torment roiled there like black smoke, always just below the surface.

'And now that you have seen, are you satisfied? I did not keep my wife in chains, if that was what you thought. I was not hiding some dungeon behind a locked door. It is just a lady's bedroom. She had everything.' He threw open the door to the wardrobe, and swept the dresses on to the floor. 'Silk, satin, feathers and bows.' And then he turned, knocking the jewel case on to the floor to join the dresses, emeralds and pearls scattering across the carpet. 'And more jewels than a woman could wear in a lifetime. She treated it all as dross, and me as well.'

Then he turned back to her, and closed the distance between them.

She stepped backwards to get away, until the wide green bed blocked her retreat.

He grabbed her by the shoulders and pushed her back until she fell on her back into the softness of the satin counterpane. And he stood over her and laughed. 'You have found the thing she liked best about this room, although if you truly wish to know Clare, you must understand that she was never satisfied to lie alone.' He reached up and tugged at his cravat until the knot came free, then cast the thing aside. 'And now, perhaps it is time for you to take a lesson, instead of giving them.' And he fell upon her.

Her mind was swirling with a confusion of thoughts. It would be bad to be caught in this room by a murderer. But even worse if she had provoked an innocent man past the point of reason. She might have pushed a peaceful man to violence by her own actions. If she cried out now, no one would see him for what he had been, only for what he had become.

She could not do that to him, for she could not bear to think her foolish meddling would be the cause of more suffering.

His lips came down upon hers, and she opened her own to let him do as he wished. He used the opportunity to take her mouth, thrusting into it, his hand reaching to twist in her hair and force her to greater intimacy.

It was totally unlike the kiss in the conservatory had been, burning through her resistance, leaving her weak and helpless, and happy to be so.

When she did not fight him, he slowed to a gentle rhythm, exploring her, teasing, trying to provoke a response as his fingers crept into her hair, loosening pins until it fell free.

The bed was seductively soft, and he was spreading her hair upon it, combing with his fingers as though readying her for sleep. And when he released her lips, a sigh escaped them, as though she wished him to continue.

He felt her tremble under him, and whispered, 'Are you afraid? For you should be. Do you know what will happen to you if I do not stop?'

And Lord help her, she did. Every touch, every thrust, every feeling it might arouse had been laid out in the letters as though they were a primer for the act that was about to occur.

He leaned away from her, staring down as if in challenge, his smile just as cold as it had ever been, but the light in his eyes was blazing like a flame. 'Perhaps your silence is permission to continue.' He slid his hand from her hair, slowly down her throat, over her shoulder, to the swell of her breast, and stopped very deliberately, cupping the flesh in his palm.

She felt a surprising wash of warmth at the intimacy, and her body tingled to life. He must have seen the response in her eyes, for he gave a small, satisfied nod. 'What is it that you really wanted in coming to this room? Not what you are likely to get. Whatever it was, you are welcome to take it, after I am through with you. It means nothing to me.' And then he began to move his hands over her, squeezing, stroking, working with his fingertips, until she was sure he must feel the nipples, which had grown hard and sensitive under the fabric of her gown. His lips settled into the hollow of her throat, teeth and tongue against the soft flesh there, and her body gave a sudden shudder, as she began to wonder what it might be like to feel his mouth wetting the fabric of her dress, or against the bare skin. And without thinking, she brought a hand up to touch the back of his head, holding him against her. The satin of the counterpane was smooth and cool against her cheek, just as his lips were hard and hot. Her head was filling with visions of what had occurred here, and what was likely to occur, and, instead of fear, she felt a trembling eagerness. She heard the voice in her head that had always urged her on, when a sensible girl would have run for safety.

Then he found her lips again, thrusting with his tongue into her open mouth as his hands reached for her hips to clutch her to the growing hardness of his body.

Almost without thinking she rubbed against him, and let the desire stab through her, wild and uncontrollable. She kissed him back then, as roughly as he was kissing her. She bit at his lips, stroked his tongue with her own and dug her fingers into the linen of his shirt, feeling the muscles underneath bunching as they strained to pull her closer. He straddled her, pinning her to the bed. Inside her skirts, her legs had parted, ready to receive him, and he steadied her hips, holding them against his erection so that he could enjoy the way that she rocked against him.

Desire was growing in her and her body grew wet as she arched against him. But the strange friction of bodies in clothes was not enough. She wanted more from him, all of him. He could take what he wanted, whatever he wanted, as long as he ended the torment of expectation.

His hand slipped into the slit in her skirt that gave access to her pocket, and she gave a shuddering gasp, knowing that his hand was even closer to her body, bringing her closer to the relief that she knew was coming.

But then, there was a crackle of parchment, and his fingers closed on the bundle of letters and drew them out. He leaned away from her and unfolded the first, taking only a glance at it before he jumped off the bed away from her, as though contact burned him. He stared down at her in horror. 'This is what they sent you for? Could they not have just asked? Do they think so little of me that we must play games over this? Will it never end? God help me, haven't I suffered enough?' He stared down at the pages in his hand and shook his head, then he stared back at her with eyes empty of emotion. 'You needn't have bothered. Now that I have them, I will deal with the things, then I will return to deal with you.'

Then he turned and stalked from the room.

Chapter Ten

For a moment Daphne fought the urge to run after him, to seize the letters from his hand and destroy them before he read them. For no matter what he had done, did he deserve to see their contents and to know the truth in such detail?

He spoke of suffering. And suddenly, she was acutely aware of how he must have felt to know that his friend and wife were together, doing what they had done.

And if her latest suspicions were correct, and it was the Duke who was guilty of Clare's death?

Without knowing it, she had fallen in league with the very people she sought to punish. She was helping her cousin's murderer escape justice. And by raking up the past, she was torturing an innocent man.

She could not imagine the Duchess perpetrating a fraud to protect her husband. The woman seemed decent and acting out of care for the children. But without having met the Duke, it was hard to know the truth about him. He might be a veritable demon, with a wife as innocent of this crime as Clare's husband had been.

Daphne stood up, still trembling from the rise and fall of the tide of emotions within her. And looked into the mirror on the dresser, to straighten her hair and clothing.

Clare's mirror.

At one time, it might have given her girlish pleasure to visit the room of her cousin, to see the gowns she had worn, the jewellery box she had spoken of, and to try some of the things on while looking into this same mirror.

But she had seen too much of Clare today. The truth had spoiled the fantasy she'd carried with her all these months. Timothy Colton was right. Clarissa had been vain and spoilt. Her husband was not the homely dullard she had claimed. After meeting him, she found it easier to believe the housekeeper. That whatever had happened on that fateful night, he had once been an ordinary man, pushed beyond his boundaries by his wife's scandalous behaviour.

But if that was true, than what did it say of Clare's influence on her?

She closed her eyes and tried to remember how it had been, before her cousin had taken a special interest in her coming out. Her parents had been more co-operative, certainly. They had all but doted on her, and called her the sweetest of daughters. She had been the apple of her father's eye, and a delight to her brothers, no matter how they had teased her.

But then her mother had decided that she needed to cast off her hoydenish ways and learn to behave like a proper lady of the *ton*. And she had encouraged the association with Clare, saying that it would give Daphne polish. The family had welcomed the money that Clare offered to outfit her for the Season. For with three brothers to establish, there was very little left when it came time to launch their only daughter. And Daphne had relished the connection for the freedoms it brought.

But after that point, her parents seemed for ever cross with her. They did not like the fact that Clare allowed her to drink champagne, nor that she always seemed to take it in excess, talking too loudly and behaving foolishly. They did not approve of the hours she kept, nor the company, nor the gowns that Clare helped her to choose.

And now she understood why her forays into Vauxhall Gardens after Clare's death had been the last straw. She had been becoming every bit as bad as they said, and had been too wilful to see the truth.

Daphne put down the brush she had borrowed and hurried out the door, closing and locking it behind her. Then she walked down the hall, trying to keep her pace unhurried, although the calm felt unnatural to her. At any moment, Lord Colton could appear and reveal all. Ahead of her in the hall, the housekeeper was looking carefully at the ground, probably retracing her steps through the afternoon. 'Mrs Sims. At last.' She put on a triumphant smile, and held the ring of keys out to the woman, who responded with an even more relieved expression. 'I found them on the floor near the school-room, after you had gone.'

'And I have been looking all over for them. Thank you, miss, for returning them to me. I would hate for the master to find out how careless I had been.'

Daphne managed a stiff nod and insisted that it was hardly a matter of concern. She suspected, if anyone in the household had reason to fear the master's reaction to the stolen keys, the blame would not rest on the poor housekeeper.

Tim paced nervously across the rug in the Bellston receiving room, then sat and tapped his foot. The gallop to his neighbour's house had cooled his desire to deal immediately with the false governess. But it had done nothing to settle his nerves, or to prepare him for the confrontation with Adam. After all this time Tim did not know whether to be angry for what had happened, or hurt by it.

He might be willing to let the evidence of infidelity pass, as he had meant to before Clare had died. What was done could not be undone. But that Adam should use such devious methods to gain the letters was a fresh injury, perhaps more hurtful than the initial betrayal. Tim would have given up the letters freely, if the Duke had wished for them back. Even with the estrangement between them, theft should not have been necessary.

And to involve the children by placing a spy in the nursery? He shook his head in disgust. Adam knew how important the children were to him, and how fragile.

That he would toy with them to achieve what he could have got with honesty made Tim's skin crawl with revulsion.

And shame as well, that the Duke and Duchess should know his reaction to the girl. She must have been reporting to her masters how easily she had ensnared him. Despite the truths he had learned today, he still felt an undercurrent of desire for her. It defied all logic. A sane man should not be wishing to lie back down with her and finish what he had started, even knowing that it was all a sham.

From the doorway there came a nervous throat clearing that he recognised as a habit of his oldest friend. Tim turned to it and rose, offering a formal bow, and muttering, 'Your Grace.'

Adam strode into the room and answered, 'Leave off with that nonsense, Tim, and tell me what has brought you here.' He offered a hand, which Tim chose to ignore, and then said, 'I suppose it was too much to hope that this was a social visit after all this time.'

'I think you know what it is about.'

'In truth, I do not.' And his friend did look honestly puzzled. 'It is not that you are not welcome, of course. Sit, please.' Adam's gestures were as nervous as his own, as he moved to a chair by the fire. 'Brandy. No. It is too early of course. Tea? Can I—'

'I do not mean to stay for long. I came to give you these, since you seem to wish their return.' He reached into his coat and withdrew the packet, thrusting it at Adam.

The Duke took the letters from him, his puzzlement

still in evidence. And he opened them. It was clear that it took only a word or two for him to recognise his own writing, for his pale skin blanched to deathly white, and his grasp loosened, as he let the letters slip to the floor. 'Oh, dear God. I had forgotten.'

'Had you, now?' Tim folded his arms in scepticism.

'If I'd remembered…if I'd even thought the things still existed…' He held out his hands in a gesture of hopelessness. 'I'd have looked for them after she died, when I was in the house. But it did not seem important at the time.' His eyes dropped from Tim's and he stooped to gather the papers. Then he threw them into the fire, seizing a poker and jabbing at the things as though he feared that they would leap out of the flames to torment him further. When he was satisfied that they were destroyed, he looked to Tim again. 'I am sorry that I ever wrote the damn things. I was a hundred kinds of fool back then.' He stared down at the poker in his hand, his knuckles going white against the metal, and then he threw it against the flagstones of the hearth.

'If you wanted them back, you had but to ask.' Tim said it softly, surprised that he could not find more fault with the man, for he knew well what fools men made of themselves once Clare had tangled them in her net.

'Want them?' Adam laughed. 'I had hoped, now that she was gone, that it was well and truly over. And I need never think of that time again. And now, this…' He looked to Tim again. 'I am sorry.'

'The governess found them.'

'Governess? You have retained a governess?' Once

again, his friend seemed without a clue, and his befuddlement almost made Tim smile. Either he was blameless, or a much better actor then he had been when he'd bedded Clare. It had been easy enough to see the truth then, no matter how Adam tried to hide it.

'Your wife hired her for me.'

Adam looked alarmed by the idea. 'She acted without my knowledge or permission. After our last talk on the day of the funeral, you made it clear that you did not want or need my assistance.' Adam looked ever so slightly hurt by the memory. That argument had been the last coffin nail in their friendship. 'I told Penny to leave you in peace. But my wife refused to believe that your edict applied to her.' He gave a kind of helpless shrug, as though to say that his wife was a law unto herself. 'I have no problem with her visiting you, of course.'

'You do not?' Tim shot him another sceptical smile. For when Adam had first married, he had been surprisingly possessive of his new bride.

'Because I know I have nothing to fear. I would trust Penny with my life. And if she is welcome in your house, than she may visit with my blessing.' He frowned. 'But if she comes to meddle in your affairs, I will try to discourage her from troubling you.'

Since it was doubtful that Penny could be discouraged, once she set her mind to a thing, Tim only smiled. 'She seems to think that I cannot manage without help. And she has told me I must take it, whether I want it or no.'

'Well, Penny would think that. She is quite preoccupied with the idea of children, now that her book is finished. Since she has none of her own, she is most interested in yours. If she is not increasing soon, I suspect that she will come to your house and teach them herself.' And Adam smiled fondly at the thought.

'So you do not think that there was any hidden motive in her sending Miss Collins to search for these?'

'Penny have a hidden motive?' And now his friend did laugh. 'My darling wife is not one to hide her feelings in subtlety and guile. Perhaps my life would be quieter, were it so. Although not as interesting, I am sure. No, Tim. If Penny had wished to see the damn things, she would have marched to your house and demanded you give them to her. Then she would have brought them back to lay at my feet, and given me no end of grief for my foolishness.'

'She knew of the letters?'

'I told her of their existence, before your wife died. Clare was threatening me with them. I thought it would be better for Penny to know the whole truth than to be surprised by it later. And then I swore that there would be no more nonsense of that sort, and that she would have no reason to doubt me. And I have been true to my word.' There was a pride in his voice, and a peace that had been absent in the days when Clare had been alive. 'If it is any consolation to you, Tim, I am a better man, now that I have Penny. If there were a way to turn back the clock, and live the past over again, it would be different between us.'

Tim sighed. 'To my eyes, it would have been much the same. Perhaps the identity of her lover would have been different, but Clare would not have changed. And I would now be sitting in another friend's drawing room, with letters very similar to the ones you destroyed.'

Adam touched his hand to his forehead, as though pained. 'You are probably right. She would have found some way to torment you. Only her death prevented her from making more trouble than she already had.' And he looked Tim square in the eye, as if to say what they were both thinking.

Do not punish yourself. We are all glad to see her gone.

Tim swallowed the shame of it. For there was comfort in remembering that, hell though his life might be, it was better without Clarissa than it had been with her. The children were better off without her. And his friend looked happier as well. Marriage had settled Adam, changing him for the better. But would he have fared as well, had Clarissa been there, attempting to insinuate herself into the union?

Adam cleared his throat again. 'About the letters. I was an idiot. I freely admit it. I cared about them only to the extent that their existence hurt those around me. If there had been any way to spare you this trip?' He shrugged. 'But I did not send a girl to your house to hunt after them, if that is what you feared. I'd like to think that, had I wanted them, I could have come to you, called upon our old friendship and asked for them openly.'

Tim felt something loosen in his chest, and a modicum of relief. 'And I'd have given them to you, of course.'

Adam seemed to relax as well. 'And now they are

gone. Neither of us need worry about the past, for it shall not be repeated, nor mentioned again.' Adam paused, and then glanced away, as though his next words meant nothing. 'I don't suppose, while you are here, that you would be interested in a game of chess? It is rather early in the day for games. And if you are busy…'

Tim replied a little stiffly, 'I had thought, after what happened to my wife, and the accompanying scandal, that you would not wish to entertain me in your home. You are the law in these parts. And I am…' He hesitated to say the word aloud.

'An old friend,' finished the Duke. 'A very old friend. Who would have been invited back into my home sooner, had I thought you would come. But now that you are here…'

Tim hesitated. There was still the damn governess to be dealt with. For if Adam had not sent her, then who?

But let the girl suffer, waiting for his arrival. Perhaps if he tarried here, she would have the good sense to run and he might never need to see her again. His reactions to her were too volatile to be predicted or encouraged. And he was tired of being passion's fool. So he shrugged to his old friend, as nonchalant as Adam had been. 'A game of chess would not go amiss. The plants will grow, even if I am not there to watch them.'

Adam grinned back at him. 'I would never know it, the way you shut yourself up in that glasshouse. Come to the study, then. The board is set, and I have nothing so pressing that I cannot set it aside for a game.'

* * *

Tim's smile faded as he walked into the entrance hall of his home. It had been a surprisingly pleasant afternoon, probably because he had got away from the past. Afternoon had turned to evening and dinner with Adam and his wife. It had grown late, and he'd been forced to ride home in darkness. It was good that he knew the old paths as well as he did, for once the sun set, there was little light from the sliver of a moon, and the growing bank of rain clouds that threatened to obscure it.

For a few hours, he'd felt almost like his old self. Then his cheerful mood had begun to fade. For he was home. There, in front of him, were the damn stairs. And, as always, the ghostly image appeared in his mind of Clare broken on the floor before him.

He turned deliberately from it, refusing to be put out of his own home by an unpleasant memory. Perhaps he did not deserve to be happy, as he once had been. But there was little he could do about it. It was foolish to start and stare at nothing, like a coward, or, worse yet, a madman, whenever he crossed his own hall.

He disguised his hesitation in care for his outer wear, tossing the coat and hat over a nearby bench so that a servant could collect it in the morning. He took a moment to brush at his clothes as he steeled his nerves. Then he turned back to the main staircase and felt his will falter as the weight on his spirit increased. The servants' stairs were just down the hall, ready and waiting for him.

But he looked up to see the governess, waiting in total stillness at the top of the stairs. She was dressed for bed, barefoot on the marble. His arrival had surprised her. She must have thought if she did not move he would not notice her.

He smiled, and remembered his discovery of her in the afternoon. *Too late for that, my dear. From now on, I will watch your every move.* She might pretend that she had the best interests of the children at heart, but what purpose did she have to search bedrooms and creep about the house when all were in bed? If Adam had not sent her, nor Penny, then who? It made no sense to think that without motive or direction, she would go unerringly to the source of so many problems and secrete it about her person.

His anger conquered his fear, and he started up the stairs, focusing on her eyes as he climbed. The truth was hidden in them, if he could manage to dislodge it. She'd lacked the sense to flee the house this afternoon, when he'd given her the chance. And now she would answer to him for what she had done.

As he stared at her, he was pleased to see her fidget. Did it bother her to be a thief and a spy? He certainly hoped so. The crime was not so grave as some. If it was only against him, he would have turned her out without a thought.

But to deceive his children, and to allow them to trust her and to become fond of her? It was an act that could not be so easily forgiven.

So he intensified his gaze upon her, and added a cold smile. He could see the hairs out of place from their tussle on the bed, and the slightly swollen look of her mouth from the kisses he had given her. She had not fought him then, had she? Probably too embarrassed by his discovery of her snooping, and wishing she could distract him from the truth. And she very nearly had.

Or, perhaps it was more than that. He could see her eyes grow large and dark at his approach, and hear a slight hitch in her breath. Was she frightened, or was that desire he saw, when he looked into those deep green eyes? And then she bit her lip in an unconscious gesture of indecision. He felt his body respond to the naïve sensuality of it. It had to be a ruse. She must know how easily she could control him and was testing the strength of her attraction.

It was to be a battle, then, to see who could uncover the truth about the other. And at what cost.

'Miss Collins,' he said, and watched her start. 'I have returned to continue our conversation. But perhaps the top of the stairs is not the best place, for you know how treacherous stairs can be.'

Chapter Eleven

Daphne felt her chest tighten with fear. Of all the places to meet him, why must it be the dark heart of the house, on the very spot where Clare had fallen? And if he was as innocent of that as she suspected, then why did he climb the stairs like a guilty man? She reached out and put her hand on the banister to steady herself.

He looked at it and laughed, stepping dangerously close to her and placing his own hand over hers. 'Frightened?'

She stared back into his eyes, wondering what had happened to the gentle man from the conservatory. 'Should I be?'

'An innocent governess would have no reason to be afraid. But then I doubt that an innocent would be sneaking around the house in her nightclothes.'

'I got up to check on the children.' That was true. For

she had felt a storm in the air, and been restless enough to come downstairs to make sure they slept well.

'The nursery is far down the hall. What reason did you have to be on the main stairs?'

The children had brought her down from her room. But the knowledge that the lord of the house had not returned from his errand was enough to keep her there. She swallowed and said nothing. But as she looked into the face of the man next to her, she suspected he knew the truth.

He sneered. 'If you wish to search my room, it is just behind you, right next to Clare's.'

'I have already done so. Since you were not in the house, I meant to go downstairs to search your study.'

He laughed, as though admiring her impudence. 'You are caught in the very act of disturbing my peace. And you show no remorse at all. Who set you upon me, and how much are they paying you? If it is money you want, I will pay you twice as much to pack your things and go.'

'There is no one else. No conspiracy to trap you.' She stared at him, searching for the man inside. 'Only me.'

'Only you.' The thought seemed to amuse him, as though he had found himself worrying at a shadow. He wrapped his fingers around her wrist, gently, as if to show her that on a moment's notice he could yank security away from her, leaving her helpless at the top of the stairs. 'Then what do you want from me? And what are you willing to do to get it? For I grow tired with you snooping through the corners of my life.'

'I want the truth. I want to know what really happened, the night your wife died.'

'Is that all?' He laughed as though she had said something funny, released her wrist and reached for a handkerchief to wipe away the tears of mirth forming in the corners of his eyes. 'And you go to such elaborate ends to gain the truth. You come into my home. Insinuate yourself into my family. Sneak from room to room, poking through our things. If you wanted the truth, you need only have asked.'

'And you would have given it to me?' Now it was her turn to smile in scepticism.

'I don't think you understand what a burden the truth can be, or the price you must pay to gain it. If you knew, you would not seek. And when you know it, I doubt you will find satisfaction.'

'But I want to know, all the same. And I will not stop until I have discovered it.'

'You want to know,' he mocked. 'Very well. Your search is over. I will tell you everything.'

A thrill went through her. For a moment, she thought she had bested him. And then she saw the look in his eyes.

'I will tell you, later. In your room. After we are finished. The time is long past when I'd have given you the truth without something in return for the trouble you have caused here.'

He was staring at her with a hungry smile that delved into her, grasping and stroking. He was waiting for her to cry off. Expecting her fear to be greater than her curiosity.

But her heart was hammering in her chest, for so many reasons. She was on the edge of a great truth, and he held the key to it all. And what was common sense, in the face of it? She should be insulted by his suggestion, just as he wished her to be. She should tell her father and her brothers. They would call the man out for it. Or run to the safety of the housekeeper, and leave on the first mail coach in the morning. She could let all know that Lord Timothy Colton was as horrible as he wished people to believe.

Or she could remain silent, tell no one and let him have what he wanted. She would finally know the answer to the question that had been haunting her for months: what had really happened to her cousin? And, more importantly, she would learn who the real Timothy Colton was and what his part had been.

When their lips met, she knew that she already belonged to him, no matter what might happen. If there was a chance that she could bring him back to being the man who had kissed her in the conservatory, then she wanted to try.

'Very well,' she said softly.

And for a moment, she saw the look in his eyes falter. Perhaps it had all been a bluff to frighten her. At his heart, he did not want her. Not in this way. But then his doubt was replaced by suspicion, and desire overcame all. 'Now is as good a time as any. Lead me there.'

'You know the way. You have been there before, have you not?'

The gleam in his eye faltered again. It was as if she had struck a wolf upon the nose, and for a moment, turned him into a dog. She turned her back to him, before she could see the wolf return, and walked ahead of him, down the landing to the servants' stairs. It was dark, and she had left her candle on a table in the hall. She did not bother to light another, feeling her way up the stairs, towards the door at the top.

She could hear his footsteps on the stairs behind her and felt the dread in her growing. Suppose she was wrong and he was the brute she had once thought. She would be giving him the chance to abuse her, as he had Clare, to use her for his own amusement. It might all be a trick, and she would be no wiser for it than before. She knew that she should turn and confront him. Tell him that she had changed her mind. If she did it before they reached the door at the top, would he retreat or simply force her backwards into her room? She suspected it was the former. For after coming to know him, she could not believe that he was as wicked as he liked to pretend.

But if she did nothing?

Once they were in the room and the door was closed it would be too late to cry off, should she find that she could not follow through with what she had promised. And yet she kept walking, listening to the steady pace of his steps behind her, glad that he could not see her tremble. When they reached the room she entered, leaving the door open behind her. She turned to face him, but could see nothing in the utter darkness of her room.

'I should not be here.' It was easier without the sight of his haunted, angry eyes. For his voice told her he was as frightened by what was happening as she was. 'Why do you not send me away?'

When she did not answer him she heard him take a sudden step forwards, and she caught her breath in a gasp.

'Do you mean to scream, then? Perhaps it will bring the servants, and I will stop. Or you could run from me and from this house, as I have asked you to do before now. It is not too late to run.' His voice was low and inviting, as he reached out and tugged at the belt that held her wrapper, pushing it open and off her shoulders, letting it fall to the floor. 'But then, you will never know the truth.'

It was wrong of him to stay, but she did not want to send him away. Now that he was so close to her, she could not seem to find her voice to say anything at all. She could smell the spicy sweetness of the flowers he had given her, still scenting the air.

But he brought his head inches from her body, inhaling deeply so that she could feel his breath changing the air against her throat. It was as though he wished for nothing more than the scent of her. And then he whispered, 'You will not speak? Very well, then. But, if you do not stop me, I will not stop myself.'

Where she should have felt fear, she felt an odd excitement. And instead of pushing him away, she arched her neck and leaned closer to offer herself to him, until his lips touched her skin.

His hand snaked around her neck and he lifted his face to hers, forcing her mouth open to accept his kiss. There was none of the tenderness from the conservatory, or even the cool lust she'd felt from him in Clarissa's bedroom, as he'd awakened desire in her.

There was just a relentless thrusting with his tongue, to prove his possession over her mouth and the rest of her. He kissed her until her body felt weak and helpless in his arms, wet and hot and as open as her mouth.

His hand dropped to the neck of her gown, and in one smooth move he ripped the thing from throat to hem, then pulled it away from her to leave her standing bare in front of him in the darkness. And then he paused. 'Scream, damn you. Don't you realise what is happening? Make me stop this.' She heard him cast the rag to the floor as he seized one of her breasts, kneading it hard. His fingers caught the nipple, rolling and pinching, and the arousal coursed like a stream through her entire body.

She realised in shock that she had reached up with her own hand to copy his movements in her other breast, to magnify the feeling. Instead of a scream, she let out a low moan of pleasure.

His hand dropped away and he was breathing heavily, as though he had just run a great distance. Then he let out a low curse and stepped away.

For a moment, she heard nothing. Then, there was the sound of her door closing, the rustle of clothing dropped on the floor and the thump of boots. She was blind in the darkness, straining to hear his approach. But there was nothing. She was alone in the dark, cold and frightened of what might occur next.

Suddenly, his mouth closed over the slope of her shoulder. She felt his teeth graze the skin and the pressure as he sucked. Then it was over and he disappeared again. The sensations raced through her body, even after the contact stopped. She reached for him, longing to bring him back to her. But her hands met empty air.

He must have been able to see better in the dark than she, for he caught her hand in his and his lips touched her fingers, his tongue flicking the tips. And then he was gone again.

Only to return and run a fingernail down her spine, from nape to hip. It made her arch her back and thrust out her breasts until they met his outstretched hands.

He was playing a game with her. She did not know the rules or the object, or who might lose from it, but it must be a game. Or torture, she realised, as his hands disappeared and his lips touched the underside of her breast. This time she cried out in frustration when the kiss ended, and it made him laugh.

She was beginning to make out vague shapes in the darkness, and could see him standing before her. So she reached out and guided his head so that his mouth covered her nipple, forcing him to settle there for a time and suckle until the trembling began in her again. Then he pulled away.

She reached out again, and he stepped away from her, and murmured, 'Close your eyes.'

She did, and was shocked again at the increased intensity of the feeling, as his fingers brushed against the place where his lips had been. Then he disappeared again. She opened her eyes, searching for him, only to feel him behind her, pulling her body tight to his, the hair of his chest cushioning her shoulder blades, his sex pressing against her, his hands travelling easily over her body. His touch was stronger now, as he cupped her breasts and stroked her belly.

It was not fair. She could not touch him in return, and she found she needed to most desperately, to kiss and stroke as well. But he wrapped an arm around her shoulders and pinned her against his body as he made free with her, letting his other hand settle between her legs.

She started back at first, for this was even more exciting than his lips on her breast. He was exploring her, fingers touching, tracing, tickling and constantly returning to the place where he knew she was most sensitive. In response, she ground herself against the hardness behind her as though her body longed to pleasure him. It made his hand press even harder against her, rubbing against her until she could barely stand it. And then his fingers thrust into her, and it was more than she had ever felt, and yet still not enough. She was grinding against him now in uncontrollable ecstasy, her body wet and trembling, and could hear herself begging him, a desperate litany of, 'Oh, please, please, please…'

Perhaps he sought to stop her pleading, for he brought a hand to cover her lips, and she seized upon it, kissing the palm. She drew the fingers between her lips, running her tongue over them, and sucking them deep into her mouth.

And then, everything happened at once. He muttered an oath in a feverish voice that was as helpless as hers, then pushed her forwards, bending her over the footboard of her bed. Her weight rested on the hand between her legs, which was spreading the entrance to her body, readying her, guiding himself. And when he felt her shudder under his hand, he plunged into her, over and over, holding her steady, urging her on, until her will broke under his and her body lost the last shred of control. She shook and spasmed; every nerve in her body seemed to explode with the feeling of him taking her. And the trembling, grasping feeling went on, and on, until she felt it in him as well. After a final surge, his movements slowed, and he pulled her upright, his arm locked around her shoulder, and his face buried against the damp hair on her neck. He was kissing her there, pressing his lips to the flesh, sighing in satisfaction.

And she sagged against him, adoring the feel of his arms around her, warm and strong. Holding her up, holding her close, his body still in hers, possessing and possessed. He was rubbing his cheek gently against her skin, as though he revelled in the softness of it.

But then he sighed again. It was no longer satisfaction, but despair. And the friction of his cheek on her body was his head shaking no, no, no, as though it was possible to ward off what he knew was coming.

She remembered their bargain, wishing that it was possible to call it back. But it was too late.

He whispered in her ear. 'You wanted the truth. Well, you have certainly earned it, my dear. You have beaten me at my own game. Very well played.'

She started away from him, trying to escape the gentle caresses, and arms that had become a prison.

But he held her close, and whispered, in the same soft

voice. 'What happened the night my wife died is just what you suspect. After years of it, I could no longer stand her taunts and her public infidelities. And so I got stinking drunk and pushed the filthy whore down the stairs.'

Then his arms dropped to his sides and he pulled away from her. And the cold and emptiness of the house seemed to rush into her, filling her with the unbearable burden of the truth.

Chapter Twelve

Tim threw on his shirt, gathered the rest of his clothing into his arms and turned to make his escape. His descent down the first flight of stairs went easy enough. But with each passing step he could feel his legs begin to give way, his stomach churning. By the time he reached the ground floor he was running, down the hall, into the conservatory, slamming the door behind him.

He dropped the bundle on to the slate floor and rushed through the room to the tiny door at the back. He threw it open, dropped to his bare knees in the garden, and proceeded to be sick behind a shrubbery.

The storm had broken while he was in the attic room. He steadied himself on his hands, letting the rain run off his hair and soak his linen, feeling the mud on his knees and between his fingers.

That had not gone well.

It would have been laughable had it not been so

utterly pathetic on the surface and so horrible at the centre. What kind of man was he, if his first experience with a woman since his wife's death had reduced him to this?

But there was so much more than that involved. He had known that coupling with some willing female was not out of the question for him, if it was discreetly done and there was no real emotion involved. But he had thought to travel down to London and avail himself of the *demi-monde*, when the need grew great enough. Instead, he had all but forced himself upon a servant. He might try to persuade himself that she had gone willingly to her fate. But at its heart, that was a lie. He had tricked her into it. He'd offered a temptation too great to resist, in exchange for her virtue. And once they were alone, he had toyed with her until she begged him to do what he had done, so that he might not feel guilt for it later.

He shook the water from his hair and hung his head again, letting the coolness wash over him, wishing it would cool his blood so that he did not wish to do the thing again. She had been smooth and tight and wonderful, twisting and pushing against him, eager to be had.

Even now he was thinking of all the ways he wished to take her: the places, the positions, the frequency. One time, and she had made him a slave to sensation, with the boundless desires and energy of youth. Before, he thought he had wanted her beyond sanity. Beyond reason. And now it seemed he wanted her even more than that.

And she had given him no sign that she would deny

him. As he'd finished, he'd heard her soft sigh of pleasure and felt the way her hand reached back to absently
stroke his flank in thanks. He had done the unthinkable.
But she was not afraid. She was not hurt, or angry,
or shocked, or revolted. She was welcoming, her head
lolling upon his shoulder, her body still close to his as
though she felt protected. And without wishing it, he
was aroused again.

And so he had sought to wipe it all away, to drive her
from him before he treated her as he had treated the last
woman he'd dared to care about. Knowing what would
happen, he had pushed his lips to her ear, and told her
what she claimed she wished to hear.

His stomach heaved again, and he was sick. He lifted
a hand from the dirt to wipe his mouth, realised that with
the mud upon it, it was likely to make things worse. So
he used the back of his wet sleeve. He tipped his head
up to catch the rain in his mouth, washed it clean and
then spat.

Now that his conscience was as empty as his gut,
he wondered if he should feel better. And surprisingly
enough, he did. He had said out loud the thing everyone
knew, but which no one was willing to say.

Perhaps she would run from the house, as she should
have before now. Or call the magistrate. Bring the Duke
and Duchess, and force them to deal with him as he
should be dealt with. At least Daphne deserved justice
for the way he had treated her. If she had wanted the
truth so deeply, he could but hope that she had a plan
to use it, once it was known.

Perhaps it was cowardly to wish her to free him of

the responsibility of ending his own life in atonement of the crime. But he was exhausted by the whole thing, so tired of living with guilt that he had become afraid to take the next step and die. Right now, she was lying in her bed, outraged at his treatment of her, shocked by his confession, angered by his departure. She could take her revenge, and it would be over.

But he remembered the gentle touch of her hands upon his body. And thought of what it would be like if things were different. Just as he had, when he had been with her—he imagined twining her fingers with his, bringing them to his lips and then leading her back to lie on her cold, hard bed. They could begin again, more slowly, learning each other's bodies, secure in the knowledge that this was just the first of many such nights.

He shut his eyes tight against the vision. It was happiness. And after what he had done, he had not earned it. Either she would denounce him in the morning, or he would send her away. But he could not keep that which he did not deserve. And he dared not risk that she might become in his care: another broken body at the foot of the stairs, victim to his drunken rage.

Daphne woke the next morning, trembling with cold, although the room was no different than it had been before. But she was different. Conscious of her body, and the air upon it. Aware of her nakedness, and her submission at the hands of her cousin's murderer.

No.

She tried to reconcile the man she had come to know

with the man she had expected and the pieces would not fit together. He'd had opportunities from the first moment to harm her. Yet he'd waited until she had given him leave to come to her room. He had begged her to stop him.

And she had not. For she'd wanted it as much as he had. When he was through, she was sure that she had not had enough. There should be more. They should hold each other in the dark room, clinging body against body until dawn broke. And when he had begun to whisper in her ear, she was expecting endearment or assurance.

Instead, he had poured out those poisonous words, like a flood to drown her passion. And she was sure that was what he had meant to do. He wanted to hurt quickly, before she had a chance to hurt him, as his wife had done. For despite what he might think, she was convinced that he was no more a murderer than she was. She was no closer to the truth than she had been on the previous day, but it was all the more urgent that she find it. While Clare might deserve justice, it was far more important that she save the living: Tim Colton and his children. They were suffering under the misunderstanding far more than she had been.

She went to the basin to refresh herself, washing carefully in preparation for the day. And she remembered his hands upon her body, the way he had coaxed her until she was mad with desire. The pleasure came upon her again, in a sudden rush that made her grab the night table for support, until the feeling had passed. But her own touch was not enough. She wanted him there to fill her, and his lips upon hers as he did it.

She glanced at her face in the mirror. Her cheeks had a healthy glow, and there was a knowing look in her eyes that had not been there on the previous day.

She put on her dress and did up her hair, hoping that the truth was not too obvious to all around her. Tim would know what it meant, of course. He might think that he could avoid what had happened. But he would have to face it, each time he looked into her eyes.

She went down the stairs to her breakfast tray in the nursery dining room, and prepared for the day with the children. She left them to work at their own projects just as she had done in the past, and found that her eyes were drawn to the window. She stared out into the garden, imagining it as it might be in spring, took up her sketchbook and drew it as she imagined. Full of life. Full of joy.

If she could find a way to end the troubles, she might be there to see it. In spring there would be flowers, she was sure. And she wondered what type were meant to express what she was feeling. There must be something quite splendid to represent the previous night.

A footman came to the door, and announced that the master wished to see her in his study. She felt a sudden flutter of alarm. Whatever was to happen between them, it was to happen now. She made sure that the children had sufficient work to occupy them and made her way to the ground floor.

He sat at the desk, barely looking up when she entered the room. There was nothing about his demeanour to say that anything unusual had happened between them, and she wondered if it was only some strange dream on her part. But then she realised that he was playing the part of the unaffected employer, just as he had done at dinner after he had first kissed her. His feelings for her frightened him. And now he would try to push her away.

He reached into the desk drawer in front of him, and removed a bag that chinked. 'As you know, Miss Collins, it was never my plan to have a governess for the children. And much as I have tried to abide by the wishes of the Duchess, my opinion on the matter has not changed. Whatever your reason for coming here, the job seems to have become something much more akin to an investigation. But now that you have discovered what you wished, I doubt you will want to remain. There is nothing further to uncover. Your services will no longer be required. I will arrange for whatever references you might need, of course. And I am willing to pay a year's salary, in addition to what the Duchess has offered you, since the inconvenience of coming here was great.'

'Inconvenience?' she said, numbly.

'Two years, then,' he said.

'You call what happened last night an inconvenience, do you?' She tried to keep the shrill tone out of her voice. Carrying on like a courtesan would not help the matter.

He flinched. 'This has nothing to do with last night.'

'Liar! You cannot even look me in the eye to say that.'

With great effort, he raised his head and met her gaze. It gave her some small satisfaction to see the guilt and shame in his eyes. If he meant to buy her off, at least he was not unaffected by it. 'I am not lying. This has less to do with what happened last night, and everything to do with what will happen in the future. If you do not go, what happened between us will most assuredly happen again.' There was defiance in his gaze as well, now. 'I wanted you. I want you still. If you stay, I will continue to take. And when I am through, it will not end well. It is far better that I send you away now, than after you have formed some false attachment to me. For it will lead nowhere.'

She laughed, her best drawing-room set-down. 'You are trying to protect my feelings, since it is too late to protect my honour. Spare yourself, my lord. I have few romantic illusions about the sort of man that turns to his servants to gratify his lust.'

Anger flashed in his eyes, and she remembered too late that he might be a dangerous man to provoke. Then his expression changed to something strange and unreadable. 'I have no illusions about my character, either. It does little good to whine that I was not in the habit of such behaviour until last night. I cannot pretend that with the act my character has suddenly transformed for the better. And I shall not lie and say that, if you remain here, you will be safe from me.

'My behaviour proves that there are no depths to which I will not sink to gain my desires. Although I detest what I have become, I cannot change it. And when I look at you, even now, I feel what little control I have slipping from me. God help me. That you were innocent does not matter. I want you still. Honour means nothing.'

And she could understand him, for she felt no different. Need for him ran through her like an ague. Taking the money on the desk and leaving was unthinkable, if it meant that she would never see him again, nor feel what he had made her feel in the dark the previous night. 'Just as my reputation means nothing to me, when I look at you. Put the money away,' she said softly. 'I will not leave.'

He stood up from his desk, and came to glare into her eyes in a way that might once have terrified her. 'If you do not go, I will put you out myself. Or worse. You know what I am capable of, should you cross me.'

'Do it, then. If you can. If you let me go, I will tell everyone what has happened.' And now she would know if he was the villain he pretended to be. She stepped near to him, reached for his hands and put them about her throat. Then she put her arms around his waist and waited for him to decide.

He froze against her, holding himself stiff and unmoved. And then there came something, from deep in his chest, that sounded almost like a sob. But when she looked up at his face, his eyes were closed, and his cheeks were dry. But she could feel him begin to shake, as though he was fighting the urge with every fibre of his being. Then he reached out and held her as well. He was gentle, so as not to disturb her gown or her hair. He would leave no embarrassing signs that he had touched her.

When he spoke, his voice was different, as though

he were a different person. 'It would be better for you if you were to go. You might be safe. No one need ever know what happened here. I swear they will not hear it from me. I would help you start again. But if you stay…' He flinched against her, and then drew her tighter. 'Oh dear God, I want you to stay. But I can promise you nothing.'

'It does not matter,' she said, surprised that she meant it.

'It does. We both know that.' He pushed her away. He turned back to the desk, and busied himself amongst its tiny drawers, removing an envelope of what looked like tea. He poured the leaves into the cup on his desk. Then he handed it to her. 'Drink this.'

She looked into his eyes, took it and drank, without hesitation, thinking too late of poison, and the sort of man that he claimed he was. 'What is it?'

'It will prevent…' he paused awkwardly '…mistakes.'

'Then you should have given it to me before today's geography lesson, for I am sure I have confused the children again.'

He managed a bitter smile. 'Not that sort of mistake. I fear you are helpless there.' He glanced at the cup, and said, in an almost scholarly voice, 'If taken regularly, there are certain herbs that inhibit gestation. If you mean to stay here, it would be best if you were to take a spoonful each morning with your tea.'

He was right to wish to avoid a bastard. And if she meant to be so foolish as to lie with a man without protection of marriage, than she need concern herself as well. He had done nothing to make her believe that there was a future in what they had done. And, some time, she might have to return home to her old life and pretend to forget what had happened between them. If that day came, it would be best that there be no outward evidence of what had occurred.

And now, the sour taste in her mouth had nothing to do with the concoction she'd drunk. She stared down into her cup. 'Very convenient that you had it handy. Did you know that I would refuse your offer? Have there been others…like me?'

'Like you?' He shook his head and stared sadly down at his desk. 'I suspect that there are no others like you. At least not that I have had the good fortune to meet. Do you mean, have I had mistresses? Yes. But not in some time. Certainly not in the house, with my family present. It was in London, years ago. And I did not need to see to their reproductive habits, for they knew more about the subject than I.'

'Then you suspected…'

'That you would stay with me?' He looked truly sad. 'I did not dare to hope. Even now, I do not know which of us is the bigger fool for continuing with this.' He glanced at the packet on the desk. 'The herbs belonged to Clare. I prepared them for her, after Sophie was born.'

'You did not want more children from her?' Which was strange, since the man adored the three he had.

'Things concerning Clare were seldom about what I wanted. We would not have had two children, had Edmund come before Lily. Although she enjoyed the getting of them, she found the whole process of carrying and birthing to be distasteful. And confinement, with no balls or friends to entertain? She informed me after Edmund that I'd got my heir and could leave her alone. She was having no more of me, if I meant to breed her like stock and keep her penned up for half the year.'

He chuckled. 'She was most put out when she came to me with news of Sophie. It was the closest I have seen to contrition. She had been careless, and had waited too long to rid herself of the problem. Now she would have to go through it all again. And she must beg me to acknowledge the child, which was a further indignity...'

He seemed genuinely amused by the story, and it was the first time that she had seen him in real mirth, when he was not speaking to his children. 'Why would you have refused?' she asked. 'You adore the girl. Don't you?' Suddenly, she was too confused to continue.

He looked at her, and the light faded from his eyes. 'You have not guessed the truth already? That is good, for I feared that as she grew it would be more evident. Apparently not.' He looked at her again. 'When Sophie was born, my wife and I had not been intimate for several years.'

'Then how...?' She'd begun before realising how naïve it would sound. If the child was not his, then it must be a result of Clare's infidelity. 'And you were not angry?'

'Resigned, more like. I knew that Clare was not with me. And I knew that she was not celibate. Only a fool would not have recognised the risk. One cannot deny nature, after all.' He looked no more interested in the idea than if it were some statistical or scientific problem. There was none of the rage she would have expected from the sort of man that might be moved to murder an unfaithful wife.

'And you claimed Sophie as your own?'

'She is my daughter in all ways that matter,' he said, effectively closing the subject. 'If ever I meant to reject her and her foolish mother, the feeling was banished at first sight of that little girl. She was as beautiful a baby as she is a child, and totally innocent of the sin of her parents. She has grown more dear to me with each passing year, and has never known another father. And I am content with that.

'But I did not want Clare to think that my patience was infinite. So once Sophie was born, I gave her the herbs and explained the advantage of regular usage. She had no more wish to be pregnant than I had to raise a collection of other men's children. There were no further problems.'

That he knew of. She wondered if he had read the letters she'd found. They might imply that there was another child on the way. Or did they refer to Sophie? Without Clare to answer, it would be impossible to tell.

'You grow quiet. Is it so shocking to you? Do you object to educating a child born on the wrong side of the sheets?' There was something in his tone that warned it had best not be the problem. 'For I wish her to be treated no differently than the other two.'

'Of course not,' she answered quickly. 'If anything,

she needs to be treated with more delicacy, and it has nothing to do with her parentage. Recent events have shocked her badly. It will do no good to try to impose discipline on an undisciplined mind at this time.'

'That is so. Your behaviour to her, your gentleness and loving attention have been quite different from what she received from the heartless woman who should have held her dear. But what else could I have expected from Clare? In all the time I knew her, she never showed a moment's care for any but herself.'

It shocked her to see the depth of bitterness and loathing for his late wife that was plain on his face. 'If you hated the girl's mother so, then why did you marry her?'

He smiled. 'The obvious reasons: she was rich and beautiful. I desired her. I was young and foolish enough to think that would be sufficient.'

He made no mention of love, even from the first. 'No wonder she grew to hate you.'

'Grew to hate me?' He smiled. 'You question my motives. But you do not think to wonder why she married me. There was never love between us. On her part, not even the physical desire was returned.'

Daphne did not respond. She did not like to think that Clarissa's behaviour over her unhappy marriage had no justification.

Tim smiled again and continued. 'I was a grave disappointment to her, you know. She and her family had such hopes for me and I failed them.'

'Disappointment? You are a baron, are you not?' It

was certainly more than she had expected, when and if she found a husband.

'A very lowly one. And that came late, after we were married. I earned a knighthood, as well.' He said it with such mock distaste that it almost made her laugh. 'For cross breeding wheat. And if you could have seen the look on my wife's face when that happened. She was horrified. She told me often enough, if she'd have wished for a husband to earn her respect, then she'd have married a cit with a fat wallet. That, at least, would have been more useful than the meagre awards I've earned with my scholarship or my poor family connections. She and her family were rather hoping that I would inherit a better title, and the land associated with it. Not hoping so much as expecting.'

'Surely not.' It made her family sound common, as though they were willing to sell their daughter for a coronet.

'I have an uncle who is a marquis. A lovely gentleman, with a weak constitution. Unmarried, at the time I met Clarissa. I told her in retrospect that if all she wanted was the title, she'd have done better for herself in seducing the old man.' He gave a short, bitter laugh. 'She told me she thought the same thing. Uncle Henry's miraculous recovery was disappointing enough. But that he should marry late in life, and father an heir?'

Tim shook his head. 'I did not mind the change in succession, for I'd given little thought to the matter before Clare pointed it out to me. She could not believe the fact. That she had bound herself to a man who was not only poor, but devoid of political ambition, was quite beyond her understanding. She was not willing to live as I am, a tenant to Bellston. But my influential friends were valuable to further her own social climbing.'

He was so very cold and matter of fact about it that it made her want to scream in frustration. It was even worse that she remembered Clare as bright, beautiful, elegant and well versed in the ways of London. She had been so witty, and always surrounded by admirers. And totally dismissive of her husband.

There had been no doubt in Daphne's mind that when she met him he would be ugly, and more than a bit of a brute. She looked again at her employer. There was nothing dull about the man. He was obviously more intelligent than her, and with a wit as quick, or quicker, than Clare's. Nor was he brutish, for his manner was easy, and his frame trim and graceful. There was none of the hesitance she expected in a man given over to learning. Had she met him in a drawing room, she would have found him an equal to any man present in looks and behaviour.

'I was a grave disappointment to her in all ways that mattered. And she was a millstone around my neck. I enjoyed her money, of course. The house was in need of repair, and I owe the success of my experiments to the wealth she brought with her when we married. The children have been a delight and a comfort to me. I was willing to bear much for their sakes, for they are my greatest achievement.'

He looked at her, and his eyes were flat and emotionless. 'But it all came with a cost. She took advantage of every chance to humiliate me, in public or private.

There was no disciplining her. If I chose to put my foot down, tried to punish her, or attempted to embarrass her, she would repay me in kind. She enjoyed watching me suffer and was more than willing to besmirch her own reputation, if it would pay me out. She even took up with my closest friend, removing what little companionship I enjoyed, and replacing it with suspicion and doubt.'

He shook his head. 'I schooled myself to hide my response to it, to pretend that none of it mattered to me. And some days, I think I even believed it myself. Other than that? The best I could manage was to keep the children away from their own mother, so that they might not see the truth. She did not mind it overmuch, for she had little patience for them. But I fear that it has harmed them permanently, to have no woman who cared for them.'

'They are unharmed, I swear,' she assured him. 'Bright, pleasant children. Co-operative and kind.'

'And is Sophie unmarked by what has happened?' He gave her a cynical smile. 'She barely speaks. And she was a little chatterbox, before I...' His throat stuck on the word. 'Before her mother died. Now she cannot stand to be in the room with me. The other children are a little better. But not as they once were. We four were a merry little family, once. Very happy, as long as Clare stayed in town. But at the last she provoked me, until I was unable to contain my rage.'

He ran a hand through his hair. 'If not for my weakness...' Then he looked up at her. 'I do not regret what I have done, so much as I regret not planning better. I can think of at least three plants in my possession right now. Untraceable poisons. I could have administered them, and been far away when they took effect. No one would have been the wiser.'

'Don't say that. You do not mean it.' She was frantic to believe the words. 'You are too good a man to be capable of premeditated murder.'

He smiled sadly at her. 'I am honoured by your belief in me, Daphne. But you do not know me so well as you think. I am who I am, and that man is not worthy of you.' He pushed the packet of herbs across the desk toward her. 'If you mean to stay, then take these with you and see that you use them. The situation is quite complicated enough, without bringing another unfortunate child into it.' Then he returned to his paperwork, and she was dismissed.

She walked slowly back to the schoolroom, tucking the packet of herbs deep into her pocket. She should be ashamed at what they symbolised. What kind of woman feared a child rather than welcoming one? But the herbs meant that he would visit her again. And for the moment, that was all that mattered. She would not think of her old life, or what would happen when she needed to return to it. For now, she would be a governess by day. And at night, she would be Timothy Colton's mistress. Each new day would be as much future as she needed.

She stopped at the door to the schoolroom, surprised at the sound of children's voices, raised in argument. It was strange, for they normally got on so well together. She had not heard a cross word between them since the day she'd arrived.

'Lily!' Edmund dropped easily into the role of leader. 'I forbid you to speak.'

'You are not the oldest, Eddy,' she muttered. 'You cannot forbid me anything. It is time. Maybe she can—'

'No. We already decided. You must not. We said nothing to the others, and we will say nothing to Miss Collins.' As she stepped around the door frame and into the room, they did not see her. They were both casting worried glances at Sophie, who was playing in a corner and oblivious to the conversation.

'But it cannot go on like this. Perhaps Father—'

'What cannot go on, children?' She stepped in between them and gave them her best no-more-nonsense smile.

They looked up at her, obviously guilty. 'Nothing.'

'Really? In my experience it is seldom necessary to be as worried about nothing as you two are. I will find out the truth eventually, you know.' She gave them a playful smile. If it was a broken window or a spoiled book, she knew of all the locations that such problems might be hidden, from personal experience.

But her friendliness had no effect on them. 'No, you will not. Because we will not tell you.' Edmund said it as though he were announcing a death, and Lily closed her eyes tightly, as though she could wish away the consequences.

Daphne went to them, going down upon her knees before them, so that she could look into their eyes. She hoped they did not suspect what had happened between her and their father. They would be far too young to understand. 'If there is something you wish to say to me, something that worries you, perhaps? You do not have to be afraid. Not of anything or anyone. No matter who it is. You will feel better, once you can share the secret.'

Lily's green eyes filled with tears. 'No, Miss Collins. Eddy is right. We promised we would not say. And telling will not help. It will ruin everything.'

So she ceased her quizzing and reached out to hug both of them.

And as they trembled in her arms, Sophie noticed nothing, sitting in her chair by the window, smiling to her papers and paints.

Chapter Thirteen

Tim went to her again, that night, after the children were in bed and the rest of the servants had retired below stairs. He had warred with himself over the visit for most of the day. Never mind that she had agreed to it, there were a hundred reasons why it was wrong. The virtue of the girl, her class, the fact that she was in the house to care for his children. She deserved better treatment. And had he still been a man of honour, it should have mattered to him.

But the stain on his soul all but laughed at the idea that he would stick at debauchery after forgiving himself for murder. If the girl was foolish enough to submit, then what compunctions need he have about using her? In the end, he let his lust overcome his judgement and focused on the vision of naked female flesh, warm and willing, waiting in the little room at the top of the house. He could lose himself there, calm the guilty voices in his head, rut himself to exhaustion and come down to sleep in his own bed. When he finally climbed the stairs and came into her room, arousal was strong in him, like a caged animal pacing behind a gate.

She sat on the edge of her bed, waiting for him. He closed the door. But he made no effort to douse the light, for he wanted to see her body. She was naked, as he had imagined her, the cold air peaking her breasts, limbs smooth and pale. He pulled off his clothing and left it in an untidy heap on the floor. Then he walked towards the bed, bare. He could feel the air raising bumps on his skin, and his hair standing up in protest. 'How can you stand the room so cold?' he asked. And then realised that, even if it mattered to her, there was no fireplace. He'd provided nothing to keep her warm. 'You should wear a nightshirt, or you will catch your death.'

She smiled. 'My only one was torn last night, and I have not yet had the time to mend it.'

He had done that to her as well. 'I will buy you another,' he blurted. 'As fine as you might wish. Sheer cotton, perhaps, or a very fine embroidered linen.'

'So that you might rip it off me again?' And she gave a small laugh. It was not the knowing sound of a courtesan, or the laugh of derision he would have got from his late wife. This was a sweet sound that seemed to say he could do whatever pleasured him, for she trusted him to bring her pleasure as well. She was looking at him through the lashes covering her slanted green eyes, trying not to appear too curious about his arousal.

And the illusion shattered in him that he could treat her as though she were a nameless stranger with no part in the matter of their coupling. She was looking at him like a bride. Innocent, but unafraid. Whether he wanted it or not, tonight she offered herself to him because she had given him her heart.

For a moment, it was easy to believe that she was his by right, the wife of his heart. There was nothing wrong or sinful about what he wished to do.

He smiled back at her, and said, 'I do not like to think you are cold because of my carelessness. Let us climb beneath the covers and warm you up.' And he pulled back the blanket and climbed into bed beside her. Soon, their mutual fumblings beneath the covers had them laughing, and far more than warm. When she was gasping with pleasure, he wasted no time in coming into her body as though he belonged there. He should not have rushed, for it was over too quickly, and she curled close to him, laying her cheek against the hair on his chest and sighing in contentment.

She'd stayed.

He had told her the truth, which should have been more than enough to send her running back to London. And yet, here she was, at his side.

His actions last night should have been enough to drive her away, if his words had not. He had tricked her out of her maidenhead. For even though she'd shown no sign of pain, there was nothing to make him believe that he was not her first lover. Tonight, she had been curious, but inexperienced.

He stared down at the top of her head, soft chestnut curls spreading out over the pillow. They looked better that way, and would look better on soft linen instead of the rough cloth here. She should be lying on down, wrapped in silk, with a roaring fire in the grate to chase away the chill.

He could give her that, if he wished. Move her downstairs into a guest bedroom. Dress her in satin, shower her with jewels. Stay in her bed so that he could feed her a breakfast of apricots from the orangery, and make her lick the juice from his fingers. But it would make her position too clearly that of a mistress.

Could he live with himself?

Instead, she was huddled in an attic, and tired from a day of caring for his children. He understood the satisfying feeling of fatigue, after a day's labour. But even at the worst times of his life, it had always been by choice. To be forced to take a position to survive… And to be forced again into the kind of service he required of her. He shook head in disgust at his own hasty actions.

She woke from her nap and looked up at him, smiling.

He gathered her close to him again.

She'd stayed.

When he'd confessed, she'd faced it without flinching. She didn't dance around it, not wanting to hear the truth, as even his dearest friend did. And she must have forgiven him for it, even if he could not forgive himself. It was the first proof he'd got that such was even possible. It gave him hope that there might be a way past what he had done, and a future after it.

And it occurred to him that there was a perfectly good way to keep her safe and warm and at his side for ever, with her honour restored. If she could accept his offer, knowing the villain that he had been, then he would put it behind him and work to be worthy of her love. They need never mention Clare again, or think of the time before Daphne had come into his house.

He could start anew.

She was nestling against him, again, and he felt her head dip as she began to doze.

He kissed her hair. 'You are tired. I should not disturb you.'

'It is nothing.' She yawned. 'The children...'

'Do you like them?' he asked hesitantly, afraid that he was overstepping yet another boundary that an employer should not cross. 'Not just the job, mind. But the children themselves.'

She gave a little start. 'Yes, I do.' She sounded almost surprised by the fact, and he wondered if this were in some way different from her last position. 'There were some difficulties at first. But they are bright and good company. And Sophie is a darling.'

'That is good. I think they like you as well.' There was one hurdle, at least. For he could not very well ask her to make a life with him, if she could not accept another woman's children.

'And how do you like me, Lord Colton?' Her lips teased his chest. Her tone was low and sultry, and went to the very core of him, stirring his body and his mind.

'Very well indeed.' He tipped her chin up, and kissed her properly, tasting her mouth. She returned the kiss, rocking gently against him. He could feel the heat rising in him, the desire to have her again. But he wanted to prolong the play. 'And am I to believe that you are growing to like me in return?'

She was kissing her way down his throat. 'Now that you have stopped trying to frighten me away, I think I like you very much.'

And he saw how much things had changed in a day, for though he had woken wanting nothing more than to be rid of her, it was now of the utmost importance to him, a matter of life and death, that he do nothing that would make her leave. 'Was it so obvious that I was trying to scare you?'

'Of course. You were nearly successful. For I do not want to say the things I thought you capable of, listening to the wind howl while lying in this bed, night after night.' Her hands were stroking his sides now, and it was only a matter of time before she touched him as he longed to be touched, and then conversation would be impossible.

'Say them, all the same. For I wish to know.'

'I thought you were a violent brute who cared for nothing but his own pleasure.' And she laughed softly.

He remembered the way he'd come to her, ready for sex but barely able to think of her by name. And lust for her mingled with a kind of sick dread.

'I thought that you would hurt me, if I opposed you.' She looked up into his eyes, and hers were as green as a cat's in the darkness. 'But now that I see the real you, the one that you hide from the world, I think my fears were quite ridiculous.'

The apprehension in him grew. And she continued,

'You are no more capable of hurting me, or anyone else, than you are of hurting the plants in your garden.'

She did not believe him.

'But...but I told you... You understand what happened here...'

She smiled her satisfied cat's smile. 'I understand what you think happened here. You feel responsible for your wife's death.'

He grabbed her hands, and held them so that she would stop tormenting his body. Then he said slowly, so that she could not doubt his meaning, 'I killed Clarissa. This is not just guilt over an accidental fall. I murdered my wife. She had preceded me to Wales. And I knew it was to be with her lover, a man I thought to be a friend. I followed. I arrived at the house. And through the windows I saw her in the drawing room, entertaining him. I went to my study and poured a brandy, even though it was still morning. Then I went to Bellston to talk to the Duchess. Adam arrived and we fought. He sent me away.'

His face tightened. 'And then I came home to my darling wife. The house was in chaos. The coach with the children had arrived, maids and nurses, bags and baggage, everywhere. So much noise, and so many people. It made my head ache, and so I had more brandy. I found Clare and we argued. On and off it went, all day and night for the better part of a week. I threatened divorce. She threatened to leave and take the children with her.' He shook his head. 'I don't know what she meant by it, other than to hurt me, for they did not mean a jot to her.'

He rubbed his temple, for his head ached at the memory. 'There was so much alcohol, and servants constantly interrupting, and the children were crying. Then there was even more brandy. And it ended with Clare, broken at the foot of the stairs.'

'That is all you remember?'

'It is enough.'

'What were you thinking, as you stood at the top of the stairs? What did she say to you, before you pushed her? What did you feel, when you saw her begin to fall? Triumph? Joy? Fear?'

'Stop!' He had spoken too loudly; for a moment he feared someone below them might have heard a man's voice coming from this room, where it had no right to be. He calmed himself, and continued. 'I know what happened. I do not need to remember the act. I remember my anger plain enough and my hatred of her. And telling her I would see her dead before I let her leave the house with the children. The next morning, I woke in my clothes in the study to the sound of more crying and the servants shouting. And there was Clare, on the floor of the hall.'

'That does not mean you killed her. It was a fall, nothing more.'

'She fell backwards, not forwards. It was plain by her injuries that she had been pushed. I was the only one in the house, Daphne.' He put his hand under her chin, and forced her eyes to meet his. 'I know the effect that strong spirits have upon me. I become violent, unreasonable. It is why I avoid them. And yet I kept taking them. I knew all along what I meant to do, and I drank until I could not stop myself.'

'No,' she said again. She refused to see the truth in his eyes: that he was capable of murder.

So he smiled and told her the real truth. 'And there is worse to come.'

'It does not matter,' she whispered.

'You are the only one who thinks I am innocent. Everyone knows what I have done. Adam is magistrate. He saw the evidence, as did Penny. He took one look, and then he ordered Penny to sit with the children. He had the body taken away and prepared for burial, and the floor and stairs scrubbed clean. He looked at me with such pity. And then he declared it an accident.'

Tim's voice broke on the last word. 'I begged him to take me to London to stand trial. I want to see justice served. If I do not pay for what I have done, I am damned for sure. But he kept repeating that it was an unfortunate accident. All for the best. And that no one blamed me.' He squeezed her hands tightly in his. 'But I blame me. The children blame me. You have seen them. The way they look at me. They know what happened. They saw too much that day for it to be otherwise.

'I must be punished for what I did to the children, even if the law will not punish me. Once I am sure that they are away to school, I will take care of it myself. They are better without parents than with the ones they were born to.' And then he began to shake. He sobbed like a damned soul, ashamed that she saw.

She reached for him, gathering his face in her hands to lay it upon her breast, stroking his hair as though he were a lost child. 'It is all right. It will be all right. What happened that day cannot be changed. And the Duke and Duchess are right as well. You are not to blame for it.'

His shaking subsided. 'And now you know why I wished the children out of this house. Even if they cannot love me, I meant to see that they were gone, and that their futures were secure before—'

'No,' she said again. 'You will not do what you are thinking. Ending yourself will leave the children in a worse state than ever. They cannot afford to lose more. They simply cannot.'

'They need to go away from this poisonous place. They are old enough to go to school, and I mean to send them.' He laughed softly. 'I told you that I was opposed to this scheme of a governess. It only prolongs the inevitable.'

'I need you.'

He shook his head. 'I have nothing to give you. If you are imagining some happy scenario, where we are together, perhaps as a family?' He shook his head. She had not forgiven him, because she believed there was nothing to forgive. And without her forgiveness, he felt his future begin to unravel again. 'Then you are more foolish than I imagined.' Just as he had been.

'I am not a fool. And I will prove it. I will uncover the truth, and set you free of your fears. There is another answer, Tim. There has to be.' It was the first time she had used his given name, and the familiarity was both startling and disturbing. It meant she thought she knew him. But really, she did not know him at all.

The time would come when she would admit that his answer was the only logical one. She would begin to doubt. And then she would run, or he would send her away.

He leaned forwards and kissed her, long and slow, but without heat. Then he escaped from her arms and her body, and sat up on the edge of the bed.

'You are going?' She stretched out an arm to him in an attempt to draw him back. The gesture was as languid and sensual as a trained courtesan's, and he wondered at how quickly she had fallen.

'It would not do for the children to see me coming down the stairs in the morning.'

She smiled. 'There are hours yet before we must worry.'

She was right, of course. He could stay as long as he liked. He could stay all night, and be damned to her reputation. He had already damned his own, by his actions. He swallowed. 'You are tired and need your rest. And there is always tomorrow.'

She yawned, and smiled. 'Tomorrow, then?'

'Of course.' He kissed her again, ignoring her hands, as they played upon his body. In time, she would see the truth, as he did. And then, when all hope for his innocence was gone, he would ask her if she still wished to make a life with the shell of a man.

Chapter Fourteen

Daphne swung her feet to the floor, as the first rays of dawn hit the tiny window. He had not stayed the night with her. But he had been with her longer than on the previous night. For a moment she feared that someone might meet him on the back stairs from her room. In any other house, it would have been most unusual to find the master creeping down the back stairs. But for once, the curious behaviour might be explained. Tim's habit of turning up in unexpected corners of the house was a change in habit, but typical eccentricity.

She smiled at the thought of him, in shirtsleeves, on his way to a cold breakfast in the conservatory. Then she reached for her sketchbook and her charcoals. She worked quickly, for her day must start soon, and there was no time for daydreaming over the master of the house.

At least not in such an obvious way as to sketch him.

In her mind he was just as he had been, cravat missing and shirt open, revealing a V of bare skin. She let her fingers linger on the place as she smudged the hollow in his throat, the shadows of muscle and bone on his chest as they disappeared behind the linen. She did the eyes next, with their sparkle of intelligence and the faint sadness that never seemed to leave them. And his smile, slightly higher at one side than the other, as though he were continually surprised by her, though delighted.

A few minutes later, she paused to admire her work. She felt she had done rather well in capturing the way his brown hair fell into his eyes as he leaned towards her, the faint dimple in his cheek as he smiled and the soft but mobile mouth. The whole demonstrated his gentleness, as well as his intelligence. In looking at the face she had drawn, she wondered how she had ever thought him capable of cruelty, much less murder. This was a portrait of a man who would be at home bent over his books, or working in his glasshouse, hands deep in earth.

She frowned. He and Clare must have known from the first that they would not suit. He would be uncomfortable in the excitement of the city, at the parties she craved. And she would be bored to tears at the estate in Wales, unimpressed by the beauty of the garden, and uninterested in her husband's discoveries. She would remain in town without him, telling all and sundry that he was a dullard and a burden, and that she had married beneath her.

It was embarrassing to admit how far she had been misled by her glamorous cousin. But it meant that she owed an even greater debt to Tim and his family for doubting them. So she rose from the bed and prepared to see to the children.

Later, Tim summoned her to the study. She was surprised to see the butler, cook and housekeeper as well. Apparently, she was there as governess, and it had nothing to do with her new, less official capacity.

Tim looked up at the servants with an air of suppressed agitation. 'I have received a letter in today's post. It seems Bellston has decided to come to dinner. He says he must take matters into his own hands, since an invitation was not forthcoming from me.' She could see by the crook of his mouth that Colton seemed both annoyed and amused by the turn of events.

'Unfortunately, I am unsure how ready the common rooms are for visitors. Can the dining room be prepared for this evening?'

The housekeeper assured him that all would be in readiness.

'And the menu?' He gave a vague wave of his hand. 'It matters not to me. He is bringing the Duchess, of course. If they mean to treat themselves as family, then they'd best not be expecting me to serve a peer. Give us whatever can be got together with a minimum of fuss. We will be retiring to the drawing room for cards, after.' He raised his head to her, as though just noticing her presence. 'And since her Grace is so fond of the children, I expect them to be dressed and present at table, and after.'

'Sir.' She tried to make the warning implicit in the single word.

'Very well, then.' He nodded, as if all were in agreement. 'You are dismissed.'

She lingered and closed the door after the others had gone.

Without looking up, he said, 'Miss Collins, do you have a problem with my request?'

'Are you sure it is wise for the children to dine with you?' she said, remembering the long uncomfortable meal of a few days ago. 'They are likely to be a nuisance.'

'And that is why their governess will be there, to prevent any problems.'

'I am to dine with you? And the Duke of Bellston?'

'And the duchess, as well,' Tim reminded her. 'These evenings always go better if there are an equal number of ladies.'

'But I am not—' She stopped herself. Of course, she was a lady. When she was in London, at least. But she could not exactly explain herself. 'It will insult them greatly, if you mean to seat a servant at the table.'

'If the Duke and his wife are bothered by the presence of a servant at table, that the Duchess herself hired, then they'd best return to their own home.'

He saw her hesitation, and added, 'My other servants know better than to cross me, when I have made up my mind. You should learn it as well.' There was something about the set of his mouth that was different from the last time he had tried to order her about like help. She suspected that he was laughing at her.

Then, for just a moment, he gazed at her as he had on the previous night. 'Wear your finest gown, with none of that muslin nonsense tucked into the bodice. Dress as a lady and preside at my table.' The last words were soft, coaxing, as though her presence was an honour to him that had nothing to do with expedience. Then his brusque manner returned. 'Do not think you can hide from me, Miss Collins. Be downstairs with the children at six sharp. Obey or be gone.' And once again he gave the invisible shifting of attention that told her she was no longer required.

Later as she was preparing herself for the ordeal ahead, she tried to quell the nervous butterflies that had taken residence in her stomach. It was aggravating of him to even suggest this, for so many reasons. She could barely stand to think what her mother would say, if she knew that Daphne was to have dinner at the very same table as a duke and duchess. The poor woman would be in alt. Considering the minor social set in which they travelled, the chances were better that she would go dancing on the moon than dining with the peerage.

But if her mother were to find that she was doing it as a servant? The horrors. She faced herself in the tiny mirror, and set about trying to do up her hair in a fashion that might match the gold satin gown she had chosen from her luggage. It was far too modest for an evening with the Duke and Duchess of Bellston, and yet too daring for a governess. And what was she to do about her manners?

It would be difficult enough to speak to the couple,

especially considering what she suspected about his Grace and the parentage of little Sophie. But though she was dressed as a lady, she must also remember to speak like a servant when spoken to, and no more than that. And to watch over the children as well. She must let nothing slip, that she was anything more to the host of the house than a loyal servant. The whole evening would be like trying to take tea on a tightrope.

But it would give her the opportunity to observe the Duke and his behaviour towards Sophie. Perhaps he would turn out to be the villain she suspected, and she could persuade Tim that his supposed old friend meant him ill by the visit. Her life would be much simpler tomorrow, if tonight she could prove the Duke of Bellston was a murderer.

The children were to be no help in the matter of decorum. For when they heard that it was 'Uncle Adam and Aunt Penny' who were visiting, they were quite beyond her control. When the time finally came to lead them downstairs, it was all she could do to keep them from running on ahead of her. As it was, they burst into the drawing room with shouts of delight. Before she was able to gather them up again, they had launched themselves upon the couple and greeted them with exuberant hugs.

As she watched, the Duke greeted each in turn, bowing to the older girl, shaking the hand of the boy and lifting little Sophie high into the air and tossing her until she laughed. As she compared the two, she could see no resemblance and no hesitation on the part of the Duke that might indicate he felt more strongly attracted or repelled by the youngest child than he did with either of the others.

When he put the little girl back down to earth, he turned his attention to their governess.

And for a moment Daphne was quite taken aback. He was the handsomest man she had ever seen, with fine pale features, black hair and sooty lashes covering deep blue eyes. And it was most affecting as he returned her gaze. It was as though she were the centre of attention, and not an invisible thing placed in the room to maintain peace during the meal. 'So this is the new governess that I have heard so much about. My wife feels that you are just what the family needs, my dear. I can only hope she speaks the truth.' He said the last too quietly for his host to hear.

And then Tim stepped forward, and offered introductions. 'Adam, this is Daphne Collins. May I present the Duke of Bellston. And, of course, you're already familiar with his wife.' He gestured in the direction of the Duchess, who had busied herself greeting the children.

She dropped a deep curtsy, and murmured, 'Your Grace', in a tone that she hoped was sufficiently subservient.

The Duke glanced at her for a moment, and then at his friend, and there was a momentary hesitation as he seemed to gather some bit of information from the silence. Then he said, 'Airs and graces are hardly necessary tonight. Please, if you are to dine with us, you must call me Adam. And my wife's name is Penny. Penny loathes formality, and will be quite out of sorts if you curtsy to her again.'

He went on for a bit about the quality of Tim's table and how he had missed it over the past months as though nothing unusual had happened between them, either before or after Clarissa's death.

Daphne had the brief, horrifying feeling that in the moment of silence, the Duke had formed the opinion that her relationship with her employer was rather closer than was normal. She turned and looked at Tim, hoping that he would give her some clue as to what was going on, and saw the look in his eyes.

He was admiring her as he might a woman of quality. As though he wished to gain and keep her approval by his actions. She had expected him to treat her as he had in the study: as a servant, to be tolerated only as long as she fulfilled her duties. And that had been at best. At worst, she expected him to do something to betray her status as his mistress. A lasciviousness of expression or a familiar touch that might indicate their intimacy.

But instead he smiled at her in a way that was encouraging, and almost shy. And when his guests were distracted by the children, he came to her side and murmured, 'See. There is nothing to be concerned about. Adam has been a dear friend to me for most of my life.' His face darkened for a moment. 'Although there has been an estrangement, of late. I did him a wrong.'

'You did him—' She shut her mouth quickly, for she was unsure how much he understood of her knowledge of the affair.

Tim was glancing at the Duke. 'But it appears that he

has decided to forgive it. And we are to go on as if nothing has happened.' He smiled sadly. 'I find that to be a great relief. Although I do not know her nearly so well, I expect you will find the Duchess to be a refreshing change from what you expected. She was the daughter of a printer, before marrying.'

'Her family was in trade?' She hoped the snobbishness did not show too clearly in her voice, for her mother would be just as shocked to hear that she had dined with a printer's daughter as she would a duke.

'Yes.' He smiled encouragingly again. 'If it gives you any comfort to know the fact, she was not born to this life. She was frightfully rich, of course. But she is not one to put on airs or think less of a person because of their birth or a need to take employment.'

'Oh. That is good.' For she remembered, after a moment, that this would have been a comfort to a true governess. But what would her mother have made of the situation now? There would have been much bowing and scraping, while at table. But when they got home, there would be a stern lecture on the tendency of great men to marry beneath themselves while gently raised ladies of a better class, ladies such as Daphne, for instance, went unclaimed.

'And I am sure she will be interested in your progress with the children's education. She is frightfully intelligent as well. She is just finished with her own translation of Homer.'

'Are you speaking of my wife's book?' The Duke's ears seemed to prick from across the room, to catch the mention. He turned from the children, and reached into his pocket. 'I have brought a copy for you, since I knew you would appreciate it. It is an early printing, of course. A proof from Penny's brother. The man still has no understanding of the material, but I must admit he has done a good job with the setting and binding.'

'Do you really think so?' The Duchess looked eagerly at Tim. 'What is your opinion? I thought, if I was seeking a more accessible translation of the story, perhaps it would do to have some illustrations, but I have not the slightest idea of how to go about getting them. I suppose I must hire an artist.'

'Oh, Miss Collins. Have Miss Collins do them.' All three of the children were chorusing the suggestion enthusiastically.

Daphne took a step back, wishing there were a way to withdraw from the room without notice. But the children did not cease their clamour.

'Could you?' The Duchess looked hopefully at her.

'Oh, I don't know. I doubt I would be good enough.' And it would be incredibly complicated to explain, once she had completed her task here and returned to her old life. Especially if she accused the Duchess's husband of murder.

'No. You must. It would be wonderful. Come and see her sketches, Uncle Adam. Come and see.' Sophie had opened like a flower in the presence of company, talking non-stop and showing no sign of shyness. She grabbed the duke by the hand and was pulling him from the room.

Too late, Daphne remembered that it was her job as governess to prevent just such an embarrassing occurrence. 'Sophie. That is quite enough. You must return to your seat, immediately.'

The Duke smiled at her. 'Do not mind her. It is quite all right, really. I have not seen Sophie in a very long time. And if this gives her pleasure?' He smiled down at the girl and gave a courtly bow. 'I am at your command, my dear. Where are these sketches? If you would like to show them to me, I would very much like to see.'

'In the nursery.' She had tugged him out into the hall before Daphne realised the girl's intent. And they had headed up the stairs.

'Do not concern yourself, Miss Collins.' The Duke tossed the phrase over his shoulder. 'She is not the least bit of a bother. We will return shortly.'

So she stood in the entry and watched. It took only a few steps for Sophie to recover from her hesitation over taking the main stairs. She gripped the Duke's hand tightly, and started up them.

The Duke showed no hesitation at all. He was smiling down at the girl, holding the banister with relaxed fingers, proceeding at an orderly pace towards the first floor, and chatting as he went.

It was a stark contrast to the way Tim approached the same stairs. There was no guilt in this man's posture at all. Perhaps her suspicions were wrong. He did not behave as if there was a reason to fear discovery. And while some might be so duplicitous as to disguise a murder, would it not have been easier to avoid the Colton family altogether, if the object was to hide an illegitimate child?

And with man and girl, side by side, she could see

no resemblance at all. Surely there would be something alike in the two, if he were Sophie's father?

But if it was not the Duke? She looked back over her shoulder at her employer, who was glancing at the stairs with the same trepidation as always.

If the Duke was not a murderer, then she was left with her original suspect, whether she wanted him or not.

The Duchess was looking over her shoulder at the retreating pair. 'My word. You have been here less than two weeks and already I see a substantial change in Sophie's behaviour.'

'Well, I…' She struggled, unable to come up with an explanation for it.

Tim had come to her side, to answer for her. 'It is all up to Miss Collins, Penny. And I must apologise for the way I treated you, when you insisted on hiring her. You were right and I was wrong. The children needed someone sensible to look after them.'

Daphne was stunned. For when had anyone ever used the term *sensible* to refer to her?

Tim was smiling at her, as though she had hung the moon and stars. 'We needed someone who could look at the situation with a head unclouded by previous events, and come up with solutions to our problems. And Miss Collins has been a godsend.'

The Duchess was staring at Tim, who hardly seemed to notice her scrutiny, for all his attention was focused on Daphne. 'I can see that.'

Oh, dear. By the look in her eyes, the Duchess could see far more. Sophie was not the only one who had been transformed since her last visit. Tim was behaving in a manner that would be most ordinary in any drawing room. The saturnine man who had been forced into hiring her had disappeared. This man was gazing upon her with the same doting pride that the Duke lavished on his own wife.

Daphne would have found it quite flattering and a sure sign of strong admiration and attraction had they met under ordinary circumstances. But to bestow such lingering gazes on one's children's governess must seem almost as mad as his earlier storming. She dipped her head in subservience, and muttered, 'Lord Colton is too kind.'

The Duke and Sophie returned to the main floor a short time later, with her sketchbook under his arm. She had a brief, irrational desire to snatch the thing away from him and argue that it was none of his affair what she might draw, or whether she displayed any skill while doing it. But it would not do to insult a peer. Her mother would be horrified that she would even consider it.

And as a governess? She should be doubly honoured that he took any notice at all.

He set the book before his wife, and opened it to the odd landscape she had drawn. Then he cocked his head and looked at her. 'I must say, the work is most singular. But I do not recognise the location.'

She cleared her throat. 'It is all of my imagination, I fear.'

'All the better, for you would have to use imagination

freely, to render the scenes from my wife's book.' He smiled proudly at Penny. 'Although she has a most vivid turn of phrase. If she can make me read Homer, then think what she will do to you.' He flipped a few more pages, to see how she had rendered the plants in the garden and the statuary there. 'And I trust you can draw people as well?'

And it was then that she remembered the sketch she'd done of Tim. Her hand was halfway to reaching for the book when he flipped the page and stared down at the image.

Tim was across the room, seeing to the children, and did not notice the sudden silence from the group standing over the sketchbook. The light in the drawing was obviously from a breaking dawn. It was soft and flattering, as was his expression. His cravat was missing, and his shirt undone. It was a view that no decent woman should have seen, much less committed to paper. What must they think of her?

Perhaps she should protest that it had been a passing fancy, and not drawn from life at all. But would it be any better that they believed she was in some way obsessed with a glimpse of her employer's bare chest? And how would the Duchess react, knowing that she had hired such a person to care for children?

But it was even worse that they think she had drawn the picture from memory of an actual event. If that was the case, it was plain what was going on in the house. And that Tim would entertain the Duke and, worse yet, his Duchess, while his mistress sat at table with them, was the gravest possible insult. She swallowed, trying to come up with some explanation that would make him turn the page.

And he said suddenly, 'It is a very good likeness, is it not, Penny?'

She adjusted her spectacles in a way that might have implied disapproval. But then it became clear that she was only wishing to get a better look at the picture. The Duchess responded, 'Most well drawn.' When she glanced away from the sketch, there was a faint hint of colour in her cheek as evidence that she had seen, understood and been amused by the subject matter. But however she might look, when she spoke to Daphne she made it clear that there was nothing worth acknowledging about the picture. 'I would be most flattered to have you accept a copy of my work, and see what you might make of it. I have ideas, of course. But I would welcome the advice of so talented an artist.' And then she smiled warmly. 'I suspect that you will be with us for quite some time, and we will be able to discuss this again.'

Daphne expelled the breath she had been holding, and murmured, 'Thank you, your Grace.'

And the Duchess reached out to touch her hand, giving it a small, affectionate squeeze. 'Please. You must call me Penny. And my husband is Adam. All the titles can get so tiresome, at times. It is good to be able to relax.'

Then her husband shut the book quietly and looked back toward his host.

Tim was giving him a curious look in response, as though he waited on an answer.

The Duke called, 'Where is the dinner you have promised us, Tim? And the wine. I have quite missed the access to your fine cellars.'

Apparently, the answer had been given, for Tim grinned back at them. 'As though you cannot afford to stock your own. I had hoped, Adam, that since you had found a wife with more sense than you possess, you'd have let her take on the accounts.'

'That is just what I have done. And now she will not let me spend on such foolishness as decent brandy. So I have come to drink yours. Gather your children.' He held out an arm to his wife and the other to Daphne. 'And I will see to it that the ladies arrive safely in the dining room.'

Daphne gingerly accepted his offer of escort. So he chose to think of her as a lady, even after the damning evidence of the drawing?

He saw her hesitation and glanced in the direction of his friend. 'It is good to see Tim so happy. I was worried that he would not recover from his wife's death.' He looked at her pointedly. 'It was very difficult for him. Almost more so than the time before her death, which was very bad indeed. And I feared for the children as well, to be raised in such a household. In your short stay here, the mood of the house is returning to what we hoped it might be. Our friend Tim deserves an end to strife, for he has suffered long enough.' Then he smiled in her direction. 'If you are the cause of it, then you are a most welcome addition to his table, and to our little circle. Tell me, my dear, do you enjoy cards? For it would be pleasant to have a fourth…'

Dinner had been delightful, as had the cards and games afterwards. And it was only when Sophie had begun to nod over the drawing she was making by the fire, and the older children yawned into the books they were reading, that the adults decided it was time to end the evening.

When Daphne made to excuse herself to help them to bed, Lily fixed her with a curious look, as though reassessing her place in the family, and offered to tend to her sister herself, so that Miss Collins could stay a while longer with the adults. Tim smiled to himself. It did his daughter credit that she could interpret the situation so quickly, without him having to enlist her help.

He could see Daphne opening her mouth to refuse, and moved quickly to speak ahead of her. 'Thank you, Lily. That is most considerate of you and very helpful.' And when he was sure no one was looking, he winked at his older daughter and she smiled back at him.

It felt natural to have Daphne there, sharing a final glass of wine before Adam and Penny departed. And even more so to have her standing at his side, as he bid adieu to his guests. His friends reached out to her with warmth, eager to put her at ease. Both the Duke and Duchess took her by the hands and kissed her cheeks, as though she was more sister than servant. Although she was still too shy to return the gesture, he felt that it would not be too long before she treated them just as warmly as they did her.

When the Bellstons were safely on their way home to the grand estate just a few miles away, he shut the door and smiled down at her, laying a hand on her shoulder in a gesture of casual affection. 'Did you enjoy the evening?'

She smiled. 'Very much so. At first, I did not think…'

'That it was appropriate?' He smiled in return. 'I saw the look in your eyes when you came downstairs. Full of doubt. It was most unusual for you.'

'Well, it is rather unusual to seat the governess down next to a duke. And given the rather unique nature of my position here…' She took a deep breath.

'You were worried that they would learn the truth?' He laughed. 'I am sure they surmised the truth, even before they arrived. Adam is not the idiot he might pretend to be. He had it all worked out before he stepped over the threshold. His wife as well. I fought and complained over you, and made no secret of the fact that I did not want or need you. And then, two days ago, I stopped complaining. Perhaps they came to make sure that I had not pushed you down the stairs.'

'Do not joke over such things.' She'd gone deathly white at his words.

'Why?' He smiled at her, the wine and good company leaving him reckless. 'It may very well be true, you know. They had reason to be worried. I have lost the right to expect full trust, even from those who admired me in the past.'

'If they do not trust you, then they are not truly your friends, Tim.'

He laughed softly to himself. 'It is flattering to have such blind devotion from you, my love. No matter how unwarranted.'

She reached out and touched him lightly on the cheek. 'I see no reason to doubt.'

He kissed her palm and then reached to catch her about the waist, pulling her close to take her lips. This was as it should be. A beautiful woman who trusted him against all reason and loved his children. And whose lips were sweeter than after-dinner port.

For a moment, she was kissing him as ardently as he did her. But then she stopped, and struggled in his arms. 'Lord Colton. Stop it this instant.'

'Lord Colton, am I? You were not nearly so formal last night. I did not think you would mind a few kisses overmuch.'

'That was last night. And this is here and now, in an entryway, where anyone might see.'

'Are you afraid to have others know the truth about what is going on between us?'

'The Duke, Adam, and his wife might know already. But the servants do not.'

'It is my house, and I will behave how I wish.' He tipped her chin up and kissed her again, open mouthed, so there would be no question of his feelings should they be discovered. 'And I wish to do this. As often as possible.' He kissed her again and again, until she forgot all arguments. When he released her mouth so that she might catch her breath, he ran a finger along the neckline of her gown, and sighed in contentment. 'You look lovely tonight. But I imagine you in satin and lace, every night. With diamonds, here and here.' He nibbled on her ear, as his fingers stroked her throat. 'Sharing my table and my bed.' She tensed at his touch, and he whispered, 'Tell me you want me as much as I want you.'

There was a pause, and then she whispered, 'I do. But...'

'But...' He nodded, for her hesitance confirmed his fears.

'It is not about you,' she insisted. 'It is all much more complicated than that. We are not married. Not even betrothed.'

It stung him to think she might reject him, and he struck back with words meant to wound. 'If suddenly your honour matters so much, I will marry you. Only to see you forfeit it again, by your association with me.'

He could see that he had hurt her, for her green eyes grew large and sparkled with tears. But when she spoke, her voice was clear. 'I regret that I cannot accept your kind offer. And before you suggest it, my reasons have very little to do with what happened to your late wife. You talk of marriage. And yet you know nothing about me, nor do you seem to care about that fact. Though you will continue to enjoy my physical company, it would be very foolish of me to expect that you will change your mind about the rest of me, and suddenly begin to care once we wed.'

And with that, she stalked up the main stairs, so fast that she was gone before he could follow.

Chapter Fifteen

Daphne pounded her pillow in frustration. It had been three days since she had left him in the hall, and it was obvious she had offended him so greatly that he did not mean to visit her again. The whole thing was grossly unfair. If she'd claimed that she could no longer bear the shame of lying with a murderer, she suspected he would have been apologetic and perfectly understanding of it. It would have appealed to his sense of tragedy.

But he could not seem to fathom that someone might have feelings to be hurt, just as he had. He supposed he could marry her, if honour mattered…

She punched her pillow again. He was not a murderer, and hardly worth saving, if that was the best he could do. Timothy Colton was a selfish lout, no better than the men she had known in London. Just like the faithless cads whose attentions Clare had trained her to encourage. It served her right that when she met someone who mattered to her, and tried to learn from her mistakes and not be a public embarrassment, it would mean nothing to him.

And yet, she could not leave. There were the children, who needed her so much more than their father did. And she had not been paying attention to them, too focused on the needs of their father. The older children were all right, for they seemed to thrive, no matter what mistakes she made.

But she had not been tending to Sophie's lessons, since the girl was happy to entertain herself, now that she had paper and pens. And Daphne had been rewarded with just the sort of pictures she should have expected when the girl had nothing specific to occupy her mind. Endless sketches of Clare, all curiously misshapen, so oddly angled and disturbing that it gave her vertigo to look at them.

She set the girl to drawing pictures of her brother and sister, of the furniture in the room, and the marble busts in the front hall. And all of them came out properly formed and natural, with nothing the least bit alarming. It was only when the little girl attempted to draw Clare that the results were wrong. Perhaps it was the fading memory that caused it. If that was true, they would run their course and stop altogether one day, once the memories held no more fear for her.

So Daphne had bundled up the pictures and stuffed them into her trunk where none might come upon them by accident. Perhaps she should simply throw them on the fire, but she could not bring herself to do it. They were Sophie's memories. It would be unfair to take all she had of her mother, no matter how horrible that might be.

Below her, she thought she heard a tread on the stairs. There was only one person who would come to her at this time of night. And without meaning to, she hoped.

It was galling to know that she could forget so easily how angry she was with him. Now that he was near, she'd managed to convince herself that the differences between them could be solved. Tomorrow, perhaps. Or at least, later this evening.

He must feel it too, for his step sounded hesitant, as though he could not help but go forward, but was not sure it was wise to continue.

He'd reached the top of the stairs now, and stopped. He did not open the door, but neither did he knock. And refusing to make it easier on him than it needed to be, she did not call out.

And then, the footsteps shuffled on the landing, turned and retreated.

She lay upon her bed, angry and frustrated. She heard the steps going down one flight, and then another, until the sound faded. He was going? Without a word of apology. Not even a whisper. No note slipped under the door. Just a pause at the head of the stairs, and that was all?

Perhaps not all. She took up her candle and opened the door, holding it low so she could see the floor in front of her. Small purple flowers, scattered like wishes at her feet. She scooped them up, into a lopsided bunch.

No book was necessary to interpret the message. They were forget-me-nots.

She gave it not another thought, running down the stairs in her bare feet, as silently as she could. She hesitated only a moment at the door that would lead her to the bedrooms. They did not matter, for she knew that she would not find him there.

Down another flight, then, as she forced all thoughts of their argument from her mind. She must believe, in her heart, that what they were doing meant as much to him as it did to her. Or how could she bear to live?

When she reached the downstairs hall, a faint light was shining from the glass doors at the end, which stood partly ajar.

She smiled. It was just as she'd suspected. He'd brought the flowers and returned to the safety of the conservatory. It was where he always came when he was unsure of himself. And it was the place where he was most like the Tim Colton that she admired. He claimed he did not mind visitors. Now was an excellent chance to put his statement to the test. She slipped into the room with him, and closed the doors behind herself with a soft click.

At first, she saw nothing but the shadows of the plants, but there was a faint glow coming from the back of the room. The stoves were lit, but there was only a single candle, near the work table. She could see Tim moving from place to place, familiar in the darkness.

He looked up as she approached, freezing in place as he watched her. 'I did not expect you.'

'You did not?'

'I was caught up in work.' He gave a shadowy gesture to the table before him. 'Some say that it is better to plant at the dark of the moon. I doubt it will make a difference. Although there is a pull on the tides. But in the seeds and the earth, it would be so small that it shouldn't matter. Still, it may be that the wisdom of those that till the earth is greater than mine…'

She crooked her head to the side, and set the flowers upon the table beside him. 'What utter fustian. You brought these to me. What do you mean by them? You cannot think that I would forget so soon?'

He wiped his hands upon his apron, in a nervous gesture. 'They mean that I am out of hyacinths. Hyacinths are better for a proper apology. I suspect that I shall continually be forcing bulbs, if I can persuade you to remain with me. I cannot help making a muddle whenever I talk to you.'

He had made her smile, and she bit her lip, trying to hide the fact. 'When you say remain, what do you mean by it? Remain in the conservatory? For though it is quite nice by day, it is well past time for us to be in bed.' Three days past time. She smiled again, at what a wicked thought that was.

He gave her an odd look. 'I often sleep here, nights. I find it more peaceful.'

'You sleep here.' Again, she feared her amazement would offend him. 'It cannot be particularly comfortable.'

'I have seen where you sleep, my dear. You must understand that comfort is hardly an issue, if one is tired enough.'

'So you work yourself to exhaustion, and then sleep in the conservatory to avoid going up the stairs.'

She saw his reaction, and knew that she had guessed correctly. 'Not every night,' he hedged.

'But often.'

'It is not so uncomfortable. There is a *chaise* near the stove. You were sitting on it yesterday.'

She walked to the back of the room, behind the screen of palm trees, and sat down upon it again. 'Here? This is your bed?'

He was obviously embarrassed, now, and went to the stone basin in the corner, carefully washing the soil off his hands. 'Silly of me, I suppose. It is really quite pleasant, once you get used to it.'

'Compared to a fine bed upstairs, with silk hangings and a warm fire. And a valet to look after your every need.'

'It is more than I deserve,' he muttered, and she could feel the darkness stealing in on him again.

'Then share the space in my bed, under the eaves. There is not much room, but you are welcome there,' she said softly. 'Use the back stairs, if the main ones trouble you so.'

'You would allow me more freedom than my own children? For you have trained them to go up and down the main stairs again, as though nothing is wrong with them. Just like they used to.'

'They are young. They can heal from anything, given the chance. And perhaps a gentle nudge such as I gave them.'

'But I am old?' He smiled sadly. 'Older than you, certainly. Thirty-three.'

'That is not so very old. And age does not signify. You are merely set in your ways. And harder to persuade than the children. Stubborn.'

She had made him smile.

'But if you are a scientist, then you must have a rational mind. When the time is right, you will abandon your fear.'

He shook his head in amazement. 'You are a nine-days' wonder, Daphne Collins. You give me too much credit. And you still treat Clare's death as though it were some sort of unfortunate accident. Can you not see that what I did was wrong? And what I have done to you is just as bad. You should not be encouraging me to continue.'

Perhaps it was true. She would have been sure, at one time. But now that she had known him, she could not manage to give him up. 'I only know that it feels very right when you are with me, and very wrong when you are not. Whatever happened, I do not believe you can be blamed for it. And if this is where you wish to be, then I would be here as well.'

She leaned back, and stretched out upon the *chaise*. When she opened her eyes, and looked up, she gasped in wonder. 'The stars.' For there, stretched out before her on the other side of the glass roof, was the night sky.

He laughed softly. 'You have discovered my secret. And I needn't feel guilty for the pleasure it brings me.

For it is available to saints and sinners alike, if they take the time to look.'

She could feel him sitting down beside her, but was unable to tear her eyes away from the sky to look at him. 'It is amazing. So dark. The stars are like diamonds. And there are so many. I have never seen a sky like this in London.'

'Because the smoke in the air spoils the view. Only when you are deep in the country and the moon is new can you see a night as black as this. And that is the best time to see stars.'

He blew out the candle that sat nearby. And as the room became darker, the stars seemed to pop from the sky in relief. She imagined she could see the distances between them, and that some were far closer than others. She reached out a hand to them. For a moment, she had been tricked into thinking she could pluck them from their places.

She could feel his hands, moving to the ties of her robe. 'I meant to resist. But I cannot help myself. Let me see you by starlight.'

And she felt the lascivious urge to feel the light upon her bare skin, as though it were sunlight after a storm. She heard him sigh, as the cold air touched her naked body, and she arched her back to let her breasts point up to the heavens. She stared up at the stars again. 'So many. And they all have names.'

'The stars?' He laughed. 'You must know that as well as I, for you are a teacher.'

She squirmed slightly against the couch. 'Well,

I know the Plough, of course. And Polaris.' She pointed.

He leaned down and turned, to follow the line of her finger. Then he took her hand and moved it. 'There is Polaris. You are pointing at Sirius, my dear.'

'Oh, my. Well, they seem very different in the sky than they do in books.'

'Do they now?' He did not believe her in the least. But he did not seem to mind it, overly. 'It appears I must teach you astronomy.' He released her hand, and reached out again to touch her shoulder. 'If you look above where you are pointing, you will see a great W in the sky.'

She furrowed her brow, wondering whether she should pretend it was clear or admit defeat.

He touched her body lightly with his fingers, at the navel. 'If this is Polaris, then…' he traced his fingers from shoulder to breast to throat, to breast, and then the opposite shoulder '…there is Cassiopeia.'

He traced it again, and again, lingering over the tips of her breasts. She shuddered at his touch and closed her eyes.

He took his hand away. 'There, now. You will never learn the stars by keeping your eyes closed. Open them again.'

She did as she was bade.

'Do you see them, now?' His lips replaced his hand, travelling gently over the path of the stars. For a moment, she was lost between pushing him away so she could concentrate, and pulling him closer, never mind the stars.

And then it was as though the great W over her head leapt into sight, so clear and bright that it was a wonder she had not noticed it before. 'I see it.'

'Very good.' He dropped another kiss into the hollow of her throat, as though to reward her. And then to her mouth, kissing slowly. She could feel the smile upon his lips. 'Now that you have found that, lower your eyes to Polaris.' His lips travelled down her body to her belly. 'And you can find Ursa Major.'

'What?' For a moment, she lost all sense of the stars, and could think only of his tongue on her body.

'The Plough.' His fingers were tracing the bowl of the dipper on her skin, curving with the handle to go lower on her body.

His touch was so gentle, it felt as though he were drawing the design on her skin with a feather. As he passed, each nerve awakened, singing for more stimulation. When she looked down, he was staring at her face, watching her reaction. 'Can you see it?'

When she looked puzzled, he pointed up towards the sky.

And she glanced up to find the brightest star, and let her eyes wander the path that his fingers had taken, feeling the skin heat as she looked at the stars. She gave a trembling sigh. 'Yes.'

'Very good.' There was amusement in his voice. 'Now let us find something else. Orion. The hunter. His arm is like so, with sword raised.' He took her right hand and raised it over her head, trailing his fingers along the skin. 'And Betelgeuse is here.' He settled his lips upon her right shoulder, sucking gently upon the skin, until she felt her breasts tingling in response. 'His throat.' He moved to demonstrate, licking at the hollow of her throat, until she twisted, trying to catch his lips with her own.

So he moved to her other shoulder, kissing it, and stroking down her arm. 'His bow arm, outstretched.' He twined his fingers with hers until she stilled.

And then he slid lower on her body. 'And the stars of the belt.'

She had been waiting, breath held, for the feel of his lips upon her breasts, but he had gone lower, and was circling her waist with kisses. And when she looked into the sky, to the stars that he had described, she could find them all. There were the lower stars, just there, where his hands were resting on her knees.

And the stars that made up the sheath. She felt her body give a shudder, as she understood where the lesson was likely to end.

For he had settled there, where there were many stars, clustered together, and kissed her as though he knew the position of each one.

She stared up into the night sky. And it was as if she could see the lights turning above her, spinning around Polaris to mark the time. He kissed, lightly at first, and then more boldly, tracing designs upon her with his tongue, sucking upon the tender flesh, delving deep, his hands stroking her thighs, and parting them wide. He held her tight against his mouth, as his tongue dipped into her, and then returned to work magic.

The sky was spinning madly now and she bit at her lip to hold back the scream she felt was coming. Her body pulsed in rhythm with the touch of his tongue and clenched to each brush of his lips. And then his fingers came into her, and the stars came unfixed and flashed before her in a jumble of brilliant sparks.

He shed his clothes then, and came to her as she trembled in anticipation, finding his place inside her as surely as if he'd never left. She touched his body, which was hard and real, moving with him and against him, staring up into the fathomless night sky as she felt him find release. Then he reached for the thin blanket that was thrown over the end of their substitute bed, and pulled it up over them. And she settled into the small space between the couch and his body, wrapped her arms around his neck and they slept.

She awoke tangled in her lover's arms, still balanced precariously with him on the *chaise*. As she moved, he rolled with her, slipped out from under the blanket and dropped bare on to the stone floor of the conservatory.

And he laughed. He looked up at her, from his seat on the floor, rested his elbows beside her on the makeshift bed and kissed her.

'What time is it?' She whispered the words, and wondered why it had taken her so long to realise the risk.

'After six, I expect. The sun is up.'

'Oh, dear.' Suddenly, her voice sounded very much the offended schoolteacher. She reached for her wrapper, quickly pulling herself back into respectability. 'I must get back to my room, before I am missed.'

'If you leave me, I assure you, you shall be missed.' He reached out to stroke her hair. 'Stay.'

'Do not be a fool. You know I cannot. I have stayed too long already. It is light. The servants will be up. And someone is sure to see me on the stairs.'

He seemed only mildly affronted by her tone. 'You needn't worry. I doubt that it is still possible to shock the occupants of this house, after what has occurred already.'

'But none of that pertained to me.'

His face quirked in an ironic smile. 'And the fact that I have borne shame means nothing to you?'

'Only because you refuse to look for the truth.' She put her hands on her linen-clad hips. 'You are innocent of what happened. And I will never believe otherwise. Never.'

'Then though you are beautiful, you are also a fool.'

The words stung, for she had feared he thought thus. 'And you do not wish a fool for a wife, so you won't have me.'

'That is not what I said,' he corrected hastily.

'Do you mean to offer for me? Answer truthfully.'

And he hesitated. But then he said, 'In the hallway, when Bellston left, I said it badly, for I made it sound as if I didn't care about you. I am sorry for that. I wish very much to offer for you. But I want you to face the facts of the marriage you will be making. If you wish to be the wife of a murderer, then I shall be happier than I deserve if you will take me as your husband.'

'I do not wish to marry a murderer. I wish to marry you. I love you, Tim. And I will not change.'

'Then we are at an impasse, Daphne. I love you as well. More than ever I believed I could. And I will live a long and full life if you will admit my crime and forgive me for it. But it will hurt too much for me to bear it, if you believe me innocent. For the day will come when you come to full understanding of the mistake you made.'

She turned and fled, running for the stairs, heedless of her condition, and surroundings.

And there, at the foot of the stairs, was Mrs Sims staring in chilly disapproval.

Chapter Sixteen

In her room, Daphne scrubbed at her face, trying to make the tearstains on her cheeks less visible. She had met the cook on the stairs as well, on her way from bringing the children their breakfast. In a short time, everyone in the household would know what she had done. She would have to face their disapproving looks in the hall and know that they thought her unfit to care for children. And what would they think of their master? Though they could forgive him a murder, there might be a limit beyond which he had travelled that would lose their respect.

No matter how sure she was of the truth, until she could prove it to Tim, there would be no marriage, no chance to redeem her reputation. Her only hope was to slip away, leaving Miss Collins behind, as a crab leaves a shell. She could go back to London, to her old life. And with no likelihood of seeing Tim or the children. For when had she seen them before?

She pulled out the contents of her trunk, ready to repack it, and Sophie's sketches fell in a cascade of horror on to the wooden floor. She could hardly bear to look down. If she left, what was she to tell the children?

She would go to Lily and explain. She would tell her that she had ill family to attend to. The girl was the oldest, and might fill in the details on her own. She suspected something, just as Adam and Penny did. So Daphne would explain, as gently as she could, that Miss Collins could not stay with them. But that they were to be good for their father, and Sophie was to be allowed to draw, no matter what the subject…

She looked down at the sketches. All Clare, all in the same dress. It was the dress she had died in, if Sophie's first sketch was to be believed. And with the toe of her slipper, she rearranged the two papers in front of her. And picked up the first drawing, to put it last.

When viewed thus, in order, the angles came right, and the story fell into place. Clare at the top of the stairs. Clare angry. A hand, holding a bit of torn cloth. Her shocked expression, as she lost her balance. Clare falling.

Clare dead.

Daphne pulled off her wrapper, and washed and dressed quickly. She ignored the breakfast, and the schoolroom, leaving the children alone without explanation. If she took time to explain, someone was sure to convince her that what she was about to do was wrong.

She went straight down to the conservatory, back to Tim.

He was sitting beside his work table, with a light breakfast and tea cup laid on a napkin on the bench beside him. He rose with his tea cup held in a hopeful gesture, as though he had forgotten the way they had parted only a few moments ago, and thought she might have returned to dine with him.

She reached out and caught him by the hand, pulling him off the bench and away from his tea. 'You must come with me. To the children. Right now.'

He rose easily at the mention of the children, obviously worried. 'Is there a problem? An accident?'

'No, they are well. But they *know*, Tim. They know everything.'

His brow furrowed in confusion.

'The night Clare died. They saw it happen.'

The china cup fell from his numb fingers and shattered on the slates. 'God, no.'

'It is true. Sophie saw everything. She has been drawing it, over and over for me. But I did not understand. The others either saw as well, or they know what she has seen. They are afraid to come to you. So you must go to them and ask.'

He looked at her as though she were mad. 'Ask them? They have suffered enough. They should not have to tell what they know. The truth would be enough to hang their father. I can live with the punishment. But I cannot die knowing that they will feel responsible for my end.'

'That is not what will happen. I am sure. If they saw

anything at all, they will be able to tell you that it was an accident, just as Adam decreed.'

He laughed. 'The accident was a polite fiction. We all know that. Adam feels guilty for allowing himself to be seduced by my wife. He thinks he can make things right between us by covering up my crime. It gains nothing to make the children relive a night they would just as soon forget. And if you care at all about my welfare or my sanity, then do not force them to denounce me.' His voice trembled. 'No wonder they could not stand to be with me. I will send them from here, as soon as I am able. And once they are gone, I will see to it, one way or another, that justice is served in the matter of Clare's death. But do not make them play a part in my downfall.'

'That is not what will happen at all. The truth is nothing to be afraid of. I am sure of it. Why are you always so intent upon taking the weight of this upon yourself? Why do you never place the blame upon Sophie's father? For he had as much reason to wish Clare dead as you did. I doubt Penny would be so patient, living next door to her husband's lover.'

'You think Adam did this?' And then Tim let out a bitter laugh. 'What utter nonsense.'

'You are too quick to protect him, after what he did to you. I understand that your friendship is deep, and that he can be a most personable and pleasant man. But that is no reason to let him free of his crime.'

'Crime?' Now Tim was truly laughing. 'Adam is guilty of many things. He has been by turns a drunkard, a rake and a wastrel. He cuckolded me, as did half the men in London. But his respect for the law holds no equal. He would be physically incapable of breaking it to rid the world of my wife. Even if she threatened him with exposure, as I know she did.'

'Did you not read the letters that I stole? She was going to Adam on the night she died, and taking their daughter with her. And he would not have wanted her, now that he was married.'

'Was she now?' He shook his head. 'Then, obviously, you are mistaken. For he had no daughter by her, nor was he likely to get one. She was not pregnant when she died. At least not by him, for they had not been together for several months.'

'But Sophie…'

He laid a hand upon her arm. 'Was another man's child. I suspect she belongs to a drawing master, if such talents are a thing that can be inherited.' He laughed again, and for a moment, he seemed sincerely light-hearted. 'Clare must have been quite angry with me if she was threatening to go to him at the end. The man was penniless, and ran like the wind when it became apparent that he might have fathered a child. From time to time, Clare made such idle threats and left the letters around to frighten me. She knew how much I loved the girl. But the idea that she might leave the comfort of our home to live as a Bohemian, with her artist…' He laughed. Then he sighed, as if he was trying to expel all the grief in his body in one great breath. 'Daphne. If the circumstances were otherwise, I would be grateful for your naïve trust in my character. If only I had met you twelve years ago, before I met Clare. I would gladly

trade the wealth I gained from my first marriage for a
chance to have a love such as yours, willing to put such
blind faith in me. But I swear to you on all that is holy,
I was the only one in the house on the night she died.
The servants would have noticed had there been a guest
and remarked on it. They might have cared enough for
her not to reveal the names of her lovers. But they care
enough for me not to hide the identity of a murderer.'

'All you have are guesses and assumptions. The children have the truth,' she said.

'It does not matter to me if they do. I forbid you from
talking to them on the matter of their mother's death.
If not for my sake, then for theirs. Let them forget.'

'Forget?' She laughed in his miserable face. 'Now
you are the one who is being naïve. They are not going
to forget, Tim. It does not matter what I say or do, they
are still living the night their mother died. Sophie especially. Have you seen her drawings? Blood and death.
It has taken weeks to get her to draw anything but her
mother's corpse. Would you have me take her pens
away, or punish her as the last governess did?'

'No!'

'Then let them tell you what they saw. Even if it is
bad, at least it will be honest. They should not have to
go through life afraid of stairs and watercolours, and
strangers. For God's sake, Tim, they should not have to
be afraid of you. No matter what they might say, you
would never love them less, would you?'

'Of course not.'

'Now, they live in continual fear of your rejection.

They think that you mean to send them away because you no longer want them.'

'That is not true.'

'But they reason like children. They do not understand that they were not to blame. They think you want to be rid of them and refuse to believe otherwise. Go to them. Go now. Tell them it is not so. And ask them for the truth.'

He wavered.

'We will go together,' she offered, placing her hand on his shoulder. 'I will be there to help you. But it must be done, for their sake, for yours, and for ours.'

He stared at her, and his eyes held the same shocked confusion that the children's did. 'And if helping them means I lose you?'

She smiled. 'You will not lose me.'

'I will if I hang for murder.' He ran a hand through his hair and gave a shaky laugh. 'It was all so much easier to contemplate ending my life, knowing that the day for the deed had not arrived. But you would have me do it now, after I have found a reason to survive.' His face was grey with fear and shock, but he rose from the desk and squared his shoulders. 'And I am so vain that I cannot let the woman I love see my cowardice. You say I am hurting the children by my inaction. And I must trust you on this, for you are their governess, and know more than I about the minds of children.'

The truth stuck in her throat. The time was coming when she would have to admit that she knew far less about children then he did. But not now. For now, she only knew what was right. 'They are your children, Tim.

You know what is best for them. In all save this one thing.'

His shoulders slumped, and she knew that she had defeated him. 'Very well, then. Let us go to them and be done with it. If they have been suffering because of my inaction, then I would not have it be for one moment more.' He went to the door, and opened it, waiting politely for her to pass through. She followed him to the main stairs, and he paused at the foot for a moment, just as he always did. Then he offered her his arm, and began the ascent. His steps were steady and unhurried, but she could see in his eye the desire to turn and run, to hurry, or to tarry. It was a struggle for him to make the trip appear ordinary.

At last they reached the top of the stairs and he escorted her down the hall, still holding her arm. And she wondered for a moment if it was for her protection or as a way to gain strength from the contact. She could see the housekeeper approaching from the other end of the hall, and the hitch in her gait as she saw the master arm in arm with the governess, about to talk to the children.

Emotions flickered across the woman's face. Shock, disapproval and then thoughtfulness. She gazed again at her employer, as though considering both the past and the future. And then she gave a small smile of approval, and continued on her way as if nothing unusual had occurred.

If Tim noticed, he made no mention of it. But it set Daphne somewhat at ease to know, if they survived the afternoon, she would not have Mrs Sims as an adversary.

He paused at the door of the schoolroom as though he still considered it possible to turn back. And then he opened the door and stood before the children.

Daphne could see by the looks on their faces that they instinctively sensed the difference in the adults and were confused by it. Without a word, the older children took a half-step towards their little sister.

'Children?' Tim looked at them for a moment as though he had never seen them before. He was staring at the worried looks on their faces, the set lines around their mouths and the frightened look in Sophie's eyes, as though it were all registering on him, fresh. Then he dropped Daphne's hand and went to them, down on one knee so that he might not be over-tall for the little one. 'It is time for us to talk.'

'About what, Father?' Edmund was curiously formal. Daphne suspected it was a ruse to buy time, for it was apparent that he knew exactly what the subject was to be.

'About the night…' Tim swallowed. 'The night your mother died. Daphne seems to think that you saw the… when I…when she fell.'

She looked at them all, her eyes travelling from face to face. Giving them a look that was all kindness and implacability. 'Tell your father.'

'If you have a secret?' Tim smiled down at them, as if to reassure them, but there were lines of strain around his mouth. 'Whatever you are concealing, I am sure it will be better if we face it together.'

'Don't send Sophie away,' Lily blurted, and then silenced herself after a glare from Edmund.

'And why would I do that?' Tim smiled again, this time with incredulity.

Sophie took a step away from him, as though afraid, and said, 'Mama fell.'

His smile became a rictus, and he flinched. 'Yes, little one. I know. And I am very sorry.' He said it carefully, not knowing how to proceed. 'But because Mama…fell…it does not mean that I am angry with you, or that you are in any danger from me. Or that I do not love you very, very much. I just think that you would be better off if you were in school, and away from here. You will find, once you try it, that it is very pleasant. And you will have such fun that you will not miss this house, or your old father, very much at all.' The last words rang false, as did his smile. For it appeared that it was difficult for him to hold even the sad parody of a grin that he had managed before.

Sophie's lip began to tremble.

'Do not punish her,' Lily blurted again, and reached to gather her little sister to her. 'Send us away, but let her stay. She is so small. And she did not know. It will not happen again. She knows better now.'

'This is not meant as a punishment,' Tim said hopelessly. 'When you are older, you will see. It is for the best. There are people better suited to take care of you than I, darling Sophie.'

Sophie was crying in earnest now, large tears sliding silently over her round cheeks. Daphne reached to comfort her, but the children closed ranks, just as they had from the first. Lily hugged her little sister and Edmund stepped between father and sisters to protect them, as though he were already the man he would become, and a match for his father. He squared his shoulders and shouted, 'Just because she is not yours, does not mean that you should not care for her.'

'Who told you that?' Tim demanded. But Daphne was sure that she knew. Where else would they have got the truth, but from their mother?

'She is not yours,' Edmund repeated. 'And so you mean to punish her, even though it is no fault of hers how our mother behaved.'

Tim took a deep, shaky breath. 'I do not blame you, any of you, for the problems between your mother and myself. And I am sorry you had to witness what you did, at the end. It was wrong to subject you to that. I think, in sending you to school, that it would be better if you were removed to an atmosphere that would be less unhealthy.'

'School?' Edmund said bitterly. 'We know the sort of school you want to send Sophie to. A madhouse is no place for a little girl.'

'Madhouse?' Tim said, helpless. 'When did I ever…?'

'Let us take care of her,' Lily pleaded. 'She is no trouble. She doesn't eat much and she's not a bother at all. And she will never hurt anyone again.'

'Again?' Now Tim was truly puzzled. 'Children. No more games. And no more nonsense about the madhouse, not even in jest. I never meant to send Sophie there. You must tell me what has frightened you so. Tell me exactly. For I truly do not understand.'

'Mama fell,' Sophie said again. And the two children looked at her in horror, as though she were not stating the obvious.

And suddenly, the meaning of the pictures became clear. And the strange angles of the drawings, as though they were from the perspective of a small child who was only drawing what she had seen right in front of her.

'Tell your father what happened that night,' Daphne prompted. 'For he knows less about it than you think he does.'

Tim flinched again, as though he did not want to know the truth, after all this time. And then he said, 'Tell me. I need to know what happened, children. I need to know the truth.'

Edmund looked at him, sullen and in challenge. 'After you fought, Mother was angry. She said that you had sent her to pack her things and get out of your sight. And she came here and told Lily and me that she wanted no part of us any more. We were our father's children, and you could keep us. But that Sophie was none of yours, and so she must go as well. Because you would not want her, once Mother had gone.'

Tim took a deep breath. 'I did not mean for her to do that. She was being hurtful.'

Lily gave a small nod. 'We did not want her to take Sophie and we called for you, but you did not come.'

Their father let out a small moan of pain.

'And she took Sophie by the arm, and dragged her out onto the landing.'

'It was hurting her,' Edmund said quietly. 'So she cried and fought.'

'Mama fell,' Sophie said again.

And Daphne could see the scene in her mind, in horrible clarity. The children crying, and mother and daughter struggling at the top of the stairs. Clare's dress ripping. And the horrible moment when she knew that she could not stop herself from falling.

She turned to Tim. And she could see the moment when he understood, as something inside him released that had been held tense since the moment of his wife's death. His features struggled between relief for himself and agony for his children. He reached forwards and pulled Sophie into his arms. 'It was an accident,' he murmured. 'Only an accident. And no one's fault at all. Is this what you have been afraid of, all this time?' He hugged her tight and murmured into her hair, 'I am so sorry, little one. So sorry.' He looked over her head, to the other children. 'I did not understand.'

'I don't want to go,' whispered Sophie.

'And you will not, sweetheart. You will stay safe and happy, right here. Isn't that so, Miss Collins?' He looked to her for confirmation, for she could see that the little girl had turned her worried expression to her, probably fearing her response.

'Of course that is so, little one.' And she smiled encouragement, although the truth was horrible. 'Where else would you belong but in your home?'

Sophie seemed to slump a little, to become even smaller than she was, as though she wanted to climb into her father's lap and stay for a very long time. But there was a hesitant smile upon her face, as though the worst had happened, and she had begun to suspect it might be all right, after all.

'And you will always be my little girl.' He looked up to his other children, and opened his arms wide to encompass them. 'You are all mine. It does not matter where you go. I am your father, and this is your home. And always will be.'

And, hesitantly, the other children stepped into his arms as well. And suddenly it was a tangle of arms and legs, and laughter and tears. And Daphne looked around, feeling lost and out of place.

And Tim looked up, over the heads of all his children, and said, 'Miss Collins?', holding his arms even wider.

And the children laughed, and turned to her as well, calling, 'Miss Collins?', and holding out their arms as well.

She froze for a moment, and then she laughed, and stepped in, joining the family. And she understood what had been lacking in the house, for the warmth and love in the hug seemed to pervade her very soul.

And Tim's eyes met hers, and he gave an incredulous little shake of his head. 'It was an accident,' he whispered again. 'A terrible accident. No one's fault at all.' And while she could feel the concern for his daughter emanating from him like a warm glow, he seemed a totally different person than the dark, tortured soul she had first met.

Chapter Seventeen

After what seemed like a long time he released them, and reached for a handkerchief to wipe his eyes and his brow.

Edmund looked at him, with sudden shyness, and said, 'Must we still go to school, then?'

Tim sighed. 'We will talk of that later, I think. The revelations of the day have given me much to think on. Perhaps next term…'

The boy seemed to sag in relief. 'And Sophie? Mother said—'

Tim stopped him. 'I would not put too much weight on anything that happened on those last days. Your mother and I were very angry at one another. What was said then changes nothing. We will not speak of it again.'

Lily smiled in understanding, and hugged her father all the harder.

'And Miss Collins will stay as well,' Sophie announced, and gave her father a hug.

And she could feel the awkwardness, coming from Tim, just as the love and protection had before. 'I think that is something I must discuss with Miss Collins,' he said.

'Yes,' she said softly, in answer. 'But now, children, you must get ready for lessons.'

'Lessons?' Tim laughed out loud. 'No lessons today. No work. We will go for a walk in the woods. And visit the orangery to see how the trees are faring.'

The children's faces shone with anticipation. Daphne looked at each in turn. 'There is a chill in the air. Go to your rooms and change into clothing that is sensible for the weather. And wash the breakfast from your hands and faces. Take care with your nails...' She let the familiarity of the routine take her, blunting out the question in the back of her mind. What would become of her, now? She had done what she had come to do, and satisfied herself as to the details of Clarissa's death.

And she could hardly fault the family, if she had been foolish enough to lose her heart as well. The man standing before her now was nothing like the dark lord who had come to her rooms. That man was gone, and in his place was a respectable father who would never have taken such liberties.

And it suddenly occurred to her that what her mother had always told her about the value of reputation might be true. She might have been able to hold his desire, but would he respect her, now that he could have any woman he wanted?

As the children moved off to care for themselves, she heard him behind her. 'Daphne?' His voice was soft, the question in the name surprisingly gentle.

'Yes?' She turned to face him.

He paused again, unsure of how to continue. And then he said, 'We have to talk.'

'We are talking now.'

'In private. After the children have gone to bed, about what will happen next between us.'

She glanced at the children, walking down the hall together. 'It would be best, if the news is bad, to inform me of it, quickly. To prevent any nonsense and false assumptions on my part.'

He gave a dry little laugh. 'How like a governess you sound, all of a sudden. Very prim and proper.'

'Perhaps it is about time for me to do so.' She frowned, thinking of Sophie's obvious attachment to her. 'I never gave thought to them, and what might happen after, even though it was my job. That should have been my first priority.'

When she looked at him, he was smiling at her, in a way she had never seen before. It was strange and soft and warm, and it made her blush. 'You honour my family with your concern. And you have given a great gift to us, with what I thought was meddling and snooping and a far from healthy curiosity about Clare. If it were not for your persistence, I would never have known the truth.'

And another flash of guilt caught her. Her motives had been just as bad as he'd thought, even if the results had been in his favour.

'And I must apologise for my treatment of you, which was coloured by my fears of the truth, and was not as respectful as it should have been.'

An odd apology. She brushed it away with a wave of her hand.

'And I would like to take the opportunity to start again, and to treat you as you deserve, as one who holds my affection, and that of my children.'

It sounded almost like he meant to pay court to her, and pretend that nothing had happened between them. And to prevent the awkwardness, she dropped a small curtsy, and said, 'Thank you, my lord,' averting her eyes and easily becoming the servant she had never thought to be.

'Oh, bloody hell.' And, for a moment, the old Tim was back. He seized her by the arms and pulled her lips to his. 'I meant to start fresh with you, now that I am free. But I cannot manage it, if you mean to change as well.' He kissed her with such force that she could hardly breathe, his hands twisting in her hair, her crisp gown rumpling under his touch, and she said, 'Lord Colton, please. The children.'

'Oh, what nonsense. The children will best get used to the way I feel about you. You have given me my life back, and my family as well. I am not going to let you drift away from me, now that everything is finally right.'

'Right?' Didn't he understand it was all wrong? For she had done wrong in coming here, even if the results were right.

He held her hand, and dropped to his knees before

her. 'I love you.' He gave a great breath, as though a weight had been lifted from his chest, and grinned up at her. And it was happy and relaxed and open. 'I have loved you for some time. But I was afraid to act. You are too good to tie yourself to a wreck such as I was. A murderer. A man with no future. I wanted better for you than I could ever give. But now?' He spread his arms wide. 'Now, it is all changed. I can be happy without guilt. And I can make you happy as well. Or, at least, I would like to try.' A shadow passed over his face. 'It will be difficult, of course. There are the children to think of. They have been through hell over this, and it will take time to recover. But you know better than anyone that what happened was an accident. You can help them see that, now that they no longer fear the discovery.'

That was true, at least.

'They are very fond of you. And now that you know the truth, there is nothing to stand between us.'

'Nothing,' she said softly, her own motives in coming there, and her real name and family, rising like ghosts from the mist.

'Is that a yes?' he asked hopefully. And then muttered, 'Or have I forgotten the proposal? Because I fully intended to ask. And it has been so strange between us. All the wrong way round. Not the normal thing at all. Perhaps you misunderstood.' He cleared his throat, and said, in a formal tone that was quite spoiled by his grinning, 'Miss Collins, it would do me a great honour if you would give me your hand in marriage.'

And once again, there was the little break in her

mind, as she recognised her alias. It occurred to her too late that Tim should really be speaking to her father over this. But he did not even know that she had a father, since the Duchess believed that Miss Collins had no family. Which meant that there was even more to explain than she thought. And she found that she could not meet his gaze. 'This is very sudden. I will have to think on it.'

'Of course.' She could hear his optimism faltering in his voice. 'It is rather out of the blue. And I meant to do it differently. Better. It is rather unfair of me to present it so.' He reached out and touched her hand. 'But I am so…happy. You cannot begin to understand. I am overcome.' And now there was a break in his voice, which was quickly mastered. 'Please, take as much time as you need. For we will have a lifetime.' He released her hand.

And when she looked into his eyes, she saw such hope, such confidence in her and in their future, that it was even more difficult to blurt the truth.

'I must go and see that the children are ready for your walk.'

'And you?'

Where was she to go? It was not really her place to walk with the family. And she was not sure if it would ever be. But she knew that the idea of a day with Tim and the children would be intensely painful to her, until she could find the right words to explain things to him. 'Today, I think it should be just you and your children. You have much to learn about each other, and it is not the place for a servant to intrude.'

He looked puzzled, as though he could not understand why her joy did not match his own. 'You know I do not think of you in that way.'

'Still, you need time alone with each other. You can manage without me, for a few hours. I will be here tonight.' She almost had to convince herself of the fact, for there was some panicked portion of her that wanted to rush to her room, gather her belongings and flee.

He nodded in regret. 'I suppose it is true. There is much we have not discussed, as a family. They have lived in needless fear for months, and I was too blind to see it.' His lips tightened for a moment, in resolution. 'I must undo any nonsense instilled by Clare, at the end. It has festered too long.'

She had a fleeting image of her dear cousin, so happy, so pleasant, and yet so vain. And so very thoughtless of those around her. 'They will be all right now that they know they have your love.'

He stared at her again. And then he smiled. 'As do you. And thank you for your confidence in me. Now go, if you must. Or I will hold you here until you say the things I wish to hear.'

Where she once might have been terrified by the threat, his words came as gentle as a caress. Without thinking, she dropped a curtsy and exited as his governess, not his lover.

It was no easier, waiting in her room. She had hoped that the things she must say would come to her, once she was alone. But her mind was a whirl of beginnings, and no clear ending. She was sorry, of course. But when he came to her tonight, would an apology be sufficient?

* * *

When at last she heard the footsteps on her stairs, she took a deep breath and sat up, still not ready to meet him.

It came as a surprise when there was an unfamiliar rap upon the door, rather than his hand upon the knob. 'Miss Collins?'

'Yes.' It was Willoby, the footman.

'I have a letter for you. From the master.'

'Slip it under the door, please.' She pulled the covers up to her chin.

She suspected he was disappointed that she did not open for him and take the letter herself. The communication was unusual, and he no doubt wanted some scrap of gossip to take below stairs. But instead there was the scratch of paper on wood as the letter appeared, and the somewhat dejected sound of Willoby's retreating steps.

When she was sure that he had gone, she got out of bed and hurried across the floor to pick up the paper. The seal was unbroken, thank God. The contents were still private. She snapped the wax and unfolded it, turning to the candle so that she could read the words.

My darling Daphne,
While I want nothing more in life than to be at your side this night, I cannot allow myself to come to you, until I am sure of your response to my question. Should it be no, I could not in good conscience share your bed. For what would it say of

my motives, or the respect and esteem I have for you, to treat you in so common a way?

You will probably think it quite foolish that I have found the value of your honour so late in our acquaintance. And perhaps it is. But I find that life was much simpler when I had no hope in the future. In my despair, I took without thinking of the consequences, for they did not matter to me. I was completely sure of myself, in thought and action. Once a man realises he is damned, he has nothing more to fear.

I am immeasurably happier than I was, just a day ago. But I find that with renewed hope, comes doubt. Did I force you to do something which you now regret? Did you only agree to save your job, or my feelings? Now that the way is clear for us to be together, are your feelings less fixed than mine?

If I have done anything that makes you unable to answer yes, with your whole heart, then please forgive me for it. If there is a way to mend the problem, if there is anything at all that I can do so that we may begin fresh, tell me it, and I will give it you.

I want nothing more than that you might know me for the man I truly am, and not the demon that possessed me for so long. My heart, my mind, all I have, I will lay at your feet. You have but to accept it to make me the happiest man in Wales.

If you will have me, then I shall always be,
    Your Tim.

She climbed into bed, clutching the paper tight to her breast, the words still echoing in her head. She wanted them to make her happy, and wished to make him happy as well. But how could he not realise that it was her unworthiness, and not his, that created the rift?

After a sleepless night she decided that the problem was all hers. She wished to soften the blow, when nothing but the whole truth would do. She arose when it was barely light, and pulled her finest day dress from the portmanteau, doing her best to shake the wrinkles from it. It was a beautiful thing of deep blue silk, embroidered all about the hem with tiny flowers. Far too impractical for a servant, which was the reason it had lain unworn for all these weeks.

She washed carefully and dressed herself. And she could see in the small scrap of mirror that already she looked different. Then, with many pins and much fussing, she managed to do her hair up in a fashion much more in tune with the way she used to wear it, when she'd had a ladies' maid and time for a proper *toilette*. With each stroke of the brush she felt a little more her old self, and a little less like Miss Collins the governess.

And she was prettier, of course. Tim deserved no less than that. But more confident, entitled to speak freely to a man who was within her social set.

A man very much to her tastes. She smiled. She suspected her father would approve as well. Tim's intelligence and good sense fairly shone from him, now that he was feeling better. He was rich enough, but not frivolous. He had a fine house, and a title as well. She suspected that, when the time came for the two to meet, his suit would be received with as much relief as joy.

And that he loved her, and she loved him in return, was almost too much to hope for. She had imagined that marriage would be as Clare had assured her, an impediment to happiness, rather than the beginning of true joy. Which proved again how little Clare knew on the subject. It appeared she was likely to have everything she might want: a man who suited her temper, and a husband to suit her family. And a family of her own, ready made—if she could make it over the difficult hurdle of revealing her true name and her reasons for coming here.

She would go to him this morning, first thing, full of humility. She would suggest that they take breakfast in the conservatory, just the two of them. The presence of his plants relaxed him, and he would be in the best frame of mind for unfortunate truths. She would tell all, and give what sorry explanations she could manage. And she would swear that there would be no more falsehoods or deceptions from her. He would have nothing but fidelity, honesty and obedience from his wife, if he wished to make the offer in his letter again, in person. She took a deep breath, and set off down the stairs to find the man she loved.

When she arrived in the drawing room, she found Tim waiting in attendance upon a guest.

It was her father.

Chapter Eighteen

She stopped in the doorway, listening to the two men, who had not yet noticed her. 'The London Collinghams,' Tim said in a stunned voice.

'I was Clarissa's uncle. Her father's brother. I assumed your late wife must have mentioned our daughter to you, for they spent much time together, when Clare was in London.'

'Of course.' His voice was faint, as though he were trying to hide the fact that he had no idea what his wife did when she was away from him. There were so many things he did not wish to hear in detail that innocent family visits must have fallen by the wayside.

'It came as a great surprise that she should be eager to visit here. She did not tell us of her intentions, when she set out. It was only when she did not arrive at her aunt's that we set about inquiring. And then, of course, we received Daphne's letter of explanation, delayed due to a blurred address.'

'Oh.' Tim's voice was still faint. Perhaps he had begun to understand, or was still merely confused by her father's strange, disapproving tone.

She stepped fully into the room, before it became any worse than it was.

'There you are.' Her father's voice held the same exasperated tone she had grown used to in London. As though whatever she had done it was faintly disappointing and not at all the course he would have chosen for her.

He beetled his brows and gave her a half-hearted glare. 'If you wished to visit a different branch of the family, I would not have objected, for I must say that Wales is remote enough to put you out of scandal's way. And one cousin is very like the next. But it is most rude of you to have given us no notice. And careless of you to send a letter that could not be read.' He glared again, as though he meant to say 'suspiciously careless'. Then he went on with his gentle harangue. 'Your mother is beside herself with worry. And I have had to track you across Wales like a wounded stag.'

She swallowed and said softly, 'I am sorry. I did not think.'

'You rarely do.' Her father shot a glance at Tim, smiling to mitigate some of the gall. 'I swear, if the girl was not so sweet natured, we'd never put up with the mischief. I hope she has not given you too much bother, in her time here.'

Tim's face was frozen as though carved in stone. At last, he managed, 'She has made up for some of the bother, and been a great help to the children.'

'Daphne helping with children?' Her father laughed then, unable to contain himself. 'What a ludicrous idea. You must have been bored out of your senses, Daphne darling, to succumb to the charms of little ones.'

'They are most exceptional children, Father. All three of them…'

But he'd turned back to Tim and was confiding, 'She really is the most selfish creature on some subjects. My wife and I have been long resigned to the fact that when she settles, any grandchildren we are likely to have from her will be raised by the nanny. If it is left to my daughter, the first handprint left on a gown, and she will put the poor mites outside with the dogs.'

'Really.' It was impossible to read the meaning in a single word. But she suspected that Tim meant to let her father ramble, just to see where the path of the conversation went.

Her father was laughing as though it were the most wonderful diversion that he had raised his daughter to be so insensible to the needs of others. And Tim was staring at her as though she were a monster. She could feel her cheeks, hot with embarrassment.

Her father ceased his laughing, and dipped his head in apology. 'I can't think what has got into the girl. We sent her to Wales as a punishment. She was nothing but trouble while in London. And, until recently, I had no idea that she had not followed instruction and gone directly to her aunt's.'

'I see.' Tim's face was deathly white, and still devoid of expression.

'I really cannot understand young women nowadays. Not even the ones in my own family. For they seem to know no bounds of decorum.' It was then that her father realised that he was speaking ill of the former lady of the house, and his tone moderated. 'But lovely, of course. Your wife was a great beauty.'

Tim nodded, giving the man nothing to rescue himself.

'And a particular friend of Daphne's. I suspect that is why she came here.'

'I had no idea that you and Clare were so close. You never said.' If possible, Tim's complexion went even whiter. And his face twisted in a sickly smile. 'Had you not heard that Clarissa was no longer living?'

'I had.' Her answer was barely a whisper.

'Oh, yes,' her father announced. 'She was most affected by it. She grieved for days about the unfairness, the strangeness that one so young, without a trace of infirmity, should die in a fall.'

Daphne touched a hand to her throbbing temple, as her father all but explained her suspicions, and the way she had declared to all in the family that it was likely to be the work of that horrible Timothy Colton.

And then, her father stopped just short of the truth, and said, 'But the children... I expect that was what drew Daphne here, and it explains her sudden change of heart. It was all out of a desire to see that they were well. I am sure that Clarissa would have wished it.'

'You are sure, are you?' Tim's smile had changed to a grimace. And for a moment, she was afraid that he would reveal all. Then he seemed to gain mastery over himself, and returned to the reliable lie. 'That is it, certainly.' He turned to her, then, speaking formally. 'Well, Miss Collingham. As you can see, after staying with us, you have nothing to fear for the sake of the children. I am quite able to care for them, from this time forth. I trust I have been able to set your mind at rest on the subject.'

'Yes.' She choked out the word, and her answering smile was as false as his. But it seemed to reassure her father that, at least this time, there would be no scandal. She had not made as complete a cake of herself as he feared.

'While I appreciate your concern, you had but to ask and I could have invited you formally to stay as a guest. Your treatment would have been much less haphazard, had we been better prepared for your visit.'

Her father accepted it as an apology, and nodded again. But she knew the truth of the words. Had he known who she was, he'd never have touched her, or trusted her with the care of his children. And he certainly would not have been fool enough to love her.

'I'm sorry.'

Her father glared again. 'As well you should be, for causing the man so much trouble.'

Tim waved his hand. 'We will not speak of it again.'

And again, her father accepted it, as a gentlemanly dismissal of the mess she had caused with her foolishness. But she suspected that the words were directed to her, and meant *I will not speak to you again.*

'I appreciate your understanding. And now, if the servants will finish packing your things, the carriage is waiting.' Father gave her a significant look.

'If I could speak to Mr. Colton for a moment, before departing?'

Her father gave an impatient sigh. 'This was not sufficient farewell?'

'In private, Father.'

Her father looked to Tim, who looked back, still impassive, and gave the slightest of nods.

'Very well, then. I will await you in the carriage.'

She waited for a moment, as her father left the room, until she was sure that he was out of earshot. And then she spoke. 'Tim, I must explain.' She reached out to touch his sleeve.

He shook off her hand and stepped clear of her grasp. 'Further explanation is not necessary. I already knew you thought me a murderer.'

'As you did yourself. But you are not. We both know that now.'

'It must have disappointed you to discover the fact. I had no idea the lengths you would go to, to prove my guilt. And I thought it was I who dragged you to do what you did.'

'Do not speak of it so,' she moaned. 'As though what we did was foul and base.'

'It was,' he said firmly. 'But now that I know of your relationship to my wife, it makes much more sense. You were not without guilt, or your parents would never have sent you from London.' He laughed. 'And I tortured myself with the notion that I had debauched an innocent. It appears that I am the more naïve of the two of us.'

'That is not true. I never… There was no one before you.'

He shrugged. 'Perhaps not. But you gave your virtue up fast enough, once you could find a reason to. You let me use you, to gain the information you craved. And you used me as well.'

Tears were stinging in her eyes to hear what had happened between them relegated to a transaction. 'It was more than that, I swear. I love you.'

'If you are a protégée of Clare's, then you are no more capable of love than she was.'

'That is not true. Perhaps once it might have been. But she was wrong. I do love you, Tim. And I love the children.'

'Do not speak of them!' His eyes narrowed. 'If I can do nothing else, I will see to it that you never bother them again. You know what I am capable of, with regards to them. Do not cross me. And do not think, for even a moment, that I will let you become a part of their lives.'

'Have you forgotten so quickly what we were talking about last night?' she argued. 'I am already a part of their lives, just as they are a part of mine. And I am a part of your life, as well.' She held her hand out to him again.

He ignored it. 'No longer.'

'You cannot send me away so easily. They need me, Tim. You need me.'

'They do not need another Clarissa. They need a

mother. Or perhaps, they need better than that. A true governess, and not some ignorant, lying sham.' He looked at her, slowly, up and down. 'And if I wish to replace what you have been to me? To find a pretty woman, to share my bed and tell me lies? Then I will find a whore. Good day to you, madam.'

And he turned and left her alone in the room, ignoring the tears in her eyes.

Chapter Nineteen

'Vouchers!' Her mother fairly sang the word. 'The patronesses have seen fit to forgive you, my dear. We are going to Almack's.' She waved the letter over her head in triumph. 'A few months away was all that was necessary. The disasters of last Season are forgotten.'

'Much has changed,' Daphne said, without much enthusiasm.

'I should say so.' Her mother nodded in approval. 'For you turned down a chance to go to Vauxhall Gardens last night, and Covent Garden the night before. And bless my eyes if I did not see you reading before the fire.'

Daphne shrugged. 'It is a quiet way to pass the time. And I have begun to suspect that there are gaps in my education. It would be wise to remedy them, lest I be thought a fool.'

Her mother laughed. 'It certainly did not concern you before. But reading is harmless enough, if not carried to extremes. I would not want to see you wrapped in a book once the Season is full upon us. That would be most unnatural.'

'Of course not.'

'Or dressed in the same gowns that you wore before. I do not wish people to think we have no money to purchase new. It will give the husband-hunt an air of desperation. Or worse yet, it will make your suitors think you do not care enough for them to put on fresh silks. And so we must shop.'

'I suppose, if we must.' She sighed.

Her mother looked at her strangely. 'Are you ill, darling?'

'No. I am fine, really.' She could not help it. She sighed again.

'Well, I think you must be ill, if you are resisting a trip to Bond Street. Your father will be incensed over it, of course. How very like a man not to see the need.'

Daphne glanced at her already too-full wardrobe. In truth, she could not see the need herself. Even her oldest dresses were hardly worn. 'It just seems so wasteful not to manage with the things I've already got.'

Her mother was giving her the look again. 'The scandal of last Season may be behind you, my dear, but I doubt that last Season's dresses will be forgotten so easily. It would never do to have every mother's daughter sniping behind their hands at your finery, in your moment of triumph. If I'd known that a month in the country would give you such bizarre notions… But never mind, it could not be helped. And now we must work to bring you back to the spirited girl you once were. For I swear, while I welcome the moderation in your character, you are most decidedly not yourself since your return.'

'I suppose.' She looked into the mirror at her own reflection, trying to see what her mother saw, and continually surprised at what she did not see. When she looked into her own eyes, the new knowledge in them was plain enough. She had expected, with a single look, that her mother would discern what had happened, and ship her right back into permanent rustication.

But no. While her father and mother had feared for her reputation before she left London, and all society had proclaimed her a hoyden, they now saw a picture of maidenly modesty. And they meant to reward her for it, whether she liked it or no.

The thought would have made her laugh, if she could bring herself to that mood. Instead, she sighed again.

He mother laid a tentative hand upon her shoulder. 'I am sure it is just a matter of re-entering society, and your mood will return to normal. I am sorry that we had to take such drastic action, my dear, and send you far from home. We missed you dreadfully, of course. And it did concern me to learn that you had stayed with Clare's family, instead of the family we had chosen for you. She was dreadfully wild, you know. We did not realise what we had done by encouraging the friendship. But hers was not the influence we sought.'

To be told this now heaped irony upon the situation. 'Oh.'

Her mother smiled. 'But I can see it has done you no real harm, and, in some ways, much good.'

'Lord Colton was most hospitable,' she lied, 'and the children were lovely.' She felt the pang of longing go through her. Did they miss her at all? she wondered. Or had they forgotten?

'And it has put you in an excellent position to receive suitors. To spend time in the country, with a family in need, and in the wilds of the country, instead of gadding about town with your rackety friends, says much about your character that is admirable. In all, we could not have hoped for a better result.'

And now she felt more like crying then ever. Her future required that she pretend she had gone to help, rather than to punish. Her mother was spreading it about that she had spent the last month as an angel of mercy to a broken man and his orphaned children, instead of tangled in the sheets with her lover. She was sure that she would go mad.

Of course, her father suspected that something other than the obvious had gone on. He had lectured her all the way back to London about the dangers of attaching herself to the household of a single man, with no sign of a chaperon. And never mind that he was family.

But her mother cared only about the improvement in her character, and gave little thought to how it might have been wrought. She went blissfully on, not noticing Daphne's melancholy. 'I must send Lord Colton a note of thanks for taking such good care of you.'

'I doubt thanks are necessary,' she said softly. 'I am sure he is too modest to think of it.'

'No thanks after such a long visit?' Her mother's eyebrows arched. 'Well, I suppose, with no woman to head the house, Lord Colton has gone a bit odd about the social niceties. But perhaps we can arrange another visit, next autumn, so that you might see how the children have grown. Or invite them here so that we all might meet them.' She smiled. 'I dare say you will be wedded by then, or at least betrothed. And the Colton family will have an honoured place on the guest list. We owe them much in reforming your character.'

'That would be…lovely. I am sure the girls would like to see a wedding.' She swallowed hard to keep back the rush of tears she felt at the thought of Tim, relegated to a front pew with the family like some sort of doting uncle, holding his tongue while another man met her at the altar.

Her mother was smiling broadly at the image formed in her mind. 'Perhaps it is not too early for me to begin the guest list. Such a large event will require planning. And once the Season is under way, we will not have time to do it justice. It is much more difficult to lay out a proper wedding breakfast than to find a groom.' Her mother exited the room in a haze of fantasy, still clutching the vouchers that were the ticket to all her future hopes and dreams.

Daphne sank back into a chair beside the dressing table, too weak to move. That was her future, and always had been. A proper Season, with no false starts, embarrassments or trips into the bushes. Suitors, an offer and a society marriage. It did not matter that her heart was in Wales. And her true family as well.

For that was how she had begun to feel. It had been such a short time. But she had begun to think of Tim's children as her own. She had helped them, and they had loved her for it. It was not her fault that she had loved in return. And was it really so strange? For little Sophie belonged to no one, and yet Tim knew from her first moment on earth that he was her true father. Perhaps that was the way, with young ones.

They had got so much better, under her care. Had the changes lasted? she wondered. No matter how she felt now, it was a small comfort to think that she had done some permanent good. But what if they felt betrayed by her sudden departure? Had everything gone back to the horrible way it was, before she'd started meddling in it?

At least now Tim knew the truth. He could move on with his life. There was no danger in marrying again. The children needed a mother. And if he had given his heart to a woman who was not worthy of him? The fact was immaterial. He was a handsome man, and wealthy as well. If he wished to remarry, then it would happen soon enough. He might even precede her down the aisle.

What did love have to do with making a future? For either of them? Clare was evidence enough that it need not enter into marriage at all.

She waited until her mother was out of sight, before ringing for her maid.

'Hannah, I need you to pack me a bag.'

'Miss?'

'And dresses, Hannah.' She looked into her closet, at the annoyingly bright array of silks that hung there. 'None of these. Could you find me something simpler?

Borrow from the servants if you must. Or remove the trims from some of my older things. Do any of the dresses remain from my time away? I know that Mother wished them destroyed, but there were a few that I would quite like to take with me. Plain dresses, such as a governess might wear.' And she felt something crack inside her, like ice on a stream in spring.

'You are going in disguise?' The maid brightened at the idea.

'Yes.' Although the way she was now felt more like a disguise than her governess clothes ever had. She shoved her lovely gowns to the side, searching the back of the wardrobe for the clothes she had borrowed from the real Miss Collins.

'And it is to be a secret. You must wait as long as you are able before giving my parents the letter that I will leave for them. Can I trust you to help me?'

The girl hesitated for a moment, and then smiled. 'Will you need a lady's maid, miss, once you get to the place you are going?'

Daphne grinned. 'If I am successful in what I mean to do? Then I certainly hope so, Hannah.'

'Then you must be sure to succeed. For your father will throw me out once he realises that I have helped you get away again. And I will be needing a position.'

Chapter Twenty

Tim threw more coal into the stove and held his hands out to the metal. Would he never stop being cold? The thermometer said that the conservatory was warm enough. Almost too warm, if he was to be honest. The air was dry. If he was not careful, the excessive heat would damage the plants.

But he was cold. He ached with it. And there was no warming.

He rubbed at the skin of his bare neck, thinking perhaps a coat and a cravat were in order, as protection if nothing else. But he hardly left the conservatory now, other than to see the children. And while surrounded by the plants, anything more than shirtsleeves and apron seemed excessive. He sat down on the *chaise* again and leaned back, pushing his face deep into the cushions. Sometimes, he thought he could catch a whiff of her perfume. Perhaps it was an orchid coming into bloom, or merely his imagination. But it was something, at any rate. And there was the vague sense that warmth lingered on the bed they had once shared.

He laughed to himself, wishing that he had taken her to his room while he'd had the chance. At least then he would be sleeping in his own bed. It would be less worrisome for his valet if he moved back upstairs.

But when he went above stairs, he found himself wandering to the end of the hall and looking up at the narrow passage that led to the attic bedroom. It would look even stranger to all concerned if he took to sleeping in a narrow bedstead, under the eaves.

He heard a rustling in the leaves by the door, and sat up quickly, before Sophie could catch him trying to sleep during the day again. The older children could see something was wrong. But they did their best to ignore it, giving him hugs, and trying to joke him out of his bad humor.

It was easier, now that they knew there was no risk to their sister. Edmund had even been talking, tentatively at least, of going to school for the spring term.

But although Sophie was better than she had been, he dare not frighten her too much with his strange behaviour, lest she relapse.

She came around the palms to where he sat, and he patted the seat beside him, and held out his arms for a hug.

In response, she climbed up beside him, and put her arms around his neck for a small wet kiss. 'Papa, are you sad?'

'Not now you are here, little one.' He smiled down at her and patted her curls.

'I am sad.'

'You are?' It was better than frightened, he supposed. And after all she had been through, he could not blame her.

'I miss her.'

He had done his best not to speak of her mother. But Clare would always be a part of their lives, and he must accept the fact. 'I know, darling.' And then he hazarded what he suspected was a bold-faced lie. 'But she has gone to a better place.'

'London is a better place?' Sophie tugged at his coat, and smiled hopefully. 'Then can we go there, too? We could visit her. I want to show her my pictures.'

'London? Visit…' He shook his head, and looked down at her again. 'We are talking of Miss Collins again?'

Sophie's hopeful smile increased, and she nodded until her curls bobbed. 'Or you could go to fetch her back.'

This was even harder to answer. For at least with Clare he could assure himself that there was an end to the conversation, and no way to bring her back. There was also no way that she could hurt them further.

But what was he to tell the girl about Daphne? 'I think she is probably happier where she is now. It was not very exciting here, I am sure. And her father said she liked the parties and balls.' It was probably true. She must have a coterie of admirers. And if he had given her a taste for carnality?

He swallowed hard, fighting the shame of what he had done. And then he had turned her off, to fend for herself against the machinations of the rakes in London. Suppose she came to harm because of him?

But he could not have kept her. His children did not need another mother like that. What proof did he have, really, that she would not have fallen to another?

Sophie tugged at his sleeve again. 'Tell her we have oranges. And strawberries. They do not have those in London, I'll wager.' She began bold enough, but her eyes had gone wide and watery at the thought of her missing friend, and her tone was softer, more hesitant. If he was not careful, she would become the little ghost she had been before Miss Collins had come into the house, convinced that her actions were the cause of Daphne's rejection.

'Would you like a strawberry, then?' He seized at the distraction. For anything was better than further questions.

Sophie smiled and nodded.

He went to the plant, and picked a handful, placing them in a handkerchief. 'There you are. Take some to your sister and brother, as well.'

Sophie took them carefully from him, and scampered out of the room, Daphne temporarily forgotten.

He would have to deal with it again tomorrow, he suspected. And at some point, he would need to explain that Miss Collins was really Miss Collingham and she was not coming back from London at all. And then he must make the child believe that it was for her own good he had sent Daphne away, and not as a punishment.

He stared at the fruit in front of him. If only it were so easy to get the memory of her from his own mind. Or to convince himself that she had forgotten him already, or been as bad as he suspected: another Clarissa ready to sink her fangs into his heart like a viper.

At least, if he could believe that the children were better off, then his own misery might not be so acute. But the house, although changed for the better, was growing just as strangely quiet as it had been before Daphne had arrived. His own sense of loss showed no sign of abating with the passage of time. And while the older children might be able to hide their displeasure for his sake, Sophie seemed to alternate between puzzled sadness and optimism that Miss Collins would be returning at any moment. While Edmund and Lily seemed resigned to the fact that they would see her no more, Sophie could not be persuaded. He dreaded to think what would happen when she finally came to realise that it was over.

Another chill went through him, and he allowed himself the luxury of a memory. Her body, pressed tight to his, as it had been on the *chaise*. How could he have sent her away?

He tried to reassure himself again that it had been for the good of the children. But what harm had she done them, in the time she'd resided under his roof? She had shown more compassion and love for them in a few short weeks than Clare had in a lifetime. They had grown, blooming like roses in the sunlight.

And he had ignored the successes and taken her

away from them, because he was angry that she had lied to him.

In her absence, he was lying to himself. It was his own heart that he feared for. She was of Clare's blood. Suppose she was more like her cousin than she appeared? She'd lied to gain entrance to his house, with the express plan of destroying him.

Instead, she'd helped him to face his fears and had healed the children. And when she had discovered the truth? She had been as eager to hide it again as he had.

Being with her felt nothing like it had been with Clarissa. He could not remember ever loving his late wife. Polite apathy and a vague sense of lust had quickly turned to loathing on both their parts, and a low-banked desire for escape. That he should be so frightened of his reaction to Daphne could mean only one thing: that he had a heart to be broken, after all this time of believing himself without one.

It was an exhilarating thought, and a terrifying one. To open himself to the woman could mean great joy, or greater heartache than he had known in his miserable life. And it might already be too late, for he had treated her abominably. She might have gone back to London, to the suitors she had left there, and chosen one who appreciated her charms. It had been weeks. For all he knew, she could be betrothed, or even married.

Or she would be, if he did not do something quickly. If he sat here brooding over her loss he would never learn the truth. He would be trapped in a limbo of unknowing, halfway between happiness and sadness, and too afraid to move in either direction.

Being without her would be no different than being with Clare.

He would go to her, and throw himself on her mercy. Or better yet, he would seize her, drag her back to Wales and force her to finish what she had begun. For whether she intended it or not, she had been well on the way to becoming wife to him and mother to his children. She had made him love her, with her sweetness and her willingness to give. If she meant to deny them, just to engage in London foolishness, then it was time for her to grow up and take responsibility for her life.

The thought appealed to him. He reached a hand to touch his face, felt the stubble on his chin and saw dirt under his fingernails. She would not want him in this condition. And he did not want to let her see what a few weeks without her had done to him, or how quickly the gains of the last month had been undone. A wash, a shave and a clean shirt would do wonders. His best coat, and a properly tied cravat. He was not the handsomest man in London, at least not compared to Adam. But when properly turned out, he had nothing to be ashamed of.

So he would clean up, and then he would head to London. He would claim it was on business, for it would not do to raise the hopes of the children if the errand proved fruitless. And he would find Daphne and bring her home.

There was a soft rapping on the panes of the door,

and the sound of his butler's shuffling footsteps as the man sought to gain his attention. 'My lord?'

He looked up, and smiled.

'A visitor.'

He cast another quick glance over his appearance. 'Stow whoever it is in the drawing room, and I will go and make myself presentable.'

'She wishes to see you immediately, and says it is most urgent.'

'She.' All his plans collapsed in a puddle of trembling hope, and then coalesced, as he realised that it could not possibly be what he was hoping for. 'Here then, and right now. Bring her to me.'

The butler stepped out of the way, evaporating into the hall. And the object of his desire stepped into the conservatory and closed the door behind her. She looked pale, and much as he felt, as though sleep had been elusive, and happiness impossible. Everything about her was more subdued than he remembered. Her hair was more controlled, her dress starched and sensible. It was a dark colour that would not show wear and would be undamaged by grubby palms. And her expression was that of a woman unsure of her position.

She dropped a curtsy that had none of the hidden arrogance of her first attempts at subservience. 'Sir?'

'Miss Collins?' And then he corrected himself, for it was not her name. 'Miss Collingham.' He wanted nothing more than to gather her into his arms. But he hesitated, just as she was doing. 'You have returned to us, against my wishes?'

'Yes.' She said it softly. 'I was hoping that during

my time away, perhaps your feelings on the subject had changed. If my old position is still open, I would very much like to have it back.'

'Your position.' Now this was an unexpected turn. 'I was under the impression, when we parted, that you did not actually need employment.'

'Not when I first came here, my lord. But now that I have left you, I find that there is not as much joy in my old life as I once felt, or as much purpose. It was an endless circle of false friends and foolishness. And if, at the end of it, the best I can hope for is an offer from a man as foolish as myself, then I think I would much prefer to forgo marriage and find some way to be of use.

'I have no references to offer.' She smiled. 'At least none that are actually mine. For those I offered you from the first were forgeries. And you have witnessed the fact that my knowledge of geography, geometry and languages are not what they should be. But the children...' She shook her head, and her eyes seemed to grow large and wavered behind unshed tears. 'Your children need a governess, just as much as they did before.'

But what of their father? 'So you need purpose, and the children need someone to watch over them. And we both know that is not the only thing that happened, when you were last here.'

'You need someone to watch over you as well.' She looked up at him, with a sad smile. 'For you are not as I remember you, Lord Colton.'

He looked down at the floor and muttered, 'Gone to seed. Just like the plants. I should take better care.'

She rushed on. 'And I would understand, if you needed to marry. For it is only right that you should have someone. Someone you could trust, who would not lie to you, or bring you unhappy memories. But if I could only have my little room under the eaves, and see the children sometimes, and bring them down to the conservatory to see you on occasion?' She swallowed. 'Then I think I should be quite content.'

'Content?' The idea was madness, and he would show her so. He closed the distance between them in an instant, and pulled her off balance and into his arms, kissing her in a way that cut off the flow of foolish words. Her mouth was as soft as he remembered, and as sweet, and her body yielding beneath the unyielding fabric of her governess dress. 'It is small comfort to offer me contentment, after what you have already given. Now that you have crossed my threshold I want you, all and unreserved, at my side in the day, and in my bed at night. I want a wife, and the children want a mother. I want a woman who I can love with all my heart, who will love me in return. If you can give me that, then stay. If you offer less, then for God's sake, Daphne, leave and give me peace. For I will go mad if I can see you each day, but cannot touch you.'

'Your offer stands, then?' She sighed into his mouth, and he could feel the spirit returning to her.

'I was horrible to you.'

'And I to you.'

'Because I hurt you.'

'But I will be better.'

'It does not matter.' He kissed her again.

She tilted her head away, not yet willing to surrender. 'And Clare. She was my cousin and my friend. And although she was not the woman I thought she was, I cannot change the happy memories of the past. Nor do I wish to. But she is gone now, for me, and for you as well.' There was a trace of question in her statement.

'She is gone. She cannot hurt me further, and I do not begrudge you your happiness. What she was to either of us does not change what we are to each other.' And she was truly gone, for when he kissed the woman in his arms, there was no shadow of the past in the bright future before him.

'I wanted to tell you, that day. After I got your letter. For I knew what my answer must be. But I could not say the words until you knew the truth. I had believed the most horrible things about you, even worse than you thought of yourself. But I had been terribly wrong, and was terribly sorry. And I wished to beg for your forgiveness, because I had come to love you more than life, and would never wish to see you hurt again.' Her words were like a balm on the old wounds, easing the ache of the past. 'But then Father came, and it was too late to explain.'

'Your father.' And he remembered that they were not the last two people on the earth together. 'Does he know that you have come back to me?'

She looked sheepish. 'I left him a note. I expect, after what has already occurred, that he will be twice as angry as he was the last time. And he was very angry with me, and none too happy with you. He will be coming along shortly, I expect. And you might be receiving a visit from my brothers, as well.'

'Brothers.'

'Three.' She smiled wickedly. 'All very large. They are rather protective, when it comes to me. They spoil me terribly, and give me my way in all things. And I am sure that they would want me to be treated honourably.'

'Then I had best work fast, if I am to deserve the thrashing they are likely to give me.' He kissed her throat. 'If it were just we two, I should rush you off to Scotland today. But I expect we shall have to read the banns in St George's in London, or some other grand church, and do this properly for the sake of your family.'

'And yours,' she reminded him. 'The children might quite like to see a wedding.' She considered. 'Although I think it is far too much bother to go back to London. If there is a small church nearby, it would suit me well. For I have grown quite fond of Wales.'

He laughed and held her close. For if there was any proof that his second marriage would be different from the first, he had heard it from her very lips. 'As long as it is soon, I do not care where. For I must have you, my love. It has been too long.'

'Then take me. For I would not wish otherwise.'

He kissed her in earnest, and she answered him with kisses of her own, her hands stroking his hair, his shoulders and his chest, until he felt the desire rising in him. The linen of his shirt was thin and her touch seemed to burn through it. She was his and his alone, warm and willing, arrayed in starched cotton like some carefully wrapped package, so many layers of cloth between him and what he wanted. He fumbled for the closures at the back of her dress.

'She is *heeeeeeere*. She is, she is, she is!' Sophie pelted into their knees like a bullet, and clung to them so that they could not part if they had wanted to. 'And Papa is kissing her!'

Daphne looked down in obvious amusement. 'Do not shout so, Sophie. While it is very good to hear you talking again, perhaps it would be better if it were not so loud. I fear you will scare your father's plants.'

The girl giggled. 'They are not like animals. I cannot scare them, see?' She ran over to the nearest orchid and cried, 'Boo!'

He used the opportunity to put distance between them, and to hide the embarrassing evidence of his desire. Focusing his mind on his responsibilities as a father, he turned to the nearby basin to plunge his hands into the icy water, scrubbing at the nails furiously with the brush and hoping that he had not left proof of his intentions as hand prints on his beloved. 'Actually, there are plants that will wilt in fear from a single touch. Now that Daphne has returned, I will find some. And perhaps she will help you to paint a picture.' He saw his two other children, hovering in the doorway, old enough to realise that they had interrupted something, but still unsure what it had been. 'Come in, you two, and say hello. For I think we all have a great deal to discuss today.'

And they ran across the threshold, obviously in no

mood to discuss anything, launching themselves on their former governess, and enveloping her in a mutual hug.

Daphne's eyes met his, over the tangle of children, and she smiled, as if to apologise for the interruption. But she seemed supremely happy to be welcomed so. She looked down at the children, smiling at them as though the separation from them had been as difficult for her as it had been for them.

They made a beautiful picture, gathered together under the leaves, the varying reds of their hair contrasting with the green and blending into each other. Some day soon he would have them painted together, just like that. His family. And he felt a completeness that he had never felt before as he put down the brush, wiped his hands on a cloth and went to join them.

* * * * *

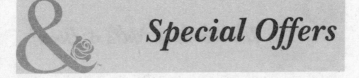
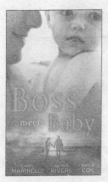

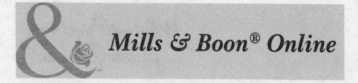